Promise of Home

Ray Harding

Canebrake Literary

1 3 5 7 9 10 8 6 4 2

Copyright © 2014 by the author.

All rights reserved.

Canebrake Literary, New Bern, North Carolina

www.rayhardingbooks.com

www.lulu.com/spotlight/CanebrakeLiterary

Printed in the United States of America

Cover photograph by Hannah Williams

Library of Congress Cataloging in Publication Data
Harding, Ray

Promise of Home/Ray Harding
    1.   Sand Ridge (NC: Imaginary Place)-Fiction 2. City and Town Life-NC –Fiction I. Title

ISBN: 978-1-312-00685-0

Thank You

To my most gracious Lord, everything good in my life is a precious gift from you.

Sandy, I could not ask for better. You make me want to be great.

To my children, thank you for being patient every time your Daddy works late to finish a chapter.

To everyone who read Back to Sand Ridge and asked for more, Thank You, I hope you enjoy your trip back.

Ray Harding

~Chapter One~

Roger Lowell turned his truck in at Marcil's driveway and pulled up to the front of the preacher's shop. It's big, wooden, front doors were swung open, and, with a quick look inside, Roger noted that the spot where the preacher usually parked his tractor was empty. He looked off towards the back side of Marcil's little farm and caught sight of the tractor parked crossways down in the path out in front of the barn.

Well Marcil, Roger thought, pulling the truck back down into gear, *That's an odd place to park.* He drove on around past the shop out to where the tractor was sitting and noticed, as he parked in the path next to it, that the engine was still running.

Roger cut his pickup's motor and then scanned the farm for sight of Marcil as he slid out. "*Marcil,*" he called, "*Marcil Potts.*" He turned round, gazing out over the pasture next to him and then the field on other side of the path, "*Preacher,*" he called again, cupping his hands around his mouth, "Hey *Preacher.*"

Propping his hands on his hips Roger turned slowly around and looked back up towards the house. He scratched his head, "Am I missing something here?" He was just about to call out again when he heard a loud bang, like someone had just clapped two flat boards together, coming from behind him. Spinning around, Roger stared at the barn for a moment trying to make some sense of things when he heard a startled shout and then three more loud bangs.

Roger took a few quick steps towards the barn as he heard another shout, and then two rusty-red hens came cackling and flapping noisily out from inside. He hopped over them as he ran up and then stopped in the middle of the open doorway as a big, speckled rooster came rocketing out past his head. Stepping a little further inside, he stopped again, hearing a deep metallic *clang,* and then, the sound of something wooden being pounded to splinters.

"*Preacher*," Roger called, as he waited for his eyes to adjust to the darkness, "*Are you alright?*" He coughed as he breathed in a headful of dust.

Roger heard another wooden crash and then some shuffling. "Watch out boy!" Marcil called out from behind a wall of hay. Roger's eyes were growing accustomed to the dark and he noticed that several of the rows of hay bales had been strewn out across the floor.

"...I got a rattler in here!"

"*What?*"

"There's a rattlesnake in here...A big one!"

Without thinking, Roger took two quick steps backwards and scanned the floor. "*Hoh,*" Marcil shouted. Roger heard a *bang, bang, clang*, and then a grunt from the preacher.

"*I got my shotgun in the truck,*" Roger hollered over the din.

"Go get it," Marcil shouted back, still pounding on whatever he was pounding on, "*Quick.*"

Roger ran back out to his truck and grabbed his shotgun from behind the seat. When he ran back into the barn, he stopped in the dusty silence, his breath coming quick as he shucked a shell into the chamber. "Preacher," he said expectantly, his voice just barely above a whisper.

"Yeah boy," Marcil Potts drawled from the darkness off to Roger's left.

Roger squinted and peered off into the dark corner, holding the twelve gauge at the ready, trying to make out the preacher through the haze. "You see him?" he said, keeping his low.

"Yeah I see him," Marcil replied, stepping out to where Roger could see him. He lifted his arm up high. Roger could see the thick silhouette of the snake hanging limply from Marcil's hand. Roger walked slowly back towards the door as Marcil came out to him. The preacher's face was covered with sweat and his clothes were dusty. Roger saw that he was carrying the better part of a broken bush-axe handle in his other hand. They walked out into the light and Marcil let out a noisy sigh. "I hope I don't ever have to do that again," he said, slowly shaking his head as he let the snake down to the ground. The rattler's body recoiled and then twitched. Roger took another step back.

"Don't you worry," Marcil chuckled, "I ain't no snake handling preacher...His brain just ain't convinced the rest of him he's dead yet."

Roger stepped up closer as Marcil stretched the snake out on the ground in front of him. "*Good night Preacher*," Roger said, "I *swornee*, that's got to be the biggest rattler I've ever seen."

Marcil pulled a big blue handkerchief from the back pocket of his overalls, wiped it across his face, and then ran it around the back of his neck. He blew out another noisy breath and looked down appraisingly at the snake.

"I bet he's close to six feet," Roger said. He emptied the shell from his shotgun and then slid it back into the magazine. Marcil knelt down beside the snake and looked it over closely. "He's a fat one," he said, "...I hated to kill him, but I got a pile of grandchildren coming in a couple days that like to play out here and I just couldn't take a chance on whether or not he was just passing through."

Roger checked the safety and then laid the shotgun down in the grass as he knelt down across from Marcil. Sliding his hand up under the snake's belly, he hefted the old serpent's weight and then, trying to wrap his two hands around its girth, he found he had to give it a good squeeze to make his fingers touch. "Reminds me of the one Mister Rufus killed out back behind Mama's house on the way to his watermelon patch when I was five," he said, giving a breath's pause, "...That was the day Elvis died."

Marcil gave Roger a thoughtful look, "That was a hot day," he remarked.

Roger sat the snake back down and then looked over toward the rattles. "Did you count the rattles yet?"

"The only thing I've counted is my blessings," Marcil said, grinning at Roger, "...And maybe how many days closer to Glory I am now, thanks to this thing." He picked up the tail and shook it, clucking his tongue, "Just can't make it buzz like they do," he said, and then held it out for Roger.

Roger looked at the snake's tail and counted. After a couple seconds he said, "Fifteen...fifteen rattles," and then looked back at Marcil, "Let me get my tape out of the truck and we'll see how long he is."

Grabbing the shotgun, Roger hopped up and went quickly off down the path.

Marcil called to him, *"How 'bout shutting that tractor down for me while you're at it."*

Roger grinned back over his shoulder and gave Marcil a "thumbs up".

Marcil was tickled at how excited Roger had become and snickered a little to himself. He remembered seeing that same grin on Roger's face the first time he had gone rabbit hunting with him as a boy.

Marcil had taken Roger and his father Jack Lowell out on a frosty December morning when Roger was ten and Roger's face seemed frozen in a perpetual grin the entire day. Even after they had had to pull Roger from the ditch of waist-deep, nearly-freezing water he had stumbled into head-first chasing after a rangy beagle pup that wouldn't come to heel. Roger rode the whole way back to Marcil's shop sitting in the floor of the truck, with the heater blowing wide open on him, and nothing on to protect his modesty but his daddy's faded hunting coat wrapped around him.

Roger came back a minute later and found the preacher there wiping his eyes with his handkerchief, chuckling softly to himself. "You want a cold drink or something," Roger asked, "I got some in the back of the truck."

"Naw, I'm good," the preacher said, "I'm just trying to get the dust out of my eyes."

Roger knelt back down and pulled on the rattler's tail, straightening out the snake's body, and then he stretched his measuring tape out along the snake's back. "Could you hold the end for me," he asked, looking up at Marcil, "I can't keep it quite straight. He's a little longer than I thought he was...*What are you grinning at?*"

Marcil pursed his lips down and shook his head. "Nothing in particular," he said, "Something was just a bit amusing to me, that's all." He looked away from Roger and let out a little snicker under his breath.

"*What did I do?*"

"Nothing."

Roger stared at Marcil, not sure if he really believed him. Marcil snickered again.

"*Alright*," Roger said, "Come on...What is it? I did *something*, I know."

"I was just remembering something."

"What?"

"A skinny little boy all puckered up in goose bumps, curled up in the foot of my truck, looking like some freshly plucked, scrawny little, Thanksgiving turkey wrapped in an old brown hunting coat, drinking down my thermos full of coffee."

Roger drooped his head and shook it with a laughing sigh. "Ahh yes," he said slowly, lifting his head and smiling at Marcil, "...One of my finest moments."

"That was a good day, Roger. You should be proud of that day...You kept smiling through that whole thing and never once complained. I've seen lots of grown men whine and moan over a lot less discomfort than that," Marcil paused and pointed a finger at Roger, "You showed your true character that day."

Roger studied Marcil's face a moment and then pulled a bright yellow foot of the tape measure out and quickly released it, letting it roll back up into the case with a metallic snap. "We ain't never gonna get this thing measured if you just sit there blowing sunshine my way," he said, pulling the first few inches of the tape measure back out. He pointed it at Marcil.

Marcil looked down at the tape measure and then the big rattler's thick, still, body. He looked up at Roger but didn't make a move to grab the tape. "We will if you move down to the other end," he remarked.

Roger chuckled and switched the tape measure around and handed the case end to Marcil. "I've had quite enough of that *other* end," Marcil joked. He held the end of the tape on the ground next to the tip of the snake's tail as Roger pulled it out and held it even with its nose.

"Six feet, one and three quarter inches," he said slowly, looking closely at the little black marks on the tape. He looked back up at the preacher. "*Dern a'mighty*," he said. He looked back at the tape for a second and then sat back on his heels and shook his head. "He's been living pretty good I'd say."

Marcil let go of the tape and it zipped quickly back up into Roger's hand. Roger noticed Marcil looked a little morose. "You really *had* to kill it Preacher," he said softly. "You're right, you can't take a chance on it with the young'uns running around... *You really can't.*"

"I know I did the right thing," said Marcil, "It just seems like such a waste." He ran his hand slowly down the snake's smooth diamond crossed back. "...Such a waste." He got himself up onto one knee and pointed at a little picked spot on the right leg of his overalls about halfway up to the knee. "You see that," he asked.

Roger looked closely and shook his head, "What am I looking for?"

"Right after you lit out for the shotgun, I kicked a bag of feed over that he had just run up behind, and when I did, he spun around and struck as I was pulling my leg back and his fangs got caught up in the leg of my overhauls." He paused and smiled at Roger and shook his head. "I had just the space to jam that bush-axe handle down on the back of his neck and take him out." He stood to his feet and looked back down at the rattler. "That was the only time he ever rattled."

"When you killed it?"

"Mmm hmm...I saw him slide down in the ditch there," he pointed out on the path on the near side of his tractor, "... Just this side of where my tractor's settin' and by the time I jumped down and chased after him he had made a beeline for the barn like he knew just where he was goin'. I run him back and forth through half the barn and he never made sound...and I mean to tell you, you'd be surprised how fast one of them rascals can move."

Roger gave Marcil a crooked smile, "...Well, I'd be willing to bet that snake was thinking the same thing about you."

Marcil chuckled deeply down in his throat and patted Roger firmly on the shoulder as he stood up.

"Well," Roger said, standing up with the preacher, "Now what?"

Marcil looked down at the dead snake. "I don't know," he said, "Seems an awful waste to just chunk him in the woods...But, I ain't got no use for that thing."

"I'll take him. I can stick him in my ice chest...I'm sure either Mister Horner or Tom Betts will want him."

Marcil made a broad sweep with his hand, "He's all yours Mister Lowell." He wiped his handkerchief across his brow once more and held up a finger. "On one condition..."

"What's that?"

"Miss Beatrice neither sees nor hears about our cat-eyed friend."

Roger twisted his fingers across his lips, "Tick-a-lock."

"Good."

Roger squatted down and rolled the rattler up into a coil and picked him up. "I still can't get over how big he is," he said over his shoulder as he headed out to his truck.

"He looked even bigger a few minutes ago," Marcil said. He turned and went back inside the barn as Roger loaded the snake into the ice chest he always kept in the bed of his truck.

After a moment, Marcil walked back out from the barn, dusting his cap off as he walked over to where Roger stood leaning against his truck sipping on a cold Champ Cola he had pulled from the ice chest. "You sure you don't want something to drink?" Roger said "I've got some more of these and a few Draught's."

Marcil looked at him for a second. "I think I *will* have one," he said, "I seem to have worked up a bit of a thirst here recently...I ain't much on Root Beer...Let me hold one of your Champs."

Roger reached into the ice chest and pulled out another cold bottle of drink and then popped the top off on the latch of his pickup's open door. "Here you go Preacher," he said, handing the dewy bottle to Marcil. Marcil took two long pulls, draining half the contents of the bottle, and then smacked his lips as he took the bottle down from his mouth. "That is good," he said. He gave his wrist a quick twist and watched the rest of the drink spinning in the bottle. "Your daddy used to love these things," he said, "... Champ Cola and a bag of salty peanuts."

"I never really cared much for it 'til I went off in the Navy...But, I shore did want one bad when I couldn't get one."

"Funny how that works ain't it?" Marcil said. He took another swallow from his drink and then propped himself on Roger's truck. "I never had much taste for the Word when I was young," he mused. He cocked his head at Roger. "My Daddy did his best to share it with me but I just let it roll. Then, after he went on Home, and I didn't have a steady supply any more...I really got to wanting it bad."

Roger stared at Marcil for a moment and then gave his head a little shake. "That's pretty hard to believe," he said.

"Why's that?"

"I've just always pictured you as having always been *you*."

"If you mean just another sinner saved by the Grace of God, then you're right. But let me assure you, I was born a downright scoundrel full of the first Adam just like everyone else." He motioned towards the battered ice chest sitting at Roger's elbow. "That weren't the first serpent I've had to slay."

Roger stared at Marcil for another brief moment and then finished off his drink. He stuck the empty bottle down in the corner of the truck bed beside the ice chest. "When Daddy told me stories about y'all when you were young, he always made you sound like the good one...like if it weren't for you he'd have either been locked up or dead in somebody's ditch."

"Your daddy was being generous."

"I think he was just a good judge of character."

"He was," Marcil agreed, "But, he was still being generous...I probbly got him *in* to more trouble than I ever got him out of."

"I'd be willing to bet the scorecards were pretty close to even on that."

Marcil chuckled and then finished downing his drink. He handed the empty bottle to Roger and Roger saw a little twinkle in the old preacher's eye. "What?" Roger asked.

Marcil chuckled a little more as he stood smiling at Roger. Roger looked sideways at him as his chuckle slowly grew into deep laugh, sneaking up from down in his belly until his whole body began to shake, and the tears crept from the corner of his eyes and ran slowly down his cheeks.

"*What?*"

Marcil stepped back from Roger's truck and shook his head, still laughing. He pulled his cap off from his head and pulled his handkerchief back out of his pocket and covered his face with it.

"What is it this time?"

"I wish I could tell you Roger," Marcil said, balling up his handkerchief. He looked up towards the roof of the barn and laughed a little more. "I really would like to tell it...But I swore to Brother Jack that I never would." He put his foot up on Roger's front tire and propped his elbow on his knee. "But I will tell you this...I never could look at my sweet Granny's floursack apron the same."

Roger's face wrinkled up, as a hundred different images of his father ran through his mind, "Oh come on Preacher," he said, "You can't just throw something like that out and leave me hanging."

Marcil shook his head. "I shouldn't have said that much," he said.

"You know it's gonna drive me crazy 'til I find out."

"You'll be alright," Marcil said, "What'd you come by for anyway?"

Roger hesitated, "Well," he said, "If you've got a little time, I was hoping to get some advice."

Marcil smiled. "Some *here's that handsaw I borrowed from you last week let me ask you something real quick* advice, or some *let's go have us a bite to eat and set a while while we have us some talk* advice?"

Roger paused a second and then smiled, "Are you in the mood for a plate of fried oysters?"

"Alright Buddy, it's your turn."

"Here you go Mister Elwood," Buddy said, as he handed the back page of the *Ormond Daily News* to the old man sitting in the chair beside him, "...Thanks for the funnies."

He stood himself up and stepped across the room to the barber chair as Furney Blalock snapped his yellowing cotton drape out into the air to shake off the last few hairs from the trim he had just done on Rudy Jenkins.

Rudy stood off to one side with a ten dollar bill folded in his hand, rubbing at the lotion that had run down onto the back of his neck from where Furney had just been massaging it into his pink scalp. "I still don't think it's fair Furney," Rudy stated. He threw a quick wink to Buddy as Buddy climbed into the chair and planted himself with a leathery creak onto the smoothly worn, deep burgundy colored seat.

Furney gave the drape one last snap and then floated it down gracefully into place around Buddy's broad shoulders and then folded Buddy's collar down into the neck of his shirt. He turned around and reached into a box on the counter, "What's that Jinx?" he finally asked, releasing the question absently over his shoulder as he pulled a paper strip out from the box.

Rudy looked over at his brother Mitchell and at Elwood Twigg. He gave his head a nod and grinned at them and then looked back at Furney and crooked a finger at Buddy. "You charge me the same as you do Buddy...and I just don't see how that's fair."

"And why is that?"

Rudy started wagging his finger at Buddy's thick head of hair. "Look at all that hair," he said, "I ain't got a third the hair that boy's got *–a fourth even*...And since that's so, you ort'n to only charge me a third or a fourth of what you charge him."

Buddy watched the three old men out in front of him as they smiled mischievously at one another waiting for Rudy to really dig in and rile Furney up. He saw Mitchell nudge Elwood in the ribs with his elbow.

"...Seems a bit *greedy* to me for you to charge us all the same when you ain't doing near the work on me as him."

"Is that a fact?" Furney wrapped the paper strip snugly around Buddy's neck and then pulled the drape up tight and fastened it into place. "Well," he continued, "Just so's you know, I only charge you two dollars for the hair cut." He stepped around the chair and took Rudy's money. He grinned at Buddy as he spun back around and stuck the cash neatly into the little metal box he kept on the counter amongst sundry bottles of assorted hair lotions, tonics, plastic combs, and the hot lather dispenser.

"Then where's all the change you owe me for all these years?" Rudy asked.

Furney pulled the top off a jar of what Buddy and Roger had always called *Mister Furney's Hick Slicker* and slid a fresh comb out of his pocket. He casually dipped the comb into the semi-clear liquid and then started combing through Buddy's hair.

"There *ain't* no change," Furney said.

"Now, I know I ain't no mathemagician Furney, but I do know that two ain't ten. So, figurin' that I started loosing my hair nigh on fifty years ago...and you been cutting it all that time," Rudy paused and pitched another wink at the peanut gallery, "...That means you owe me back a toe sack full of money. I'm bound to be due near six or seven hunert dollars by now."

Furney was undaunted, "You didn't let me finish," he said dryly, "...I only charge you two dollars for the hair cut." He slid the comb into the chest pocket on his coat and whipped out his scissors. "The other eight's the finder's fee."

Rudy slapped his thigh as he and his two cronies burst out laughing.

Buddy chuckled and grinned up at Rudy.

"*He gotcha there Rudy*," Elwood cackled.

"*He shore did*," Mitchell agreed.

Rudy snorted, "*Finder's fee*," he shook his head and laughed some more, "You're too much Furney." He stepped over towards the door and lifted his hat up from off the rack on the wall. "Come on Mitchell," he said as he sat the hat on his head. He opened the front door and gave Furney a wave. "You got me a good one Furney," he said, chuckling to himself. "A finder's fee," he repeated to himself as he stepped outside. Buddy could still hear him laughing as Mitchell walked out and closed the door behind them.

"That was a good one Mister Furney," Buddy said as the old barber started appraising his head.

"I been waiting to use it," Furney said, "I got it from your father." He sat one hand on top of Buddy's head and tilted it forward a little.

"*You did?*"

Furney nodded, and pulled Buddy's head back up straight. "Uh huh," he said, "...Last time he was in here for his haircut he asked me if what he was paying me was for *cutting* his hair or for *finding* it."

Buddy chuckled. "I'll have to tell him you used it," he said, "It was a good one."

Furney turned Buddy's head slowly back and forth, examining the hair on each side. After a moment he said, (*somewhat accusingly* Buddy thought) "You've trimmed this yourself."

Buddy cleared his throat quietly, "*Well*," he replied, "Hillary said it was looking shaggy."

"You shouldn't go so long between cuts," Furney replied firmly. He breathed heavily on his scissors and then shined them on his sleeve, "Don't butcher your hair Buddy," he said, "Don't do that."

"Yessir," Buddy mumbled guiltily. He adjusted himself uncomfortably in the chair.

"You shouldn't just hack away at hair with any ol' thing... You really shouldn't."

"Yessir," Buddy mumbled again.

Furney leaned around and studied Buddy's head for another long moment, sighed, and then leaned back out and cocked his head over the other way.

"I was just wanting you to–"

"I know what you want Buddy," Furney interrupted, snipping his scissors in the air over Buddy's left ear. "You ain't got to tell me son. I been cuttin' your hair the same way since you were nine years old. I know how to do it."

"He don't do but *two* haircuts no how, Buddy," Elwood chimed, "One bad, and t'other worse."

"Hush up El-*wood*," Furney said, "Or I'll do Buddy's the bad and yours the worse." He sat his hand on Buddy's shoulder. "Now you relax and I'll get you whipped in two shakes."

"Yessir," Buddy said flatly as he settled down into the chair. He flicked the cover back and forth on the little metal ashtray that was built into the armrest of the barber chair with his thumb as Furney went to work on his head.

"What are you so nervous about son?"

"*Sir?*"

"What are you so nervous about?"

"*Me?*" Buddy said, still working the ashtray lid, "I ain't nervous."

"Then why are you trying to flick the shamrock off my ashtray?"

Buddy closed the ashtray and rested his hand down over it and chuckled quietly. "I didn't even realize I was doing that," he said as he slowly started tracing the outline of the shamrock that was pressed into the chromed steel lid with his fingertip.

"You, Tilley Peters, and Little-Paul Edwards all do that when you first sit down," Furney stated, "...Like your scared I'm gonna whack off an ear or something."

"Sorry Mister Furney."

"That's alright Buddy," Furney said, patting Buddy's shoulder. He gave Buddy's right ear a little tug, "I ain't lopped one yet," he said. He sat his hand gently on top of Buddy's head "Just relax, son."

Buddy glanced up and caught a glimpse of the barber pole out on the front of the shop through Furney's front window. A memory in his mind washed Buddy back to the Blalock's Barbershop of his childhood and a visit there with his father. His father was there for the bi-weekly touchup he always had done on his now gone flat-top and the slick straight-razor shave that he still swore was the mark of a true barber. Buddy remembered standing out on the cracked sidewalk in front of the bench that had *Furney's Resting Place* painted across the backrest in tall green-with-gold-trim letters. His father had just walked inside and Buddy was standing there on the neatly swept sidewalk watching the barber pole spin slowly around in its glass case, marveling at how the red and blue stripes seemed to run in a never-ending spiral up, up, up.

Buddy chuckled almost silently to himself, picturing his father sticking his head out of the shop sometime later and saying, "Come on son, Mister Furney's waiting on you." Buddy had had no idea how long he had been standing out there, mesmerized, with his mouth gaped open watching that silly pole spin, but he new it must have been a while because his father had already gotten his trim, his shave, and his two hot towels...And, he vaguely remembered a man, whoever it had been hadn't registered at the time, stepping out of the shop and saying good morning to him on his way to his car.

"So what's the story on your buddy Roger," Elwood asked across the room, drawing Buddy back to the present. Furney pushed Buddy's head forward and started evening up the hair at his collar.

"...I don't see him around as much as I used to," Elwood finished.

Buddy peered up through his eyebrows, "That makes two of us Mister Elwood," he said, his chin bouncing on his chest. "He's a little tied up with things these days."

"That's what I hear," said Elwood.

"It looks like the love bug's running epidemic in the Lowell clan," Furney added, "Ellis Spruill was in here day before yesterday and he said that he seen–" Furney stopped and looked up towards the front door as Will Wells came in.

"Hey Mister Furney," Will said cheerfully, "Hey Buddy."

"Will," Furney replied.

"Hey Will," Buddy said.

Will closed the door and looked down at Elwood, "Hey Mister Elwood." He stepped over to Furney's beat-up old refrigerator and opened it up. He pulled out a bottle of Cherry Zipper and popped off the top in the opener on the side of the refrigerator and took a big swallow, "Anybody else want anything," he asked.

"I'll take some of that belly-wash," Elwood said. He pointed a long, knobby-knuckled, finger in Furney's general direction, "You can take your *Champ Cola*," he said, "I've said it before and I'll say it again...Cherry Zipper's about the finest beverage that the Ormond's Treat Bottling Company *In*-corporated ever stuck in a bottle..."

Will grabbed another bottle and popped off its top as the old man spoke. He handed it over to Elwood as he finished pontificating on carbonated beverages; "...Lime is for pie, *Cherry* is for drink..."

"That's the last cold Zipper, Mister Elwood," Will said, "*Anybody else want anything*?"

Furney gave his head a little shake as he went back to his work. Buddy waved no. Will sat his drink on top of the refrigerator and grabbed a full six pack of Cherry Zippers from off the shelf by the front door and stuck it in the refrigerator. He grabbed his drink as he closed the door and took another big swallow. "What's the word for the day Mister Furney?" he asked as he went back over and sat down next to Elwood.

"Truculent."

"*Truculent*," Elwood said. He grinned at Will, "I know that one...it's when you borrow somebody your pickup." He stamped his foot on the floor and guffawed loudly, nudging Will, "Get it?"

Will nodded and smiled at Elwood. "Yessir," he said, "I get it."

"What's it really mean?" Buddy asked.

"It means savage, harsh, or cruel," said Furney, "...But most people use it referring to someone who's being belligerent."

"Truculent," Buddy said, "That sounds a bit better than ornery...I'm gonna have to remember that one."

Elwood said, "Furney, I've always wondered; where do you get your words from?"

"The good ol' Oxford Unabridged."

"Is that the same one you used to look at when we were in school?"

Furney snipped at the front of Buddy's hair. "Mmmhmm."

"You ort to see that thing," Elwood told Will. He held his hands up in front of him, one about ten inches up over the other, "...It's got to be *that* thick."

"Sounds like the one at the library," replied Will. "There must be eight pounds of words in it."

"I'd just about bet cash money that Furney here's read every word in it, too...Ain'tcha Furney?"

"I don't know as I've read 'em all," Furney said, "But I've put a pretty big dent in 'em."

"I always liked *pulchritude*," Buddy drawled nobly, "It must have been five or six years ago you learned –I mean *taught*– me that one...I just ain't never had a good chance to use it, yet."

"What's it mean?" Elwood asked.

"Comely or beautiful," Furney said, rather poetically.

"*Really*? It sure don't *sound* like it would mean that," Elwood said. He looked over at Will. "What woman do you know who'd want to hear that she was eat up with the pulchritude...Sounds more like an infected toe to me," he added, "Or maybe how a doctor'd tell you you got the hoof and mouth."

Will winced up his face and gave his head a little shake. "Ugh," he groaned, "That's bad...Speaking of hooves Mister Elwood; you got Miss Hilda a deer yet?"

"Not yet," Elwood replied. He shook his head sorrowfully, "I'm quite *crestfallen* about it." He looked over at Furney, "How 'bout that'n there Furney."

Furney looked over at Elwood and nodded his approval. "It's good to know you've at least learned *one* from me in all these years."

Elwood turned back to Will, "I've learned a few more than that," he said, "I just like the way that one sounds...

Crestfallen," he repeated slowly, "Kindly rolls off the tongue, don't you think."

"I reckon I'm liking it a bit better than *pulchritude.*"

"Of course you do," Elwood said, "But anyhow, what was I talking about?"

"I asked you if you'd got a deer yet...Seems like I've seen tons of them running around this year."

"Me too, but, I think I've bred them Walkers to run too fast," Elwood said, "...I can't seem to get a decent shot at one these days."

"I've told you you need to get rid of them things and start still-hunting Wood," Furney said, "You ain't shot a deer over them hounds in five years."

"I know, I know, but I just love to hear 'em sing...And if the Good Lord had a'wanted me sitting in a tree he'd a'topped them all off at about three feet."

Furney stopped cutting Buddy's hair and looked over at Elwood and chuckled. "Then get a tape," he said.

Elwood shook his head at Furney, "Don't you ever get outta here?" he said, "Nobody uses tapes anymore Furney... even I know that."

"Then get yourself a CD," said Furney, "...It'll save you a ton of money, not to mention a whole lot of fuss. You can listen to it while you're sitting up in your shrub and pretend it's your hounds running another deer that you're not gonna shoot." He tilted Buddy's head back up straight, "Don't slouch son." He ran his fingers along Buddy's part and lifted the hair on either side of it up straight and; *snip, snip* went his scissors. "So," Furney Blalock drawled, "You were saying you don't see much of Roger anymore either, huh?"

Buddy snorted a bit of hair off that had just fallen onto the end of his nose. "Not really," he said, "I mean, we all get together every now and then..." Buddy paused for a moment and tried to remember the last time he and Roger had done something together just the two of them. After a few seconds he cocked his head a little to one side and said, "But, I really couldn't tell you when the last time I saw him was."

"Hold still son," Furney said, "Or we'll be calling you *Patches* for a week or two."

"Sorry."

"Don't give him an excuse Buddy," said Elwood.

"I remember it used to be seemed like you never saw one of you without the other," said Furney.

Elwood said, "Well, no offense meant to you Buddy, but who would you rather be settin' round giving the sweet eyes to...Her or you?"

"Y'all must be talking about Maggie and Roger," Will said, "Robin seems to think they're quite the ticket."

"The boy shore could do a lot worse," Elwood commented.

"*She* could too," Buddy said.

Furney stopped his cutting and looked at Buddy oddly.

"*What*," Buddy said, catching Furney's expression in the mirror on the far wall of the barber shop, "What's wrong? *What's wrong with my hair?*"

"She's a catch alright," Elwood stated.

Buddy watched Furney's reflection as he stood motionless staring at his head. "*My hair*," Buddy repeated, his voice rising nervously, "*What did you do to it Mister Furney... What's wrong?*"

"Sweet girl," Elwood continued, talking to himself now, as much as anyone else, "And some kind of purty."

"*My hair...*"

Furney finally shook his head and made an irritated face, "Calm down Buddy, *nothing's wrong with your hair*. I just ain't never heard anybody comment on how a *woman* could do a lot worse than the man she's got, *that's all*." He fell silent again and stood with his scissors poised at the back of Buddy's head for a moment and then gave his head another little shake and shrugged.

Running his comb up through Buddy's hair, Furney started trimming again, "But, you're right Buddy," he said thoughtfully. He paused his trimming again as he cocked his head over to the other side for a second and then went quickly back to work. "...She *could* do a lot worse."

Furney stopped again and looked over at Will and winked. "If his voice goes up that high again," he chuckled, "I think one of us'll have to tear a corner off his man-card."

ȣ

"No, really Maggie, I'm not going to feel left out," Lydia said, "My doctor said that I could deliver any day." She swung open the back door on her old Land Rover and stepped out of the way for Maggie to put a tub of clothes inside. "I can just see us all down in Oleander and my water breaking in the middle of Julia Davie's or some other such place I can't afford to be shopping in."

"Are you sure?" Maggie said. She put one foot up on the trailer hitch and rested the tub on her leg, "You're not due 'til the twenty-eighth right?"

"Yes, but with twins, they say that I could go any time from now until then."

"But you went two weeks over with TJ didn't you?"

"Yeah, I did...but he was my first –and he wasn't twins."

Maggie leaned inside the Rover and slid the tub up against the back of the back seat, "Hey," she said, "I didn't know this thing had seats in the back like this." She stood herself back up and faced Lydia, "That's pretty cool; you could carry all kinds of people in there."

"Terry used to haul TJ's whole Scout Troop off on camping trips with it. They'd all fight over who got sit in the back," Lydia said. She stared inside for a moment and then took a deep airy breath.

Maggie laid her hand on Lydia's shoulder and then rubbed it up and down Lydia's arm, "I'm sorry Baby...I didn't mean to stir up any memories."

Lydia sighed and then turned back to Maggie, "That's alright Maggie," she said, "They're good memories." She smiled softly, "Nothing but *good* memories."

Maggie took a long breath and then let it out sharply, "It's hard," she said, "I know it is..." She looked closely at Lydia and a flicker of a smile passed across her face, "Do you remember what Grandaddy used to say about hard courses?"

Lydia nodded, "I sure do. He always said 'A course that's hard *still steers'*."

"It does," Maggie said, "And it *will* get easier...I promise."

"I know it will," Lydia said quietly, "It already has... *if only just a little*." She laid her hand on the back of the car, "At least I can drive this thing without crying now."

Maggie nodded. She raised her eyebrows sharply and rested her hand on her chest, "I finally gave up on James's truck," she said, "...I held onto it for three months and gave it to his father."

"I had thought about selling this," Lydia said, "But, I didn't think TJ would have been able to handle it...and besides, with so many of them running around this town I'd have *still* had constant reminders."

"*I know*," Maggie said, "I'd never seen one when I moved away, and then when I came back it seemed like you couldn't sling a dead cat around here without hitting one of 'em."

"Roger told Terry that he thought it was a requirement that you had to have one if you wanted to join the club at Bird Hollow."

"It sure looks that way."

Lydia turned and slowly looked over her husband's car and then sighed and smiled back at Maggie, "I think I'm glad I didn't sell it."

"I do sometimes wonder if what *I* did was the right thing."

"I don't think there is a right or wrong thing to do," Lydia said, "You do what you have to do to survive...And besides, it's still in the family. You know Jimmy will get it back someday." She paused and looked closely at Maggie.

"*What?*" Maggie said.

"You know I couldn't have made it through these last few months without you Maggie," Lydia said softly, "You've been an angel."

Maggie's eyes moistened, "I'm pretty sure you'd have done fine," she said, "But I'm glad you feel that way just the same."

Lydia reached out and pulled Maggie close, "Trust me," she said, hugging her tightly, "I couldn't have."

Maggie held tightly to Lydia for a long moment. "Okay," she finally said cheerily, pushing back from Lydia, "...That's enough. Today's not the day for mushy-mushy." She held Lydia at arm's length and smiled brightly, "It's the day for good times and baby-stuff. Let's get the other tote loaded up, then we'll go get us a bite to eat, *and then*...It's off to Ormond for an afternoon of pink blankets and Noah's Ark." Turning loose of Lydia, Maggie spun on her heels and headed up the walk, "I'll be right back," she chirped.

Lydia watched her cousin as she went back inside. She rubbed at her belly and let out another sigh, stopping her hands as she felt a slow bulging kick from down low in her abdomen.

Maggie's big Chesapeake came ambling slowly up into the yard and sat himself down at Lydia's feet with a burly grunt. Lydia smiled down at him, "Hey big boy."

Doc looked up at the sound of Lydia's voice. His big brown eyes blinked twice and then he yawned noisily. Lydia reached down and squeezed the base of one of his ears starting his tail swishing happily back and forth.

Lydia looked up as Maggie came back out of the house carrying another purple plastic tub. "Nice of you to join us, Doc," Maggie said as she came down off the porch. "...Did Merv run out of scraps?" She stepped past Lydia and slid the tote into the back of the Land Rover, "Mr Deel cooked a pig yesterday and I haven't seen Doc since the first whiff of cooker smoke made it over from next door night before last."

Doc looked up at Maggie and then lay down and rolled onto his back. Maggie smiled down at him and rubbed his stomach with her foot. Doc's tongue lolled out the side of his mouth.

"You are just rotten," Maggie said. She rubbed a few small circles with her toe and then bent over and rubbed his chin, "You even smell like barbecue." She rubbed his face in her hands a moment longer and then stood herself back up. "Well Lydie," she said, "...I think I'm about ready to eat...How about you."

"You know I am," Lydia said. She patted at her stomach, "It seems like I just can't get enough in me these days."

"Well you *are* eating for three."

Lydia slid her hands down to her hips and patted them a couple times with the flat of her hands, "I don't think they're quite getting all of it, though."

"*Oh please.* Girl you look great...I blew up like Herschel Landry when I was pregnant with Sarah."

"*Herschel Landry,*" Lydia cackled, "I hadn't thought of him in years...*Drime* that boy was *huge*...There ain't no way you were that big."

"You want to bet on that?" Maggie said, "...It took me the better part of ten months after she was born to get back to my pre-baby size, even *with* nursing." She closed the car's back door and shook her head, "With Jimmy I craved peanut butter, snow peas, and the occasional sausage and mushroom pizza. *But with Sarah...*it was *Burgers, Burgers, Burgers.* We had this little twenty-four hour diner near our neighborhood that served the biggest, juiciest, hand-pattied hamburgers you've ever seen. Oh, they were awesome."

Maggie half-closed her eyes and rolled her head around on her shoulders and let out a groan, "I just could not get enough of 'em." She rested her hand on Lydia's arm, "And I'd get a craving for them thrown on me at the worst times," she chuckled. "James made many a Two-AM run for half pound packages of flame broiled goodness and a side of spicy curly-fries."

"Now, that's a good man."

"He took good care of me," Maggie said. "I don't know what it was, but, I'd get crazy when I was pregnant. He put up with *a lot*."

"I just can't see that," Lydia said, "Miss Cool that you are."

"Miss Cool?" Maggie said, "*Ha.* I don't know where you and Hillary have come up with that mess...Let me tell you, I was a wreck. With Jimmy, I got obsessive about cleaning, but then the smell of any kind of cleaner would make me so sick to my stomach that James ended up having to keep my 'Cleanliness Jones' fixed himself *and* keep my food cravings satisfied at the same time...He'd have to change the sheets just about daily because I was always munching on something at night. He'd wake up with cracker crumbs in his hair or pizza crusts up under the pillow, and he'd just get up and strip the bed without comment."

Maggie paused and laughed loudly, "I woke up one morning when I was about seven months along with Sarah after he had made a burger run for me, and I rolled over and he had a hamburger dill slice and half a dozen sesame seeds stuck to his cheek...I tried to slide out of bed and get the camera, but, you know how easy it is to sneak when your belly's out to here-" she held her hands out in front of her stomach, "He woke up as I was trying to get down on my knees next to his side of the bed, and he caught me and scraped the pickle off and threw it at me before I could snap the picture."

"That would have been great to stick in her baby book."

"I was gonna put it on the birth announcement."

"Even better."

"He made me a sundae a day or two later and put some pickle chips on it to try and get back at me, but I actually liked it."

Lydia made a face.

"I know," Maggie said, "Ain't it nasty...I think it must have been the salt or something." She shook her head, "I think I'd puke if I even *tried* to eat something like that now."

"That makes two of us."

Roger backed his truck in the shell-covered parking area on the side of his shop and stopped it with the tailgate just outside the open doors. He cut the motor and the revving sound of a motorcycle engine came to him from inside the shop. He chuckled to himself as he slid out, "I wonder if Joey could use a cold beverage."

Reaching over into the bed, Roger opened the lid on the ice chest and peered down inside at the big rattler that he had half-buried in the ice. He stuck his hands down in and pulled a cold bottle out from the bottom of the ice and sat it down in the bed of the truck. With a quick glance over his shoulder, he grabbed the snake with both hands and lifted the thick body free from the ice, chuckling to himself again as he rested the snake back down and adjusted its big spade-shaped head so that it looked like it was about to strike.

The engine revved in the shop again as Roger let the lid back down and picked his drink back up. He stepped over and hopped up into the doorway and quickly reached over and popped the top off the bottle with the opener on the workbench.

Roger downed a quick swallow, snickering darkly as he looked over to the back corner of the shop and saw Joey silhouetted in the open rear doors, standing over Terry's Triumph, wiping his hands with an old rag as he listened to the motor run. Joey grabbed the throttle and revved the engine once more as Roger made his way back to where he was working.

Roger said, "*Hey Junebug.*"

Joey gave a start and jerked his head around to face Roger. "Hey Chief," he said, smiling crookedly.

"Sounds good."

Joey stuffed the rag down into his back pocket and then revved the engine again. He held the throttle open briefly and then let it idle, smiling at Roger, "It does, don't it." He looked briefly back down at the bike and then turned back to Roger, "Have you had a chance to ask Miss Lydia about me taking it out every now and then?"

"No, not yet."

"I don't want to be a pester, but you know it really needs to be run through the gears...What I do here around the shop just don't cut it."

"Don't worry," Roger said, "I'll ask her."

"Don't if you think it'll bother her."

"It'll be alright...Did you get yourself something to eat or have you spent your whole dinner working on it?"

"I had some cheese and crackers."

"You want a drink," Roger asked, "...I've got some Draughts in the truck."

"Yeah," Joey said, "I *could* use a drink." He cut the engine and then picked up another rag that was laid across the seat. He took the rag and wiped across the top of the shining fuel tank and then took a step back and stared down admiringly at the racer. "*Man*," he said, "This thing is *so* sweet."

"So are you," remarked Roger.

Joey looked up at him and rolled his eyes, "You got drinks..."

Roger took a pull from his drink and then nodded affirmatively. Joey draped the rag across the handlebars and then headed through the shop. Roger followed a couple steps behind him, barely able to contain himself. He stopped a second and put his hand over his mouth to stifle himself as he pictured Joey opening up the ice chest.

Joey stopped at the door and looked back towards Roger.

Roger hunched over and faked a sneeze.

"You alright?"

Roger kept his hand in place covering the bottom half of his face, "Mmhmm."

Joey looked at Roger half a moment longer and then stepped outside. Roger went quickly to the door and stood there as Joey walked over beside the truck.

"I thought you were gonna run them stabilizers over to Will," Joey said, motioning towards the big metal stabilizers that he had laid in the bed of Roger's truck earlier in the morning.

Roger cleared his throat, "That *was* my plan," he said, "But I, I, got a little side-tracked."

"*Oh*," Joey said, turning his attention back to the ice chest.

Roger was about to explode as Joey laid his hand on top of the ice chest and then turned back in Roger's direction and said, "Did you get up with Preacher Potts?"

Roger propped an elbow on the doorjamb and tried to look casual, "Mmhmm."

Joey stared at Roger, "Are you sure you're alright?"

Roger took another pull from his drink and drank it down slowly, "Yeah," he said, staring down at his shoes, "...I'm fine." He studied his feet intently as he crossed one over the other, silently dying inside as he waited for Joey to open the lid.

Joey flipped the lid back as he held his gaze on Roger. Roger looked up and could just see the head of the rattlesnake from where he was standing. He thought he was going to bust if Joey didn't hurry up and look in at it.

Joey stared at Roger a moment longer and then shrugged. He turned and looked down into the ice chest and grunted an easy, "Hunh," as he reached over and nonchalantly picked the big snake out from the chest and held it out over to one side as he leaned himself over a little further to peer down inside. He reached down into the ice with his free hand and fished around 'til he found a bottle of Draught's and pulled it out. Then, without missing a beat, he unceremoniously plopped the chunky rattler back into the ice, flipped the lid closed, swapped the drink to his other hand, and shook the water from his wet one as he walked back towards Roger like nothing had happened.

Roger stared at Joey in disbelief as he stepped up into the shop, popped the top off his bottle, leaned himself back against the workbench, and took a cocky swig of root beer.

"*Alright*," Roger said, "Who told you?"

"Told me what?"

"You know what...about the snake."

"*Snake?*" Joey straightened up and glanced around on the floor, "*What snake?*"

"That's funny."

Joey took another swallow of his root beer and grinned. Roger sat his empty drink bottle on the workbench behind Joey and shook his head. Joey chuckled as Roger turned and walked outside. He turned his drink up and chugged it down and then planted the empty bottle down on the bench next to Roger's and then strutted himself out to where Roger was standing looking down into the ice chest.

"Sorry Rog," Joey said, "Bernie Revels heard about it from somebody and came by hoping to see it...when you started acting all quare on me I figured you were trying to get me."

"Well ain't you just the clever one."

Joey looked in at the rattler, "He is a real beaut ain't he? What'cha gonna do with him?"

Roger grabbed the snake around its neck and lifted it halfway out of the ice, "I was thinking about making Mama a matching bracelet and head band for Christmas."

"I can see that," Joey nodded, "...Have the rattles hanging in the middle of her forehead." He held his hand up to his forehead and wiggled his finger between his eyebrows. "...But it might clash with that alligator hide vest she always wears."

Roger chuckled, "Yeah, you're probbly right. You think maybe Granny Jack might like some snakeskin boots?"

"Oh she'd love some, but you'd have to kill another one first; she's got really big feet."

"*Boy,*" Roger drawled, "She'd break one of 'em off in your butt if she heard you say that."

Joey shook his head.

"You don't think so?"

Joey gave his head another shake. "Uh uh...Granny Jack's not a butt kicker," he said, karate-chopping the air behind Roger's neck, "...She's a rabbit chopper."

"That's a good thing to know," Roger said. He looked at the snake again and then let it slide back down into the ice chest, "I'm gonna run by Herron's and see if Tom wants him and then carry Will's stabilizers down to him...You want to ride?"

Joey looked at his watch, "I reckon I'd better not. I wanted to work on the thing for the bell a little and I need to finish up cutting those rake handles Willie Prescott ordered."

"Did the stainless come in today?"

"Yessir, right after you left...Mickey said to let you know how much he appreciated you understanding about the short and everything."

"It weren't no big deal," Roger said, "I mean, it ain't like he asked for his truck to get broken into."

"I told him not to worry about it."

"Good...Well let me run. I should be back in a little while. But, if I'm not, I'll see you in the morning."

❧

"*Hey Wes*," Roger called out as he stepped out onto the dock at the Wells' family fish house.

Wesley Wells Jr. looked over at Roger from where he was sitting on the gunnels in the stern of the *River Lady* looking up into the boat's rigging. He gave Roger a nod and then hauled his legs over the side of the boat and stepped down onto the dock.

Roger looked up at the deep green nets hanging up overhead from the boat's outriggers, "Those look like they've just been dipped," he said.

"Just finished getting everything back up this morning," Wesley said, as he stepped over next to Roger. He pointed past the *Lady* down the dock to the boat they called *Precious Time*, "We're gonna start getting Will set back up tomorrow."

"Well," Roger said, "My timing must be getting better. I got his new stabilizers in the truck...Where do you want 'em?"

Wes tugged absently at the bill of his weathered cap and then propped his hands on his hips. He looked at Roger for a second and then let his gaze wander around the near side of the dock under the shelter that was built out from the back of the fish house. "I reckon we can just set 'em out here behind the grader," he said, jerking a callused thumb at the long stainless steel rig they used to grade clams.

"Alright," Roger said. Wes followed him as he turned and headed himself back out front to his truck. Roger stepped from the loading dock down into the bed and picked up one of the stabilizers and set it up on the dock. Wesley squatted down on his heels and eyeballed his cousin's handiwork. "What'cha think of 'em?" Roger asked as he set the other stabilizer on the dock in front of Wes.

A short, deep chuckle rose from Wesley's throat. "They ort to do the trick," he replied. He chuckled again, "Will said he was gonna have you make him some *real* floppers, and he weren't kidding."

"Does that boat roll *that* bad?"

"It's worse than some," Wes said. He grabbed up one of the big metal fins and stood himself up, "Daddy's fussed over that boat since we brought it back from Mississippi...." Roger hopped up next to him and picked up the other stabilizer. Wes continued, "He said that if he'd a known just how round they built her bottom he'd a never bought the thing." Roger followed as Wesley turned and headed back out towards the back of the fish house.

"Why's he kept her so long, then," Roger asked, "I mean, why didn't he just sell her?"

Wesley looked at Roger and gave him a little half shrug and cocked his head over to the side. They walked around and sat the stabilizers down behind the fish house. "I don't know, Roger," Wes said, after he had set his load down and straightened himself back up, "You know Daddy..." He paused and turned back out towards the river. Stepping over to the edge of the dock, he stared out over the calm waters for a moment, watching the reflection of the soft, lazy clouds that seemed to be floating easily over the surface.

Roger watched Wesley for a moment and thought about how much older Wesley had always seemed when they were growing up. *He's what,* Roger thought, *Ten...Twelve years older than me.* Roger laughed to himself and shook his head, remembering how he had always called Wesley *sir* when he was younger and had been just a little bit afraid of his quiet, stern-faced, cousin. But then, Wesley had been the first one to come see him when Roger had come back home from the Navy, *and* he had been the first one there when the cancer had finally taken Roger's father.

Roger went over and stood next to Wesley. He looked out and saw a jumble of tiny, silver-sided, baitfish jump in a group out in the river just past the bow of the *River Lady,* and then caught a dark, metallic-blue, flash as something bigger made a dash just under the slick surface after them. Roger privately noted that he was grateful *not* to have been born a little silvery-sided baitfish.

"He got attached to it," Wesley finally said of his father, speaking out over the water, "For some reason he says it reminds him of Grandaddy." He glanced Roger's way and then looked quickly back out over the river. "He's never said how," he continued, "...or why, but sometimes, you know things just kindly mean something without you really knowing why...I think it's that way with *Precious*."

Roger noted for the first time how sweetly Wesley said the name *Precious*. "Would you–"

"Hey y'all," called Will from behind them.

Roger and Wesley turned around to see Will's bright smile as he came over to them with his hand out towards Roger, "How's it going, man," he said cheerfully.

"Not too bad Will," Roger said as he reached out and gave Will's hand a quick shake. Roger gave Will's head a quick once over, "Got your ears lowered, I see."

Will turned Roger's hand loose and crooked his fingers up in his hair and scrubbed quickly at his scalp. "Yeah I did," Will said, "Furney made shore I got my money's worth, too."

"I believe that's probbly the shortest I've ever seen it," Roger said, "That there looks like a summertime haircut." He looked around the sides of Will's head again. "I think I can actually see a little scalp here and there."

"I asked him if Wesley had called and told him to scalp me." Will cocked his gaze at his big brother, "Of course he denied it...But I still don't know as I believe him."

"I hope you thanked him," said Wesley, "He finally gave you a *man's* haircut." He took a step back and appraised Will and Roger. "Y'all wear your hair like you think you're still seventeen." He held his gaze on his brother, "You got a wife and two young'uns," he added, "It's time for you to start looking like somebody."

"*Ahhhh*," Will groaned nasally, "You don't know what you're talking about," he said, dismissing Wesley's statement with a wave. He looked over at Roger and then grinned back at Wesley, "We're too pretty for crewcuts."

Wesley rolled his eyes and walked off down the dock chuckling. Will grinned at Roger, "He let me know where that goat was tied a *long* time ago."

"I know...How many times did he call us Moppy and Shaggy? And what was it he called Buddy? *Wilhelmina?*"

"He didn't think much of Buddy's mullet did he?"

"He let him have it good every chance he got."

"Oh man...let *him* have it. If you had any idea how many times he offered to buy me some curlers and hairbows...If I had a dollar for every time I bet I'd be a millionaire by now."

"You mean to tell me you're not?"

"I realize it may be hard to believe...but, alright now, *brace yourself Roger*...No...No I'm not."

Roger mooned his eyes as he grabbed his chest, "The shock...I don't know if I can take it." He shuffled his feet around, swooning. "Wait, stop, stop the bus," he said. He held his arms out mockingly, steadying himself, "Does this mean I don't get the six figures I was hoping for for the flappers."

"*Six figures*," Will reached out and grabbed Roger firmly by the shoulder and made his voice serious, "Try hard to understand this friend," he said. "Unless more than half of them are behind a decimal point," he shook his head somberly, "It's...it's just not gonna happen."

Roger pained his expression, "But, but," he stammered, "I need that money, don't you understand, I've got marble statuary ordered, urns, fountains...and a pin-ball machine."

Will let his hand fall from Roger's shoulder and laughed, "*Urns?* Oh man, have you ever missed your calling. A pin-ball machine I can see, but...*Urns.*"

"What, you don't think I need urns?"

"Just what would you do with urns?"

"Set them out on the Grecian-Styled portico I'm having added to the front of the shop."

"*A Grecian portico*," Will laughed again, "I see. Now it's all starting to make sense to me...and, what about the statuary?"

"They're for out by the pool."

"The pool? You got a pool at the shop too?"

"Oh no. That's at home, out in the baroque garden."

"I didn't know you had a baroque garden," Will said, "When did you get that?"

"I haven't got it yet," Roger said, "I've got to get the house torn down first."

"You're tearing down your house?"

Roger nodded grandly, "*Oh yeah*. Gonna build me an I-talian villa," he said. "And everybody knows you can't have an I-talian villa without statuary by the pool in the baroque garden."

"You know, I was just telling Elwood Twigg that very thing a little while ago."

"I'm not the least bit surprised. Elwood Twigg has always been very forward thinking and *quite* cosmopolitan."

"Have you told anyone else about your big plans yet?"

"Oh no, I want it to be a surprise." Roger said, he cast two quick glances back each way over his shoulders and then leaned in close to Will. "I wouldn't want people finding out and then the whole town doing it," he whispered. "You know how everybody around here latches on to a new idea...I want it to be unique."

Will nodded, "Understood."

"But," Roger sighed, standing back up straight, "I guess I'll just have to wait a little while longer now." He looked over at the stabilizers he had built for Will, "I really thought those were going to put me over the top...Those were supposed to be the ticket to make me enough money to turn The Dream into a reality." He pursed his lips over to one side and nodded his head sorrowfully, "*Oh well...*Such is life...Maybe those scratch rake handles..."

Will let out a little chuckle, "Just what have you been reading?"

Roger smiled, "You think I can't come up with this stuff on my own?" He sniffed noisily and wiped away an imaginary tear, "That just hurts Will."

"You can come up with some stuff," Will said, "but, I don't remember any of your creativity ever going into such high-browed endeavors....Seems like most of your big ideas always involved somebody's drawers ending up run up the flagpole with Ol' Glory or Mister Sanders getting mooned from the top of the gym...If you have cultivated and redirected your talents to the design and construction of a fine European inspired estate, well...I'm sure we'd all be most impressed."

"Joey's been reading a lot of architecture books lately," Roger confessed.

"*Really?*"

"Mmhmm...That's about all he's done for the past three or four months," Roger said, "He had one in the shop yesterday about some old Italian inspired villas in Florida. He was talking about how he'd like to do something like that around here some day."

"In Sand Ridge?"

"I don't know about in Sand Ridge...He's talked about either up in Ormond or down on the waterway near Pearl Island."

"Well how about that."

"Maggie's been trying to get him to see about signing up for some classes up at Glenfield."

"Good for him," will said, "...Not to change the subject but I ran into Buddy Vander at Furney's this morning."

"It's about time he got Furney to fix his hair," Roger said, "I don't know what he was trying to do..."

"He got it straightened I'd say...I think this warm air has got Mr Furney thinking summertime. Anyhow, the gals at the barbershop were gabbing about you and Maggie when I got there and Buddy got to saying that he never sees you anymore."

"*Really,*" Roger said, "That's odd...We see one another all the time."

Will gave a little shrug, "He weren't griping about it or anything," he said, "Somebody must have asked him about you and Maggie before I came in. After I set down I heard him tell Mister Furney that he couldn't really remember the last time the two of y'all did anything *just* the two of you... Like I said, he weren't griping about it or poor mouthing you or anything...Just stating facts." Will paused a second and then added, "To be honest with you, he really sounded pretty depressed about it."

Roger propped his hands on his hips and looked down into the water, "I wonder why he would..." he trailed off for a moment as he tried to remember the last time he and Buddy had done anything together. After a few seconds, he lifted his gaze up toward the clouds, and then turned back to Will. "You know," he said, "*I* couldn't tell you the last time we did anything together either." He shook his head and then looked down at his feet. He kicked a bleached out scallop shell off into the river and watched it drift slowly down to rest on the sandy bottom, "I've gotten so wrapped up in Maggie–" he stopped himself and looked back up at Will, "She comes by work with something for me to eat just about every day...I've been joking her," he chuckled, "... Calling her my 'Number One Sammich Maker'...Buddy and I used to get together a couple-three times a week and grab a bite and hang out for an hour or so. I guess it has been a pretty good while since we've done that."

"I didn't think he'd say anything to you about it," Will said, "I mean, he probbly wouldn't have even said anything today if he hadn't been getting questioned about y'all for the latest issue of the Sand Ridge Society Report."

Roger grinned at Will, "Gotta keep the gentry abreast of the comings and goings of the well-to-do."

"I figured you'd want to know."

"Yeah," Roger nodded, "I reckon I ort to call him," he said, "I appreciate it Will."

~Chapter Two~

Iris rubbed her wrists softly against either side of her neck as she walked back into her bedroom and sat herself down on the edge of the bed. Kicking off her slippers, she slid her feet down into her shoes, pushed her slippers up under the edge of the bed, and then checked herself in the mirror one last time before she stood to her feet. As she turned around and was smoothing down the bedspread where she had been sitting, she heard the quiet rapping of a small hand on her door. She smiled to herself as her niece's son's voice came through the door; "*Aunt Iris...*" he whispered noisily. She heard another little knock and another noisy whisper; "*Aunt Iris?*"

She reached over and pulled open the door. TJ smiled up at her, "*Hey.*"

"*Hey,*" Iris whispered back.

TJ glanced over his shoulder and then stole into her room and pushed the door closed behind him, "Hey," he said again.

"Hey."

"You fixin' to go?"

"In a minute."

"Can I ask you something?"

"Sure."

"Can you take me shopping after I'm done with my school today?"

"What kind of shopping?"

"Christmas. I want to buy Mama a present."

"Getting started a little early ain't you?"

"I don't want to wait until all the good presents are gone."

Iris held back a chuckle. She grinned at TJ, "Where do you want to go?"

"Someplace nice."

"What do you want to get her?"

"I'm not exactly sure," TJ confessed, "But, I want to get her something nice. Daddy always used to help me."

"Oh," Iris said softly. She touched TJ's face and smiled down at him, "I can't *this* afternoon; I've got to meet with the Parade Committee when I get off work."

TJ's shoulders slumped as his eyes went sad and he let out a little sigh.

"I'll tell you what, though," Iris said, "I'll take an afternoon off one day next week and we'll sneak you off from your mama...*How's that sound?*"

TJ's face brightened and he gave Iris a quick nod.

"I'll tell your mama I need an assistant for the afternoon and we can ride up to town and find her something very special."

"*Great.*"

"It'll give you a few days to figure out what you want to get her, too."

TJ stood staring through Iris with a crooked little grin on his face. She could tell his mind was working on something. After a few seconds he brought his focus back to her and asked, "Do you think we might could get us some taffy while we're there?"

Iris smiled and nodded at him and then reached out and pulled her bedroom door back open. "I don't see why not," she said, "Let's just plan on it. We'll get us something to eat and maybe an Indian Pudding at Pierce's and a bag of Taffy for the ride home."

TJ peeked out into the hallway and then looked back up at Iris with his finger over his lips. "Don't forget," he said, "...Our secret...I want to surprise Mama."

Iris turned an invisible key in the imaginary lock on her lips and then tossed the key back over her shoulder. TJ's smile widened even more as he turned and went out into the hallway. Iris followed him out and then stopped as he glanced down towards the stairs and then looked quickly back up at her, "You're sure you won't forget?"

Iris made an X over her heart. "Cross my heart," she said, "...And, I promise, I won't breathe a word to her about it." She knelt down and held her arms open to TJ. TJ fell against her and she hugged him tightly, as he crushed his face down into her neck. TJ held tightly to her a moment and then leaned his head back, "You smell nice," he said, grinning at her.

Iris lifted her wrist to her nose, "You like my perfume, huh?" She breathed in the scent and then held her wrist out to TJ. He sniffed at it and grinned again. "*That* is called China Musk," Iris said.

"It doesn't smell musty."

Iris laughed, "Not must, *musk*."

"It doesn't smell musky, either."

"No, it doesn't, does it."

"Where'd you get it?"

"At a store in town."

"You think Mama might like some if it?"

"Maybe…And now that I'm thinking of it, the store where I got it has lots of nice things for ladies. We could stop in there and see if there's something she might like."

TJ smiled broadly and nodded, "Yeah," he said, "I want to get her something nice like that."

～

Roger pulled his truck in and parked in his usual spot outside his shop and cut the motor. He leaned over and rolled down the window on the passenger side and then opened his door and slid out. Joey rolled back the big side-door and stepped outside munching on a muffin as Roger closed his door and came around the front of his pickup.

"Morning Chief," Joey said.

"Morning," Roger answered, *"Where'd you get that muffin?"*

"Huh," Joey grunted. He took another bite off the top of the cinnamon and brown sugar crusted muffin and squinted up at the morning sun. He stood there silently for a moment, chewing on the bite of pecan filled goodness and letting the sun warm his skin and then he looked back at Roger and swallowed.

Roger piqued his eyebrows and gave Joey a questioning look.

"What?"

Roger glanced down at the remains of the jumbo sized muffin Joey was holding in his hand, "Where'd you get the muffin?"

"Oh yeah, the muffin," Joey said, wanderingly, "…Uh, Roslynne…Roslynne dropped some by. They're really good."

"Some?"

"Yeah, there's some more in the shop."

"I wonder what brought that on."

"What?"

Roger slouched his shoulders and looked sideways at Joey, *"The muffins."* He shook his head, *"How long have you been up?"*

"Since six."

"That was a rhetorical question."

"Oh."

"Did you get the coffee started?"

"Si...Tenemos café."

"Have you had any of it, yet?"

Joey crammed the last part of his muffin into his mouth and nodded his head. He held up two fingers, "Two cups," he mumbled.

Roger grinned at Joey, "Maybe I should switch back to caffeinated," he said. He turned and went inside the shop and on to the office in front with Joey following behind him. Joey picked his coffee cup up off the workbench on his way by and gulped the last few swallows to wash down the rest of his muffin.

Roger pulled open the top drawer on the file cabinet and grabbed his coffee mug from inside. He held the mug out for Joey and then sat himself down at his desk after Joey had poured it full.

"Mister Albret called after you left yesterday," Joey said, as he set the coffee pot back in place on the back table, "He said he mommicked his trailer and wants you to take a look at it."

"Did *he* say mommicked? I can't picture Mister Albret saying mommicked."

Joey gave a little chuckle and shook his head, "No, actually, I think he said he shivered it, or skivered it or some such truck as that...I told him to bring it on by today."

Roger pointed at the molasses jar sitting on the table next to the coffee pot and Joey picked it up and handed it to him. Roger twisted off the top and watched the steam swirl slowly up from the coffee as he poured some of the dark syrup into it. Joey sat the plate of muffins Roger's younger sister Roslynne had dropped off earlier on the desk in front of Roger.

"You didn't pull an Agnes and just sprinkle a spoonful of grounds in on yesterday's did you?" Roger asked as he stirred the molasses in.

"*No*," Joey said, "I used all new this time."

"Thank goodness." Roger took a sip of his coffee and looked the muffins over. "Man, these look good," he said,

"She sure made 'em big enough." He picked one up and took a big bite. "Mmm," he groaned, "That's moisty."

"*Moisty?*"

"Uh huh...Got to be the moisty-est muffin I've ever had." He took another bite and chewed a bit and then sipped his coffee and swallowed it all down. He took another bite and closed his eyes and savored the taste as he chewed. "Mmm," he groaned again, "It's like it's got a whole stick of butter in it."

"I told you they were good."

"I'll have to give her a call and say thank you," Roger said, "...I could get used to this." He spun his chair around to face Joey. "I tell you what Joey," he said with a grin, "...I'm getting downright spoiled. Between Maggie bringing me dinner just about every day, Mama calling me to stop by for sausage biscuits or eggs and grits nearly every other day, and you bringing Granny Jack's breakfast extras three or four times a week..."

Joey grabbed another muffin and held it up, toasting Roger with it. "Well, you won't hear me complaining," he said. He took a bite off the muffin and chewed it up, "It does make you wonder though," he said, swallowing down the bite, "We must look pretty pitiful...All these ladies wanting to take care of us."

Roger took another swig of his coffee, "Let me look at you," he said. Joey stood still a moment and then slouched over a little and sucked in his cheeks. Roger grinned at him and then shook his head, "You're shore pitiful," he said, "But, I don't know if that's it." Joey sucked his stomach in and drew his shoulders a little further forward and wrinkled up his face miserably, "How 'bout now?"

"Maybe," Roger chuckled, "Have you been walking around town like that?"

"I don't think I could if I wanted too," Joey replied. He shuffled around in front of Roger with his stomach and cheeks sucked in and bent halfway over. He kept flashing a pitiful, wrinkled up face at Roger as he moved back and forth, "What'cha think Rog," he muttered, "Sickly...pitiful?"

Roger's chuckle built up into a quiet laugh, "You looked sickly and pitiful *before*," he said, "Now you just look demented."

Joey knocked his knees together and hugged his stomach; "How 'bout this...Is this better." He closed his eyes down to tight slits and rolled his head back, "Feed me," he pleaded, "Feed me...*Sammiches*...Please Maggie...*Please*...I need *me* a sammich maker...*Please*...*Sammiches*."

Roger leaned back and almost flipped his chair over as he burst out in a loud peal of laughter. He dropped his muffin back down onto the plate and covered his face with both hands.

Joey sucked his cheeks back in and watched Roger carefully. Every time he saw Roger start to peek out at him through his fingers, he would wince up his face again and shuffle back and forth. After almost a minute Roger leaned over with his elbows on his knees, silently shaking his head with his eyes closed; his body hitching as he tried to stifle his laughter. Every time he seemed to be getting himself under control, Joey would start shuffling his feet and the sound would send Roger into another fit of convulsive laughter.

"You're killing me," Roger finally wheezed, waving a hand in Joey's direction, "You gotta stop." He leaned back in his chair again, holding onto his stomach with tears rolling down his cheeks. He looked up at Joey. Joey hitched up his pants and gave another jerky little shuffle. Roger covered his eyes as his body started hitching again, "I'm gonna kill you if you don't stop."

Joey held his elbows out crookedly from his body and shuffled stiffly back towards the door to the shop, "Gotta catch me first."

Roger grabbed a handful of pens and pencils from the cup on the desk and threw them, bouncing them off the back of Joey's shoulders just as he was hunching his way into the shop.

Joey faked a stumble and then swooned himself back around to face Roger, "*Oww*," he drawled pathetically, grabbing at the back of his neck, "*My pancreas*, I think you've bruised my pancreas."

Roger picked up a *Carolina Offshore Action* magazine and slung it in Joey's direction. Joey watched it hit the floor out in front of him and slide to a stop at his feet. He looked up at Roger and grinned, "Nice throw Grandpa. My old Aunt Ethel can throw better from her wheelie-chair than you."

"You don't even have an old Aunt Ethel."

"Yeah, I know, but if I did she'd bring more heat than you, *Rags*."

Roger jumped up towards Joey, "I'll bring you some heat," he said. A hop and two long strides and he had Joey in a headlock, rubbing his knuckles across the top of Joey's head. "*Grandpa*," he growled, "I've got your Grandpa."

Joey pulled and set his weight back and tried to hop himself out from Roger's grasp, tugging at the arm Roger had clamped around his head, and groaning in mock anguish.

"Don't tell me," Roger laughed, "Now I'm *mashing* your pancreas, ain't I?"

Joey pried his head loose and took a quick step back from Roger as he straightened himself up, massaging his ears as he grinned at Roger. "*Oh, my kidneys*," he moaned, "I can't believe you'd noogie all over my poor kidneys."

"You had Mister Porter for Biology didn't you?"

"Uh huh...Advanced Biology, too."

"He'd be so proud."

"Of course he would...he prepped me for Med School."

Roger squatted down and started picking up pencils. Joey stepped over in front of him and shuffled his feet a little, eliciting a low chuckle from Roger and then he knelt down and picked up a pen. Roger arched an eyebrow at him and grinned, "That was hilarious."

Joey picked up another pen and handed it to Roger. "I'm not kidding," Roger said, "I think that little show you just put on was one of the funniest things I've ever seen."

Joey stood himself up and looked down at Roger. He sucked in his cheeks and rolled his eyes around waiting for Roger to look up at him. Roger picked up the last of the pencils and stood himself up. He looked at Joey and started chuckling again. "No more," he said, poking at Joey's ribs with the eraser end of a pencil, "Please, my sides are already hurting."

"Can you ask a bird to say tweet, tweet."

"No, but I can marinate him in a nice vinaigrette and grill him over hickory charcoal."

"So, what's the agenda for today," Joey asked, "Am *I* or are *we* going out to Bird Hollow?"

Roger winced and shook his head, "I had forgotten all about that," he said. He rubbed at his chin for a second and looked around the shop, "I reckon you can handle that yourself...I've got a few things I need to take care of this morning." He looked at his watch and then looked back out over the shop, patting at the ends of the handful of pens and pencils with his free hand and considered his thoughts for a moment, "Yeah," he said, turning back to Joey, "Why don't you finish up your breakfast and then go hook up the trailer and run on out there...Hopefully you'll be done and back in time for sammiches."

Roger stared at Joey for a few seconds waiting for a response. After a brief silence he asked, "*Well*, is that alright?"

Joey looked oddly at Roger but still didn't answer.

Roger snapped his fingers toward Joey, "Hey, man. Are you alright?"

"Huh?" Joey grunted, "Yeah, I'm alright...Why do you ask?"

"Because you've been just a little odder than usual this morning and you're standing there staring at me in silence with this look on your face like you just now realized that you put on wet underwear this morning."

Joey fidgeted a bit and an uncomfortable look crept into his expression.

"What's up?"

"Nothing," Joey said, "...Nothing." He glanced back and forth from Roger's face to the floor in front of his feet, "I've, uh...It's just that I've sort of already got some plans for dinner today."

"That's fine," Roger shrugged. "No reason to get all weird....So what are you doing?"

"Nothing," Joey replied vaguely.

Roger cocked his head to one side and probed Joey's face with a stare.

"I mean, I'm gonna eat," Joey added, finishing his statement with a high, nasally chuckle.

"That makes good sense," Roger quipped, "Who with?"

"*Who with?*"

Roger nodded.

"With, uh..."

The telephone on the wall over the workbench rang and Joey jumped at the sound, "I bet that's Mister Albret," he said, "He sounded like he might call and talk to you before he brought the trailer in." He spun around and went quickly over and answered the telephone. Roger watched him in puzzlement until Joey turned to him and said that it was Mister-Lester-Winslow-wanting-to-know-about-some-metal-grating-for-the-fire-department's-brush-truck-and-would-you-like-to-talk-to-him-in-your-office?

Roger grinned at Joey and said sure and went back into his office and dropped the pens and pencils back into their cup as he sat down at the desk and picked up the telephone. Joey hung up and Roger listened for a few minutes as Lester Winslow talked about the Volunteer Fire Department and it's new-to-them Brush Truck, the renovations at the Methodist Church, the lobster pie he had eaten over the summer in Maine that he still swears is just about the best dang thing he ever put in his mouth, and how he thinks *for sure* that the Sand Ridge High Golden Panthers ought to be in contention for the State 1A Championship this year. When Lester had finished, Roger hung up the telephone and wrote a note to himself about the grating Lester wanted and then picked up his coffee and walked back out to the shop to find that Joey had hooked up the welding trailer and gone.

☙

"So anyway," Roger said into the telephone, as he threw a quick wave out through the open side door of his machine shop to the old gentleman who had just pulled up outside, "...I said all that to say this: I thought we could grab us a hamburger or something at Douglas's and then, if you want to, you could ride to Ormond with me afterwards."

"That sounds good to me Roger," Buddy Vander said, "All I had planned to do tomorrow was mowing Judge Hassell's dove field and then I was going to service my tractor...I can change oil and stuff when we get back."

"You're sure this won't put you out," Roger asked. He leaned back against the open door frame and held his hand outside, catching himself a palmful of sunshine. He watched as Albret Heath, the *Commander*, as most of the people in Sand Ridge called him, slid out of his hunting car, followed by his two big Llewellyn Setters.

"No," Buddy replied. "It ain't no thing. But, you could help me out a little bit though."

"How's that?"

"Would you mind reminding me what you look like so I'll know you when I get there...It's been so long–"

"Ha Ha," Roger said, "I'll see you at Randy's at 11:30."

"11:30," Buddy repeated, "I'm really looking forward to it Bud...I'll see ya."

Roger hung up the telephone and stepped outside. Albret Heath stepped over to Roger with his hand outstretched. His dogs stood flanking him, staring up at Roger.

"Sorry to make you wait Mister Albret," Roger said. He took Albret's hand and gave it a firm shake.

"That's quite alright," said Albret, in his smooth British brogue, "I've naught else to do at the moment." Albret was a little taller than Roger and built lean. He was wearing a tan corduroy suit, and a light grey checked shirt with a dark green knit tie. Albret had a long handsome face with bright blue deep set eyes that seemed to twinkle out at you from under the bill of his shooting cap.

Roger turned the Commander's hand loose and patted one of the dogs on the head, "So you're having a little trouble with your beagle trailer, huh?"

Albret pulled at his mustache, "I'm afraid I've pretty well buggered it up, Roger." He patted the top of the trailer he had hooked behind his meticulously maintained Land Rover. "I got mired behind the Rector's in the greenway between Tippett's Branch and Doctor Donley's. I was in a bit of a rush and I worked a bit harder than I should have to get it out."

"Let's just see what you've got here," Roger said as he walked with Albret over towards the front of the trailer.

Roger looked at the trailer tongue, cocking his head as he considered the ugly new bend the commander had twisted in it.

"There's a crack along the edge of the tank, too," Albret said. He knelt down and pointed up under the edge of the body, "...I wouldn't have thought I could do it, as stout as you two built this rig."

Roger squatted down on his heels and looked closely up at the small crack. He leaned himself a little further over and looked up under the frame, checking for any further damage. "It looks like it's just the tongue Mr. Albret," he said, "Boy, is it ever clean up under here." Albret's dogs crept up and began crowding Roger, sniffing curiously about his back.

"I gave it a good wash after I got it home," Albret said as he stood himself back up. Looking down at Roger, he clucked his tongue twice and his dogs looked up at him. He pointed at the ground behind himself and they both stepped around and sat down obediently at his heels.

Roger looked around underneath the trailer a few seconds longer and then got back up. He smiled at Albret, "It looks like it's mainly the tongue... *That's* the big thing. The wiring to the lights and the plumbing to the water tank should be easy fixes..."

"Do you have time to make the repairs?"

Roger nodded, "Oh, absolutely. We can probbly get started on it tomorrow...It shouldn't take all that long to fix. And I think we've still got some of that paint you ordered for it left, so, everything will still match up just fine."

"Excellent."

"I imagine we'll have you back on the trail by Monday afternoon."

"Would you like me to drop it here?"

"If you could, how about pulling it around to the back. Joey's got my pickup out at Bird Hollow welding that lip on y'all's pitch-kettle."

"Was he able to get the cook top made?"

"Yessir, he sure did," Roger said, "Once he's done today, it'll be all ready for the oyster roast on Saturday."

Albret smiled broadly. "That's capital," he said, "...Just capital. It's been such a dry fall; they should be good and salty."

"We had some last week," Roger said, "And they were about the saltiest I've ever had."

"Did you catch them yourself?"

"No, I always get them from my cousin Jeff. His are all selects," Roger said. He paused and gave a little chuckle, "He's got him a secret hole somewhere that he won't let me or anybody else know where he's getting them. But, he let's us get 'em for half of what we'd have to pay at the fish house, so I don't mind his secrecy."

"I wonder who's supplying the club's," Albret said rhetorically. He looked through Roger for a moment and then gave his head a little shake and asked, "So, you said I should pull around to the back?"

"Yessir."

Albret looked at his dogs and nodded his head towards the car. "Load up," he said crisply. The dogs trotted around and hopped up in through the open driver's door.

"Just pull on around," Roger said, "I'll meet you back there."

Roger walked back inside and made his way to the back of the shop. Albret was just backing in from the street around the big live oak at the back corner of the shop as Roger slid open the back doors. He waved Albret back and then held up a hand, stopping him just outside the shop.

Roger uncoupled the hitch, unhooked the plug, and tilted down the jack as Albret climbed back out and walked around to him. "What year is this thing," Roger asked as he lifted the hitch clear of the ball on the back of the Land Rover.

"The Landie...She's a Sixty-Seven."

Roger gave the olive colored jeep a quick appraisal. "It looks brand new," he said, "How long have you had it."

"Madeleine and I took the train up to Warwickshire in March of 1967 and drove her back home to Dartmouth," Albret replied, "This was the first car we ever owned together."

"You've sure taken good care of it."

"It's been stripped down to its frame and completely rebuilt twice."

"Wow."

"I'm a bit sentimental when it comes to this car," Albret said, "...We've seen plenty of adventures together."

"I've heard they're tough as nails."

Albret grinned at Roger, "It's been mired up over the sills in mud on four continents," he said, "...Completely submerged in two different rivers, had the back glass kicked out by a mule, been rammed by a cape buffalo, had its back seats eaten by a honey badger, was nested in by a Derbyshire Redcap, had tires flattened by an angry mother lion *and* a crocodile, and was once shot on a grouse hunt by a member of the royal family." Albret paused a moment and let out a little chuckle, "But, I think the hardest thing it ever had to do was to survive through my three raucous boys learning to drive."

Roger smiled and nodded his head, "Speaking of boys," he said, "I want to thank you for being so good to my cousin's little boy Mister Albret...You've really done a lot to ease his father's passing."

Albret turned his face into the sun and breathed in deeply, "That boy and I share some common ground." He turned back to Roger, "I wasn't much older than he when I lost my father...He was *my* whole world then."

Albret pulled off his shooting cap and tapped it absently against his thigh. "I was one of six children," he said, "Doctor John Powell and his wife Maria were dear friends of my parents' who were unable to have children of their own. So, when my father died, they stepped in to help my Mum, and I, being the only boy, got most of John's attention. He and my father shared a great love of the countryside; they had been shooting and fishing companions for years. He was a wiry, almost frail looking man, but, he had the heart of a Welsh Black." Albret paused a moment, chuckling quietly at a memory, and then looked at Roger with that little twinkle in his eye, "...The day of my father's funeral, he took me for a walk and he said to me, 'Brettie, are you still breathing? You most certainly are...Then you're not licked yet.' That was the way he looked at life, and as much as he taught me later, I'd say *that* lesson was the one which has meant the most to me."

Albret set his cap back in place on his head and propped himself against the trailer, "When your friend Buddy shared with me what had happened," he continued, gazing off down towards the river, "I felt that it was my opportunity to do for someone else what John had done for me." He looked at Roger and grinned, "But it has all really turned out to be yet another blessing for *me*."

"He's a neat little guy."

"He's sharp," Albret said, "Doesn't let anything slip by him...And the questions he asks..."

"Lydia said that his father was the same way; he was going to know everything there was to know about anything he came in touch with."

"My middle son Randall is like that too," Albret said, "and so is *his* son. They make you realize how much you really don't know that you *thought* you did with all their questioning."

"It's great to be humbled by ten-year-olds, ain't it?"

"Keeps me on my toes, Roger," Albret replied. "I like to have answers to *give*," he said, and a little gleam came into his eyes, "Never stop learning, never stop becoming all you can become." He paused a second as if he wondered if he should complete his thought and then smiled again and said, "Who you become is a gift that you give to yourself... *Virtus*, Roger...Become all the man that God has made you to be. It's the *Art* of manliness."

"I'll have to remember that," Roger said, "Was it from Dr Powell too?"

Albret smiled and gave his head a little nod. He rapped his knuckles twice, lightly on the roof of the trailer, "I'll be going now," he said. He stuck his hand out, "It's been a pleasure."

Roger shook his hand, "I'll give you a call when we're done with it, Mister Albret."

"Thank you," Albret said, "Just leave a message with the Missus if I'm out." He turned to go and then stopped and turned back to Roger, "Oh," he said, "I almost forgot. Have you been able to find the book for Miss Maggie yet?"

"Not in my price range yet," Roger said, "But, I've not given up...I've still got a couple more shops to check."

"I do wish you would just let me give you one of mine," Albret said, "Then we'll be sure you'll have it to give for Christmas."

"I appreciate it Mister Albret," Roger said, "But I know the books you've got are worth a lot more than the ceiling we've set for Christmas gifts."

Albret's brows knitted as he folded his arms across his chest. He took a step back from Roger and quickly looked the trailer over and then turned back to Roger. "Why don't we just do a bit of barter for it then," he said, "Trailer repairs for Karen Blixen."

Roger chuckled lightly, "This ain't going to cost that much to fix," he said, "I really appreciate the offer Mister Albret, but–"

"How about for my second edition, then...It's not signed, but it's a very nice copy."

Roger eyed Albret Heath as he thought for a moment. "Alright," he said, "It's a deal. But, I'm reserving the right to knock a little bit off the price of whatever you bring in here for me to do next time."

Albret stuck his hand out again. "Good," he said, smiling as Roger gave him another firm shake, "Maddie will be so glad to know that your Maggie's going to be getting it for Christmas...I'll bring it with me when I come to pick up the trailer."

"I appreciate it," Roger said, "I'll call you when she's ready."

Albret touched the brim of his cap and turned once more to go, "Take care, Roger."

~

"Alright Mr. Wells, we're almost finished."

Wesley Wells let his breath out in a sharp puff as he leaned forward and pulled his boots on again. He pulled the shoehorn out from behind his heel and handed it to Monica Harris, the occupational therapist who had been treating him since he came home from the hospital. She smiled at him and then watched as he, with very deliberate motions, looped and tied the laces on one boot, and then the other. He finished and sat himself back up, grinning.

"That's great," Monica told him. She paused for a second. "...That's the last thing on your list you know."

"I told you I weren't gonna be wearing Velcro shoes the rest of my life." He pointed over to the clunky, white sneakers, with the wide straps criss-crossed tightly across their tops, sitting over on the floor by the front door and said, "You can carry them things off with you when you go."

Monica stood up and looked over across the living room to where Mary Wells had just sat herself down. "I talked with the PT earlier," Monica said, "She said she was discharging Mr. Wells." She turned back to Wesley and smiled, "I'm really happy *and* a little sad to say this, but, I really don't think you're going to need *me* any more, either."

Wesley looked closely at Monica and appraised her for a long moment. "So, this is it," he said, thoughtfully, "Well, Miss Harris, I can't thank you enough for all you've done."

"You don't need to thank me Mr. Wells. You're the one who's done all the hard work." Monica smiled broadly and pushed her hair back behind her ear, "I'm just really glad to have been able to see all your progress, and to have been able to get to know you all as well as I have." She turned back to Mary, "I don't usually get the opportunity to get to know my patients' families like I have yours," she said, "You have a very nice family. It has truly been a wonderful experience coming out here these past few months."

Mary nodded. She looked at Wesley, smiled softly, and said, "We are blessed."

"Do you mind if I–" Monica was interrupted by a bang on the screen door. They all turned to see a furry, black head stick in through the gap that had just been made in the door, and then a scruffy little dog wriggle his way into the house. The dog ran in and across the room and bounced off of Monica, leaving a wet tongue mark on the thigh of her slacks, circled round Mary, and then headed back toward Wesley.

The little dog's left ear came to rest, flopped over the top of his head as he hopped up and planted himself in Wesley's lap. "Hey Boy," Wesley said, rubbing his hand firmly back and forth along Huff's back.

TJ snatched open the door and stomped sullenly into the house, the front of his shirt and pants stained with black mud. "What's the matter, Honey," Mary asked him, "*What's happened to you?*"

TJ looked up at his grandmother with black ooze dripping from his chin. His eyes were fiery. "Huff tripped me up," he fumed, "We were racing home around the pond and he tripped me up." He pointed angrily at his furry playmate, "*You cheated!*"

Monica looked down at the little mixed-breed and was almost certain that she saw a smile flash across the dog's face.

"Now TJ," Mary said soothingly as she made her way over to TJ, "You know dogs don't think that way." She touched her husband's shoulder and then scratched the top of Huff's head on her way by Wesley's chair, "...He just took the shortest route he could see." She pulled the dish towel out from where she had it hanging at her hip over her apron strings and gently wiped the muck from TJ's face, "I bet just as soon as he heard you say the word 'home', he just lit out for the door and never looked back...Hold your chin up for me now."

TJ lifted his chin and worked hard at keeping his face sour as Mary finished getting the last of the mud out of his eyebrows. He looked over at Huff and frowned again, "For somebody who don't think that way, he sure does look awful proud of himself."

Monica reached down and pet Huff's head and then rubbed briskly under his muzzle. She looked over at TJ and smiled, "I can take this little pest home with me if you want to be rid of him," she said, "He reminds me of a little Scottie I had when I was a girl."

TJ's eyes darted back and forth from Monica's face to Huff's, "N...n...no," he stuttered, "That's alright. I...I'm not *that* mad at him." TJ looked at Huff again. Huff raised one paw and waved it at him to shake. TJ's eyes softened and he grinned slowly, "I don't reckon he *really* meant to do it." He stepped over and grabbed Huff's paw and gave it a little shake, "...Did you boy?"

"Alright," Monica said, "but you let me know if you change your mind...I'll come right back down and get him." She stepped over to the kitchen table and slid out a chair, "Mr. Wells, I've just got to write down a few notes and then I'll be out of your hair." She sat herself down and flipped open the notebook she had brought in with her earlier.

Wesley said, "We hate to see you rush off Miss Harris."

"We sure do," said Mary, "Can you stay and visit with us a bit?"

Monica looked up at Mary and then checked her watch. "I've got an eval scheduled for 3:30," she said.

"Is it here in Sand Ridge?"

Monica nodded, "Yes ma'am." She flipped a page back in her notebook. "Let's see...where was that? Yeah, here it is... on West Surrey Road... *Nineteen* West Surrey Road."

Wesley clucked his tongue, "Probbly Lizzie 'Beth Tich..."

Monica looked closely at the notebook page. "Mmm hmm, Elizabeth Tich," she said, "So it is *Tich* and not *Tick*...I was wondering when I read it."

Wesley looked up at Mary and then turned back to Monica, "She's a pistol," he said, "...Fell off her back porch and broke her hip *and* her shoulder." He shook his head, "Tripped over one of her cats..." Monica wrinkled her brow at him as he gave a dark, little chuckle. Wesley caught her look and shook his head at her. "I ain't laughin' at *that*," he said. "I was just laughin' at her husband...He was so mad at that cat; while Lizzie was in the hospital, he pure-t went to work on the local cat population." Wesley shook his head again and grinned at Monica, "*Generally speaking*, Charlie Tich is one of the kindest, most mild-mannered fellas you'll ever meet. But, for nearly two whole weeks last month, he was whackin' and stackin' cats to beat the band."

"*Oh Wesley*," Mary said, waving her dish towel at her husband, "She doesn't want to hear that mess." She turned back to Monica, "Can you come back and have some supper with us when you're through...Since we won't be seeing you any more."

"Well, why won't you be seeing me anymore? I was hoping that I might be able to stop by just to visit every now and then," Monica said, "...When I'm out this way."

Mary looked over at Wesley and smiled at her grinning husband. "Of course you can," she said, "You're welcome here anytime."

"I'm certainly glad to hear that. I'd really miss seeing y'all, and I'd hate to think that I wasn't going to get to see those twins when they come...After coming out here and watching Lydia growing for the last few months." Monica took a deep breath and sighed, "I just love babies," she added wistfully, "And besides that, what in the world would I do for fresh eggs?"

"I could always send you off with a setter to take home," remarked Wesley.

"How much longer is it supposed to be now 'til the babies come MeeMaw?" TJ asked.

"They're due the twenty-eighth," Mary said, "But, with twins, it could be any time."

"How come?"

"Because there's twice as many babies taking up the same space that *one* little one did before," Mary said, pinching at TJ's ribs. TJ giggled and hopped a step back from his grandmother. "Why don't you run on out back and get some clean clothes on," Mary told him, "Your laundry's folded up on top of the dryer." She patted TJ on the head and sent him on his way down the hall. Huff jumped down from Wesley's lap and followed TJ out to the back porch.

Mary rested her hand tenderly on Wesley's shoulder, "We'd still like you to come back for supper today, if you can," she said.

"We *shore* would," Wesley agreed.

"I think I can," Monica said slowly, "I'd like that very much." She bit down on the end of her pen and ran through her schedule in her mind. "Yeah," she said brightly, "I'm sure I can."

"Good, good," Mary smiled, "Can you be back here by around five-thirty?"

Monica asked, "How far is it to the Tiches'?"

"'Bout five minutes door to door," Wesley replied.

"I should be able be back here by five-thirty then."

Wesley reached out and Mary helped him to his feet. He looked over at Monica, "I've gotten to where I look forward to seeing you come by young lady...I think I'm actually gonna miss our torture sessions," he said, watching Mary as she walked off into the kitchen.

"*Uh*," Monica grunted. She slouched her shoulders and pinched her eyebrows down tight, "*Torture sessions?*" She cocked her head at Wesley, "After all that big talk about how much nicer I was than the PT...The truth finally comes out." She looked over into the kitchen at Mary and made her voice jealous, "I bet he's been blowing all that sunshine at her for the past six months too, hasn't he?"

Mary had just taken a pound cake out of the oven and was gently sitting it down on a pad on the counter. She turned around to face Monica with a grin on her face, "He liked Donna just fine," she said, "...But, he didn't ask me to make *her* a pound cake."

Monica looked over at Wesley with a flattered grin on her face. Wesley whistled airily as he examined the ceiling.

"*Mr. Wells...*"

Wesley slid his hands down into his pockets and took a couple casual steps toward the kitchen.

"...You remembered the pound cake."

Wesley stopped and looked over a Monica. "Yeah," he said, "I did. But, you'll have to settle for some of Miss Mary's *canned* briarberries this time, though."

"Oh, I think I'll manage it just fine."

"I kindly figured you would."

"Now, what is that supposed to mean," Monica said coyly.

Wesley gave Monica a little half smile, "Nothing much," he said, "Except that, for a skinny girl, you're just about the eatinest thing I've ever seen."

"I can't help it if Mrs. Wells is such a good cook. Coming here is like going to my grandmother's down in Brunswick."

"Don't pay him any mind, Monica," Mary said, "I'm glad you feel at home."

"I really wish I had more patients down this way...I'd love a reason to *move* down here."

Wesley said, "Well, I can think of four or five young men I know would love to have a shot at giving you a reason to move here...As a matter of fact–"

"Now don't you go playing matchmaker," Mary scolded, "You know better..."

Monica flipped her notebook closed and stuck her pen back behind her ear. She slid her chair out and checked her watch as she stood to her feet, "I'm going to go ahead over to see Mrs. Tich so I'll be sure and be back by five-thirty," she said, "Can I pick up anything to go with supper for you while I'm out?"

"No, I believe we've got everything we need," Mary said, "But, thank you."

"Alright then..." Monica crooked her notebook up in her arm and patted Wesley on the shoulder as she made her way to the door, "I'm proud of you Mr. Wells," she said, "... You've certainly come a long way."

"Alright TJ," Lydia said as she came into her son's bedroom, "It's about time for bed."

TJ was leaned back against a pile of pillows at the head of his bed with a book open in his lap. Huff was stretched out on the bed next to him.

"...What'cha got there?"

"It's the book Mister Albret gave me."

"It is, huh?"

TJ looked up at Lydia, "Yes ma'am," he said, folding the book closed in his lap. "It's *Kim*...It's by the same man that wrote the poem Daddy gave me to hang up on my wall." He pointed up to the framed copy of "If" he had hanging over his dresser.

Lydia sat down on the bed next to TJ and put her arm around his shoulder. She pulled the cover open on TJ's book and noted the signature on the first page. "Well, this book's autographed," she said, "Let me see it for a second." Straightening herself up, she took the book from TJ's hands and opened it back up. She held it out in front of her belly and flipped back the cover page; *MacMillan & Company Limited*, she read, *London 1901*. She looked over at the autograph: *Dearest Nil, May your adventures take you as far as your imagination will. Your Friend, Rudyard Kipling*

Lydia glanced over at her son. "Did you say he *gave* this book to you, or he *loaned* it to you?"

TJ smiled brightly at her, "*Gave it*," he said proudly.

"You didn't *ask* him for it did you?"

TJ's brow puckered and he shook his head no. "No ma'am," he said, "*I wouldn't do that*." He looked down at the book and then back up into his mother's eyes, "He told me it was his daddy's book...He said he hoped that I'd enjoy it as much as *he* did when he was little."

"Well, *are* you enjoying it?"

TJ nodded, "Yes ma'am, I sure am...It's *real* good. It's about an orphan boy in India; he's a British spy. I'm only up to chapter four, though."

Lydia gently closed the book again and slid it back into TJ's lap, "You take good care of this TJ," she said, "It was very, *very* thoughtful of Mr. Albret to give this to you."

"Don't you worry, *I will*."

~Chapter Three~

"Yeah Fox," Roger said, as he slid himself out from the booth. He fished through his wallet and dropped a couple dollars tip on the table and then picked his cap up from off the seat, "I hate you didn't get to see Buddy, too." He put his cap on and shook his head, "It ain't at all like him not to show up for a meal."

Frankie Lee slid out from the booth and stood up beside Roger, "Well," he said, "Tell him I said hey anyhow...Maybe I'll see him next time I'm in town." He patted Roger on the shoulder and walked off towards the front door of Douglas's.

"Yeah," Roger said, following Frankie out, "But, who knows when that's gonna be."

Frankie looked back over his shoulder at Roger and grinned, "Country mouse don't have much reason to come to the big city, Boss."

"*Big city*," Roger chuckled. He looked over to the man and woman behind the counter and gave them a little wave, "See you Randy...Zoë."

Frankie pushed the door open and pulled his sunglasses down into place from off the top of his head as he stepped out into the bright sunshine. Roger followed him out and the few steps down the sidewalk to Frankie's truck. Frankie faked a shiver as he rolled up his shirt sleeves, "Hard to believe it's November."

Roger said, "Almanac says it's gonna be a white Christmas."

"I better break out my Long Johns then."

"You go right ahead," Roger said, "I'm holding out. Until I see frost...mine are staying in the attic. I don't want to jinx it." He stuck his hand out and Frankie gave it a firm shake, "It's good to see you Fox...Don't be such a stranger."

"Ain't nobody stranger," Frankie grinned.

Roger grinned back at Frankie, "'Cept me." He stepped down into the street and headed across towards where he had parked his pickup over on the other side.

"You take care Roger," Frankie smiled, "*Hey*. Come on down to the Point some time," he said, "I'll take you out and we can do a little fishing."

Roger stopped in the middle of the street and turned back to Frankie, "I don't know as I can afford for *you* to take me out fishing," he said, "...I mean; your prices were high *before* they wrote you up in *Southern Inshore*, I can only imagine what you charge now."

"Ain't nothing a high roller like you can't handle."

Roger waved Frankie off and then turned and walked on across the street and climbed in his truck. He reached up and grabbed his cell phone from the sun visor as he closed his door behind him. He hit the speed dial for Buddy's cell and then gave another quick wave out the window to Frankie as Frankie backed away from the curb and drove away. Buddy's voice mail picked up and Roger hung up, dropped the phone down on the seat, and sat silently for a moment staring out his side window down the street.

Roger thought about Buddy and had an uneasy feeling down in the pit of his stomach. He just couldn't figure why Buddy hadn't shown up after the big deal he had been making about Roger never going to eat with him anymore. Running over their conversation from the day before when he had called Buddy and asked him to grab a bite to eat that day and then ride up to Ormond with him in the afternoon, he was sure that they were clear on their plans.

He cranked his truck and backed out into the street, deciding to ride by the hardware store to see if Buddy had gotten tied up with somebody there.

Roger cruised past the parking lot at *Sand Ridge Builder's Supply and Hardware* and didn't see Buddy's truck. He stopped in the road out in front of the store and called Buddy again on his cell. *Come on Buddy,* he thought, *pick up.* Buddy's voice mail picked up again and Roger hung up. He dialed his shop and asked Joey if he had heard from Buddy.

"No sir Cap'm."

Buddy's mowing Judge Hassell's dove field, he thought. He stepped down on the gas and headed his truck down the road toward the Judge's farm out on the eastern side of town. He glanced down Bridge Road toward Maggie's and then rounded the bend and pressed his foot down a little firmer on the gas and sped his pickup up the road as it straightened out past Bird Hollow.

Roger chewed the inside of his lip and wondered at why he was so worried. If Buddy hadn't seemed so excited about spending the day with him, maybe he wouldn't have been concerned, but something just didn't feel right.

The old tobacco barn at the edge of Judge Hassell's dove field came in to view as Roger rounded the last curve and he scanned the field for Buddy on his tractor. He pulled his truck up and stopped at the gate, still looking for his friend as he slid out and went to open the gate. He unhooked the chain and swung the gate open and took a couple steps forward and looked the field over again. With his gaze, he followed the oddly crooked line at the edge of the last strip that had been mowed across the field. And there, on the low side of the field, back towards the creek he saw the back end of Buddy's tractor with one of the back wheels off the ground and the bush hog pointing high into the air. He had a sudden sinking feeling in the pit of his stomach and remembered his father telling him about Tom Abernathy running himself over with a tractor when his father was a boy. He squinted his eyes down hard but didn't see Buddy anywhere and found himself praying that Buddy was over on the other side of the tractor trying to figure out how to get it out from where it was stuck.

Spinning around, Roger got quickly back behind the wheel and drove his truck across the field towards the tractor. About half way across, he slammed on the brakes. He looked again, back to where the mowed line began to go crooked and then cut the wheel hard and jammed his foot down on the gas. The pickup whipped around as the engine roared and the tires slung dirt and grass out in trails behind the truck. He shook his head and squinted down hard again to be sure. As he drew closer, what he thought he saw grew clearer...there was Buddy, lying on his side in the freshly mown stubble with his arm part way up, waving his hand weakly. His hand was covered in blood.

Roger flew the truck up beside Buddy and was out before it came to a complete stop. He jumped over his friend and was down on his knees staring into Buddy's swollen face in a second.

"*Where are you Buddy?*" he said quickly.

Buddy's eyelids fluttered; "Judge Hassell's," he whispered.

"Where's it hurt?"

Buddy opened his left eye just a narrow slit and groaned. "All over Rog," he hissed, taking a shallow breath, "...More than anywhere else."

Roger looked him over. Buddy's face was swollen and red and he was bleeding from his scalp. His left leg was twisted out at an odd angle and the end of a broken stick was poking out through the thigh of his jeans. He noticed some red welts on his arms.

"Did you get into some hornets?"

Buddy nodded weakly and started to roll onto his back. Roger grabbed his arm and stopped him, "Buddy," he said, "Don't move...You stay just like you are, okay?" Buddy stopped and groaned again, "It hurts to breathe," he whispered airily.

"Okay Buddy," Roger said, "It's okay." He looked Buddy over again and then continued, "My phone's in the truck. I'm gonna go get it and call the Rescue Squad. *Don't move.*" He jumped up and ran to his truck, grabbed his phone, and dialed 911 as he came back and knelt down in front of Buddy.

"I need the Sand Ridge Rescue Squad. My friend has had an accident with his tractor. Yes, yes," Roger said impatiently, "Put me through. Yes, no, no I haven't. Please just put me through." Roger paused a moment for the transfer and then said, "Miss Berta, this is Roger Lowell. Buddy Vander has had an accident and we need the rescue squad...We're out at Judge Hassell's dove field...Yes," he rested his hand gently on Buddy's arm, "Yes, Yes ma'am, yes ma'am, no ma'am I haven't, yes ma'am...Tell Rob to turn in at the first gate and come straight across the field, he'll see my truck...yes ma'am...He says it hurts to breathe...I don't know, no, no ma'am, I can't tell...yes ma'am...Thank you."

Roger flipped his phone closed and dropped it into his shirt pocket. He leaned in close and stared into Buddy's face. It hurt him to see the pained look on his friend's face. "They're on the way Buddy," he said, "Hang in there."

Buddy's brow furrowed deeper and he strained a whisper; "Can you get my wallet?"

"*Your wallet?*"

Buddy grunted painfully and gave another weak nod. Roger leaned over him and slid Buddy's wallet out of his back pocket. He sat back down and held it up for Buddy to see.

"What do you want me to do with it?"

Buddy took a shallow breath and let out a slow wheeze. Roger leaned his ear down close to Buddy's mouth. Buddy whispered, "Keep it for me...there's a note...in it for...for Hill...if I die..."

A chill ran down Roger's spine that sent a shiver through his body, "You're not gonna die Buddy." He heard the siren from the ambulance wailing in the distance and got himself up on one knee and looked past his truck to the open gate, "They're coming Buddy."

Buddy reached out and grabbed Roger's hand. Roger leaned back down close to Buddy's face. "*Promise...*" Buddy said "...Promise you'll give it to her."

Roger looked up as the Rescue Squad pulled into the field and quickly stood himself up and waved them over. Buddy coughed and then groaned painfully. Roger looked down at the worn leather wallet in his hand. He could just barely make out the word *Daddy* that had been carved onto the front fold. He slid it into his back pocket and knelt back down with Buddy as the ambulance came to a stop in front of them.

"I promise," he said.

੭

"Maggie," Roger said, "Is Hill there with you?"

"Yes why?"

"Keep smiling and be calm."

"*What is it Roger?*"

"I'm in my truck following the Rescue Squad to Ormond."

"Mmm hmm..."

"Buddy's had an accident...I don't know how bad he's hurt."

"Okay," Maggie said coolly, she looked over at Hillary and nodded her approval of the blouse Hillary was holding up for her, "So...anything interesting happening today?"

"He stirred up some hornets while he was mowing at Judge Hassell's and somehow he fell off the tractor and it ran over him."

Maggie choked back the urge to gasp, "*Well*," she said, forcing herself to keep a steady tone, "How about that." She winced up her face and shook her head at the skirt Robin was holding up for an opinion, "...*And then?*"

"I don't know exactly," Roger said, "It hurt him to talk... When I found him he was laying out in the middle of the field. His tractor's down at the edge of the field halfway over in the creek."

"How's he doing?" Maggie asked, trying to keep her voice bright.

"He's hurting pretty bad and he seems pretty scared."

Maggie replied, "I would imagine so," she paused and smiled at Robin, "Yeah, that one looks good," Roger heard her say, "Hey y'all, I'm gonna go outside for a minute...I'm losing my signal. Alright, I'll be right back. I'll tell him." Roger heard a quiet chuckle that he thought was from Hillary and then the muffled sound of movement. After a couple seconds Maggie said, "Okay, I'm outside, what do you want me to do."

"*First*: Stay cool. Then, tell Hillary what's going on and then *you* bring everybody home...I don't want Hillary driving."

Maggie paced back and forth on the sidewalk out in front of the store, "Understood...How bad do you think he is Roger?"

"I have no idea," Roger said, his voice breaking. He cleared his throat and took a long breath, "I need to go," he said, "Tell Hillary not to worry...I'll call you."

"*Roger?*" Maggie waited for a moment and then realized he was already gone. She flipped her phone closed and stood on the curb watching a young mother unloading a baby from the back seat of her car. *How do I tell Hillary,* she wondered, *Oh dear, sweet, Lord, please help him.*

"Look at that TJ...Can you see their little faces?"

TJ leaned in close to the monitor. Wrinkling up his face, he pointed at a green glob on the screen, "Is *that* a face?"

"It sure is," Kim, the ultrasound technician, said. She froze the screen and then moved an arrow around and pointed it at the other pale face, "That one is sucking its thumb, see?" She clicked again and the screen came back to life, "She just pulled it out again."

Lydia giggled and then TJ laughed as the babies shook and then squirmed tightly together a moment and then settled back down. Lydia watched the expression on TJ's face as he studied his two baby sisters closely. She nudged him gently with her elbow, "Pretty neat, huh?" she said, "Aren't you glad you decided to come?"

TJ stared at the screen until he was able to make out clearly what he was looking at, "*Hey,*" he blurted, "That one just stuck her tongue out!"

"I bet you'll be seeing a lot of that in the years to come," Kim remarked.

TJ kept staring at the screen. "I think this one's covering her face," he said, pointing down towards the bottom of the image. He paused a moment and glanced up at Lydia. "Can you make 'em move again Mama? They're not doing anything now."

"How about we listen to their heartbeats," Lydia suggested. "...Could we do that Kim?"

"Sure," Kim said. She clicked her computer and then adjusted a knob and the room was filled with the deep, rhythmic, swishing of the twins' hearts beating. TJ's eyes grew wide.

Kim moved her hand around on Lydia's stomach until a heart was plainly seen in the middle of the screen, "And *there* is the source of half of that ruckus," she said. She moved the arrow around the screen and counted, "One, two, three, four chambers...now let's check your sister Little Miss." She moved her hand around again and quickly brought up another pulsing miracle for TJ to see, "One, two, three, and four. How's that TJ?"

"Can you do *me*...I want to see mine."

Lydia laughed, "I don't think Miss Kim can do yours today Sweetie."

"*Can she next time?*"

"There isn't going to be a next time," Lydia said, "The next time we see these babies, we'll be holding them in our arms."

TJ looked glum.

Kim said, "Tell you what we'll do...I've got this little monitor that we use just to listen to the babies' heartbeats." She looked at Lydia, "If your mother doesn't mind, when I'm done with her, I'll squirt a little jelly on it and hold it on your chest and let you hear yours beating."

"That's fine with me," Lydia agreed, "How would you like that TJ?"

TJ's face brightened, he flashed a broad smile and nodded his head enthusiastically.

"Good," Kim said, "I'll be done in a just a few more minutes and then we'll let you take a listen..."

❧

"Alright TJ," Lydia said as she pulled into the hospital parking lot, "Finish up that milkshake...We can't take it on the tour with us."

"Yes ma'am," TJ said, sucking a big slurp up through the straw, "May I ask you why I can't take it on the tour with me?"

Lydia pulled up and backed into an empty spot under the limbs of a big longleaf pine down near the end of the lot. "Yes you may," she said, cutting off the motor, "...Because I don't think that–" She stopped in the middle of her sentence and gave her head a little shake. She smiled down at her rounded-out belly and then gave a sighing little snicker as she struggled to get herself turned around enough in the seat to look back at TJ face to face.

"*You know what*," she said when she finally got herself situated, "I've changed my mind...you *can* take it with you. *What's the harm?*"

TJ smiled and took another draw on his milkshake. His eyes twinkled as he swallowed it down, "That's just what I was thinking... *What's the harm?*"

Lydia reached back and pinched at his knee with her knuckles. TJ squirmed up against the door and quickly drew his knees up away from her, giggling.

"You think you're pretty funny, don't you," Lydia said.

"Mmm hmm," TJ nodded, sticking the straw back into his mouth and slurping loudly. Lydia feigned at his knee again and he threw his door open and popped out onto the pavement. He slammed the door and ran around and opened Lydia's door for her.

Lydia handed TJ her purse and then worked her way out of the Rover. He handed her purse back as he closed the door and then held his hand up for her to take. She slung her purse up over her shoulder and smiled down at him as she took his hand. "Thank you sweetie," she said, "You make me feel like *such* a special lady."

TJ's cheeks flushed and he dropped his gaze down to his shoes. Staring down, he nudged a smashed bottle cap with his toe for a long moment until Lydia gave his arm a gentle tug. TJ looked up slowly at his mother and smiled shyly.

"That's just another way that you're like your daddy," she said.

TJ's smile widened briefly and then he dropped his chin again. When he looked back up into Lydia's eyes, his smile was gone. "I sure do wish he was here," he said.

Lydia put her arm around his shoulders and pulled him to her, "Me too sweetie," she said softly, holding him close, "Me too." She took in a long, deep breath and then let it out slowly. Leaning down, she kissed him on top of his head and then lifted his face up to hers and smiled brightly.

She hesitated for a second and then said, "*You know what?*"

"What?"

Reaching down quickly, Lydia grabbed TJ's milkshake and pulled it up to her mouth, "*This–*" She took a noisy pull at the straw as TJ tried to get the cup back from her.

"Hey!"

"*I* paid for it," Lydia joked as she took down a big swallow and then held it out of his reach for a moment longer before handing it back. TJ snatched the cup to his chest and gave his mother a look that was meant to be menacing. They heard the sound of a siren coming up the road and both turned to see the Sand Ridge Rescue Squad pull in and head around to the emergency entrance.

"Isn't that Uncle Roger's truck," TJ said, pointing at the red pickup that was following behind the ambulance.

"I believe it is TJ..." Lydia replied, concern flashing across her face. She fell silent as she followed the two vehicles with her gaze. She looked back down at TJ, "Let's head over that way," she said, leading him quickly across the parking lot towards the side entrance of the hospital.

Cradling one hand up under her stomach, Lydia stepped up onto the sidewalk and then tromped across the natural area that ran between the parking lot and the hospital. She saw Rob Tilley hop out of the cab of the ambulance and run around and open up the back doors as two nurses came out from the hospital to meet them.

TJ held tightly to his mother's hand and dodged azaleas, "Mama," he said, half-tripping on a broken off limb that was partially hidden in the pine straw, "I thought we weren't supposed to walk through the–"

Lydia cut in, "It's alright this time," she said, "This is an emergency." She saw Roger trot over from where he had parked and then saw Gregory Parke step out from the back of the ambulance. Keeping her eyes focused on the back of the ambulance, she hustled her steps and weaved between two big camellias, "*Roger*," she called, as she came around them and stepped into the grass, "*Roger Lowell.*"

Roger turned around gravely and found Lydia's face.

"What's going on," she said as Rob and Gregory pulled the stretcher out from the back of the ambulance.

Roger turned back around away from her without speaking and then, between the nurses, she caught a view of Buddy's face. Stopping cold in her tracks, Lydia's knees went weak, "*Oh dear God...*" She reached out and grabbed TJ's shoulder to steady herself as a strong flutter ran down through her stomach and then settled into a cramping in her low back.

Roger turned back to Lydia as the ambulance crew wheeled Buddy inside. Seeing how pale she had gone, he stepped quickly to her side, and put an arm around her waist and grabbed her free arm with his other hand.

"Take a deep breath, Baby," Roger said. Lydia noticed his voice was shaky. "Let's get you to a seat."

Roger guided Lydia over and sat her down on a bench just outside the emergency room doors. TJ stood next to Roger and glanced nervously back and forth from his mother's face to Roger's.

"Are you alright Lydie?"

Lydia nodded and took another slow breath as she rubbed at her belly. She stared at the ground for a moment as her hand made slow circles on her stomach. Roger's gaze went nervously from Lydia to the emergency room.

Lydia looked up at him, "What's going on Roger?"

"Buddy ran himself over with his tractor."

Lydia covered her mouth her with her hand and swallowed down hard. The image of Buddy and Hillary's prom picture popped into her head. "*How did he...*" she shook her head, "*...How bad is he hurt?*"

Roger's jaw clenched. He cleared his throat, "I don't know. He said it hurt to breathe and it looked like there was something wrong with his leg."

"Have you called Hill?"

"Yeah, I mean, I called Maggie..."

"Oh yeah, they all went down Oleander this morning." Lydia winced her face. "It'll be at least four hours before they can get up here."

Roger took a step back and squinted his eyes, trying to peer through the reflection on the windows into the hospital.

"Go ahead Roger;" Lydia said softly, "I'm okay."

Roger stared into the window a moment longer and then looked back down at Lydia, "Are you sure...I don't want to leave you if–"

"I'm fine Roger, really...go ahead."

Roger hesitated; he took a step back closer to Lydia and then looked back over towards the big glass emergency room doors.

Lydia said, "I've got TJ here with me...You go ahead. I'm fine." She reached up and grabbed Roger's hand, "I'll call Hillary and let her know we're here...go ahead."

Roger gave her one more long look and then turned and hurried into the hospital. Watching him disappear inside, Lydia let out a long sigh, and then reached out to TJ. She pulled him down onto the bench beside her and put her arm around him and gave him a hug.

Roger leaned back against the windowsill with his arms folded across his chest and watched as Buddy drifted off to sleep. He continued watching as the blanket across Buddy's chest fell into a slow rhythm of rising and falling, rising and falling. Buddy's nurse stepped back into the room and walked over next to the bed. She smiled politely at Roger and then looked Buddy over, "How long has he been sleeping," she asked quietly.

"Just a minute or two."

The nurse nodded and smiled, "Good," she said, turning as she headed for the door. Stopping about halfway across the room, she turned back to Roger and said, "My shift is over in about twenty minutes," she said, "I probably won't be back, but I'll be down at the nurse's station finishing up my paperwork if you need anything."

"Thank you," Roger smiled, "I appreciate it." He watched the door close behind her and then turned back to Buddy. He watched his friend sleeping for a moment and then sat himself down in the chair that was sitting at the foot of Buddy's bed and leaned his head back against the wall.

Buddy's eyelids fluttered as an odd look passed across his face. Roger wondered what he was dreaming. Buddy's face tightened as a tremble started in his chin and worked its way up across his face in a wave.

Roger smiled, thinking about a time when they were about fifteen and they were on their way back in from a grouper trip they had taken with his Uncle Charlie. Roger had wedged himself up in a corner in the cabin and had fallen asleep to the hum of the big motor droning down belowdecks. After Roger had dozed off, Buddy took a squirt bottle of mustard from the little fridge Charlie kept his provisions in and squeezed a yellow line of it around Roger's mouth as he slept. It had been Buddy's half-stifled laughter that awakened Roger when they were still a couple of miles out from home. Coming out of his sleep, Roger had felt a tickle under his nose and then smeared the mustard all over his face when he went to rub it away with the back of his hand.

Roger remembered how he had suddenly noticed the odd way his Uncle Charlie was staring at him, and then Buddy finally completely losing it and laughing himself out of his seat and onto the floor. *What I wouldn't give for a jar of mustard when he wakes back up,* Roger thought. He shook his head and grinned, "I love you Buddy," he whispered, "... you big knucklehead."

Roger was still sitting at the foot of Buddy's hospital bed, with his head in his hands when the door to the room swung open. He jumped up as Hillary swept in and went quickly over to Buddy's side. Roger watched her silently as she stood over her husband and stared down into his face with puffy, red eyes.

Roger waited a minute and then stepped softly around the foot of the bed and stood next to Hillary. He put his arm around her shoulder and she slowly turned to look him in the eyes. She smiled thinly up at him, "How long has he been sleeping," she whispered.

Roger glanced up at the clock on the wall over the head of the bed and then looked back at Hillary, "About fifteen, twenty minutes, maybe...he went out pretty quick after they got him in here."

"Good," Hillary said. She looked back down at Buddy and reached out to touch his hand. Stopping herself, she drew back, clutching her hands to her chest as she turned back to Roger for a second before looking back down at Buddy, "I just want to look at him for a minute," she said softly.

Roger nodded. He watched Hillary's face as she stared lovingly down at Buddy. "I don't think I've ever been so happy to see him sleeping," she said wistfully.

Roger chuckled and gave his head a little shake, "Things shore can get put into perspective in a hurry sometimes, can't they?"

Hillary's eyes rimmed with tears. She crossed her arms and then sniffed loudly and rubbed at her nose with the heel of her hand. Roger pulled her back in close to him and kissed the top of her head.

"Thank you for all you did, Roger."

"I didn't do anything."

Buddy stirred and let out a low groan and then slowly opened his eyes. He looked up at Hillary and his mouth turned up a little at the corners, "I was just dreaming about you."

Hillary's face broke into a grin, "*Hey Bear,*" she sighed. She took Buddy's hand and sat down on the edge of the bed beside him. Roger heard movement behind him and turned to see Maggie standing in the doorway. He turned back and watched Hillary lean over and kiss Buddy passionately on the lips.

Stepping back, Roger turned towards the door. Maggie looked into his eyes and smiled. Roger took one last look back and then Maggie took his hand and led him out into the hallway.

Roger pulled the door closed behind him as he walked out and then propped his hands on his hips as he stepped over and leaned himself back against the wall across the hall from Buddy's room, "It's good to see you, Maggie."

"It's good to be seen."

Roger leaned his head back against the wall and chuckled. He reached up and rubbed his face and then massaged the back of his neck before letting his hands fall loose at his sides. Maggie took hold of his hands and gave them a squeeze. Roger rolled his head around on his shoulders and then looked fully into Maggie's eyes. He felt a warm rush run through the pit of his stomach and smiled to himself, still wondering in the newness of being in a life with Maggie. "Well," he remarked, "I reckon this kind of screws up your Christmas shopping."

Maggie searched his face and then arched her eyebrows at him as he smiled at her. She heard another little chuckle down deep in his throat.

"*Well,*" he said, "*It does, don't it?*"

Maggie snatched his cap off his head and swatted him playfully with it, "You are *so* bad," she said, swatting at him again. She dropped the cap back down on his head, pinched his chin, and then leaned up and kissed him on the cheek.

Roger straightened up his cap as Maggie took a step back away from him, "I'm sorry my phone died," he said, shaking his head, "I reckon I need to get myself a car charger."

"That's alright, Lydia kept us updated."

"Is she still here?"

"She left right after we got here. She looked tired. Heck and Lina-Mae, Mister Denny, Miss Lynn, and Richard and Pat and a few other folks were down in the cafeteria."

Roger nodded and then rubbed his stomach, "Have you eat yet?"

Maggie shook her head, "No, I haven't...How 'bout you?"

"Not yet."

Maggie grinned as she heard a rumble from Roger's stomach, "Hungry?"

"Like the wolf."

"Do you want to go get something?"

"Yeah," Roger said, "You want to go and get some barbecue?"

"Sounds good to me...Let's do a last check on Buddy and then we'll go."

"You think it's safe to go back in there?" Roger asked, "Things were getting a wee bit sultry when you pulled me out."

Maggie cracked a playful smile, "You want to listen through the door?"

Roger cringed, "*Eeww*...Just call the room. If they don't answer, we'll just leave."

Maggie nodded, "Good idea." She pulled her phone out from her back pocket and hit redial for the hospital, "Room 513 please," she said and twitched her nose at Roger, "It's ringing..."

Roger watched Maggie's expression as she listened to the rings. She held up four fingers and mouthed: "*Four...Five... Six...*" She flipped her telephone closed and smiled slyly at him, "I think maybe we ought to just go on and grab us some supper..."

≈

Roger sat up in his bed and swatted at his alarm clock, knocking it to the floor. He rubbed his face as his telephone continued to ring. Yawning noisily, he rubbed a knuckle into one eye as he reached over and picked up the receiver, "Hello..."

"Hey Roger, its Buddy."

Roger cleared his throat and threw his legs over the side of the bed, "Hey Buddy," he said sleepily, "Everything alright?"

"I can't sleep."

Roger bent over and picked the clock up off the floor, checking the time as he set it back in place on the nightstand, "It's three-fifty-seven."

"*It is...Wow.* I had no idea it was so early. I figured it was at least four-eleven. Look, Roger, I need you to do something for me."

"Sure Buddy," Roger said, thinking to himself that his best friend was sounding a little bit loopy, "What do you need?"

"I need you to get some flowers for me."

"*Do what?*"

"Some flowers," Buddy repeated.

"You called me at four o'clock in the morning to tell me you want me to buy you some flowers." Roger stifled another yawn with the back of his hand and then reached up over his head and stretched.

"You said to call you if I needed anything."

"And you need flowers at three-fifty-seven."

"Yeah," Buddy said, "Well, sort of. You see, I've just been laying here thinking and I want you to get some flowers for Hillary for me. Can you do that?"

"You don't want them right now do you?"

"No," Buddy said. Roger heard him let out a little chuckle. "You can wait and get 'em in the morning."

"Thank you."

"You reckon I ort to call Roslynne and tell her what I want?"

"No Buddy," Roger quickly replied, "I really don't think you ought to do that. You can either tell me what you want now or you can wait and call her when the shop opens."

"What time is that?"

"Eight, I think."

"What's the number?"

"I don't know off the top of my head," Roger said, "Why don't you just tell me what you want and *I'll* call her when they open."

Roger waited as Buddy fell silent for a few seconds and then he said, "Okay Rog, here's what I want: I want something that's pretty, and it needs to be about this tall, and I want it–"

"*Buddy...*"

"What?"

"I'd be willing to bet money that you've got your left hand floating in the air somewhere out in front of your face, but for the life of me, I can't see you through this telephone."

Buddy chuckled goofily, "Oh yeah," he said, "My bad...I don't want some big gaudy looking thing," he continued, "But not *too* small, either...About yay big." Buddy paused and laughed at himself again. "Sorry," he said, "...Did it again. Just have Roz make it kindly medium sized, and have her put some orchids in it. Hillary really likes those."

"Have you got a budget for it in mind?"

"Uhhh...Nope."

"*Really?*"

"Yep."

"Anything else?"

"Uh, yeah, make sure there's a nice card."

"Will do Chief."

"Thanks Roger," Buddy said, "I owe you one...Oh yeah, this is top secret."

"*Top secret?*"

"Yeah, I don't want Hillary to find out. I want it to be a surprise."

"Not a problem."

"Great. I owe you one."

"You already said, and no you don't. I'll see you in a few hours."

"Bye."

~Chapter Four~

Joey stepped out the front door of the machine shop and then stopped abruptly and pointed at Roger. Giving his finger a quick shake, he turned and went back inside. He came back out after a minute and trotted over and climbed into Roger's truck. Roger smelled cologne.

Roger backed his pickup out into the street, "What was that all about?"

"*Nothing*," Joey replied, "I just forgot something."

"Right...We've got to run down to the flower shop real quick and pick up some flowers for Buddy."

"Yeah, I know."

"Oh yeah...How'd you know that?"

"Roslynne."

"When did you talk to Roslynne?"

Joey propped his elbow out the window and stared down the street, "Clear this way."

"Yeah," Roger said, pulling his truck out onto Commons. He pulled up to First Street and waited for a moment, "When did you talk to Roslynne?"

"Uh, just a few minutes ago," Joey replied, "She called the shop to see if you were there just before I came out."

"Oh," Roger said, wrinkling up his brow, "...that's odd." He pulled out onto First and drove down towards the flower shop. "I had *just* talked to her," he said, more to himself than to Joey, "...Just before I left the house." He pulled up to Kelton's and parked out front, "Did she have something else she wanted to tell me?"

"Huh..." Joey looked surprised, "Oh, no, not really."

Roger pursed his lips and then tapped at the steering wheel with his thumb, "What are you so jumpy for?"

"Huh? Me?" Joey said, fidgeting in his seat, "I'm not jumpy...what makes you say I'm jumpy?"

Roger shook his head and chuckled. He looked Joey over a moment and then shrugged, "Well anyhow...she said she'd have the flowers ready for us by the time we got here."

Joey popped his door open and quickly climbed out. "I'll go get 'em," he said, slamming his door. He hustled across the sidewalk and as he opened the door and went inside, Roger noticed for the first time that Joey's strawberry blond hair looked a little *styled*.

"Slicked up and ready for the big city," Roger mused. He looked down the street and saw Timmy Ramsey up on a ladder hanging a big Christmas star on a light pole. Timmy had backed his pickup up to the pole and stood the ladder up in the back. "Now *that*," Roger said to himself, "looks like an accident just waiting to happen."

Roger watched him for a moment and then, just across the sidewalk from where Timmy was balancing himself precariously and struggling with some loosely hanging silver garland and a long, dangling power cord, he saw his Uncle Clarence come out the front door of the Café with his cousin Byron. Clarence and Byron stepped down onto the sidewalk and stared up at Timmy with identical expressions of amused interest on their faces.

Roger chuckled at them to himself and called out, "*Hey B.*"

Byron turned Roger's way and smiled as Roger waved out the window at him. Byron nudged his father with his elbow and pointed in Roger's direction. Clarence looked down Roger's way and gave a little nod and then placed his old brown hat carefully into place on top of his head. Roger opened his door and slid out as Clarence and Byron Lowell came down the sidewalk to speak to him.

"Hey Griz," Byron said, "How's Buddy doin'," he asked as Roger closed his door and stepped up onto the sidewalk.

"Hey Uncle Clarence," Roger said, raising his voice a little so the old gentleman could hear him, and then he turned to Byron, "...Pretty good," he replied, "...All things considered." He shook his head, "He really dodged a bullet this time."

Clarence pulled his pipe pouch from his hip pocket and opened it up carefully, "Reckon it weren't his time," he said, pulling his pipe and an old brass lighter out from the pouch.

"I don't reckon it was," agreed Roger.

Clarence packed some fresh tobacco into his pipe and then flipped open the lighter and lit it up, "I heard he got into some hornets," he said, puffing firmly to get the pipe going.

"That he did."

"Do *you* know what happened," Byron asked, "I've heard so many different versions of it...Nathan said he heard that Buddy was trying to jump off to get away from hornets and didn't jump far enough. Red Beck said he got knocked off by a limb down by the creek and then John-Boy told me that somebody had told *him* that Buddy had knocked *himself* off swatting at some ground-bees he had stirred up."

Roger crossed his arms, leaned back against the fender, and propped his heel up on the front tire, "Well," he said, "It was as much because of a box turtle as anything else."

Byron wrinkled up his forehead and cut his eyes over at his father. Clarence Lowell puffed at his pipe and shrugged. Byron cleared his throat and looked sideways at Roger, "*Do what?*"

Roger cocked his head over to one side, "Seriously... Buddy told me that he had gotten down off the tractor to move a box turtle out of the way and he walked through a muddy, wet spot on the way back to his tractor. It wasn't ten seconds later that he got into the hornets, or bees, or whatever they were and he was riding along standing up, steering with one hand and waving them off with his other. He hit the split brake to spin the tractor around and get out of the field, and when he did, his foot slid off and he slipped down and spun around in front of the back wheel. He said the lugs just grabbed a hold of him and pulled him right under. The wheel ran right up both his legs, his stomach, and his chest. He jerked his head over at the last minute and kept it from running over that." Roger stopped briefly and shook his head. He stared down at the ground for a moment and then looked back up at Byron, "It's just a miracle that he didn't get caught up in that bush-hog."

Byron stuck his hands down in his pockets and gave a shiver. He shook his head and looked over at his father again and then back to Roger; "*Dern.*" He took a deep breath and then blew it out slowly as he stared off into the sky over Roger's head.

Roger's cell phone rang. Byron's hand went to his hip. He tilted his phone, checked the screen, and then gave his head a little shake and looked at Roger, "I think that's you Bud."

"Ooh, I better get that," Roger said, "It might be Hill." He spun around and reached in through his open window and grabbed his phone. He looked at the number for a second with a puzzled look on his face and then flipped the phone open, "*Hello...*Oh hey Fox..." Roger turned back around and leaned himself back against his truck. "Frankie Lee," he said to Byron and then returned to the call; "Yeah Fox..."

Clarence and Byron returned their attention to Timmy while Roger spoke, "Yeah," he said, "I could probbly handle that...I thought your uncle did all your welding for you...He is? Well that's tough...Yeah...Yeah. Not a problem...He had a little tractor accident," Roger continued, "No, no, he's doing pretty good...He spent the night at the hospital...I don't know. I'm headed up that way now...Sure, sure, I'll give you a call...Yeah, I'll tell him. Alright, just come on by...Alright then, we'll see you." He flipped the phone closed and tossed it in on the seat. Byron turned back to Roger. "Sorry 'bout that," Roger said.

Byron shrugged and shook his head, "No big deal...So, how bad was he hurt?"

"Not as bad as you'd think," Roger replied, "He busted his head open pretty good –sixteen stitches worth– and he got stung I don't know how many times." He patted at his face and then held his hand out about two inches from his right cheek; "His face was swollen out to here." He dropped his hand down and ran his knuckles up and down the left side of his chest and continued; "He separated his ribs from his breastbone on this side, and he's got a mildly cracked pelvis and a dislocated hip."

"I swornee Roger, it's a wonder he ain't dead," Byron said, "...I just can't see how in the world that bush-hog didn't *eat him up.*"

"All I can say is it's a miracle."

"*And a half...*" Byron gave his head another little shake, "Well, look Roger," he said, "We'll let you go, but tell Buddy if there's anything we can do to let us know."

"I will," Roger raised his voice a little louder again, "It's good to see you Uncle Clarence."

Clarence worked his pipe around to the corner of his mouth and then spoke out of the other corner, "You too son," he said, "You tell Buddy to take care, and that I'll be praying for him." He stuck his hand out and Roger gave it a firm shake.

Byron patted Roger on the shoulder, "We'll see you," he said, "Tell everybody I said hey."

"I will," Roger nodded, "*Oh hey,*" he said loudly, as Clarence and Byron turned to head back up the sidewalk, "*Uncle Clarence.*" Byron and Clarence stopped and turned back to face Roger. "Do you know anything about my daddy and a floursack apron?"

Clarence pulled his pipe from his mouth and studied Roger briefly. His eyes drew down and then he burst out into a high, cracking, laughter as he turned and continued slowly up the sidewalk. Byron watched his father for a moment and then looked at Roger and shrugged before he trotted off to catch up with Clarence. Roger followed them with his gaze as they walked away, watching Timmy fight the star at the top of the ladder as they went.

Roger chuckled as he watched them go. "*Man, that story must be a doozie...*I have got to find out–" he snapped his fingers, "*Oh yeah,*" he said, interrupting himself as he remembered why he was there. He looked over at the front door of the flower shop and then checked his watch, "*What in the world is taking him so long...*"

Hopping back up onto the sidewalk, Roger strode over to the shop's front door and peered in through the window. Joey and Roslynne were leaning in close to one another from opposite sides of the flower-arranging counter with their faces only a few inches apart. Roger watched in amazement as they smiled giddily at each other, lost in their conversation.

"*What in the world is going on in there...*" Roger whispered. He watched for a few seconds longer and then took a step back and clapped his hand to his forehead, "*I don't believe it...*" He ran his hand down his face and then stuffed both hands down into his back pockets. He looked back up the sidewalk; Timmy was climbing down the ladder into the back of his truck with the star looped over his shoulder.

Should I go in there, he wondered. He spun around and stared back in through the glass, *I just don't believe it.* He grabbed the door-handle and stood there for a moment with one foot up on the doorstep, poised to barge in on them. He leaned forward to push open the door and stopped as an idea came to him.

Letting his hand fall, Roger pulled himself back and went quickly to his pickup. He climbed in and tooted the horn twice and then made a move to be climbing back out as Joey came hustling out of the store. Roger pulled his door closed and watched Joey as he got in. Joey sat down and slammed his door; his cheeks were flushed red along the cheekbone.

"That took a little longer than I was expecting," Roger said.

"Huh," Joey grunted and wrinkled up his forehead. "Yeah," he said, turning Roger's way and giving a couple nervous nods of his head, "Yeah...Roslynne got a little busy." He smiled crookedly at Roger and then stared back out the windshield.

"*She did?*" Roger said, "Well, that's funny, I didn't see another soul even go in there." He cranked the truck and then pulled on his seatbelt. He looked over at Joey and then straightened up in the seat and crossed his arms. Joey pulled his seatbelt on and waited in silence almost a full minute for Roger to back the truck out and go. He started drumming his fingers on his bouncing knees and then glanced Roger's way out of the corner of his eye. He cleared his throat, "*Well,* I reckon I'm ready if you are."

Roger turned slowly in Joey's direction and cocked his head back a little; looking down his nose at him, "Are you *sure* you're ready?"

Joey nodded his head slowly, "Uh, huh."

"You're *all* ready..."

Joey's eyebrows drew down together as he continued nodding.

"You're sure you wouldn't like to go back inside and see Roslynne real quick."

Joey squirmed uncomfortably and shook his head, "No... Uh uh."

"Hunh," Roger grunted, "You can't think of any reason to go back inside."

Joey shook his head again. His face had lost all its color and his expression looked like he was walking up the stairs for a brief visit with a man in a big, black, hood.

Mmmhmm, Roger thought, *I reckon I saw exactly what I thought I saw.* "Well Joey," he drawled, "I think that maybe you should go on back in there." He nodded his head dramatically, and sucked at a tooth, "Yep...*I shore do.* I think you ought to slide your sweet smellin' self right back on in there and talk just a little bit more with Miss Roslynne."

"Why would I want to do that?" Joey's voice cracked and sounded very small.

Roger lifted one eyebrow ever so slightly and cocked his head at Joey, staring silently at him for a long moment. He chuckled inside as he watched little beads of nervous sweat pop out on Joey's forehead.

"So you can get the flowers we came down here to pick up."

≈

"Thanks Roger," said Buddy. He gave a little grunt as he pushed himself up in the bed a bit higher. "Just put them over here on the table by the telephone," he said to Joey, "I don't really want Hill to see them when she comes in...I want to surprise her with them."

Joey walked around the foot of the bed moved a water pitcher out of the way and set the arrangement down. He looked at it for a second and then turned the vase a quarter turn, "How's that?"

Buddy grabbed the one-eyed teddy bear his little girl had left with him and set it on the table in front of the bouquet, "Can you see it over by the door...when you come in?"

Roger walked backwards over to the door and shook his head, "Only if you were looking for it."

"Good," Buddy said. He looked back at the flowers for a second and then rested his head back down on the pillow, "I really appreciate it...Hillary loves orchids. How much do I owe you?"

Roger shook his head as he stepped back over beside the bed, "Don't worry about it, Buddy, Roslynne said they were on the house."

"She didn't tell Raechel, did she?"

Roger shrugged, "Couldn't tell ya."

"I didn't even see her there," Joey said.

"Well, she's bound to find out," Buddy said.

"It is *her* store," Roger reminded him.

"I know; I know...I just want them to be a surprise."

"I don't think she'd tell," Roger said, "Besides, Hillary wouldn't believe her if she did."

"You're funny."

"Oh, I almost forgot," Roger pulled Buddy's wallet from his back pocket, "Here," he said, handing it to Buddy, "You might want this back."

Buddy took it and held it for a second before opening it up and looking inside.

"I only took a couple dollars," Roger said.

Buddy gave him a look.

"*What*? I was hungry...And the way you let on, I just *knew* you weren't going to be needing it."

Buddy grabbed an extra pillow from between his leg and the bed-rail and tossed it at Roger. "That's just *wrong*, man," he said, "...There I was, laid out there in that field about to die and you're running all over half of creation using my wallet for a cashpoints." He shook his head dramatically, "And I thought you were my friend." He let his face droop and rolled his eyes up toward the ceiling as he let out a pitiful sigh and lay still for a moment. He looked over at Joey, "You'd never do something like that...Would you?"

Joey shook his head, "Not me."

Buddy smiled up at him sappily, "I didn't think so," he said, "You'd be a *good* friend...Would *you* be my friend?"

Joey stared down at him for a moment and then looked over to Roger and started laughing.

Buddy turned to Roger, "He has obviously been spending too much time with you...The boy can't even manage a two minute conversation." He turned back to Joey, "Get out now while you still can or he'll be the pure ruination of you." Buddy gestured at himself, "You see what *my* association has done to me don't you."

"They better get you off the pain pills, quick," Roger remarked, "Before you dig too many holes for yourself."

"What are you talkin' about? I ain't had the first pill all morning."

"*You haven't*...Well then, are you sure the tractor didn't get your head?"

The telephone on the bedside table rang its loud, chirping, ring.

"*Ahh*," Buddy smiled, "the cricket phone beckons." He reached over and picked the phone up off the table, "Hello... Hey Roz," he rested back down onto the pillow with his free hand propped up behind his head, "Yeah, they're great...

just what I wanted...Uh huh, yeah...I really appreciate it...I owe you one, girl..."

Roger noted to himself that he had never *ever* heard his friend Buddy Vander call anyone '*Girl*' in his entire life.

"Bye, bye," Buddy said, laying the phone back down on the table. He flipped his wallet open and checked the inventory, "At least all my credit cards are still here." He pulled the pictures out and thumbed through them. Stopping on the picture he kept of himself and Roger together in their first little league baseball uniforms, he stared at it for a moment and chuckled softly. He smiled up at Roger, his eyes moistened, "Thanks for coming to find me."

Roger looked over at Joey and then back down into Buddy's eyes, "You don't need to thank me, Buddy."

"I know." Buddy looked at the picture again and smiled, "I know that things weren't as bad as I thought they were Roger, but, I want to tell you something...I really thought that I was going to die. I've never felt like that before." He looked back up at Roger and smiled self-consciously, "And I kept thinking that, if I *did* die, I knew you'd take care of my family...I had no doubt." Buddy paused and glanced over at Joey and then turned back to Roger and continued, "I knew you would come and help me," he said, "You always have. And, when you did, I was glad that you were there with me."

"You don't need to be saying all this stuff Buddy," Roger said.

Buddy nodded firmly, "Yes I do," he said, "...*Did you read my letter?*"

Roger shook his head.

"I knew you didn't...Why not?"

Roger looked confused. He stared at Buddy for a moment without answering and then said, "Because you said it was for Hillary."

Buddy nodded again and pointed at Roger. "*Right,*" he said, "But, you wanted to didn't you?"

Roger slid his hands down into his pockets and cocked his head a little to one side, "What's this got to do with anyth–"

"*Oh, just answer the question*...Isn't that what you always tell me...'Keep all the extra and just answer the question.' Well *you* just answer the question."

"Yeah Buddy," Roger said, "I did want to...I wondered what my best friend's dying words to his wife would be."

"But you didn't."

"No, I didn't, *so what?*"

"It would have been wrong. So, no matter how much you wanted to, you didn't." Buddy smiled a broad smile mixed of love and pride at Roger, "You do what's right, and I love you for that. No matter what, you've always done what's right. I always know that I can count on you Roger, and I love you for that. I am a better person for you having been my friend." He smiled and chuckled again, "I want you to know that -*our whole life*- it has made me proud that people know you are my best friend."

Roger glanced back over at Joey. Joey looked honestly surprised at what he was hearing, "Do I need to leave," he asked.

"No," Buddy answered quickly, "Don't leave. I've got something to say to you too."

"*Me*," Joey said, "What did I do."

"It's more what you're *not* doing, than what you *are*...Well, maybe it is sorta what you are doing. I don't know...Maybe it's both."

"What in the world are you getting at now, Buddy," Roger said, "And what's this all about...What's got into you?"

"I'm talking about Joey sneaking around with your sister, for starters."

Joey jumped and flashed a fearful look at Roger, "*Hey*," he nearly shouted, "I'm not sneaking around with anybody. I swear Roger...I'm not sneaking around with Roslynne, or anybody."

"You are too," Buddy said, "Have you forgotten that my mother-in-law is the biggest gossip in town...*Telephone, Telegraph, Tell Lina-Mae.*"

Roger set his hands on Buddy's bed rail and leaned over towards Joey with a stern look in his eyes.

Joey took a step back and pressed himself back against the wall. He shook his head slowly, "I swear Roger, we are *not* sneaking around."

"What *are* you doing, then?"

Buddy shot his hands up between them. "Hold it, hold it, *hold it*...I still have the floor here, and I'm not done."

Roger looked down at Buddy and then stood himself back up and crossed his arms across his chest. Joey could see the muscles in his jaw working as he gritted his teeth.

Buddy continued; "What I was going to say was; Joey needs to stop this sneaking and just go on and court the girl right out in the open in front of God and everybody." He paused and looked back and forth from Joey to Roger, "This *sneaking* business just makes it look like y'all are doing something you shouldn't be doing and that makes it look like y'all *are* doing something you shouldn't be doing."

Roger shook his head and looked down at Buddy, "*What?*"

Joey held his right hand up like he was taking an oath and said, "We are *not* doing something we shouldn't be doing, Roger. *I swear.*"

Roger looked back over at Joey and then took a deep breath and leaned back over on Buddy's bedrail. He bowed his head and stared down at the scallop-shaped O-C-M-H symbol printed repeatedly across the bedspread. Joey stared across at the top of Roger's head as it began to wag slowly back and forth. Finally Roger let out a long, noisy sigh and looked back up at Buddy.

"Why are you saying all this?"

Buddy reached up and rested his hand on Roger's and smiled warmly. He stared at Roger in silence for a moment and then he gave Roger's hand a squeeze before letting his fall back down to rest at his side, "Because it needs to be said," he said softly, "...I love you Roger. I always have. You're not *like* a brother to me; you *are* a brother to me." He glanced over at Joey and then turned back to Roger and chuckled, "I realize now that I was nowhere near death. But, when I was laying out there curled up in that field, I was sure that I was about to die, and it occurred to me that I had spent– No," he shook his head with frustration, "...Not spent –*Wasted*– my whole life being scared."

Again, Roger Lowell looked genuinely confused; "What do you mean you've *wasted* your whole life being scared," he asked, "*Scared of what?*"

"Scared of everything," Buddy replied, "Scared of *doing* anything, scared of *saying* anything, scared of life."

"I'm not sure I'm following you Buddy," Roger said, "The only two things I've ever known you to be afraid of where Hillary and the cemetery."

Buddy rolled his eyes, "How many times do I have to tell you...I'm not afraid of the–" He stopped himself and grinned crookedly up at Roger, "Okay, maybe I am a *little* afraid of the cemetery. But, who could blame me, after that mess y'all pulled on me in Cub Scouts." He turned to Joey and jerked his thumb at Roger, "Did I ever tell you what he did to me?"

Joey glanced at Roger and shook his head.

"Him and Philip Register, and Ellis and Paul took a–"

"Wait, wait, wait," Roger interrupted, "We're getting off track here, *I* never did anything to you. *I* just came up right there at the end...and besides, *your* version of the events has changed so much over the years that I've got to the point that I'm not so sure that you were even there. So, let's get back to *you* and why you think you need to stop being so afraid of everything that you suddenly realized you were all afraid of and that me or nobody else in this town ever knew you were afraid of."

Buddy turned briefly back to Joey and said, "Remind me to tell you about it sometime...It was wrong man, just *wrong*."

Roger made a face and shook his head at Joey, "Buddy," he said, making his voice sound fatigued, "You're killing me...Would you just please explain this great epiphany of yours. I don't understand how you can say that you've never done, or said, anything, when, in all actuality, you never shut up and in nearly everything I've ever done, you've been right there beside me."

"Roger, *man*, I've never *really* done anything. Sure, I've been here and there with you and, yes, I do talk a little much at times, but, nothing that really matters. I have spent my whole life either following along or hiding in a corner for fear of what would happen if I didn't..." Buddy paused a moment as he found the controls on the bedrail and pressed the button to lift the head of the bed. He stared into Roger's eyes until he had raised himself up to sitting and his face was nearly level with Roger's. He let go of the control and then held his hand up in front of him and started counting off on his fingers, "A: Have you ever seen me be spontaneous? No...Two: Have you ever heard me give somebody, *anybody*, a piece of my mind? No...D: To your knowledge, has Warren-Rainey-Vander-the-Second ever done any *thing* to surprise any *one*? No." He chuckled sarcastically at himself and shook his head, "Buddy just doesn't do such things." He made a disgusted face; "You remember when you all went off to The Cool Spot out at Cash Creek...that *first* time?"

Roger nodded.

"Why do you think I didn't go?"

Roger shrugged; "Seems like you said you had a stomach ache or something..."

"Didn't you ever wonder why I suddenly took ill every time everybody paired up and went out there to go dancing? Or how 'bout spring break senior year...I was the only one that didn't go down to Carroll's Island. And, how many times have you ever seen me dance with my wife, huh?" Buddy paused and waited for Roger to respond.

Roger shook his head and gave him an exaggerated shrug, "I don't know Buddy..." he said, "*Never*, I reckon."

Buddy pointed at him and gave a long, dramatic nod; "That's right. *Never*...You've *never* seen me dance with her; I was always so scared of looking foolish 'cause I couldn't dance, that I would rather sit on the sidelines and watch you, or Fox, or Randy Douglas dance with her...Do you understand what I mean." He paused again, considering his words, "Would you believe that, as of last Friday afternoon,

I have thirty six thousand, three hundred seventy two dollars and fifty six cent in my savings account?"

Roger's eyes opened wide. He gave his head a little shake, "I wouldn't have if you hadn't just said it."

"My house is paid for, my car is paid for, my truck, my tractor, my mowers, my trailers...all paid for. In addition to my savings, I have consistently put six thousand dollars per year, every year, into my retirement since I turned eighteen years old...*And*, I have never bought my wife, my precious, beautiful, loving, wife –with the exception of a pitiful excuse for an engagement ring and dinky little wedding band– I have never bought her one piece of jewelry...And, do you know why? I'll tell you why. Because I was always afraid that something might happen *tomorrow* and that I would need that money. Can you believe that? Not *one* bouquet of roses. Not *one* slinky, little, silky. Not *one* real vacation..."

"Hillary loves you Buddy. She's happy with you."

"Roger, in fifteen-and-a-half years of marriage I have never dressed myself up, slicked myself down, and taken her out for a night on the town. I haven't shown her how much she means to me because *I* was afraid *I'd* look stupid trying to do it...Hillary deserves better than that." He shook his head emphatically, "Well buddy, let me tell you this, when I found out last night that I *wasn't* gonna die, I made a decision...Yesterday was the last John Brown day that Buddy Vander's gonna live afraid. If I look stupid, *so be it*, if I sound stupid, *so be it*. Life is way too short..."

Roger chuckled, "You ain't gonna get a perm and start wearing silk shirts are you?"

Buddy and Joey burst out laughing.

"*Naw, man*," Buddy said. He laughed a little longer and then made his face serious, "Unless you think it'll help."

Roger stepped around to the foot of the bed and cocked his head at Buddy. Buddy gave him a little smirk and chuckled softly, "Just kidding."

Roger fell silent as he spraddled his legs and crossed his hands behind his back. He stared down at Buddy's feet for a long moment and then gently grabbed hold of them as he slowly raised his head, "Buddy," he said, "You need to give Hillary the note."

"I thought you said you didn't read it."

"I didn't."

"Then why do you think I should give it to her?"

"What does it say?"

Buddy opened his wallet and pulled out the note. He looked at it for a few seconds and then held it out to Roger.

Roger looked at it and then shook his head, "That's not what I meant...What does *that* note say?"

Buddy dropped his hands into his lap and stared at the note that he had written for Hillary on their tenth anniversary and never given to her. He thought about what he had written.

Roger said, "Think about all that you just told us, Buddy...Giving her that note is part of all that." Roger straightened himself up and slid his hands down into his pockets, "You can buy her some jewelry," he said, "Get her some flowers. Wine her and dine her..." Roger motioned towards the note with his chin, "But, I'd be willing to bet that what's in that note right there would mean a hundred times more to her than anything your money could buy."

Buddy looked at Roger and then nodded slowly. He handed the note to Joey, "Would you pull that little store note out and stick this in the flowers?"

Joey took the note and swapped it out for Buddy, "What do you want me to do with this one," he asked, tapping the little white envelope in his hand.

"Chunk it," Buddy said firmly. He looked at Roger and grinned, "Starting today; I'm grabbing life by the ears and kissing it square on the mouth."

❧

"What time are you bringing Buddy home?"

"I'm not sure Maggie," said Hillary. She rolled over and glanced at the clock on Buddy's dresser, "It's already going on ten o'clock; I've got to get moving."

"What time did you finally get to bed last night?"

Hillary switched the telephone to her other hand as she rolled onto her back and stretched, "I don't know," she said, stifling a yawn with the back of her hand, "...Somewhere around three I believe. After I got off the phone with you I took a shower and then ate half a carton of freezer burnt ice cream and then laid here in the bed telling God how thankful I was that I still had a husband–

"I'm sorry Maggie...I didn't mean to—"

"It's alright Hill," Maggie said, "I understand, I'm thankful you still have a husband, too."

Hillary paused a moment to consider her words.

"Go ahead Hill," Maggie said, "It's alright...This isn't about me."

"You're a great friend Maggie."

"So are you, Hillary."

"I mean it, Maggie."

"I know you do Hill."

They both fell silent for a moment and then Maggie sighed noisily and said, "So anyway..."

Hillary pushed herself up and slung her legs over the side of the bed. "Anyway," she said, yawning again.

"...Back to Buddy..."

"Yeah...I woke up around eightish and called him. He said the Doctor was going to fill out a discharge when he finishes his morning rounds, so he can leave anytime after noon. I had intended to get myself up after I talked to him but I just couldn't seem to make myself get going."

"So, how did he sound?"

"He sounded great," Hillary replied. She hesitated and then went on, "He was, I don't know, I thought he was medicated when he first started talking, but, he said he hadn't had anything since what they gave him when he first got to the room last night."

"He's probably tired," Maggie said.

Hillary rolled her head around on her shoulders and heaved a heavy sigh, "He didn't sound tired," she said, "He was rather chippy, to be honest with you."

Maggie thought about Buddy for a second and then said, "He's probably just happy to be alive."

"I'm not sure that's it," said Hillary.

"Really," Maggie said, "*Why?*"

"*Well*," Hillary hesitated, "The conversation was just kind of odd."

"How so?"

"He told me I was a great lover."

"*What?*"

"Yeah," Hillary said, "you heard right."

"Would you care to tell me," Maggie chuckled, "Just how it was that he came out with that."

Hillary chuckled quietly as she stood to her feet, "Well," she replied, "He answered the phone and we talked a little bit about how he was feeling and then I asked him how he had rested. He made his voice kind of low and smooth and made a reference to what I had done when y'all left his hospital room and how a man couldn't help but rest well after something like that..." Hillary stopped as Maggie let out a little snicker, "*What?*"

"That's about the closest thing to something dirty I've ever heard of him saying."

Hillary walked over and pulled open the window shade, "He didn't say it like it was dirty."

"I didn't mean it like he was being dirty," Maggie said, "But you know, the Barry White talk...Buddy just doesn't say stuff like that."

"I know, and then he told me *that* –the good lover part– and he said that he meant that I had *always* been one."

"And what did you say?"

"I told him thank you and that he was too."

Maggie laughed.

"What are you laughing at?"

"I'm sorry," Maggie said, "But do you really need to ask me that? I mean, come on, I'm just hearing this conversation of yours in my head and...not to mention the uh, you...Uh, well, you and...I was wondering...What possessed you to uh, to do...*that.*"

Hillary turned herself around and leaned back against the window and thought for a moment. "I don't know Maggie. When he opened his eyes and looked up at me... After spending the whole afternoon thinking he was going to die and realizing that he was going to be fine...all the emotions running around inside me...I just climbed into the bed with him and, well...It was all I could think to do."

Maggie paused again. "Well," she said, giving another quiet little chuckle, "I'm sure glad we didn't walk back in there."

Hillary laughed, "You're not the only one."

"Was that the only odd thing he said?"

Hillary said, "The whole conversation was a little bit weird, but, other than that it was more his affect than anything else."

"Did you ask him if he was alright?"

"Yeah, a couple times...But, he just kept saying he was fantastic, no, *superb*...That was the word, *superb*."

"Well that's good...right?"

"Yeah," Hillary replied, "It is good...but still weird."

"When are you going up?"

"Whenever I get myself up and ready."

"Are you taking the young'uns?"

"No, I didn't see any reason to pull them out of school, but, Mama's gonna bring them home this afternoon."

"Alright then, I'll see you later. You call me if you need anything."

"You're doing enough Maggie."

"Call."

"I will...I'll see ya."

"Bye *Lovergirl*."

⁊

Roger circled his truck around the block once and then pulled it down the alleyway beside the antique store that sat across the street from Richmont Family Jewelers. He cut the motor and looked over at Joey.

"We were gonna tell you Roger," Joey blurted, "Honest we were..." somehow he managed to sound very nervous *and* very excited at the same time, "...And, and, I promise we're *not* sneaking around. I mean, I know what it must look like and all, but, we're *really* not doing anything." He took a deep breath and then tugged at the collar of his shirt, "It's as hot as all get out in here."

Roger turned his face away from Joey to hide his grin. He bit down on his bottom lip and then turned back to Joey, "When were y'all planning on coming out with it?"

"About three months ago."

"*Three months ago*...How long has this been going on?"

Joey replied sheepishly, "Since May."

Roger shook his head and muttered to himself, "Where have *I* been for the last seven months?"

"You've been a little preoccupied..."

"Yeah, but how in the world could I have missed something like this since May?"

"I guess it's kind of hard to see what's going on around you when you've got your head in the clouds."

Roger studied Joey a moment and then nodded his head, "Yeah, I guess it kinda is." He twisted himself around in the seat and smiled at Joey, "Look Joey, I apologize if I came on a little strong at the hospital...I was just caught off guard by the sneaking around comment and my Protective-Big-Brother self took over."

Joey's body relaxed as he let out a loud sigh; "So, you're not mad at me?"

Roger shook his head, "Naw man, I'm not mad. How could I be mad? I just found out that two of my favorite people in the world have gone all sweet on one another."

"*Boy*, is that ever a relief."

"Now," Roger added, "...If you break her heart...That's another matter entirely."

Joey's face flushed as he broke into a grin. "You *definitely* don't have anything to worry about there," he said, "I'd have to be a pure fool to let that girl get away."

"That's good to know," Roger said. He gave Joey another quick smile as he pulled his keys from the ignition and opened his door. Jiggling his keys in his hand, he arched his eyebrows at Joey and let out a sharp, nervous, breath, "Alright," he said, "Off to the jeweler."

Roger slid himself out and quickly closed his door behind him as he headed around the back of his truck towards the street. Joey hopped out and started to follow until Roger stopped suddenly at the back corner of his truck bed and spun around towards him with a perplexed look on his face, "One more question," he said, "*If you don't mind my asking*...How exactly did this whole thing come about?"

Joey stopped and grinned at Roger, "It's kindly your doing," he said.

"How's that?"

Joey leaned his back up against Roger's tailgate and rested his elbows up behind him. "*Well*," he began airily, looking off distantly over Roger's head, his mouth still a wide grin. He propped his heel up on the back bumper; "... You remember when you were going over to Buddy and Hillary's that first time for *The Big Meal* with Miss Maggie and you sent me over with your truck to help Roz move that furniture out of the Merrits'?"

Roger nodded.

"Well, I guess the ol' Stoop charm was just more than she could take."

Roger rolled his eyes. "Yeah," he drawled, "I'm sure that was it." He paused briefly, thinking back about that day, "*Didn't you take Roscoe over there with you?*"

"Uh huh," Joey nodded, "...*Why?*"

"I was just thinking...I reckon you would look pretty charming with only him to compare you to."

"Ha ha."

"Anyhow," Roger said, "So what happened?"

"Nothing really," Joey grinned, "I mean, we were just getting everything moved into her little place and I was really having a nice time talking with her while we were working, which, to be totally honest with you, *really* surprised me." He paused a second and looked self-consciously at Roger, "I have never had *any* girl, let alone one like Roslynne pay me any mind," Joey pointed at Roger and then crooked his thumb back at himself, "So let me tell you, Joey Stoop was *all about* keeping the conversation going."

Roger smiled and nodded at Joey, "Gotcha."

Joey pinched nervously at one of his shirt buttons as he continued; "When we were about finished moving the big stuff, I was really starting to sweat about how I was going to keep things going, and then Roslynne said something about wanting to pay us for helping her, and all the sudden I got an idea." Joey paused, arched an eyebrow, and gave Roger a sly grin, "I gave Roscoe two dollars and sent him on his way–"

"*Two* dollars," Roger said, "That's all you gave him was *two* dollars..."

"He's lucky he didn't just get a ham sandwich and a road map," said Joey, "I was really about ready to smack him one good time."

"*What for?*"

"For him ogling Roslynne the whole time we were there and for him constantly making cracks to me about how he was going to be going back later to help her *arrange things,*" Joey set his jaw, "...*That's' what for.*"

"*Ahh,*" Roger said, "So that's why he hasn't been around in so long."

"Yeah, that's part of it," Joey said, "...but, I have also come to realize that we never really had all that much in common in the first place; we just happened to be two little outcasts who lived on the same shabby little street." He crossed his arms across his chest and let out a sigh, "Anyhow, I told her that the only way that she could pay me would be by riding over to the beach for some ice cream." Joey paused again and chuckled to himself; "I didn't know *what* she was gonna say. She stood there thinking about it for a minute and then just about the time I figured she was gonna start laughing in my face, she looked up and smiled at me and says –real sweet like–, 'Sure Joey, that sounds like fun.'"

Joey bent over and let his arms fall loose down in front of him and then stood himself back up, clutching his chest dramatically. He grinned broadly at Roger and took a couple wobbling steps from side to side. "*Man,*" he said, mooning his eyes, "I liked to have *fell out.*"

Roger laughed. "I know the feeling," he said, "That's nice Joey...I'm glad."

Roger started towards the sidewalk again, but then stopped himself once more and cocked his head at Joey.

Drawing his eyes down to slits, he jutted out his chin, and pointed at Joey, "So, you mean to tell me that you've been dating *my* sister, in *my* truck, right under *my* nose, since last May, and I had no idea..."

Joey shrugged up his shoulders and arched his eyebrows as his lips drew back into a wide grin, "*What can I say?*"

Roger shook his head. "I shoulda known something was up," he said, "The way you've been keeping my truck so clean for me." He propped his hands on his hips and wagged his head at Joey, "Goodness of your heart," he muttered, "...*Please.*"

"You wouldn't have wanted me carrying your baby sister around in a dirty pickup would you?"

Roger looked sideways at Joey, "Didn't I *pay* you a couple times for washing it?"

Joey checked his watch and whistled, "Wow, look at the time," he said, jamming his hands down into his back pockets as he headed himself up the alleyway.

Roger stepped in beside Joey as he passed and grabbed him firmly by the back of the neck. "You know what," he said, giving Joey's neck a little squeeze.

"No...What?"

"I think, when we're done in the jewelry store, that, *you* are *really* gonna want to strut on over to Marvin's and buy *me* a *big ol'* steak and cheese, and a *big ol'* order of fries with a *big ol'* glass of tea to wash it all down."

"*I am?*"

Roger stopped on the curb and nodded, "Uh huh...And, after that, you're probbly going to jump right up and suggest that we go right back across the street to the Friendly Freeze, where you would like to treat me to one of their delicious hot-fudge-turtle-cake-sundaes."

"*You think?*"

"I *know.*"

≈

Roger's phone rang as he pulled in the gate at Mossback. Taking his foot off the gas, he let the truck coast up the long drive as he checked the number on the screen. He smiled to himself and then flipped the phone open, "Hey Mag," he said, "...I was just talking about you."

"*Hey Maggie,*" Joey said loudly towards Roger's phone, "... *It was mostly good.*"

Roger made a face at Joey and shook his head. Maggie said, "Tell Joey I said Hey back..."

"Maggie says hey back Joey," Roger said.

Joey smiled and then pointed a finger out towards a flock of about two dozen guineas scratching their way across the drive out in front of Roger's truck.

Roger nodded his head at Joey, acknowledging the flock of white-headed, gray-flecked birds as Maggie said, "So, what you were saying was *mostly* good, huh?"

"Not really," Roger said, throwing Joey a wink, "...You know how he exaggerates. It was only *partly* good at best." He chuckled a little and stopped the truck in the path to give the guineas a moment to move out of his way.

"Are y'all on the way home yet?"

"Yeah," Roger said, hitting two, quick taps on the horn to hurry the guineas along, "As a matter of fact, we just pulled into Mossback." He watched the birds move quickly off to his left and then started the truck forward again.

"Well, how's Buddy look to you?"

Roger pulled up in front of the big plantation house and parked, "He looks pretty good. His face is still a little puffy, but to be honest, you wouldn't even know that he just got run over if nobody told you."

"That's good. Hillary said they were going to release him this afternoon...She was hoping to be heading back home by three-thirty, four o'clock."

Roger checked the time on the radio. "Well," he said, cutting off the truck, "they might be on the way home by now...I'd better get on the stick if I'm gonna get his tractor out and over there by the time he gets home."

"Are you sure you don't want to use my jeep?"

"No, I really don't think it'll do it. And, Dickie already said I could use one of his tractors."

"Alright," Maggie said, "...But it's yours if you need it."

"Thanks...Anyhow, am I gonna get to see you later?"

Maggie thought for a second, "No," she said, "I don't reckon so, unless you want to meet me at Buddy and Hillary's."

"What time are you going over?"

"'Bout five-thirty..."

"I might be over there when you get there," Roger said, "*If* we can get Buddy's tractor out."

"Have you got any plans for supper?"

"Not really."

"Would you like me to bring you some clam chowder? I've made more than enough for the Vanders...I can put some in a bowl for you, and it wouldn't be a thing for me to whip up an extra pan of cornbread for you, If you'd like."

"You don't have to do all that," Roger said.

"It's no problem."

"I know you spent all morning shucking clams and dicing potatoes."

"I'd like to do it for you Roger."

Roger paused for several seconds, slowly letting out a long breath. He rested his head back against the back glass and smiled, "That'd be nice Maggie...I'd appreciate it."

"Great. Well, I'll see you there, then."

"Alright, we'll see ya."

"Oh," Maggie said, "Before you go..."

"What'cha need?"

"Did Buddy say anything *odd* to you?"

Roger glanced over at Joey and then looked back out through the windshield, "Why do you ask?"

"I'm just curious. Hillary told me that he seemed a little odd when she talked to him on the telephone this morning."

Roger looked over at Joey again and chuckled, "He was a bit on the quare side," he said, "But I wouldn't be too worried about it."

"You wouldn't?"

"No, and if Hillary's worried, tell her not to either."

"Really?"

"Yeah, Buddy just realized he's in love with a great girl and he wants to make sure she knows it." Roger paused a second and then said, "That's a smile I'm hearing right now isn't it?"

"See you in a little while Roger…"

"See ya Mag."

Joey leaned over towards Roger, "*Bye Maggie.*"

Roger held the phone out towards Joey, "*Bye Joey,*" Maggie said.

Roger backed Buddy's tractor up under the shelter on the side of Buddy's barn and cut off the motor. Just as he was climbing down, Joey stepped around the corner of the barn and said, "Hey, did you see Buddy? He's standing out there on the front porch."

Roger wrinkled up his forehead and shook his head, "Naw," he said, "I sure didn't. Was he there when I pulled in?"

"I don't know, but, he was when *I* did."

Roger stepped out from under the shelter and saw Buddy standing, slightly stoop-shouldered, on the front porch of his house with a nearly grown fox squirrel perched up on the back of his neck. Buddy gave them a little wave and a thin smile.

Waving back as he and Joey walked across the yard, Roger called out, "*Hey Bud.*"

Joey looked at Roger and asked, "Should he be standing out here like that?"

Roger shrugged his shoulders, "If he can, I reckon he can."

"Thanks for getting my tractor for me," Buddy said, as Roger and Joey came up the walk. He stuck his hand out to Roger, "Was it much trouble?"

Joey glanced at Roger and chuckled.

"Shoot no," Roger said, stepping up onto the porch and taking Buddy's hand, "The only trouble was hanging on… Joey liked to snatched it out from under me with that big Cat Dickie let us use."

Joey looked at Buddy and grinned, "I ain't never driven a tractor that big," he said, "I didn't have the slightest idea it had that much power."

"The size of the chopper that was hooked to it when we got it should have given you *some* idea," Roger said dryly. He turned back to Buddy, "Have you ever driven one of those big track-jobs they use in their impoundments?"

Buddy shook his head no.

"They're pretty neat," Joey said.

Roger touched Buddy on the shoulder, "So...how ya feeling?"

Buddy nodded slowly and forced himself to stand up a little straighter. A little black squirrel head with a white face popped around from the opposite side of Buddy's head to take a closer look at Roger. "Pretty good," Buddy said quietly, nodding again, "...Pretty good."

"Good," Roger said. He reached up and scratched the top of the squirrel's head with his index finger, "Look...If it's alright with you and Peaches, we're gonna go back over to Judge Hassell's and run the Cat back over to Mossback and then we'll be back...You need anything before we go?"

Buddy forced a deep breath and shook his head no. He looked over towards his barn and Roger noticed an odd look flash across his face.

Roger followed Buddy's gaze and noted that you could just see the front end of Buddy's tractor from where they were standing. He turned back to Buddy, "You still love it?"

"I love everything Roger," Buddy remarked. He paused a moment and then turned back to Roger and was opening his mouth to say something else when Hillary stepped out the front door onto the porch behind him.

"Hey Roger...Hey Joey," Hillary said. She smiled at them both as she stepped up next to Buddy and laid her hand on his back. Puckering her lips, she made a little squeaky-chirping sound and the squirrel hopped over onto her near shoulder. "Bear," Hillary said gently, "You promised, if they let you come home, that you wouldn't overdo it...You need to come back in and get in the recliner."

Clenching his jaw, Buddy shuffled his feet around to face his wife and gave her a wincing, crooked smile. He leaned in and kissed her, "I love you, Babe."

Buddy turned to Roger, "I'm good," he said, "...See you in a bit. Thanks." He turned slowly and walked himself deliberately back into the house without protest. As the screen door creaked closed behind him, Hillary turned to Roger. "*Well*," she said quizzically, "*How 'bout that.*"

"*Yeah*," Roger agreed, "How 'bout that."

Roger followed Maggie out onto the Vander's front porch, still talking back over his shoulder to Buddy. Stopping just outside the door, Maggie elbowed his ribs and then pointed off to the side yard, directing his gaze toward the sound of the hollering children. Roger looked to see Joey fall down to his knees with Maggie's two *and* the Vander's two children piling on top of him. Joey had a huge grin on his face and was laughing loudly.

"Don't break him," Roger yelled, "He's a delicate thing and I need him for work tomorrow."

Jimmy McKenzie grabbed Joey in a headlock as Buddy's son Rainey tried to get Joey in an arm-bar. Sarah and Abigail climbed up his back, digging heels into his ribs.

"*Hey, Hey*," Roger called, "*Rainey*. No judo." He looked back inside, "Rainey's trying to get Joey in an arm-bar."

Hillary stepped over to the door and walked around Roger onto the porch. "Rainey!" she hollered, "What have I told you about that...Turn him loose."

"*Everybody* turn him loose," Maggie added firmly.

"Ever since he got his orange belt, all he wants to do is grapple with everybody," said Hillary, "He's about to drive me crazy."

Roger touched his hand to his forehead and then waved at Buddy. He turned and rubbed Hillary affectionately across the back of her shoulders as he walked by her. Stepping off the porch, he smiled and told her, "Let me know if y'all need anything."

"You know I will Roger...Thank you for everything."

Maggie reached over and gave Hillary a hug, "I'll see you tomorrow."

"*Oh*," Hillary said, "I almost forgot...The children's bag. Hold on just a sec." She ran back into the house.

"Come on y'all," Maggie called out across the yard. She watched Roger walk out across the yard smiling at the children as he headed to his truck. He stopped in front of his pickup and leaned back, propped against the grill with his arms crossed over chest and watched them crossing the yard behind Joey. He chuckled quietly as they all came up and stood in front of him, "Y'all got to ease up on Joey a little," he said, "He ain't gonna be worth two skips all stove up."

"We weren't stovin' him up," Jimmy said.

Roger arched his eyebrows in mock amazement and then pinched them down close, "*You weren't?*" He pointed at Joey. "Look at him," he grinned, "He can't hardly stand up straight."

"Awww," Rainey drawled, "...He always looks like that."

Roger threw his head back and laughed loudly. Joey feigned to go after Rainey and Rainey took two quick steps back and braced a stance, holding up his fists. Joey dragged a foot as he stepped over next to Roger and propped himself laboriously on the hood. Roger looked sideways at him and gave him a little wink. "Yeah Rainey, I reckon he kinda does, but, he weren't limping like he is *before* I brought him over here."

Maggie stepped down from the porch and Roger looked over and caught her watching him. Maggie felt a little flutter as they made eye contact and she flashed Roger a smile. Roger smiled back and held his stare for a long moment. Maggie rested her hands in the small of her back and cocked her head a little to the side, keeping her eyes on Roger.

"Here you go," Hillary said as she came back outside carrying a big, blue, duffel bag with a faded golden panther printed on the side.

Maggie spun around and looked blankly at Hillary, "*Huh?*" she said, snapping back from her bliss. Hillary caught Maggie's expression and then glanced out at Roger. She smiled to herself as she came down next to Maggie, "It's nice, isn't it?"

Maggie looked at Hillary a few seconds and then a smile slowly crept its way back across her face, "Yeah," she replied softly, "It really is."

"I'm happy for you Maggie," Hillary said. She looked back out at Roger and then back to Maggie, "I feel like giving you both a hug."

Maggie rolled her eyes at Hillary, "You're silly, you know that?"

Hillary grinned and nodded her head sharply, dropping the duffel bag down in the grass next to her feet. She reached out and pulled Maggie in tightly. "I know it," she said, stepping back to look at Maggie. Her eyes rimmed with happy tears, "It's alright though, isn't it?"

"Yeah," Maggie smiled. She glanced over at Roger and then covered her face with her hand. She looked back at Hillary, "I just can't stop smiling," she said, "I just about can't stand myself, I'm so happy."

Hillary flashed Maggie another silly grin and shrugged her shoulders up high, "Can I hug you again?"

Before Maggie could answer, Hillary had reached out and given her another big hug.

"Alright Hill," Maggie said as Hillary turned loose of her, "I need to get going... *you* need to go be with your husband."

Hillary took in a deep breath and stared at Maggie's face for a moment, "Alright," she sighed. She gave her head a little shake and then picked the duffel bag back up and handed it to Maggie, "All their stuff should be in there."

"Are you sure I can't keep them for you tomorrow night, too?"

Hillary shook her head, "No, that's alright Maggie. I appreciate it, but Aunt Mamie's gonna have them over the weekend."

"Oh that's right," Maggie said, "...This weekend's the first weekend in November. This spring weather is really screwing me up."

Hillary smiled, "Yeah, me too. But, it's already time for the big kick-off to the holiday season. Uncle Den's cooking a pig for Sunday afternoon."

"You want me to carry them out there for you, then? I can stop by and pick up some clean clothes and then shoot them out to Tanner's Run."

"Uncle Den's gonna pick them up when he brings the eggs in."

Maggie's eyes widened, "*Oh hey,*" she said, "Do you know if he's got any of those goose eggs?"

"No, but I can call him and see...Why?"

"I'm baking a yellow cake for Daddy's birthday Saturday. That one I made with the goose eggs has spoiled everybody."

Hillary nodded, "They *are* rich, aren't they...How many layers are you shooting for this time?"

"I'm hoping sixteen; I got twelve last time. Miss Marion brought a twenty to the last covered dish at church." Maggie shook her head, "I don't know how she does it."

"I don't either," Hillary said, "They're just ain't no way I can compete with that. I got one up to eight and after that I kept tearing up layers...I finally gave up trying. The Vanders will just have to be happy with three." She paused for a second and glanced down at her wedding band. "Anyhow," she looked back up at Maggie, "I'll give Uncle Den a call later and have him to bring you some if he's got any."

"That'd be great," Maggie said, "Could you give me a call and let me know either way when you talk to him." She passed the Vander children's bag to her other hand and then headed down the walk toward her jeep, "Come on y'all," she said to the children, "Let's roll."

Rainey and Abigail Vander waved happily at their mother. Hillary smiled and waved back and then stepped back up onto the porch and watched the four children pile into Maggie's jeep, "You better behave," she called.

Rainey and Abbey waved at her again, "*We will.*"

Maggie walked around and stuffed the duffel bag down behind the back seat. "Thanks for supper," Roger said as he came over next to her, "This is a good step in getting you out of the dog house."

"The *dog house...*why am I in the dog house?"

Roger made a motion in Joey's direction with his head and said, "'Cause you knew about Roslynne and loverboy over there and didn't tell me."

"You should pay better attention."

"Maybe I pay too much attention..." Roger said, he opened his eyes wide and stared down at Maggie, "To the wrong things."

Maggie sparkled her eyes and bounced up onto her toes, pushing her face up close to Roger's. "I don't think that's possible," she said, reaching up to tweak his nose.

Roger swatted at her hand, "Man," he said, "I can't believe the size of these mosquitoes." He waved his hand slowly around his head and then made a move over Maggie's. Maggie took a step back as Roger made an exaggerated wave her way, "Pesky, pesky, pesky," he said.

"You know it's just the females who draw the blood don't you?"

"Oh, I know," Roger drawled, "Trust me, *I know*."

"You are really cruisin' tonight, Mister."

"Is that bad?"

Jimmy leaned over and stuck his head out of the Jeep's driver's side window, "Can we go now Mama?" he groaned.

Maggie turned his way, "We're going."

Roger touched her on the arm, "You want me to drop your Hot Bag by tomorrow?"

Maggie turned back to him and thought for a second, "Sure. Why don't you come by around dinnertime...I'll fix you a sandwich or something."

"You're gonna spoil me if you keep this up Number One."

Maggie rocked back on the heels of her boots and smiled up at Roger. "Maybe that's my plan," she said, "I mean, I gotta get out of the dog house somehow."

"Yeah," Roger nodded, "You shore do." He looked into Maggie's bright eyes and stopped for a moment.

"Mo-om..." came another groan from in the Jeep.

"Well," Roger sighed, "I reckon I'd better let you get going." He looked over at Joey, "You 'bout ready?"

Joey rubbed his stomach, "Si senor," he nodded, "...Tengo hambre."

"Muy bien," Roger smiled. He turned back to Maggie, "I think the CDs are working better for Joey than they are for me."

"Stick with it," Maggie said, "Es no muy dificil aprendar."

Roger squinted his eyes down and wrinkled his face as he translated in his head. He thought for a second, "That's easy for you to say," he grinned, "...Es...*muy* dificil...por yo." He reached his arm around her shoulders and gave her a hug, "I'll see you tomorrow...*twelvish.*"

Maggie brushed a kiss against his cheek, "I can't wait."

Roger glanced down at Maggie's feet. "I really like your boots."

~Chapter Five~

Lydia rolled onto her back, stretched her arm up over her head, and flexed her fingers. Opening her puffy eyes, she stared up at the ceiling fan spinning silently overhead, as she tried to shake free the tingly, pins-and-needles feeling from where she had just been sleeping on her arm. "*Uughh,*" she groaned, pumping her arm as she rolled slowly to her other side.

Kicking off her covers, Lydia paused a second and listened as a rustling sound passed down the hallway outside her door. She felt a kick down low in her abdomen and took a deep breath, "...There has got to be a better way to do this Lord," she muttered.

She looked down for her slippers in the puddle of blue moonlight on the floor next to her bed as she let her legs down over the side and sat up. "Maybe I should just sleep with them on," she said; as she found them waiting right where she had kicked them off after her last trip to the bathroom. She shuffled into the bathroom and came back out a half a minute later and headed downstairs.

Halfway down, Lydia saw the light from the back porch shining into the hallway. Mary's voice came floating softly into the hall as Lydia reached the bottom of the stairs. "It's alright sweetie," Mary said, "...These things happen."

Oh no, Lydia thought, *he's wet again.* She stopped in the hall just inside the back door. She heard a click and then the sound of the washing machine filling with water.

"Did you have that dream again?" Mary asked.

"Yes ma'am," TJ answered softly.

Lydia's heart broke. She leaned back against the wall; *I hoped we were past this...* She heard the lid on the washer close and then her mother say, "I'll take care of the rest of this. You want a little snack before you go back to bed? I think there's still some tapioca left from dessert...Look at me TJ. There's nothing to be embarrassed about...Come here."

Lydia peeked around the corner and saw her mother, wrapped in her housecoat, kneeling down, holding TJ tightly to her breast. Her mother's gray hair was flat on one side. TJ's face was buried in Mary's collar. "Don't cry sweetie," Mary said softly, "...it's alright. Don't cry." Lydia watched them for a moment and then leaned back against the wall. She felt a tear roll down her cheek.

"I love you sweetie," Mary said and then there was a brief pause, "Look at me...That's better. Everything's gonna be just fine...Are you sure you don't want something...Is your knee feeling better? Good...Alright then, if you don't want anything, then I reckon we ort to get you on upstairs."

Lydia heard her mother stand to her feet and she turned and went quickly down the hall and stepped around the corner out of the light. She listened as TJ and Mary came in from the porch and then made their way up the creaky steps. When they reached the top Lydia went back down the hall and waited for her mother at the foot of the stairs.

After about ten minutes, Mary appeared at the top of the stairs and smiled when she saw Lydia waiting for her. She came down and held her finger to her lips when Lydia started to speak. She stepped off the stairs and gave Lydia a hug.

"Thank you Mama," Lydia whispered.

Mary clicked the light off in the hallway and then led Lydia down to the kitchen. Lydia took a seat at the table as Mary turned on a light and pulled a pot from the cabinet.

"He wasn't quite asleep when I left him," Mary said quietly. She sat the pot on the stove and got the milk out from the refrigerator, "He tripped in the sheets when he came off the stairs and fell down right outside my door." She poured a few cups of milk into the pot, put the milk away, and turned on the stove. Lydia watched as little blue fingers of flame flickered to life under the pot. Mary stirred some honey and vanilla in with the milk and then came over and sat herself down next to Lydia.

"He had already stripped and made up his bed and washed up and changed his pajamas and was coming down to throw it all in the wash," Mary said. She paused and shook her head, "I almost hated to get up," she sighed, "I knew he'd be embarrassed."

"I'm glad you did."

"He had that dream again."

Lydia nodded and then rested her face in her hands and rubbed at her temples.

"He's going to be fine Baby," Mary said. She caressed Lydia's back across her shoulders, "It's just going to take time."

Lydia looked at Mary, "I know Mama. I just hate it for him."

"I know you do."

Lydia said, "I wish there was something I could do."

"You're doing all you can do," Mary said, "Just keep reminding him how much he's loved...that's what he needs."

Lydia looked deeply into her mother's eyes. Mary smiled and then got up and turned off the stove. She got down two of their big hot chocolate mugs and poured them full of the warm milk and then grabbed a shaker of cinnamon and dealt each mug a quick shake.

Coming back over, Mary sat the mugs down on the table as she sat back down. Lydia picked hers up, tested the temperature, and then took a sip. "That's just right," she said. Feeling the warm milk settle down in her stomach, she took another sip, and curled her feet around one another as her body gave a little shiver. "At least it's cool at night," she said.

"You want me to turn the heat up?"

"No, I'm fine. It's plenty warm upstairs, and I know Daddy likes it cool when he's sleeping."

"I'll be glad when it gets cold enough for a fire," Mary said, "How 'bout you?"

Lydia nodded and took another swallow of her milk. "Daddy said the woolie worms were especially fuzzy this year," she replied, "But I'm starting to doubt they know what they're doing."

Mary said, "I remember once when I was a little girl it staying really warm like this...I mean, you know as well as I do that it doesn't get *really* cold and stay that way until January and February...but, it was warm like it is now, up near eighty nearly every day...Right up through Christmas." She took a big drink of milk and continued, "Then, right between Christmas and New Year's it just dropped. I think we had something like three feet of snow fall on New Year's Eve, and then about four days later it was back up in the sixties and everything was just soaked." She smiled at Lydia, "We were pretty well shut off, so many trees went down on the road between here and the highway during the storm...It was nearly a week after the snow melted before anybody could get in or out that way."

"Let's just hope it doesn't turn out like that this year."

"We'll just have to wait and see."

"I guess so," Lydia said. She drank down the last of the milk her mother had fixed for her and pushed her chair away from the table, "Thank you for the milk Mama, I think I'm gonna get myself back to bed now."

"You're welcome," Mary said, she glanced up at the ceiling, "I hope TJ's gone back to sleep."

"I'll check on him," Lydia said, She noticed a pensive look pass across Mary's face, "...Unless *you* want to."

Mary smiled, "I'll walk you up." She stood to her feet, took their mugs to the sink, and then followed Lydia back down the hall. "Have you thought any more about what you want to name your girls," she asked Lydia quietly as they started upstairs.

Lydia slowed and turned to look at her mother. "I have some ideas," she said coyly, and then continued on up the stairs.

Mary waited until they were at the landing at the top of the stairs and then said, "But you're still not sharing?"

Lydia winked an eye and then grinned at her.

"Oh fine then," Mary said.

Lydia leaned over and kissed her mother's cheek, "Good night Mama," she whispered, "I'll see you in the morning."

Mary stood at Lydia's door until Lydia had worked herself back into bed and snuggled the covers up under her chin. "Good night Baby."

"Are you sure you don't mind me coming with you," Joey said, "...'Cause you know you can drop me at Granny Jack's...She's always fine to feed me."

"No Joey, I don't mind...Every time I see Maggie doesn't have to be a romantic interlude you know."

"I know," Joey said, "I just don't want to be the fifth wheel."

Roger turned onto Bridge Road and grinned over at Joey. "You're a *third* wheel," he chuckled, "And I already told her you were coming, too. She said she'd throw an extra chicken breast on the grill."

"Ooh, is she doing the grilled chickie with the pepper jack things?"

"...On her fresh baked sourdough rolls."

"Oh man, those are so good. You know, I was never a big fan of the sourdough 'til I had some of Maggie's rolls."

"You should tell her that," Roger said, "It'll make her feel good." He pulled into Maggie's driveway and parked behind her jeep. "Grab the Hot Bag for me please," he said as he opened his door and slid out. Maggie came out onto the porch as they walked up to the house. "Hey Maggie," Joey called.

"Hey Joe," Maggie said, "Hey Roger. I just brought the chicken in off the grill. Big slices of Pepper Jack are wrapping themselves nicely over each piece right now as I speak," she smiled, "...I hope y'all are hungry, I didn't realize how big the pieces of chicken were until I put them in the marinade. I had to use the next size up bowl from what I usually do to fit 'em all in."

Roger stopped at the foot of the steps and looked crookedly over at Joey, "I ain't gonna get a lick of work outta him this afternoon then." He looked up at Maggie and shook his head, "He ain't worth half a toot on a full stomach."

"Aww, come on," Joey drawled, "You're one to talk." He grinned up at Maggie, "When he comes back to work from out here eating with you, he comes waddling into the shop with his belly all pooched..." Joey paused as he puffed up his cheeks and leaned himself back trying to make his stomach poke out. "After about thirty minutes, I've got to go squirreling him out of some hidey hole he's crawled up in to take himself a nice long siesta."

Roger rolled his eyes, "Oh, give me a break. You're the one who's always crashed out in the back of my truck from twelve-thirty to two...laying out there happy as a dead pig in the sunshine."

"That's a nice visual," Maggie said.

"Well, have you ever seen one," Roger asked.

"*What*, a dead pig in the sunshine?"

"Yeah."

"No, in point of fact I haven't."

"Well, I'm here to tell you; they're the happiest looking thing you'll ever see," Roger said, "Grinning bigger'n anything."

Maggie gave her head a little shake, "I'm afraid I'm having a little trouble believing that one Roger."

"I'm serious," Roger said, "Watch this." He turned to Joey, "Smile great big."

Joey smiled broadly.

"Do it a little more," Roger said.

Joey grinned a little wider.

"...Little more."

Joey strained his grin back even more, pulling his lips tightly back across his teeth and squinting his eyes down to tight little pink lines under his thin strawberry eyebrows.

"Push your nose up."

Joey took his thumb and turned up his nose.

"*That's it,*" Roger said. He pointed at Joey, "They look just like that." He turned back to Maggie, "Look at that smile... Now ain't that about the happiest thing you've ever seen?"

Maggie looked at Joey for a moment and then grinned at Roger. "Yep," she chuckled, "That's sure happy, alright."

Roger looked back at Joey and stared at him for a second. "His cheeks aren't as full as I'd like," he said, "but his color is right on...Yep, that there is about as perfect a dead pig as you're likely to see...Without having to deal with the smell."

Joey's lips started to quiver.

"You can stop now Joey," Roger said, "Breathe."

Joey blew out a forceful breath and opened up his eyes, "*Whew,*" he said, "I thought I was gonna pass out for a minute there."

Maggie smiled, "Don't go doing that," she said, heading back into her house, "I made a banana cake with cream cheese icing for desert."

Joey pumped his eyebrows at Roger, "That woman speaks my language."

🙎

"So what do you think of my idea."

Roger stopped at the foot of Maggie's front steps and smiled back up at her, "Which one is that?"

Maggie stopped at the top of the steps and hung her toes over the edge, watching Joey climb into the cab of Roger's pickup. She crossed her arms and looked down at Roger with a smile, "About us all going out to eat or something... You gave me one of your classic Roger Lowell non-answers when I brought it up."

Roger propped himself on the railing and studied the polish on Maggie's toenails.

Maggie wiggled her toes, "Don't you think it would be nice?"

Roger reached out and tried to pinch Maggie's big toe. Maggie took a quick step back and wagged a finger at him. Roger snapped his fingers and made a disappointed face.

"*Well?*"

"I think it'd be weird to be honest with you."

"No it won't."

"Yeah it will."

"Why?"

"Because it's Roslynne and Joey."

"So."

Roger glanced out towards his truck and then looked back up at Maggie, "*It's Roslynne and Joey.*" Maggie chuckled at him. "There's nothing weird about it," she said, "It's sweet."

Roger took a deep breath and slowly shook his head, "I'm still trying to get my mind wrapped around the whole situation," he said, "I feel like that guy in that story."

"Which guy?"

"*You know...*the one in that story."

Maggie stared at Roger blankly. She leaned her head over to one side and shrugged up her shoulders, "Which story?"

"*Aww*, you know," Roger said, "That one about the guy that that stuff was going on right under his nose and everybody else knew that it was going on but him."

"*Oh*, that one."

"You know the one I'm talking about?"

"Nope."

Roger shook his head, "I'll think of it later."

"Think about my suggestion."

Roger looked back out at his truck. Joey had his head laid in the open window and started making an exaggerated snoring sound when Roger looked his way. Roger rolled his eyes and then looked back up at Maggie. He made a pitiful face, "*...It's Roslynne and Joey.*"

"Bye Roger."

Lydia mashed the button on the telephone and laid it down on the table, "That was Miss Rose," she said, turning to her mother.

"I kindly thought that's who it was," Mary said, peeling the last bit of skin from the potato she had in her hands. Glancing over at Lydia, she dropped the skin into the bucket she kept for Wesley's chickens and then quickly quartered the potato and dropped the pieces into a pot of water on the stove, "How's she doing?"

"She's good," Lydia said, "...And she's decided that she *is* coming."

"Well, that's wonderful," Mary said. She picked up another potato and started peeling.

"She's flying in Friday-week after Thanksgiving," said Lydia, "And she's thinking about staying on right through New Year's."

"Wait 'til TJ hears..."

"Oh, no," Lydia said, "Please don't tell him. I want it to be a surprise."

Mary smiled at Lydia, "I'm sure that he'll be tickled to death to see her," she said. Lydia came over and pulled her mother's fold-out step stool out and sat down on it next to Mary. She rested her elbow on the counter and propped her head on her hand, "Miss Rose said that she had a big surprise for *us*, too."

"It's going to be really nice to have the house full for Christmas again," Mary said. "I know you might find this hard to believe...but Christmas was always my favorite time of year." She split the potato into quarters and dropped the pieces in with the others, "This is going to be the first *Christmas* I've had in a long time."

Lydia rested her hand on Mary's arm.

Mary turned and smiled softly at Lydia, "I'm sorry I didn't give you Christmases like my mama gave me."

Lydia chuckled quietly. "It's funny Mama," she said, "I think I understand Terry, now."

Mary looked at Lydia a little closer.

"He used to tell me to stop thanking him for things that he was doing for me..." Lydia looked down at her stomach and then reached out and grabbed at the trim on her mother's apron. "I love you Mama," she said, looking back up into her mother's eyes, "You don't have to say you're sorry for that anymore... *You don't*...Every day we spend together now is a new memory of us that I have to look back on."

Mary took a long slow breath as she stared into Lydia's face. "Thank you Baby," she said, "But I'm going to say I'm sorry one more time...I'm sorry, that I can't take the credit for having such a wonderful daughter."

Lydia smiled at her mother, unsure of how to respond. After a few seconds, she stood herself up beside Mary and set her hands on her mother's shoulders, "What is it that Reverend Whit always says," she asked, "...'You've got to let go and let God'."

Mary leaned her head over against Lydia's.

"You know what Mama," Lydia said, "I've thought about what I wanted out of life, and how I wished things were and how they could be. But, I know that everything happens for a reason...I have faith in that. It's really hard to swallow sometimes, and I can't say that I am happy with the way everything *has* been or *is*, but I *do* know this: if things had been different for us...if you had been different...I really don't believe that I would appreciate what I have with you now even half as much as I do."

Mary straightened up and looked at Lydia through tear-rimmed eyes.

"To be completely honest with you Mama," Lydia said, "I used to wonder why Daddy ever married you...You two always seemed so different. More than just the opposites attract kind, but, now...now that I've gotten to really know you –the real you– I have no doubts why."

"*Mary*," Wesley's voice called from the front porch. Lydia and Mary turned to see Wesley come in the front door carrying the day's mail. He looked their way and grinned as he stepped inside. "Mary," he said, sounding a little winded, "I met Emmett Dingle at the foot of the driveway..." He tossed the mail onto the kitchen table as he made his way across the room, his smile growing as he came closer to his wife and daughter. "He said he couldn't get in the mailbox again," he paused and took a breath and then fished delicately around in the pockets of his vest, "That silly speckled hen laid three more eggs in there and kept pecking at his hand when he tried to slide this stuff in."

Pulling his hands back out, Wesley gently handed three tawny eggs to Mary, "I don't know what I'm gonna do with her," he said, "...I've got fifty dollars in a dern chicken coop and that silly bird won't stay out of the mailbox."

Lydia noticed how deliberate her father's motions still seemed, "Well, look at the bright side Daddy," she said, "At least she's not nesting up under your truck anymore."

"Yeah," Wesley nodded, "That's true. But it took a fourteen mile ride and her nearly getting killed to break her of that...I didn't think the feathers would ever fill in on the back of her head."

"Whatever it takes to get the job done," Lydia grinned, "Right Daddy?"

Wesley glanced over at his wife and then turned his eyes back to his daughter, "If I'd have known that I'd be hearing all of my *wiz-dom* spouted back at me on a regular basis all those years ago," he said, "I'd have quoted more Poor Richard and less Poor Wesley."

"Why is that?"

"I don't know," Wesley shrugged, "Mine just don't sound too sage."

"Sure they do."

"No they don't...They sound like some cranky old know-it-all codger who figgered he had more smarts than everybody else."

"I don't think so," Lydia said, "They've gotten me through a lot of tough spots through the years." She paused and grinned at her father, "But," she added, "I *could* start delivering them with an accent...You think that might help?"

Wesley shook his head no.

"Why not? You know how everybody thinks people with accents sound smarter than we do."

"You can't do accents."

"Sure I can."

"*No you can't*," Wesley said, "I've heard your accents... Gypsy...Italian...Scotsman...Every last one of 'em comes out sounding like an angry Aunt Soolie on a bad drunk."

"*Daddy*, Aunt Soolie didn't drink."

"I didn't say she did," Wesley replied, "But if she had, your accents would sound just like her when she did." He stopped for a second and his smile widened, "If she'd ever had to listen to your *Liza Doolittle* she'd have probbly asked for a couple good stiff ones, I'd bet."

Roger followed Maggie up onto the Vander's front porch and sat himself down in the high-backed rocking chair next to Buddy. "I'll just sit right here with my good buddy 'til you're done Mag," he said.

"I'll only be minute," Maggie said as she disappeared inside.

Roger rocked his chair back and looked at Buddy. He thought Buddy's face looked a little thinner than normal. "You're looking a bit thinner," he told his friend, "...And you look like you're sittin' up a little straighter today."

Buddy leaned his head back against his chair. "I'm feeling a lot better, Roger," he replied. He rolled his head around to look at Roger, "If you'd a' told me three days ago that I'd be feeling as good as I do, I'd have said you were crazy."

Roger nodded, "That's good."

"I mean, my chest is a little sore right through here..." Buddy ran his knuckles up and down the middle of his chest, "...Mostly on the left side...And my hips are still achy. But, other than that, I feel fine."

"Are you able to take a deep breath?"

"I have to really make myself, but, yeah I can." A purposeful look came across Buddy's face and he straightened himself up a little and gripped the chair's armrests as he slowly filled his lungs with air. He held the breath for a few seconds, took it in a little deeper, and then let it out slowly.

"How was that?"

Buddy's body relaxed a little, "Better," he said, "I've done that a few times today. That was probbly 'bout the best one."

"Maggie said Hill said you took a little short walk this morning, too."

"I took Peaches for a little walk," Buddy said. He gave Roger a half smile, "...Over in the cemetery."

Roger leaned himself back away from Buddy and opened his eyes wide, "*Well, look at you*," he said, sounding honestly surprised, "I don't know what's the bigger surprise...You going for a walk so soon after your accident or the fact that you went for a walk in the cemetery."

Buddy smiled proudly at Roger, "I actually *sat* on the edge of Fischweller's vault and ate a bag of peanuts with Peaches," he said.

Roger stared at Buddy in amazement, "*Who are you?*"

"I told you I was making a change."

"That's a pretty big start."

Buddy grinned, "I figured 'Go big or go home'."

Roger chuckled; he reached his hands up and grabbed the top of the seatback behind his head. "So," he said, "What's next? You got an appointment at Amanda's to get your highlights..."

"How'd you know?"

Roger looked around his elbow at Buddy and slitted his eyes down tight. Buddy made his face serious and sat silently staring back at Roger.

After a few seconds Roger said, "Please tell me you're kidding."

Buddy looked at Roger a moment longer and then smiled. He rolled his head back around and looked out into the yard, "When are you going back in to Ormond?"

"Wait a minute...You didn't answer my question."

Buddy turned back to Roger, "Technically, you didn't ask me a question."

Roger dropped his hands into his lap and then slid his chair around to face Buddy, "Okay," he said, "Are you *really* getting your hair highlighted?"

"No."

"Good."

"...*Permed.*"

Roger winced up his face and leaned in closer to Buddy, "You can't be serious."

"*Why not,*" Buddy said, "It was your idea."

"I was kidding."

"So am I."

Roger blew out a frustrated sigh, and let his head fall, dropping his chin down on his chest.

Buddy chuckled as Roger stared down at the porch shaking his head, "It's as bad as talking to yourself, ain't it?" he remarked.

Roger looked up at Buddy and then clapped his hand over his eyes. He dragged his hand slowly down his face and then pursed his lips and gave his head a tiny shake, "Is this how it's gonna be," he asked, "...With the new Buddy?"

"You don't like the new Buddy?"

"Not particularly," Roger said, "He reminds me too much of me...One smartass in this act is about enough."

"Eureka!" Buddy said loudly. He gave a little wince as he grabbed at his chest and grunted softly. He cleared his throat and settled back in his chair, "Thirty-five years," he said airily, "...Thirty-five years and you're finally admitting it."

Roger straightened up and leaned back towards the front door, "*Maggie,*" he called, "You 'bout ready?"

"Oh come on Roger."

Roger smiled, "I'm just messing with you," he said. He looked closely at Buddy, "You can be whoever you need to be. I'm just glad you're still here."

Buddy rolled his eyes and dismissed Roger's comment with a wave. "I picked that up from you, too" he said slyly, and waved again, "How you like it?"

Roger sat quietly for a moment and then said, "Do I really do that?"

Buddy nodded.

"Well, I hope I look cooler than *that* when I do it."

"I don't think that's possible...I'm the Lord of Cool."

Roger grabbed his stomach and laughed loudly, "I think you need to get that put on your license plate."

"*Hey,*" Buddy drawled, drawing the word out slowly into two syllables, "That's not a bad idea." He held his hands out in front of him with the ends of his thumbs touching one another, framing the front bumper of his truck parked out in the driveway between them, "The Lord of Cool...*Yeah,* I like it. That's much better than 'I *Heart* My Tractor'."

"So anyway," Roger said, "What did you want to know if I was going to Ormond for...you need me to run an errand for you?"

Buddy stared off across his yard for a moment, basking in his future coolness.

"*Buddy.*"

"Huh?"

"Land the plane dude."

"I'm here...What did you say?"

"I asked you why you wanted to know when I was going back up to Ormond. Do you need me to do something for you?"

"Right," Buddy replied. He shook his head, "No, I want to go with you."

"Sure," Roger said, "What'cha got in mind?"

"Umm, let's just say that I've got a few purchases I need to make." He looked in through the living room window and then beckoned Roger to lean in close with a tilt of his head.

Roger shifted in his chair and moved his head over next to Buddy's. Buddy lowered his voice, "Are you going back to Richmont's any time soon?"

Roger glanced over toward the front door and then leaned back in close to Buddy, "Yeah," he said, I'm supposed to go back on Thursday," he said quietly. He glanced over his shoulder again and then flashed Buddy a smile, "Besides the sizing, *it's* supposed to be ready then. They want me to come in and make sure they've got it just how I want it. If it's right I'll bring it home."

Buddy pumped his eyebrows up and down, "*Al-right,*" he drawled and smiled broadly at Roger, "So, when are you gonna pop–"

Buddy stopped as the screen door pushed open and Hillary and Maggie came out onto the porch and walked around in front where they were sitting. Roger and Buddy sat up quickly and stared up at them in silence. Hillary and Maggie glanced back and forth at their faces. Hillary looked over at Maggie and then stared down at Buddy, "Did we interrupt something?"

Roger and Buddy looked at each other and then stared blankly at the two women and made no response.

"Oh, I've seen those faces before," Maggie said, "...Y'all ain't been out here nippin' at the orange extract have you?"

Buddy grinned at Roger as Roger swayed himself in his chair and faked a hiccup. "I don't know what you're talkin' about Occifer," Roger slurred, "We ain't been extricting any oranges."

Buddy chuckled, "Honest we ain't youronner," he sloshed, and rested his hand over his heart, "And to be extract, *I mean*, exact...We ain't even got a norange."

~Chapter Six~

"*Oooh*, there goes a good one." Lydia said. She stopped at the foot of her bed and grabbed onto her stomach.

"Do you think it's a real one?"

Lydia considered it for a moment and then shook her head, "No," she said, "I'm pretty sure it's just another Braxton-Hicks." She finished shaking her pillow down into the pillowcase and tossed it up against the headboard, "I seem to recall having more trouble holding a conversation during the real ones."

Iris fluffed the other pillow and set it next to Lydia's.

"I was wondering," Lydia said, "...Am I allowed to ask what you and my son are going to be doing today?"

Iris pulled the cover up over the pillows and glanced at Lydia out of the corner of her eye, smiling as she tucked the bedspread neatly down around the pillows. "No," she said, "You're not...As if I need to tell you, though."

Lydia picked the throw pillows back up from the chair and arranged them in place on the bed. "Just promise you won't let him buy me a bunch of chocolate," she said, "I'm going to have enough trouble getting back into my clothes as it is."

"Gotcha...Do you have any suggestions as to some direction I might steer him –*if* I were taking him shopping."

"To be honest with you," said Lydia, "I haven't got any idea." She walked around and sat herself down on the foot of the bed, "He's been asking me these somewhat subtle, leading questions for the last two weeks, and I can't think of a thing I want."

"How about some chewing tobacco?"

Lydia grinned and shook her head no.

"*Pipe cleaners?*"

Another shake no.

"*Zincs?*"

"Unh uh."

"Bottom paint."

"Maybe candy isn't such a bad idea."

Iris sat down next to Lydia, "We'll come up with something."

Lydia gripped the rail at the foot of the bed and lifted her feet out straight, "I can't wait to get my ankles back."

"I don't know," Iris said, cocking her head to the side as she studied Lydia's legs, "You do kankles very well."

"Thanks a lot."

"Well, you always used to complain 'cause you thought they were too skinny."

"You won't ever catch me doing *that* again, that's for sure." Lydia lowered her feet back down and pumped her toes up and down, "This is miserable."

Iris's face brightened, "How about a spa day," she said, "...For after. TJ can get you a gift certificate for Hazeltine's."

"I don't know," Lydia said, scrunching her face, "Isn't that a little expensive?"

"Come on Lydie, you deserve a nice massage and spa treatment." Iris hopped up and faced Lydia, "Just picture it," she said, lifting her hands out in front of her, a little above Lydia's head and then slowly moving them out away from each other in an arch, "You're laying there, looking out that big picture window over the river. There's some breezy, acoustic, summertime, toes-in-the-sand music playing soft in the background and you've just gotten out of that nice, hot salt-bath and you've got that just-showered-after-the-ocean feeling and you're getting ready for your full body massage."

"Wait a minute," Lydia said. She pointed at her chest, "Does this massage table have holes in it for my two poor we-need-a-break-'cause-we're-nursing-twins-eight-times-a-day boobs? 'Cause if it doesn't–"

"Thanks a lot for the visual."

"Nice huh, wait 'til it becomes reality."

"You want me to check and see if they do a European Breast Massage while I'm downtown?"

Lydia burst out laughing, her stomach bouncing up and down in her lap, "Is that even a real thing?"

"I don't know," Iris said, "Billy McKee offered me one on our one and only date. He claimed he learned," she paused as she gave Lydia a little wink and made quotation marks in the air with her fingers, "'*The Fine Art*' in chiropractor school in Tampa."

"*He didn't go to chiropractor school.*"

"I know that...He was working with his Uncle Reuben running water taxis...and I told him so."

"And what did he say to that?"

Iris made her voice deeper, "*Does that mean you don't want one?*"

Lydia rolled her eyes, "That *dog*," she chuckled.

Iris said, "Yeah *really*...And he seemed so charming." She shrugged, "So, what do you say to the spa day, do you mind if I steer your little man in that direction?"

Lydia looked down at her ankles again, "No, I guess not," she said, "If it's not too expensive...Oh," she jerked her head back up and looked at Iris, "If you happen to go by Seaport Antiques while you're that way, could you check and see if they still have those red depression-glass, tea sets for me?"

"Sure, you want me to get all four of them for you if they do?"

"If you could," Lydia said. She thought for a moment, "That'll give eight settings, right?"

"I believe so."

"Yeah, get all four if they still have them."

"Am I sneaking them in?"

Lydia nodded, "I've never seen Mama make such a big deal about something as she did those. I'd really like to surprise her with them."

"If you want, I can go ahead and get them wrapped...I'm sure that the First Baptist Ladies have got their deal set up downtown."

"I don't know," Lydia replied, "Wrapping the presents is one of my favorite parts of Christmas. I love fixing up all the ribbons and bows. I'd hate to miss all that."

"I know you would," said Iris, "But if something happens, you might not be able to wrap presents."

"Like what?"

Iris looked down at the rounded belly sitting heavily in Lydia's lap. "Those pumpkins you're smuggling just might decide it's time to come out and meet the family early," she said, "...That's what."

"Oh yeah," Lydia said, she smiled and looked down at herself. "I find it hard to believe myself, but, I keep forgetting I'm pregnant."

"I can't imagine how."

"I know it's crazy," Lydia said, gently cradling her stomach, "It kind of sneaks up on you and you get so used to the feeling."

"Can you imagine if you just woke up the next morning like that?"

Lydia laughed. "There sure wouldn't be any question as to whether or not you were pregnant," she said, "So much for all the home tests."

"I'm sure there a few moms out there who'd gladly trade it for the morning sickness."

"I know," Lydia said, "I've had some friends that I was convinced they were gonna die from dehydration...This one friend of mine, Nancy Willis –she was a teacher at the school where I worked in Hadley– I was standing in my class one day and I glanced over and she's crawling down the hall past my door...She had just told me earlier in the week how bad her morning sickness had been with her first two and that she was expecting it to start any day...Bless her heart, I saw her like that at least three times a week for the next six weeks."

"Are you serious? Why didn't she just stay home?"

"I think I remember her baby was due about fifteen weeks before school let out for the summer and she was trying to save up her sick time for when he came so she wouldn't have to come back for the last three weeks of school."

Iris shook her head, "I don't know as I could do that."

"Maybe you'll be like me and you won't have to."

Iris stopped and cocked her head at Lydia, "I'm afraid you're leaving out a very important part of that equation," she said.

"Don't you worry about that," Lydia said, "I've got this feeling that that's going to work itself out very soon."

Iris sat down in the chair and stared oddly at Lydia for a moment, "What makes you say that?"

"I just have this feeling that something magical is going to happen this Christmas."

"What makes you think your magical feelings have anything to do with my current lack of romantic interests and *not* the arrival of two very special little babies?"

"I just do."

Iris looked at her quizzically.

"I don't know," Lydia shrugged, "I can't explain it. You know how you kept telling me to have faith when Daddy was sick, and how you said that you just were so sure something good was coming from all of it?" Lydia paused and then stood to her feet, "You remember I kept asking you how you knew and you just kept telling me that you just *knew*...That you could *feel* it...I've got a feeling just like that now...Down in the pit of my stomach."

"That's probably gas."

Lydia laughed, "Or worse..."

"Well," Iris said, "I really do appreciate the encouragement, but, I'm afraid that I just don't share your faith in this. I mean, the possibles around here are some pretty slim pickins."

"Things can change at any minute."

"I know," Iris sighed.

"They can," Lydia said, "...They *do*." She patted her stomach again, "I hate to keep drawing attention to this, but, I was convinced I'd never have another baby..."

"And here you are with two on the way."

Lydia nodded, "And look at Daddy...and Mama." She smiled down at Iris, "Terry used to say that life was like the weather, 'If you don't like it,' he'd say, 'Just wait a minute... *It'll change.*'"

Iris stood herself back up and patted Lydia's belly. "Well," she said, "One thing I am sure of is that I am *so* looking forward to holding these babies."

"Me too," Lydia said, "But I am going to miss this...It makes you feel so special...The way people treat you, you can't imagine how nice everyone is."

"It's a special thing, Lydie" Iris said, "What a wonderful time of the year to be expecting."

"Terry always wanted to see me pregnant at Christmas," said Lydia. "He had this picture of me in a black velvet dress; my belly out to here, drinking hot chocolate by a roaring fire...Every time he'd tell me his *vision*, I'd just laugh and tell him he was crazy, but he said he couldn't imagine seeing anything more beautiful."

"Black *is* slenderizing," said Iris.

"Nothing's *that* slenderizing."

Roger pulled around the corner and spotted Joey and Roslynne walking down the sidewalk along Commons Street headed towards the waterfront. He stopped his truck in the street under the boughs of the big live oak that grew off the back corner of his shop and watched them for a moment. Roslynne had a hold of Joey's arm and was smiling at him as Joey was pointing at something out in the river. The sight of the two of them together hit him in a way he hadn't expected and he started chuckling, "*Ho-ly Mackerel*," he said. He started to drive down next to them but changed his mind and went ahead and pulled in at his shop instead.

Parking in his usual spot, Roger leaned over and rolled down the passenger window and then slid out and went inside. As he walked past the workbench, he noticed an open cardboard box sitting there with some DVDs inside. He picked one up off the top of the stack and read the cover; *Marco Rebahno's Cage Fighter Workout*. Roger picked up another DVD; *Marco "El Tigre" Rebahno's Fighting Fit Workout*. "*What in the world is this*," he said, flipping the lid on the box over with one of the cases. He saw that it was addressed to Buddy, but it had his shop's street address.

Roger looked back at the DVD cases. A sweaty young man with dark, brooding, eyes scowled at him. He was standing close with his hands out as if he was about to grab you from the cover. The young man was turned just enough so that you could see that he had a leopard with its fangs bared tattooed on his right shoulder. Roger sat the DVDs down and picked up the last two from the box; *El Tigre's Cardio Workout* and *Marco Rebahno's Complete Fighter... Take your training to the next level*. Roger stared at the picture on last case. Marco had a one inch cut set precisely on his sweaty cheekbone and was looking exceptionally rugged as he stared fiercely out at the purchaser of his "Most complete training system ever!" Roger chuckled and stacked the DVDs back into the box.

He walked on into the office to pour a cup of coffee and had to stop and smile when he saw the fresh pan of coffee cake sitting next to the half empty coffee pot. He noticed that there were two pieces gone from the cake and then saw the two empty cups sitting over on his desk.

Grinning to himself again, Roger fixed himself a cup, sat down at the desk, and stared out the front window at the brilliant blue sky. He sat there for a moment and thought about his little sister's new romance as he watched a handful of seagulls pass overhead heading east towards the river. He heard the birds calling to another flock flying towards them from the north.

"I reckon you're just gonna have to get used to it Roger," he told himself as the two flocks joined and then continued on out of sight. "Not that you've got much choice..." he chuckled.

He picked up the Christmas card they had gotten in yesterday's mail from Down East Machine and Tool Supply and smiled at the Santa Claus on the front in welding goggles repairing one of the runners on the sleigh. Roger stared at the card for a moment and then hauled himself up from his seat and went over and opened the front door. He pushed the big Chatham Block Company brick over in front of the door to keep it propped open with his foot and then stepped out onto the front step in the sunshine just as Marvin Carter came down Pine Street in front of Roger's shop in his flatbed Chevrolet hauling a load of new crabpots.

Marvin looked over and saw Roger standing there and stopped short, "*Hey Big Man,*" he said, leaning himself out the window, "How ya doin' this fine morning?"

Roger took a sip of his coffee as Marvin spoke and then smiled at him as he swallowed it down, "Just peachy," he said, "How 'bout you?"

"If I was any better there'd be two of me."

"Looks like you've been busy," Roger said, motioning towards the fresh, green-meshed crabpots stacked high on the bed of Marvin's pickup. He stepped down and headed out into the street, "...Those yours or you delivering them to somebody else?"

Marvin craned his neck around and stared at the crabpots for a moment like it was the first time he had ever seen them, "Oh them," he said, turning back to Roger, "...They're for Darvell Coombs...I've just about given up crabbin', I'm staying so busy building pots."

Roger stepped up next to Marvin's truck and propped himself on its big, side-view mirror, "Is that good or bad?"

Marvin scratched at his wiry blonde beard, "It's good I reckon," he said, "I can work right there in the yard under the shelter and not have to get rained on or beat by the sun all day...That coffee sure smells good."

"You want a cup? We got a fresh pot on."

"Sure."

Marvin grabbed a plastic mug from the seat next to him and popped the top off, "Watch out," he said to Roger as he reached his arm out and poured the remnants of yesterday's coffee into the street. Roger took a step back and then Marvin shook the last drops free and handed the mug to him. Roger looked at the battered mug and read the side, "Nethercutt's Net and Fisherman Supply...Where'd you find this? They went out of business what, twenty years ago?"

"It was up under the decking in that Horace Brothers I bought off of Lou-Mark Tilley back when I got out of high school," Marvin said, "Pretty cool ain't it."

Roger nodded, admiring the cup, "Mister Nethercutt was a good man," he said, "It was a real shame when that place burned..." He stood there for a moment and then gave his head a little shake and looked back up at Marvin, "Let me get you some coffee."

Marvin backed his truck and then pulled up in front of Roger Lowell's front door as Roger went inside and poured the mug full. After a few seconds, Roger stuck his head out and asked, "I forgot, how do you take it?"

"Two spoons of sugar."

"*No milk?*"

Marvin shook his head. Roger disappeared for a few more seconds and then came back out and handed the cup to Marvin. "Thanks Roger," Marvin said, he took a swallow, snapped the lid back on the mug, and then took a sip through the little hole, "We can't seem to keep coffee, pimento cheese, or dill pickles in the house since Gina's daddy moved in with us...And I hain't been by Randy's yet this morning."

"Don't mention it," Roger said, "How's he doing anyway?"

"*A lot* better," said Marvin, nodding slowly, "He's pretty much on the oxygen all the time now, but he can get around about like he pleases."

"That's good to hear."

"Well, I better get going Roger," Marvin said, "I've got to run another bunch of pots down to Hall's Point after I drop these off." He lifted the mug and tilted it at Roger, "I really do appreciate the cup of coffee."

Roger held his cup up and gave a half nod, "It was good talking to you Marvin," he said. "Tell Gina I said hey," he added as Marvin backed back out into the street.

"*Will do*," Marvin replied, he threw his arm out the window as he stopped his truck, "See ya."

Roger waved and took another swallow of his coffee as he watched Marvin turn and drive up Commons, heading off towards the Landing. As Marvin's truck cleared the intersection, Joey came walking back around the corner, whistling happily to himself. He waved when he saw Roger. Roger toasted him with his cup and then drank down what coffee was left.

"*Howdy*, Doodie," Joey said as he came up to Roger. Joey's hair was styled again.

"Good morning," Roger said, "I don't reckon I need to ask how you're doing today do I?"

"If I was any better there'd be two of me."

Roger laughed.

"What?"

"Nothing...How's Miss Roslynne this morning?"

"Fine as frog's hair."

"Is that coffee cake she baked for everybody or just her sweetie pie?"

"*Well*," drawled Joey, "If you're extra nice, Sweetie Pie will share."

"That's mighty kind of you," Roger said, heading back inside. "*Oh*," he said, stopping in the doorway and turning back to Joey, "Before I forget," he said, pointing at Joey through the handle on his coffee cup, "I talked to Lydia yesterday afternoon and she said it would be fine if you wanted to take the bike out every now and then. Just for you to be careful, 'cause they're dangerous..."

Joey's face broke into a grin; "Awesome," he said, "...I've got to get a helmet –Roslynne would kill me if she found out I drove that thing around without a helmet."

Roger bit his lip as he turned and went back inside. *Get used to it big boy*, he thought, *just get used to it*. He topped his cup off and stirred in a little more molasses and was getting himself a piece of coffee cake when the telephone rang. Joey picked it up as Roger put his piece of cake on a plate and then took a bite.

"Lowell's," Joey said, "Joey speaking...Good morning Mister Hicks, what can I do for you?" He covered the mouthpiece with his hand and mouthed to Roger that it was the jewelry store. Roger sat his plate back down.

"Yessir," Joey said, "Well he's right here if you'd like to speak with him...Sure...Thanks, you too," he handed the phone to Roger and then walked off into the shop.

Roger said, "Good morning Mister Hicks...Fine and yourself?" He pinched the phone up between his face and his shoulder and grabbed his plate and cup and moved them over to his desk and sat down, "Really? Well that's great."

Joey came back in with the cordless phone. "Thanks," Roger mouthed as he took it from him. He clicked it on and then swapped it out and handed the old corded phone back to Joey to hang up. "...Yessir, I can do that. That's not a problem...Any time today...Great...I'll see y'all this afternoon sometime then...Alright, thank you."

Roger had a wide grin on his face as he clicked the phone off and set it down on the desk. He looked at Joey, "You reckon you can handle things by yourself today?"

"Yeah, what's up?"

"They've got Maggie's ring done so I need to run in to town."

"That was quick."

"The jeweler had an order canceled so he got to it a lot sooner than he was expecting."

"That's great...can you pick me up a Rolex while you're there?"

"Sure," Roger said, picking the telephone back up, "I'll put it in the glovebox when I pick up your Jag." He dialed Buddy's number and put the phone to his ear, "You wanted silver with red leather, right?"

"And twelve cylinders..."

"Hey Hill, good morning," Roger said. He smiled at Joey and gave him a thumbs up, "I was calling to see if you wanted me to run Buddy to the doctor today." He leaned back in the chair and turned it slowly in a circle, "...No I don't mind; I just found out I've got to run to town myself... Yeah, put him on." He turned back to Joey, "Do they make 'em with anything less?"

Joey shrugged.

"Hey Buddy, how ya feelin' this morning...Great. Did Hillary tell you what I asked her...Yeah, Richmont's called this morning and *it's* ready...Yeah, they got it done early... What time's your appointment." He checked the clock on the wall, "You want me to come on over and get you then?" Turning the chair back toward the desk, Roger took a bite of coffeecake, "Alright," he said, tucking the coffeecake into the side of his mouth, "I'll be there in about thirty minutes, see ya."

Roger clicked the phone off and sat it back on the desk as he took a sip of coffee. Swallowing down the coffee and cake, he turned back to Joey, "That takes care of that... Don't forget; mum's the word about the you-know-what. If anybody asks all you know is that I took Buddy to town for his checkup."

Joey winked one eye closed and flashed an O-K at Roger, "You got any idea when you'll be getting back."

Roger shook his head, "It shouldn't be too late, but, Buddy mentioned something the other day about having to make some purchases while we're in town so I don't know. Why, what'cha need?"

"Well, I was figuring on finishing up the frame for the churchbell this morning and then I was planning on us taking it over there this afternoon."

"*Oh yeah*," Roger said, wincing up his face, "Sorry J, I forgot all about that." He leaned on the desk and propped his chin in his hand as he thought for a moment, "Did you call Reverend Whit and tell him you'd be bringing it today?"

Joey shook his head no, "I didn't want to call him until I knew I was done."

"That's probbly better…If I remember correctly, he wanted at least a day's notice to let the contractor know so they can do whatever it is they need to do to get it back up in the roof." Pausing for a second, he stared down at the floor, and then looked back up at Joey and continued "Go ahead and finish it up and then call out to the church. See if he'll be ready for it tomorrow and we'll take it over then."

"Okay," Joey said, "But that's about all I had to do for today."

"That's fine. Just hang around 'til about three or so and if nothing comes up you can swoop."

"Sweet."

"Oh," Roger remembered, "What's the deal with the package for Buddy in the shop? I forgot to ask him about it."

"I don't know," Joey shrugged, "Deek dropped it off first thing this morning," he said, "I opened it before I realized it wasn't ours." He chuckled softly, "I was standing there reading the covers trying to figure out what you where doing ordering something like that when Roslynne got here." He paused and gave another chuckle, "And when I actually read the box, I got pretty tickled."

"You didn't let Roz see them did you?"

Joey shook his head, "No, uh uhn…I figured he wanted it a secret or he wouldn't have had it mailed here."

"Good."

"We catching the usual," Roger asked Buddy as he slid in and planted himself down into the booth. Buddy slid in on the other side and stared at Roger like he had something he wanted to say, a little crease showing across the middle of his forehead.

"Well," Roger said after a couple seconds of silence, "What'cha say?" He smiled, "…We splitting a large Hawaiian-eye?"

Buddy stared at him a second longer and then gave his head a little shake and grabbed himself a menu, "I don't know Rog," he said airily, flipping the menu open. He read down the first page, "I think I might get something off the menu."

"*Okay*," Roger said, staring at the top of Buddy's head as he read the menu. He grabbed the menu that was stuck in between the napkin holder and the condiments, opened it up, and read the weekly lunch specials. He glanced up at Buddy, "The Stromboli looks good."

Buddy kept reading and didn't answer. Roger stared back down at the menu and pretended to be reading it, "How 'bout some cheese sticks?"

"I don't know if I'm in the mood for cheese sticks," Buddy replied, as much to himself as to Roger, "I think I'm gonna try something a little lighter today."

"Like what...*a salad?*"

Buddy shrugged, "Maybe."

Roger made a show of pinching his own arm to make sure he was awake, but Buddy was too involved in the menu to notice. A waitress in a bright pink shirt with a Christmas tree decorated with tiny Italian flags and *Buon Natale* printed across the front came over smiling at Roger and asked them what they wanted to drink and "...Can I interest either of you in an appetizer? The stuffed mushrooms are very good."

"I'd like a sweet tea," Roger said, "And, I think I'd like to try some of those mushrooms, please."

"And for you sir..." the waitress said, turning to Buddy.

"Ice water, please," Buddy replied, smiling politely up at her.

"Would you care for an appetizer?"

"No thank you."

"Alright," the waitress said cheerfully, turning back to Roger, "I'll be right back with your drinks." Buddy quickly picked the menu back up in his big square hands and went back to it like he was studying for a mid-term exam as she turned and headed for the kitchen. Roger watched her go and then turned back to Buddy, "How 'bout we split a medium instead of a large."

Buddy looked up at Roger, "I think I'm gonna get a salad," he said warily.

"*A salad*," Roger said, "*Yeah right*...You gonna get 'em to pour you some gravy on it?"

Buddy's eyes rolled around in their sockets, "Come on man," he said, "I'm serious."

"Really?"

"Yes, *really?*"

"What in the world for?"

Buddy thumped the menu down on the table, "I want to lose some weight, Roger," he blurted, "...That's why."

Roger sat back in the booth, caught off guard by the intensity suddenly coming at him from across the table.

Buddy shook his head almost in disgust, and then glanced around the room. He leaned towards Roger and brought his voice back down, "I'm tired of being fat...I'm tired of being *Comfortable*...I'm tired of being *Good Ole' Buddy Bear*." Buddy sneered at the nickname and spoke the words as if they left a bad taste in his mouth.

"I don't understand, Buddy," Roger said, "*That's you*...I like you...I like Buddy Bear." He paused a moment and then added, "*Everybody* likes Buddy Bear."

Buddy's mouth creased, "Not *everybody*."

"Not everybody?" Roger said. "How can you say that? Everybody likes Buddy Bear."

Buddy leaned back away from the table. "*I* don't," he said. He rested his head against the back of the booth, gazed up at the ceiling and let out a heavy sigh, "You can't understand Roger," he said distantly. He looked back down at Roger, "...I want Hillary to look at me the way women have always looked at you...the way Maggie looks at you. I want *my wife* to look at *me* like that, and as long as I look like *this*," he gestured at himself, "...That ain't gonna happen."

Roger chuckled self-consciously under his breath, "*What women are looking at me*," he said, "*I've never seen anyone looking at me.*"

Buddy's head rolled to one shoulder, "Please," he said, "Be serious."

"I am."

Buddy considered Roger briefly, "Look, your eyes ain't brown and I weren't born yesterday, so let's keep the who-ha to a minimum...You know as good as I do that –*and the Lord only knows why*– women have always seemed to find you nice to look at." Buddy stopped and stared down at the menu lying on the table in front of him. "You wouldn't understand what it's like," he said quietly, pushing the menu around in little circles, "I'm afraid one of these days, Hillary's gonna realize she settled for a lot less than she deserved." He turned the menu sideways and then squared it up with the edge of the table.

Roger took a deep noisy breath and held it, silently ashamed of himself. "I'm sorry Buddy," he said, "I didn't mean it to hurt you."

Buddy smiled, "You didn't hurt me Roger. But you have to understand, I was serious when I told you I wanted to make a change. I've been thinking about it for a while. Running myself over was just the catalyst that finally got me going...I mean to do it."

Roger thought for a moment and then said, "*You lied to me.*"

"No I didn't."

"Yes you did, you lied to me."

"When?"

"When I picked you up this morning...You told me those DVDs were for Rainey." Roger pointed a finger at Buddy, "They're for *you* aren't they?"

Buddy grinned embarrassedly.

Roger shook his head, "And that whole story you conjured up about Rainey's *Judoka* recommending them to you–"

"*He did,*" Buddy interrupted, "Sort of...just not for Rainey..."

Their waitress stepped over and sat their drinks and a little plate of lemon wedges between them. "Your mushrooms will be right out," she said to Roger before quickly heading off to a young couple who had just come into the restaurant.

Buddy picked up a wedge and squeezed the juice into his water, "Kenny," he said, laying the mashed out pulp back down on the edge of the plate, "*Rainey's Judoka,* is really into these body-weight exercises...He's always talking them up to his students during their classes and he's into these Brazilian training methods. A couple weeks ago, I asked him if he had any recommendations for some training for someone who wanted to get into shape and he threw out a few names and then I found an ad for those DVDs in the back of one of Rainey's martial arts magazines. I remembered that Marco dude's name from Kenny..." Buddy stopped and looked out the window, watching a small group of nicely dressed women crossing the parking lot headed toward the front door of the restaurant. He watched as several of their stares lingered on his friend Roger. He turned back to Roger with a smirk and then took a long swallow from his glass of water, "You really don't see it do you," he asked.

Roger looked at him blankly.

Buddy took another quick swallow of water, sat his glass back down very slowly, and looked Roger straight in the eye, "I'm not going to be *comfortable* anymore."

Roger sat and silently admired the determination on his friend's face, "Alright then Buddy," he said firmly, "I'm in for this grand adventure with you."

Buddy smiled at Roger again.

Roger picked up a lemon wedge and squeezed it over his tea. He took a slow drink and then set his glass down; lining it up on the ring of condensation the glass had left on the table. He looked at Buddy and the corners of his mouth curled up, "But, you're really still not getting a perm... Right?

Roger stepped out the front door of the Richmont Family Jewelers and caught sight of a familiar car parked along the curb on the other side of the street. He stood under the awning, holding a little red bag by its braided gold rope handles and got very nervous. Glancing down the sidewalk, he wondered which store Buddy had slipped off to. He glanced at his watch, "Come on Buddy," he muttered, "You said you'd be back in ten minutes." He stepped out from under the big green awning and shaded his eyes with one hand as he peered off down the sidewalk, "Why couldn't you have just waited for me to finish with the jeweler," he said under his breath, "Maybe I ort to just go wait in my truck..."

A breeze blew up from the waterfront, skittering a handful of leaves along the sidewalk past Roger's feet as he ran through the downtown stores in his mind, trying to reason where Buddy might be.

"*Roger.*"

Roger gave a start. He spun around on his heels to find Iris and TJ standing behind him. TJ was carrying a big brown bag with the outline of flowers stenciled across it in both hands. Roger clutched his little gift bag tightly and had the sinking feeling of being caught red handed at something.

"Hey," Iris said as she reached up and hugged Roger's neck. She pecked a kiss on his cheek, "Fancy seeing you up here today."

Roger grinned nervously and then tried to look casual as he shifted the bag and his hands out of sight around behind his back, "Hey Iris," he said, "...Yeah, it is." He smiled down at TJ, "Hey Slick."

"Hey Roger," TJ replied, grinning up at Roger over the top of the bag.

"So," Roger said to Iris, "What are y'all doing up here today?"

"Getting in a little bit of early Christmas shopping," said Iris, "How 'bout you?"

"I brought Buddy up for his doctor's appointment–" Roger pointed back over one shoulder with his thumb and then quickly stuck his hand back down behind his back.

Iris glanced past Roger down the sidewalk and then looked back up at him, "Did you lose him somewhere?"

"Uh, no, or yeah, I mean, I was in the store here–" Without thinking, Roger pointed at the jewelry store with the fancy little Richmont's bag. He saw Iris eye the bag and quickly snatched it back down behind his back. He felt his face grow warm and wondered if his cheeks were turning red. "...And he," he tried to avoid eye contact with Iris as he continued, "He, uh..."

Iris's face broke into a huge grin, "*Did you just buy somebody some jewelry?*"

Roger scratched at the back of his neck and stared down at his feet.

"Oh come on Roger, don't worry, I won't tell..."

Roger slowly brought the little gift bag around in front of him as he looked up and smiled wincingly at Iris. *Thanks a lot Buddy*, he thought and cleared his throat.

Iris took a step towards him, "Can I see?" she asked, mirroring Roger's movements as he took half a step away and then worked himself around until his back was to the street. "It's just a little thing," he said.

Iris glanced down at the bag, "It's not a little *round* thing is it?"

"Hey Mister Buddy," TJ called, gazing down the sidewalk between Iris and Roger.

Iris and Roger both turned to see Buddy coming up the sidewalk to them. He waved, "Hey TJ." He looked at Iris, "*Hey girl.*"

Roger had to stifle down a little chuckle. Buddy held a hand out to Roger and gestured towards the Richmont's bag, "Thanks for holding my bag for me," he said, "Sorry I took so long."

Roger looked down at Buddy's hand and then pursed his lips as he looked back up at him. Buddy pumped his hand and held it out for Roger again. Roger leaned in a little closer to Buddy and lowered his voice, "She already knows it's mine dude."

Buddy let his hand hang motionless in the air for a second and then ran it back through his hair and grinned foolishly at Iris. Iris cocked her head and eyed him closely, "Nice try," she said.

Buddy shrugged, "It was worth a shot," he said. "That's one nice ring, huh?"

"*Buddy,*" Roger smacked Buddy's arm, "She didn't know it was a ring."

Iris bounced up on the balls of her feet, "*A ring...*" She gave Roger another hug, "That's so great," she said, grabbing his arm, "You don't have to worry Roger, I won't breathe a word." She looked at TJ, "...And TJ won't either, will you buddy?"

TJ nodded and then shook his head and grinned. He held his hand up and gave Roger his three-fingered salute assurance, "Scout's honor."

Iris turned back to Roger and smiled again, "I promise Roger...Not a peep."

"Thanks Iris. This is kind of a big deal for me."

"Of course it is," Iris said. She rested her arm across TJ's shoulders, "You can count on us."

Roger looked down at TJ, "I appreciate it TJ...I owe you one."

TJ stuck his hand out and Roger gave it a firm shake. TJ said, "Don't mention it."

"*Well,*" Iris said, "Are you gonna let me see it?"

Roger pulled the box out from the bag and stuck the bag up under his arm. He opened the box and then carefully pulled out a little, hinged, velvet-covered box.

Iris rested her hand over her heart as Roger pulled the lid back. She leaned in to get a closer look and then *Ahhed* quietly. She took Roger's hand in hers and stared at the ring and then looked up at him and smiled broadly, "Oh Roger," she said, "It's beautiful." She glanced at Buddy and then looked back down at the ring, "Those look like two gold feathers holding the diamond."

"Roger came up with the design himself," Buddy said.

"It's beautiful Roger...Maggie is going to be so happy."

"You think she'll like it?"

"Oh, she'll love it," Iris said. She looked back up into Roger's eyes, "*And* what goes with it."

Roger smiled and closed the box, "Listen," he said, "Nobody knows a thing about this except for Joey and us–"

"Don't worry Roger," Iris quickly told him, "*Really*...Not a peep."

&

"I'm *real* sorry Rog," Buddy repeated for the twelfth time, "...Me and my big mouth."

Roger placed the Richmont's bag down on the floor between his toolbox and the surplus ammo can that he used to carry his jumper cables, some extra gloves, and a couple half-rolls of duct tape, and then covered it with a faded canvas fishing hat. He pushed the seatback back up into place as he stood himself up and grinned at Buddy. He grabbed Buddy's shoulder, "Let it go man. Iris won't tell. That secret's as safe with her as that ring's gonna be in the cannonball."

Buddy said, "I know she won't tell, but I still feel bad, just the same." He stopped and shook his head, "My big flappin' jaws..."

Roger chuckled and then shut the door on his pickup, "Little steps," he said.

Buddy stared at him for a second and then smiled, "I know...I've been thirty-five years in the making, I'm not going to be new Buddy in a week."

"Right...Now let's go finish your list."

"Ain't you gonna lock her up?"

Roger paused and glanced around, "Well, I reckon I better." He opened the door back up and flicked the lock and then quickly closed the door, "I bet I could count on one hand the times I've done that since I bought her."

Buddy said, "It's nice...ain't it?"

Roger nodded, "I'm afraid we take it for granted sometimes Buddy."

"We've shore got it good," Buddy said, "I can't imagine what it must be like for people who live in places where they're afraid to go out at night or they feel like they've got to keep everything locked up tight as Dick's hat band or somebody's gonna take everything they've got."

"It's a real blessing."

"That's right," Buddy agreed, "The Lord's been good to us Roger." He stuck his hands down deep into his pockets, "I need to find a pot."

"*Huh?*"

"A pot," Buddy repeated, pulling a five dollar bill from his pocket. He scanned the street. "Where did we see that Salvation Army dude with the trumpet?"

"I believe it was a French horn."

"Yeah, that too...Where was he?"

"Over on the corner across from the big Presbyterian Church I think. We saw him when we first drove in, right?"

"Yeah," Buddy said, "That sounds right...I've got a feelin' to put some money out there."

"Well, we have to go right by there to go to that dress store you said you wanted to go look in."

"Well let's roll, then," Buddy said. Roger followed him as he turned and crossed the street. "You know," Buddy said, half turning to Roger as they stepped up onto the sidewalk, "I've never thought of myself as selfish before, but right now, I feel like I've been one of the most selfish people in the world."

"I've never thought you were selfish."

Buddy stopped and looked at Roger.

"You'd do anything to help somebody," Roger said, "I've never known you *not* to lend a hand."

Buddy's head tilted over to one side as he thought for a moment, "That may be true Roger," he said, "But, it just came to me that God has blessed us with a peaceful, bountiful existence that so many other people don't have..." He stopped and paused for a breath, "In my entire lifetime that has never really crossed my mind." He threw his arms out, "...I mean, I'm trying to lose weight for crying out loud. There's probbly people right here in Ormond that don't know if they'll be able to keep the lights on *and* put some food on the table by the end of the week."

Reaching back, Buddy snatched his wallet out from his back pocket and looked quickly inside. He whipped out a fifty dollar bill and snapped it back and forth in front of Roger as he jammed his wallet back into his pocket, "That's more like it," he said, "I just ordered my wife a pair of twelve hundred dollar diamond earrings; I think I can give fifty to my Brothers in the Salvation Army."

Roger stood staring at Buddy with his mouth gaped open like he'd just been pole-axed right between the eyes.

Buddy tromped off down the sidewalk and left Roger standing there staring at no one. Half way down the block, Buddy turned and called back to Roger, "Come on man. Let's roll. You're burning daylight."

Roger shook himself out of his stupor and went down the sidewalk after his *new* old friend. He caught up to Buddy just as he reached the curb across the street from where they had seen the man with the French horn. Roger looked across and saw that he had been joined by a heavy-set woman with a trombone, a piccolo player with a bushy, red beard; and a tall, cadaverous-looking man holding a cornet.

"Looks like they've got the whole band out now," Buddy said, stepping out into the street. The little ensemble broke into a lively version of God Rest Ye Merry Gentlemen as Roger followed Buddy across against the light. The man with the French horn gave Buddy a nod as he stuck the two folded bills down in through the little hole on the shiny, red pot. The cadaverous gentleman touched the shiny brim of his natty, black cap and then went quickly back to working the valves of his horn. "Halleluiah," the lady tromboner said between breaths, "God-bless."

Buddy paused just long enough to give them all a smile and a hearty "*Merry Christmas*."

Roger sidled around past the red-bearded piccoloist and followed after Buddy again.

"That felt good," Buddy told Roger as he came up beside him, "But I did kind of miss hearing the pot clank."

"Next time you'll have to swap your fifty out for nickels and dump *them* in," Roger said, "That ort to give you a good clank."

"I'd say it would," Buddy chuckled. He stopped in his tracks and stood stock still in the middle of the sidewalk. Roger stopped a couple steps ahead of him and turned around. Buddy was standing with his eyes closed and his head tilted back slightly, breathing deeply, sucking the air in noisily through his nose.

"What is it Buddy," Roger asked, "You alright?"

"Fresh apple bread," Buddy replied, "Don't you smell it?"

Roger sniffed and caught a whiff from the bakery they had just passed. "Yeah," he said, stepping back to where Buddy was still standing, "...Smells good."

Buddy winced his face and gave his head a little shake. He opened his eyes slowly and looked at Roger. "You know what I just realized?"

"What?"

Buddy said, "That I must have picked just about the worst time of the year to try to start losing weight." He rubbed his hand around in a circle on his stomach, "Salad don't stick with you as long as it should." He took another deep breath and closed his eyes again. "...I think I can smell a pumpkin pie, too."

Roger eased in closer to him and spoke into his ear, "What's your goal Buddy?"

Buddy took another deep breath, "One eighty," he said firmly, "...by Valentine's."

"Well...what are you gonna do about it?"

Buddy cracked open one eye and grinned at Roger, "Keep walkin'?"

Roger smiled, "Keep walkin'."

ॐ

"I know I blew it for you with Iris, but I'm shore glad we run into her," Buddy said, stepping out the front door of The Town Shop and down the sidewalk with Roger.

Roger said, "Why's that?"

Buddy shifted his packages around in his arms, "I wouldn't have had the slightest clue as to what size dress to get for Hillary," he said. He pinched his brow down tight and looked sideways at Roger, "How do women know stuff like that? I mean, I know what size shirt *you* wear, but I've known you my whole life, and I can read what size britches you need right off the back of your jeans, but she rattled off Hillary, and Maggie...My mama, *your* mama, my sister, *your* sisters, and three or four other women I'd forgot that I was even kin to...*How do they know?*"

"Beats me," Roger shrugged, "I'm just glad they do...Iris saved me a whole lot of hem-hawin' to find out sizes for Christmas presents."

"*Tell me,*" said Buddy. "Hey...have we got time to finish out the list we came up with?"

"If you want to...I told Joey to take off if I wasn't back by three."

"Great."

Buddy shifted his boxes again and pulled a piece of paper out of his pocket, "You gave me some good ideas," he said, looking over his list, "I'd like to go ahead and strike while the iron's hot." He stopped and grabbed Roger's arm, "Hey, I just got another idea...Do you think I should start going by Warren?"

Roger had to work very hard at his poker face again. Looking down at his shoes, he ran his hand up and rubbed at the back of his neck as he carefully considered his words. "Buddy," he said, slowly raising his head to look Buddy full in the face, "Warren's a good name...A real good name. But, I really think you should just stick with Buddy. I know you're kind of reinventing yourself and all, but people have been calling you Buddy since you were in diapers...I mean, you've just always been Buddy. I really don't know how you could get everybody to call you Warren."

Buddy thought for a moment, chewing on the inside of his lip, and then directly he said, "I reckon I should just stick to trying to change *me.*"

Roger pointed at Buddy and winked, "*That,* my friend, is one of the great secrets to living a happy life."

~Chapter Seven~

Roger opened the door to the flower shop and glanced up at the little, jingling, brass bell hanging overhead as he stepped inside. "*Welcome to Kelton's,*" Roslynne called from somewhere in the store. Roger thought she sounded a bit flustered, "Hey Roz," he called back, "It's me."

"Hey Roger," Roslynne said, "Come here real quick...I need some help."

"Where are you?"

"Over here...behind the tree."

Roger looked and saw a hand waving at him from behind a big Christmas tree on the other side of the store. "It shore smells like Christmas in here," he said as he made his way across the store. He cocked his head as he walked up to the tree, "Is this thing leaning?"

Roslynne peeked around the tree at him and rolled her eyes, "I am *so* glad you're here," she said, "Please grab this thing."

"*What?*"

"*The tree*...I've been standing here like this for the last ten minutes trying to get it back up in the stand right without the whole thing toppling over on me."

Roger reached his hand in through the boughs and grabbed the tree, "I got it."

Roslynne let out a noisy breath and dropped her arms. She pushed some hair back out of her eyes and shook her head, "I told Raechel not to let Martin put this big thing in that cheap little plastic stand..." She squatted down and pulled the skirt back away from the tree, "*Oh great*," she groaned, realizing the skirt was soaked. She leaned herself over a little further and looked up under the bottom limbs at the stand, "...At least the skirt soaked up the water."

"What's wrong?"

"The stand's got a big crack in it. There ain't no way it's gonna keep this tree up."

Roslynne studied the broken stand a few seconds longer and then sat down on her hip on the pine-planked floor, closing her eyes as she rubbed her fingers slowly across her forehead.

"It's a pretty tree," Roger said.

Roslynne let out another low groan and then pulled her hand out away from her face and slowly opened her eyes.

"You alright?"

Roslynne said, "I think I just smeared sap all over my forehead." She rubbed her thumb against her fingers and then held them to her nose and sniffed, "Yep," she said flatly and then patted the back of her other hand against her forehead to feel the sticky.

"Merry Christmas."

Roslynne chuckled, "Thanks." She looked up at Roger, "Got any suggestions?"

"Get a menorah."

Roslynne chuckled again, "Got any *other* suggestions?"

Roger looked the tree over, "I can run over and get you a real stand from Nathan's."

Roslynne looked in at the broken stand again.

"He's got some of them big heavy green ones."

Roslynne looked back up at him, "Are you sure he's got them?"

"I saw 'em when I was in there yesterday."

Roslynne rubbed at the stickiness on her hands and then stood herself up purposefully in front of Roger. She reached in and grabbed the tree with her sticky hand as she looked up at her big brother and smiled, "Turn your cap around so I'll think you're on your way back."

Roger let go of the tree and grabbed the bill of his cap and spun it around backwards, "One, good, ol' fashion, made-in-the-USA, genuine, cast iron, Christmas tree stand coming right up," he said, and then trotted over to the door and snatched it open. Stepping one foot out the door, he turned back to Roslynne; "I'll be right back," he winked, "... Don't go anywhere."

About fifteen minutes later, Roger hustled back into the flower shop carrying a big green tree stand, "Miss me?"

"What took you so long?"

Roger knelt down and started loosening the big screws in the stand, "Ben Stilley."

"Oh."

Roger stood up and grabbed the tree, "I did the best I could."

"I'm impressed you got away from him as fast as you did."

"Tell me about it...Alright, when I pick it up, pull that plastic thing off the bottom and slide the new one under it."

"Gotcha."

Roslynne knelt down and pulled the old stand off the tree as Roger lifted. She shoved the old stand out of the way and slid the new one into place. "Alright," she said, "You can let it back down now."

Roger let the tree down and Roslynne started tightening the screws against the trunk. "I believe this one's gonna do the trick," she said, "...That daggone Martin."

"You got 'em snugged up yet?"

"I'm screwing the last one in...Alright, you can let go."

Roger turned the tree loose and took a step back. "That looks pretty good," he said.

Roslynne stood herself up and looked the tree over, "It does, doesn't it?" She stepped around towards Roger, still studying the tree, "Can you lean it just a little bit this way?"

Roger adjusted the tree, "How's that?"

"Perfect. Now, can you move the whole thing this way about a foot?"

Roger sat down and put his feet up against the tree stand and pushed the tree slowly towards Roslynne, "Tell me when."

"Keep going...alright, *when.*"

Roger stood back up and stepped over beside Roslynne. "It looks nice," he said.

Roslynne stared at the tree for a moment with her arms crossed in front of her and then she slowly rested her chin on her fist, "I think we need to turn it that way a little."

Roger cut his eyes at her.

"*What?*"

"*I* think it looks great right where it is," he said, "*Right there.*"

"Are you sure?"

Roger nodded, "Absolutely," he said, "That tree, absolutely, positively, does *not* need to be moved. It doesn't need to be moved, rotated, tilted, twisted, angled, nudged, pointed, leaned or manipulated in any way. All it needs is to be plugged in and watered."

Roslynne smiled at him, "You don't have to beat around the bush, Roger. Just come on out with it and tell me how you really feel."

"You Lowell women are hard on a Christmas tree," Roger said. He gave his head a little shake, "It's a wonder we ever had one with any needles left on it by Christmas the way y'all made me and Daddy keep *adjusting* the dern things."

"We just want it to look its best."

"Yeah, but y'all weren't the ones that had to live with your hands covered with sap for three straight weeks *every* Christmas."

"A little sap never hurt anybody."

Roger grabbed Roslynne's hand by the fingers and gave it a little shake, "I'll remember you said that."

Roslynne pulled her hand away and tried to pinch Roger's nose. "Watch it girlie," Roger said as he swatted her hand away, "You better play nice...Remember, *Santee's watching.*"

Roslynne scrunched her shoulders and darted her eyes around the room. "Oops," she said, looking up towards the ceiling, "Sorry Santa, I was only messing."

"I don't know what you're looking up there for," Roger said, sweeping his arm out towards the street outside, "I believe *your* Santa Claus is about two-tenths of a mile up that way in a big green brick building on Commons."

Roslynne's gaze followed Roger's arm out through the intersection and up the hill. When she turned back to him, her cheeks were flushed a little pink and Roger caught a twinkle that he had never seen before in her eyes. He stared down into her face for a moment and then she wrinkled up her nose and grinned at him.

"So you really like Joey, huh?"

Roslynne's grin grew a little wider and she gave her head a quick, little nod, "It's kinda crazy, ain't it?"

"On the surface, maybe," Roger agreed, "But I know you both too well, and to be honest with you, when I really think about it, it makes perfect sense."

Roslynne reached her arms up around Roger's neck and hugged him tightly. She gave him a quick peck on his cheek and smiled brightly at him. "Thanks big brother," she said, "I'm sorry if it's been a little weird for you."

"Don't worry about it," Roger said, "I'm used to weird... And while we're on the subject of things that are a little weird, I've got a favor I need to ask."

Roslynne stepped back and looked sideways at Roger, "I was wondering what brought you down the hill to see me so early this morning."

"First off, whether your answer is yes or no, you have to promise," Roger paused and shook his head, "No; you have to *swear*, that you won't utter a word of this to anyone."

Roslynne's eyes drew down to slits, "Now you're really starting to prick my curiosity."

"I'm serious," Roger said, "This is really important...You swear to keep it secret?"

"Sure," Roslynne said, "You know you can trust me Roger."

Roger hesitated.

"I swear Roger...not a word. What's the favor?"

"Buddy needs you to teach him to dance."

Roslynne grabbed her stomach and burst out laughing.

"You know it ain't *that* funny."

"That is absolutely *not* what I was expecting," Roslynne said, still laughing. She grabbed Roger's arm, "The way you were carrying on, being so serious and all...You'd have thought you needed help secretly disposing of somebody's remains."

"Well this *is* serious," Roger said, "...Not as serious as *that*, but still serious." He paused and shook his head at his sister's continuing chuckles. "Can you do it?" he said, "I mean, twelve years of Miss Nancy you ort to know how to–"

"You don't expect me to teach him ballet do you?" Roslynne burst out laughing loudly again.

"*Law, no*," said Roger, "...Couple's dancing."

Roslynne took a breath and wiped under her eyes with the back of her hand. "Whew," she sighed, "That's a relief. Why's he need to learn how to dance?"

"He's got big plans for New Year's Eve" Roger said, "He wants to romance Hillary, and, *you know*," he shrugged, "Kind of...sweep her off her feet."

"Well," Roslynne said to herself, "That explains that..."

"Explains what?"

"Did you know that he's bought her flowers three times since he ran himself over with that tractor?"

"No I didn't, but it really doesn't surprise me." Roger paused, "When he was in here, did you happen to notice anything different about him?"

Roslynne thought for a moment, "I don't know," she said, "Like what?"

He glanced back over his shoulder towards the door and turned quickly back to his sister, "Listen," he held up a finger and pointed it briefly at Roslynne as he continued, "...And this is part of the not-uttering-a-word deal, *alright*?"

Roslynne nodded, "Sure."

"After I tell you this, it'll only be Buddy, Joey, you, and me that know anything about it and it needs to stay that way."

Roslynne felt an odd flutter of excitement down in her stomach at being included in something that had a hint of the clandestine to it. She gave Roger another nod, "Sure," she said again, "You can count on me, Roger...mum's the word."

"Buddy's kindly trying to, umm, how do I put this? He wants to, uh...Re-invent himself."

"*Really*...that's awesome. Good for him."

"I'm glad to hear you say that," Roger said, "I think you can really be a big help to him...More than just the dancing."

"*I* can?"

Roger nodded, "Yes. He wants to cultivate himself some style, and you've always had a knack for knowing what works."

Roslynne was honestly flattered, "Thank you Roger," she said, "It's nice to know you think that."

"Well, it's true," Roger said, "You know what looks good."

"And again, thank you."

"Do you think you can do it?"

Roslynne considered the idea for a moment and then asked, "Where and when I am supposed to do this? I mean, have y'all thought about how to keep Hillary from finding out? 'Cause, I'm guessing this is gonna take a lot of work, and we don't have all that much time between now and New Year's...especially if you take out the days for celebrating Thanksgiving and Christmas. It's gonna take a lot of work just to keep it a secret."

"So, you'll do it?"

"If you can find me some size seven-and-a-half steel toed dancing shoes, I don't see why not."

Roger heaved a sigh of relief, "Thanks Roz. I did not want to have to be the one to rain on Buddy's dreams."

"Is the dancing part *that* a big a deal to him?"

"You have no idea," Roger said, "...He's *never* danced with her."

"Never?"

Roger shook his head.

"So when does he want to get started?"

"As soon as possible," Roger chuckled, "Like you said, he's gonna need *a lot* of practice."

"Well that brings me back to my question," said Roslynne, "How are we supposed to do this *and* keep it a secret?"

"You're gonna do it at the shop," Roger said, "I talked about it with Joey and he volunteered his place. Buddy said he could meet you anytime, so if you want to do it on your dinner break, or after work, or mix it up and do it at dinner some days or wait 'til after work other days, it's up to you."

"Buddy's willing to miss his dinner to learn to dance," Roslynne snickered, "He *must* be serious."

"He is *very* serious," Roger said, "He's started eating salads."

"With or without gravy?"

Roger shook his head at Roslynne and chuckled darkly. She walked over and picked up the wet tree skirt, motioning for Roger to follow her as she headed for the back door, "Can I ask what brought all this new Buddy business on?"

"I don't know that I can really explain it," Roger said. Roslynne stopped in front of the back door, holding the dripping red and green checked skirt out away from her and waited for Roger to open the door for her. Roger paused and gave Roslynne one of his silly half-grins, "For a while there I thought the tractor might have run over his head."

Roslynne grinned.

"It's actually a little bit of a lot of different things," Roger said as he stepped past her and opened the door. Roslynne stepped out and draped the skirt over the railing on the back steps. She looked at the skirt for a moment and then came back up the steps to Roger, "It's not one of those mid-life crisis things is it?"

"Don't you think we're still a bit too young to be starting on those?" Roger asked as they walked back inside.

"I don't know Roger," Roslynne said wistfully, "You know they say every calendar year is like seven years for a man?"

"Oh, ain't you just the funny one."

"I do know what works, don't I."

"I knew somehow that I was going to end up regretting giving you a compliment."

"Anything you say can and will be used against you."

Roslynne grabbed the mop handle as she bounced past the storeroom and rolled the bucket out in front of her into the front of the store. "Seriously," she said, "Why is he suddenly wanting to change himself? I mean, he's just about the nicest person you'd ever want to meet." She started mopping, "And every time I see him, I just want to give him a big ol' hug." She smiled at Roger, "Buddy's like a butterball turkey...you just gotta love him."

"What you just said is the probbly the main reason he's wanting to do this," Roger said, "He told me he's tired of being Mister Comfortable Buddy Bear."

"I like Buddy Bear...Everybody does."

"Well, I know one person who doesn't."

Roslynne plopped the mop into the ringer and gave it a squeeze, "That's too bad..." She glanced at Roger and then looked the floor over where she had just mopped, "I think that's about got it," she said, "Do you see any I missed?"

Roger scanned the floor and shook his head, "Looks good to me."

"Well, I can go up to your shop and meet him today if he wants to go ahead and get on with it."

Roger thought for a moment and then said, "Unless you hear from me otherwise, come on up at dinner. He's supposed to be bringing his tractor down sometime this morning for us to do some work on it, so y'all can put your heads together and work out the details then."

Roslynne leaned on the mop handle and smiled at Roger, "This is kind of exciting," she giggled, "It's like we're doing a makeover on him."

"I think that's pretty much what he has in mind. He's trying for an all new Buddy."

"What all is he planning to do?"

"For starters, he's going all out this year for Christmas and New Year's."

Roslynne leaned in conspiratorially, "What's he doing?"

"Well," Roger said, "He's bought tickets for him and Hillary to the Ormond Historical Society New Year's Ball, and he's booked them for two nights in a bed and breakfast on the river downtown in the historic district–"

"*Nice.*"

Roger nodded, "Yeah, very nice."

"Which one?"

"You know the great big brick one with the triple-decker porches that sits right on the waterfront...The one with the pavilion that goes out into the river."

Roslynne's brows went up, "Oooh," she said, "The *Captain's Manor.*"

"Yeah, The Captain's Manor, that's it. Have you ever been in there?"

Roslynne shook her head, "No, but I've heard it's really, *really* nice."

"Really nice doesn't come anywhere near it," Roger said, "We went in there the other day for Buddy to make the reservations," Roger arched up his eyebrows and shook his head slowly, "Until you see it, you can't imagine...The place is *huge*...I lost count of the rooms, and I'm sure this shop would easily fit into any one of them. Twelve foot ceilings and mahogany floors. They've got this one room that takes up the whole third floor right by itself...It's got four sets of french doors across the back balcony overlooking the river, the biggest four-poster bed I've ever seen, a huge clawfoot tub that I'd bet would hold half a dozen people," he paused and blew out an airy whistle, "Talk about some gracious living...Whoever gets that room, gets served their own private breakfast, special in the room all by themselves... *Buddy got that one.* And I'll just let you guess how much that one cost on New Year's."

"I'm impressed," Roslynne said, "What else?"

"Let's see," Roger counted on his fingers, *One*: "...A horse drawn carriage from *The Captain's* to the Ball and back. *Two*: Supper on New Year's Day at the Schooner. *Three*: An afternoon couple's dinner cruise on the *Star Chaser* with mini concert by some jazz singer *with* ensemble during the cruise on the second."

"*Holy Mackerel...*What in the–"

"*Wait*," Roger said, "That's not all. Between The Lady of the House and the Town Shop, we spent over two hours shopping and he spent almost five hundred dollars on a slinky midnight blue dress for the ball, and an ooh-la-la silk nightgown and robe for at the B&B."

Roslynne's jaw dropped.

"And I don't even know *what* he paid for the earrings he bought."

"Earrings?"

"Diamonds."

Roslynne stood staring at her brother in astonishment, "Unbelievable."

"I think I watched him spend more money in one day than I've seen him spend over the last thirty years put together."

"Inconceivable," Roslynne lisped.

Roger cocked his head at his sister, "I do not think that means what you think it means."

Roslynne grinned, "That never gets old, does it?"

"It hasn't yet," Roger said, "Look..." He stepped off towards the front door, "Let me get going...Come on up the hill at dinnertime, alright."

"I'll be there."

Roger stopped at the door and called back to Roslynne, "*Hey Roz,*" he said, stopping her on her way back to hang up the mop.

"Yeah?"

"I've got an idea...Just wait here for your loverboy...I'll send him down to get us a pizza from Roland's, and y'all can walk up together, alright."

"Sounds good," Roslynne said, "See you."

"Bye."

❧

Roger stood in the open front door of his shop and watched Joey walk off down the street with Roslynne. He paused a moment and listened: he could still hear music and some somewhat heavy-sounding footfalls coming from upstairs. Chuckling quietly to himself, he thought about the strange new world he had become a part of, "I will be so glad when I can talk all about this to Maggie," he said.

Putting his hands up against the door frame over his head, Roger leaned out the door, and stretched his back. He shook his head and let out a contented little sigh as he thought about Maggie, "And, I thought getting things together with you was a change..."

Roger straightened himself up and crossed his arms across his chest as he propped against the doorframe and stared out into the street. He pictured Maggie standing there in the middle of Commons soaking up the sunshine that warm day last spring. *I reckon you could say that that was the day that things really got started*, he thought, *What a ride it's been...what a year.* He smiled to himself, remembering the sound of Maggie's voice when she had called him late in the evening on the day of Terry King's funeral; how she had sounded just a bit shaky as she said hello. Roger hated talking on the telephone, but he had gladly spent four hours that night, sitting on his kitchen floor, leaned back against the cabinet, telephone to his ear, listening to the sweet melody of her words.

"I would have set right there and listened to four hours of dead silence as long as I knew it was you on the other end of the line," he had told Maggie when she called him at his shop the next day to apologize for keeping him up so late.

Roger pictured the way she looked three weeks later when they had finally gotten together for the first time: she was standing barefoot in the Vander's living room in a white cotton dress that just stopped him cold as he came in through the front door. He stood there, staring at her with his heart pounding in his chest, wondering, *How can I possibly go on another day without this amazing woman being mine?*

And now she is, Roger thought, "...Almost." He glanced over to the old cannonball safe bolted to the floor in the corner, "If I can make it through the next few weeks, this will certainly be one year that is going to go down in the Roger Lowell *One to Remember* book."

He ran how he was going to ask her through his mind and then a thought came to him; *What if she doesn't say yes?* He had never even considered it. Everyone else seemed so sure that she would, and, up until that moment, so had he. The thought seemed incredible to him, but...

He turned his gaze up toward the sky, "Lord," he said, "You know that I'll go along readily with whatever you've got planned, but, you know I'm trying to do right in this, I sincerely hope that the next few weeks–"

"Who you talking to?" Buddy asked as he bounded into the room behind Roger.

Roger gave a start and turned around. Buddy was smiling happily and his face was flushed a deep red. He had beads of sweat across his forehead and dark blue circles of sweat spreading out from under both arms of his faded denim workshirt.

Roger smiled, "Just a little conversing with God," he said. He smiled at Buddy again, "Well what do you think? How was lesson number one?"

"I think it went well," Buddy replied, "...All things considered." He chuckled self-consciously, "I think I might've gotten Roz's toes a couple times."

"Well, she didn't appear to be limping too badly," Roger said, "But you know, sometimes it takes a while for tissues to really start to swell up."

"I hope I didn't hurt her too bad."

"I don't think you did any permanent damage."

"I really think I'm gonna get the hang of this," Buddy said. He held one hand out and held the other up in front of his chest as he held an imaginary partner, "Look at what I've already learned." He closed his eyes and made a few shuffling steps around Roger's office. Stopping himself in front of the coffee maker, he looked at Roger and asked, "What do you think?"

"That's pretty good Buddy," Roger said, "I'm impressed."

"Really?"

Roger nodded, "Yeah, really."

Buddy grabbed his imaginary partner again and watched his feet as he danced a few more steps. He looked up at Roger and grinned, "This is gonna be so cool," he said, "You *know* Hillary's gonna just fall out."

"That's gonna make it kind of hard to dance with her."

"It would wouldn't it," Buddy snickered. He held his hands out around his partner for a moment longer and then let his hands fall. "Look," he said, "Have you got some scrap tubing around I could have a piece of? I need a piece about three feet long."

"Sure. What'cha need it for?"

"I want to put a pull-up bar up in my barn. That way I can do some exercises without having to come all the way over here."

"I thought you didn't want Hill to know what you were up to."

"You know she never goes out to the barn."

"Still hasn't gotten over The Great 'Possum Incident, huh?"

"Nope."

"You can take a piece of that that I'm building the cage for your tractor out of when you go," Roger said, "It's good heavy-walled stuff. You won't have to worry about it bending on you."

"Thanks," Buddy said. He pinched the front of his shirt and fanned it in and out and made a face, "*Phew*...I'm gonna have to get some stronger deodorant. I never realized you could work up that much of a sweat ballroom dancing."

"How are you planning on covering up your lovely aroma and hiding all the stinky clothes from your wife until New Year's?"

"I hadn't even thought about it," Buddy said, "I'm not used to being so deceptive...It's taken every bit of sneaky I could conjure up just to figure out how to *not* get my usual portions at mealtime."

"How's that working out?"

"It's tough. I'm not too sure she's believing that my chest gets sore if I eat too much."

Roger laughed and shook his head. "Yeah," he agreed, "I'd have to say that one may be a little tough to swallow." Roger paused and then said, "Hey, why don't you be honest –hold on," he held up a hand and cut Buddy off before he could interrupt, "...I don't mean everything. Just tell her that the doctor recommended you drop a few pounds, so you're cutting back just a little."

Buddy considered Roger's suggestion a moment and then nodded. "That's an idea Roger," he said, "It might would take the load off –*Especially* at Thanksgiving."

"And, the doctor *did* say that," Roger reminded him.

"Yeah, but he was only agreeing with me when I told him I thought I needed to."

"Either way, he said it, so you're not having to waste all your creativity making up some cockamamie story to tell her as to why you're not eating so much anymore."

"I'll have to think about it...but I'm still gonna be a big old stink-wagon by the time I get home every afternoon. How am I gonna explain that? She knows I ain't got that much heavy work right now."

"If you need to use the shower here or at my house you know you're welcome to," Roger said, "And you can leave a change of clothes too. I'll be glad to throw them in the washer for you in the evenings."

"Oh man Roger, that would be great. I really appreciate it."

"Just don't expect them starched and creased," Roger added, "'Cause, I don't do creases."

~Chapter Eight~

"He's been really sweet," Hillary said, "*Really*, I don't remember him ever being this sweet to me –even when we were first married– but, he...he's still just...well, *odd*."

"Roger said he hadn't noticed him being odd about anything," Maggie said as she took the last book from Hillary and slid it into the bin out on the sidewalk in front of the library. She rolled her window up and pulled her jeep back out into the street, headed out of Sand Ridge.

"Come on, Maggie," said Hillary, "Do you really think he'd say so if he thought Buddy was acting weird?"

"I asked him, Hillary." Maggie said this as a statement.

"*So*," Hillary said, "You know how men are. They have to follow The Code."

Maggie chuckled at Hillary. "Look," she said, "After you mentioned it again yesterday, I was a little curious so, when I talked to Roger later, I asked him right out if he thought Buddy might have been acting a little quare lately, and he said that he really didn't think so." Maggie paused briefly and then added, "He might not bring it up on his own if he did, but I'm pretty sure that if I ask him about something directly he'll answer me honestly."

"Okay," Hillary said, "Maybe he *would* tell you," and then her eyes widened, "*Or*...maybe he knows something's going on and he's in on it, too."

"Oh come on Hillary."

"No really. Think about it. Who else would be in cahoots with Buddy but Roger?"

"Have you gone crazy?"

"No."

"Then think about what you're saying. They've got Roger's picture in the dictionary next to Boy Scout."

"*Maggie. You* think about it. When somebody as predictable as Buddy suddenly isn't...something's up."

"What do you mean something's up...Like what?"

Hillary shrugged indecisively and gave her head a shake, "I don't know."

Maggie smiled to herself and pressed down on the gas, speeding the jeep across the Earley Creek Bridge so that it gave a good bounce as she came off on the far side.

"You just *have* to do that, don't you?"

Maggie looked at Hillary out of the corner of her eye and grinned, "You know I do."

Hillary fell into silent thought for the next few minutes until Maggie had driven them well out of town and then she said, "It's as if he's done something that he feels really bad about, and he's trying to make up for it."

Maggie gave her head a shake, dismissing Hillary's comment and said, "Hillary, we're talking about Buddy."

"Oh, I see," Hillary said, "Who else would want him."

"That's not what I meant at all," Maggie said. She looked over at Hillary, "My mind wasn't even going there."

"Of course not."

"It's not that he's not desirable," Maggie said, "It's just..." Maggie paused a second and then said, "Buddy's rock solid, Hill. You know he is. Don't let a little oddness on his part make you think otherwise."

"That's exactly what all those blind-sided women always say."

Maggie took a deep breath and exhaled noisily, "Hillary, you know good and well that *if* Buddy even remotely considered doing something as stupid as that, that Roger would plant his foot so far up his butt you'd be looking at the sole of a size twelve brogan every time your husband smiled at you."

Hillary chuckled and gave Maggie a half smile.

"Don't stress yourself out."

Hillary stared at Maggie and her eyes glistened, "I'm sorry Maggie," she said quietly, "You're right." She glanced back out the windshield and then turned back to Maggie, "I know you're right. I just don't know why he's been so strange about things lately. I've never had any trouble just looking at him and knowing exactly what's on his mind, or just asking him something and getting twenty minutes of *The Life and Times of Your Man Buddy Vander* in response...But lately, I've been trying to get him to tell me what's going on with him and he just seems sort of evasive."

Maggie glanced over at Hillary as the jeep approached the intersection with the Ocean Highway, "In what way?"

"Ever since he came home from the hospital, I can't get him to tell me anything about himself...How he's feeling, what he's thinking, why he's not eating..."

"He's really not eating?"

"Not much."

"Not much for him or..."

Hillary chuckled again as Maggie stopped her jeep at the intersection and looked left down the empty stretch of four-lane highway, "Not much, *period*," she answered, "...Not even at Thanksgiving."

"Did anybody else notice?"

"I overheard my mother ask him if he was feeling alright and then he kinda mumbled something about his doctor saying he should think about losing a few pounds."

"So he's trying to lose some weight."

"I don't know," Hillary shrugged, "He didn't tell *me* the doctor told him to lose weight." She shook her head and made a face at Maggie, "When I asked him about it, he told me his chest still hurt him a bit when he eats too much."

"And you didn't believe him?" Maggie asked as she pulled out onto the highway.

"No. Not really."

Maggie glanced back over at Hillary and then turned back to the highway, "Maybe it does," she said, "It hasn't been *that* long since his accident."

Hillary's brow pinched down tight and her mouth turned down at the corners as she shook her head at Maggie again, "It doesn't seem to bother him any other time."

"*Oh, no,*" Maggie said, "You're making your Mrs. Groat face."

Hillary stopped and considered herself briefly and then clapped her hand over her mouth and winced her face, "Sorry."

"You haven't been looking at your husband that way have you?"

Hillary dropped her hands into her lap, "I don't think so."

"...'Cause it would explain a lot if you have," Maggie joked, "I mean, if I was Buddy and you were looking at me like that, I surely wouldn't want to tell you much of anything either."

"That's very constructive."

"*I'm just saying...*"

Hillary sighed breezily and turned her face slowly back towards the windshield. Maggie watched her out of the corner of her eye and snickered quietly to herself as Hillary pulled down the sunvisor and made her Mrs. Groat face at herself in the mirror on the back. After a few seconds Maggie said, "Told you you looked like Mrs. Groat."

Hillary flipped the visor back up and stuck her tongue out at Maggie. She slouched back in the seat, "You are *not* funny."

"I am too."

"No you're not...and I don't look like Mrs. Groat."

"You say."

Hillary pulled the visor back down and scowled at herself in the mirror again, "Okay," she said, "Maybe I do look a little like her..."

"But *only* when you do that."

Hillary flipped the visor up again and brushed her hair back, "I know one thing," she said, "I'm gonna have to make very sure that I don't make *that* face anymore."

"Should I smack you if you do?" Maggie asked, swishing her hand back and forth in the air between them.

"I'm thinking no."

"Can I punch your arm?"

"Uh uh."

"How 'bout I pinch you?"

"No."

"Flick you?"

Hillary shook her head.

"You are just no fun anymore."

"Sorry."

Maggie said, "That's alright. I still love you."

"Thanks."

"Now, back to Buddy... when you ask him things, what does he say that's evasive?"

"Different things."

Maggie looked over at Hillary and waited for her to elaborate. After a long moment she finally said, "Well...like what?"

Hillary squirmed in her seat a little and smiled uncomfortably at Maggie, "Just...different things."

Maggie drove along, rounding a long bend in silence as she waited again for Hillary to provide her with a little more information. After a minute's waiting, she turned back to Hillary, "Come on," she said, and held her hand out, "What *things*?"

"Well," Hillary began, "...He'll usually give me a compliment, or ask something about me, or he'll just say something to me that's supposed to be romantic, or kind of...umm," she turned her face away towards the side window and mumbled, "...Sexy."

"*What*," Maggie said, leaning herself over towards Hillary a little, "What was that? He says something that's romantic or kind of *what*?"

"You heard me."

"I'm not sure that I did," Maggie said, "You were mumbling a little there at the end. Would you repeat it for me?"

"No I won't," Hillary said, "You heard me just fine."

Maggie looked sideways at Hillary and made her voice low and growling, "So," she said, rolling her shoulder saucily, "*Are we still a good lover?*"

Hillary's face was stone. "Yes," she said, "*I* am...And *you're* still not funny."

"So what's wrong with him complimenting you? Maybe he read an article or something."

"Because a lot of it seems like he's already got these things he says planned just to throw me off," said Hillary. "You know, like he's thought it out...like he's thinking, 'Okay, if Hillary asks me about *this*, then I'll pay her *this* compliment,' or, 'if Hillary says *this*, then I'll say *this* sexiness.' " She paused a second and then added, "But what makes it seem evasive and not just some awkward, corny attempt at romance, is the different things he seems to be consistently choosing not to want to talk about. I've tried to figure out some connection, but there isn't one." She shook her head, "He just doesn't make sense."

"*Like what?*"

"Well, *first*, he doesn't want to talk about anything about himself: how he's feeling, what he's thinking...*anything*. I'll say, 'How's your hip feeling?' and he says, 'Your hair looks really pretty that way.' I ask, 'What did you and Roger do in Town this morning?' and he winks real slow at me and says, 'I really like how those jeans fit you.' "

"Maybe they went shopping and he doesn't want to give away what he got you for Christmas," Maggie suggested.

Hillary cocked her head to one side. "A flannel nightgown, two sets of footies, and a bottle of *Cocoanut Breeze* body lotion," she said, "The only thing that changes is the wrapping paper."

"Well, maybe you're in for a surprise this year."

"Mmhmm...And monkeys could fly out of my butt."

"You don't know," Maggie said, "Maybe I'm right and he's just trying real hard not to give it away."

Hillary stopped and thought for a second and then said, "Alright, I'll give you that...maybe, *just maybe* he's gonna do something different, but what about talking about our holiday plans? You know how he's all about the endless get-togethers and food-fests over the holidays...Any other year, he starts, *oh I don't know*, sometime around Labor Day talking about what-all we're gonna do in December...

Well now, anytime I try to bring up plans it's '*Ooh Pretty Lady sexy, sexy, ooh la la.*' "

Maggie snickered a little and tried unsuccessfully to fix the picture in her mind. "*Really,*" she said, dying inside wanting to know exactly what Buddy had been saying, "What kind of things does he say that are sexy?"

Hillary thought for a second and then her cheeks turned pink. Maggie grinned, "*What?* Come on, tell me."

"Like last night," Hillary said, "We were laying in bed kind of spooning and I asked him if he was still planning on us going to Terry and Natalie's after the fireworks on New Year's and he said–"

Hillary stopped herself and cleared her throat.

Maggie glanced over again, "Said what?"

"You wouldn't believe it."

"Try me."

"He said–" Hillary closed her eyes down tight and gave her head a little shake, "I can't say it."

"Yes you can."

"No, I can't," Hillary said, turning her face back towards the window, "It's all too embarrassing."

Maggie let out a groan and rolled her eyes, "*Come on* Hillary, aren't you being just a little melodramatic?"

"No. If it was you you'd feel the same way."

"Maybe so, but it's not me, it's *you,* so just tell me."

Hillary took a breath, "Okay," she said, "But you've got to promise me you won't laugh."

"I can only promise you that I'll *try,*" she said glancing over to Hillary, "Just tell me."

Hillary paused a moment, "Alright," she said slowly, "He said–" She stopped herself again and laughed embarrassedly, covering her face with her hands.

Maggie could see glimpses of Hillary's cheeks in between her fingers growing a deeper shade of pink by the second. "*Oh come on Hill,*" she said, "It can't be *that* bad."

Hillary's hands dropped into her lap. She smiled crookedly at Maggie and opened her eyes wide; "*Oh yes it can,*" she said, her head bobbing in a jerky nod.

Maggie said, "Well *you* brought it up. You can't bring something up and tell me how I won't believe it and then not tell me what it is." She made a move for her cell phone, "I'll just call Buddy and ask him what he said to you last night. *He'll tell me.*"

Hillary's hand shot out and she grabbed Maggie's wrist, "Don't you dare!"

"Then tell me."

Hillary let go of Maggie's wrist and took another, deep, cleansing breath. She opened her mouth and then clamped it back down and shook her head. "I can't," she said, "I can't bring myself to say it."

Maggie took her foot off the gas and knocked the jeep out of gear. "Fine then," she said, as the jeep slowed and she coasted over onto the shoulder, "I'm gonna just pull right over, and we'll just sit here on the side of the road until you do."

"Come on Maggie. Are you really gonna make me tell you?"

"After all this buildup, you can't just leave me hanging like this."

Hillary stared at Maggie for a moment and then turned and stared out the side window into the woods beside the highway as Maggie brought the jeep to a stop. "Alright," she said, "but you can't look at me when I tell you."

"Are you serious?"

"Yes."

Maggie rolled her eyes and then turned her face towards the road, "Alright, I'm not looking."

Hillary turned in her seat towards Maggie and spoke quickly, "He told me that snuggling up next to me was like cradling a bouquet of *lavender and vanilla moon petals.*"

Hillary heard Maggie's forehead bump against the window as she fought to stifle a laugh. She could hear little puffs of air jetting out between the fingers Maggie had clamped tightly across her face. She thought about Buddy's declaration as she stared at the curly brown hair shaking on the back of Maggie's head. She felt her embarrassment melt into amusement as she watched Maggie's shoulders hitching up and down as she struggled to keep herself from bursting out in laughter.

"Did you hear me," Hillary asked, feeling a chuckle welling up inside. She leaned forward to get a look at Maggie's face as she poked at Maggie's ribs. "...*Moon petals*."

Maggie swatted at Hillary's hand without looking back. She shook her head emphatically. Hillary could see tears rolling down Maggie's bright red cheeks.

"*Vanilla* Moon Petals," Hillary drawled.

"I heard," Maggie wheezed, still swatting at Hillary, "I heard."

"You can look at me now."

Maggie shook her head, "No I can't."

Hillary poked her again, "Sure you can."

Maggie turned slowly to Hillary, tears making tracks from the corners of her eyes. Her mouth trembled as she worked hard to hold back her laughter.

"Aww," Hillary chuckled, "just go ahead and laugh."

Maggie pursed her lips and took a deep breath as she held up a hand, "No," she said, clearing her throat, "You were right...this is no laughing matter. I mean if your husband is working so hard to throw you off his trail that he's willing to pull out the–" Maggie stopped and clamped her mouth shut. Her nostrils flared as she sucked in a breath and steadied her voice, "Lavender moon-petals-"

Maggie threw herself over the steering wheel, buried her face in her arms, and bawled out loud peals of laughter.

"And vanilla," Hillary chuckled, "Lavender *and* vanilla."

Maggie sat back with both hands over her face, "*Oh lordy-mercy*," she groaned, leaning her head back against the rest and dropping her hands into her lap, "...*Moon*-petals." She rolled her head around and looked at Hillary, "...No wonder you're worried."

Hillary chuckled. "I guess I could be being a little overly dramatic," she said, "But when I got home from Mama's yesterday and he had Sade playing on the stereo, I just didn't know what to think."

Maggie's eyes flew open wide, "*He was playing Sade?*"

Hillary nodded, "He met me at the door and said I was his *Sweetest Taboo.*"

Maggie covered her face again.

"I reckon sweetest taboo and lavender and vanilla moon-petals in one night was just more than I could handle."

Maggie sat snickering behind her hands with her head back against the seat composing herself. After a long moment, she sat up and turned to Hillary, "Mid-life crisis Hillary. He's having a mid-life crisis."

Hillary furrowed her brow.

Maggie said, "If you think about it, it makes perfect sense."

Hillary shook her head slowly, "I don't know, Maggie. I don't think Buddy's the mid-life crisis type. And besides, he's too young for something like that yet."

"Normally I'd agree with you, but they say that sometimes some dramatic occurrence in someone's life can start something like that."

"I don't know..."

"It makes sense to me. Just you wait. He'll be pulling up in the driveway in a hot little convertible any day now."

❧

"Wow, Buddy, a new car."

"I wanted to get her a convertible but this one was such a deal..."

Roger said, "And you said it was a sixty-five?"

Buddy nodded, "Hillary's always liked these," he said, "She wanted one when we were in high school, but you know, her mamma and daddy couldn't afford to buy her one."

"She likes koalas too doesn't she?"

Buddy wagged his head at Roger, "You're funny."

Roger stepped over towards the passenger side front fender and squatted down, admiring the lines of the little Karmann Ghia, "It shore is straight."

"The fella I bought it from did a full restoration about three-and-a-half years ago. He took the whole thing completely apart and re-did everything...took him nine months. He gave me an album full of pictures of the whole project," he motioned towards the car with his thumb, "It's inside on the seat."

Roger studied the car, "It almost looks green in this light."

"That's because it *is* green."

Roger glanced over at him and then stood up, "I was sure it was black until I really got to looking at it," he said as he stepped over and looked in the open passenger side window.

"I thought it was too, but the man said it was *Roulette Green*. He said it's the darkest green you can get."

Roger reached in and caressed the upholstery and then leaned his head inside. He looked out through the windshield at Buddy's smiling face, "It almost smells new in here."

"It ort to," Buddy said, "The interior's only six months old."

Roger watched Buddy as Buddy's eyes worked their way over the car. Roger saw the little smile Buddy had and thought about how his friend always seemed to have a little grin on his face lately that made him look like he had some happy little secret that only he knew. He wondered what Buddy was thinking. "How'd you get it in here without Hill seeing it?" he asked.

Buddy jammed his hands down deep into his pockets and then gave his head a little shake and pulled them quickly back out again as he made his way around to the driver's side door. "You know what I read, Roger?" he said, studying the palms of his hands. And before Roger could answer, he continued; "A gentleman shouldn't go around with his hands stuffed in his pockets."

Roger pulled his head back out and straightened himself up, "Yeah?" he said, "Where'd you read that?"

"Did you see the little cover under the dash that covers the CD player?"

Roger looked at Buddy in silence for a second, wondering if he had intentionally ignored his question and then shook his head, "No I didn't."

"I know; it's pretty cool. If nobody tells you it's there, you can't really even see it."

Roger looked back inside. "I don't see it."

Buddy pulled open the door and squatted down. "It's right there," he said, pointing to a barely noticeable bulge under the dash just to the right of the shiny, pearl-colored knob on the end of the stick shift.

"Oh," Roger said, "Okay, I see it now."

"If you give it a little bump, it opens up so you can see the stereo."

Roger looked at Buddy and nodded. "Neat. So, how'd you get it in here without Hill seeing it?"

"The guy brought it out in a trailer after she and Maggie left this morning. We backed it out of the trailer right into the barn."

"You're pretty slick ain't you."

Buddy looked at Roger and nodded. "I'm learning."

"Next question is, how you gonna keep it a secret?"

"She don't come out here."

"I know that...But the young'uns do. And you know when they see it, one of em's bound to say something about it."

"I'm gonna keep the barn locked until Christmas," Buddy said. "My plan is to come out here before Hillary gets up on Christmas morning and pull it up in front of the house," he gave his head a little nod towards the front of the car, "... and put a big bow on the hood."

"Wouldn't that be the boot?"

"Huh?"

"*The boot*," Roger repeated. He jerked his thumb towards the back end of the car. "If the motor's back there then wouldn't that make *that* the hood?"

Buddy thought for a moment, "I hadn't ever thought about it," he said, "I guess it would at that."

"You better get your mess straight if you're gonna be a VW man," Roger joked, "Them people are serious about their cars now."

"Yeah I know," Buddy said, "You ort to purchase one sometime." He shook his head and whistled.

"He was proud of it, huh?"

"You'd a thought he was selling his only child."

"That bad, huh?"

"I probbly would've come out cheaper if I had been buyin' his young'un."

Roger slid himself in and sat down in the passenger seat. He looked closely at Buddy, "You ain't gonna get yourself in a bind over this New Buddy Christmas are you?"

Buddy stared blankly at Roger for a moment and then smiled and gave his head a little shake, "Naw man...I'm good."

"You sure?"

Buddy smiled, "I know what you're getting at Roger. But I haven't gone *completely* off the deep end," he chuckled, "I've actually got a plan."

Roger raised his eyebrows and eyed Buddy.

Buddy smiled again and then slid into the driver's seat and closed the door. "Thank you," he said, "I appreciate your concern. But seriously, I *do* have a plan. I've got all this stuff budgeted, and I'm *not* spending my children's college fund."

"Alright," Roger said, "I was just checking."

Buddy said, "I know...*It's all bueno.*" He reached up, grabbed the keys, and smiled a big, goofy, just-turned-sixteen-and-got-my-first-wheels grin, "You want to hear this baby run," he said, "It's got dual carburetors..."

~Chapter Nine~

"Alright sweetie, time's up," Lydia said as she came back into the living room. TJ looked up from his test and grinned at her.

"Can I please have just a couple more minutes?" he asked.

"You're not finished yet?" Lydia said with some surprise as she stepped over beside where TJ was sitting on the floor in front of the coffee table. She looked down at his math quiz as TJ turned the paper right side up for her. Lydia saw that the left half of the paper was covered in an unfinished rendering of the Nativity.

TJ looked up at her and smiled, "No ma'am," he said, "... Well, yes ma'am, I *am* done with the problems, but I haven't finished the picture I was drawing for you."

Lydia sat down on the sofa, and then rested a hand across TJ's shoulder as she lowered herself down to the floor to kneel beside him. "They're all right," she said as she looked his answers over, "But I can only see half of your work." She turned the paper back sideways, "Those wise men look terrific...Why didn't you get your art pad to draw on?"

"You said not to get up until I was finished."

"But you are finished."

"I wasn't when I started drawing."

Lydia chuckled, "The picture's really nice, but you know I like to see your work."

TJ looked back down at the paper, "You *can* still see it," he said, "...See right here." He pointed at one of the problems he had worked out, "That's a six–" He looked a little closer, "No that's that sheep's eye and part of his ear." He pointed at another spot; "Thirty-one divided by..." he trailed off and then grinned his crooked grin at Lydia, "Sorry Mama, I just felt like drawing you a picture."

Lydia hugged TJ tightly to her, "That's okay," she said, picking up the paper. She held it up in front of her, "I guess we can let it slide this time."

Kissing the top of TJ's head, Lydia laid the paper back down, "Help me up and then go wash your hands," she said, "I've got us some sandwiches made and then we're taking us a field trip."

TJ jumped up and grabbed Lydia's arm, "Where to?" he asked, as he tried to snatch her to her feet.

"Easy buddy," Lydia groaned as she worked her way up off the floor, "Don't yank my arm out of socket."

"Where are we going Mama, huh, where?"

"It's a surprise...now go wash your hands and come eat."

TJ took off down the hall to the bathroom and was back down at the table with wet hand prints across the front of his shirt by the time Lydia had their water poured. He hopped into his seat and took a big bite of his sandwich as

Lydia sat down. "Unh uh," she said, and pointed at his sandwich, "*Down...Ask the blessing, please.*"

"Sorry," TJ said. He set the sandwich down, washed the bite down with a swallow of water, and then bowed his head. Lydia watched him and then bowed her head as he began to pray.

"Dear Jesus. Thank you for this beautiful day and for our food. Thank you for Mama and our babies and please keep us safe on our field trip. Amen."

"Thank you," Lydia said.

TJ tapped his toes on the floor beneath his chair as he took another bite of his sandwich and then stuffed too many potato chips into his mouth.

"You're not excited are you?"

TJ nodded his head and then swallowed down hard, "Can we run and get Huff from Grandaddy?"

Lydia shook her head, "We don't need to take Huff where we're going."

"Where's that?"

"The airport."

"*In Ormond?*"

"Mm hmm...We're going to watch some planes take off and land and we're going to go inside and see people coming in from off the planes and all kinds of things."

"That thounds neat," TJ said through a mouthful of sandwich."

"Good," said Lydia, "...This is going to be a very special day."

"How lond do we deth to sday?"

"Don't talk with your mouth full...I guess we'll probably stay for an hour or so."

TJ forced down his food and then gulped some of his water, "That's not very long," he said, "How are we gonna get to see everything in an hour?"

"Tell you what," Lydia said, "We'll stay long enough to see everything you want to see. Okay?"

TJ smiled and nodded his head.

"Well eat up then," Lydia said, checking her watch. *We should be right on time*, she thought, "...We'll get going as soon as we finish."

"Wow Mama," TJ said loudly, pointing out his window at the jet that was just touching down on the runway, "Look at that...It flew down right over us...and now it's landing."

Lydia glanced at TJ in the rearview mirror, smiling to herself as she turned in off of the Monk Creek Causeway and then crossed over the bridge onto Phillip Garris Drive. *He is going to be so excited*, she thought, *I can't wait to see the look on his face when he sees Miss Rose.* She drove under the *Ormond/Garris Regional Jetport* sign and stopped at the guardhouse. She could hear some soap-opera playing loudly from a television set inside the little building as the window slid open. The heavy-set guard spun his big-jowled face in her direction and smiled broadly at Lydia. "Hey Baby," he said cheerfully, "How you doing?"

"I'm doing really well Dip," Lydia replied, "How are you doing?"

"Can't complain," Dip Bailey said as he turned the volume down on his little television. He squeezed himself up into the open window and motioned behind Lydia, "Is that your boy?"

Lydia glanced back over her shoulder and then smiled proudly at Dip. "Sure is," she said, "...that's my TJ. TJ say hello to Mister Bailey."

TJ pulled himself away from the planes shuttling around the tarmac and smiled politely at Dip. "Hello Mister Bailey," he said. He unfastened his seatbelt and slid over to the driver's side and stuck his hand up over his mother's shoulder and out her window. "It's a pleasure to make your acquaintance," he said.

Dip took his hand and gave it a shake; "Likewise little man." He turned TJ's hand loose and raised his eyebrows at Lydia.

"Mister Bailey went to school with me," Lydia told TJ, "He's from down Hall's Point."

"That Booming Metropolis," Dip said breezily. "So what brings you out today," he asked, "Y'all taking a flight? Picking somebody up?"

"We're having a field trip," TJ answered.

"*A field trip?*" he grabbed a clipboard down from beside the open window. "There weren't anything on the sheet today about a school group coming in..." He flipped up the top page and quickly looked over the next one.

"Oh, it's just us," said Lydia.

"Just y'all two?"

"Uh huh," Lydia nodded, "We home-school."

"*You do?*" Dip said, looking terribly relieved as he hung the clipboard back in place, "Well how 'bout that." He gave his head a slow nod and then said, "*Oh,*" like he had just remembered something important. He spun his chair around and checked the screen on the computer next to the television. "Look," he said, turning back to Lydia, "There's a flight scheduled to be leaving in about fifteen minutes..." he reached down and grabbed something from out of a drawer and handed it to her. "Hang this from your rearview mirror, and..." he pointed to a little parking area next to a fence near the runway. "Drive over to that arm there and I'll let you through, and you can park over there and see it take off. That's probbly about as close as you can get without being out there on the line."

"Well, thank you Dip," Lydia said, surprised. "That's very nice of you. Are you sure it's alright for us to be over there? I mean, we won't get you into any trouble will we?"

"*Naw,*" Dip drawled and pointed again, "You see that silver Dodge right there?" Lydia looked back over and nodded. "That's my pickup," Dip continued, "...You see that grassy spot past that?" Lydia looked and nodded again.

"...You just park right down there and you won't be in anybody's way...Alright?"

"You're sure."

"Positive." Dip paused and held up a finger, "...As long as you don't forget to give me my pass back before you leave."

"Thanks Dip."

"Don't mention it," Dip said, "...Everything's been running on time today –surprisingly enough– so you'd bes' get on over there if Little Man wants to see it." He leaned back and checked his computer again, "And there's another flight coming in about ten minutes after that departure, so y'all can see some coming and going up close."

Lydia checked her watch, *That must be Rose's flight*, she thought, "Where's that one coming in from?"

Dip checked the computer; "DKX," he said, "...East Tennessee."

"Can we get inside from that way or do we need to go around to the front?" Lydia asked as a car pulled up behind her.

"There's a set of double doors on the end."

"How long does it usually take everyone to get in once the plane lands?"

"From the time they turn at the other end of the runway, they're usually in the terminal and waiting to pick up their luggage in about fifteen minutes."

Lydia thanked Dip again.

"You're welcome," Dip said, waving her on, "Pull up past that arrow and then cut back around to the arm. I'll lift it when you get over there."

≈

Lydia was sitting with her legs hanging out the back of the Land Rover letting her feet swing easily back and forth and thinking about Terry as she stared at a fire ant mound that was piled up around the base of the fencepost just out in front of her.

"What's so funny Mama?" TJ asked from where he was standing up on the roof rack.

"What?" Lydia said, snapping out of the memory.

"What are you laughing at?"

Lydia leaned herself a little further out and shelved her hand over her eyes to shade them from the bright sun as she looked up to where TJ was perched on the car's roof. "Was I laughing?"

TJ looked down at her through the big binoculars he was using to watch for planes. Lydia could see his eyes magnified through the lenses. "Your head's huge," he laughed, "You look like a cartoon...Say something else."

Lydia said, "My, what big eyes you have," precisely enunciating each syllable.

TJ pulled the binoculars down from his eyes. "You've got horse teeth."

Lydia curled her lips back into a wide grin and then blew out a noisy breath, vibrating her lips horse fashion.

"Do it again," TJ said, lifting the binoculars back up to his eyes. Lydia whinnied and blew out another horse breath. "I can see spit flying off your lips," TJ said.

Lydia slumped her shoulders and looked sideways at TJ, "*Oh, that's nice,*" she said.

"Do it again."

Lydia shook her head; "Not hardly." She sat back down and pumped her feet up and down. "I do miss my ankles," she said wistfully, "Y'all are welcome to come back anytime."

She heard the sound of a tractor and looked up to see a tall, stoop shouldered man wearing a ratty ball-cap come driving past on a red tractor. The man nodded his head and touched the bill of his cap when he saw Lydia sitting there by the fence. Lydia smiled and waved back as he drove on by.

"Are you gonna tell me what you were laughing about," TJ asked, "Or is it another one of them grown up things that I won't understand 'til I'm older?"

"No. I didn't even realize that I was laughing...I was just remembering one time when your daddy was putting out pine straw around the house and he was toting a bale up against his belly that he didn't know was full of fire ants." Lydia paused and chuckled. "I was putting out some flowers and all the sudden I hear him holler and I look over and he's tossed the bale halfway across the yard and he's snatching off his shirt, smacking at his stomach as hard as he can go." Lydia stopped again and chuckled a little harder, "As I jumped up to see what was the matter..." Lydia's chuckle grew, "He snatched his pants off right out there in middle of the front yard..."

"They got in his pants?"

"*Oh they sure did...*He was just smacking away and I said, 'What do you want me to do?' and he yelled '*THE HOSE... THE HOSE...QUICK, GET THE HOSE!*' And while he was hollering, he stumbled over toward the house as best he could with his pants all down around his ankles, and then he stood there smacking at fire ants while I sprayed him down."

"Did they get him bad?"

Lydia chuckled to herself again as she pictured Terry coming in to the bedroom from the bathroom that night with nothing on but about forty pink splotches of strategically placed calamine lotion. "Not *too* bad," she finally said, "...But bad enough."

It had been *so* hard for her to keep a straight face when he handed her a cotton ball and the bottle of calamine. "There's a few I can't see to get," he had told her meekly, "Would you mind getting them for me?"

Oh, the look on that poor man's face, she thought, *I really shouldn't have laughed at him.* She covered her face with her hand and shook her head...*But when he bent over the bed...*

After a couple minutes, Lydia thought she could hear a plane somewhere off in the distance. She called up to TJ; "Have you seen anything, T?"

"I saw three Canadas fly over the treetops towards the river; six mallards jumped and went off that way when that man that came by here on the tractor drove down past that little pond over yonder; and a few minutes ago I saw a little yellow airplane with big green letters on the side that said N-C-F-S circle around *that* way," TJ replied, staring off over a distant treeline through his binoculars. He held the binoculars with one hand and pointed with his other hand in the direction of all the activities he had witnessed as he spoke.

"How 'bout now? I thought I heard another plane."

TJ gave the horizon a scan. "I think I can see something off towards town...I think there's a plane coming...Yep there it is...It's starting to turn. I think it's gonna circle around to come in and land."

"Good," Lydia said, sliding back out of the Rover, "After it lands we'll go in and watch everybody coming in and then we'll see what happens from there."

"It's coming around."

Lydia looked down and straightened her clothes and then closed the back door. She looked up at TJ and then looked off over the pines to watch the plane.

"I think they just let their wheels down...Wow, it looks like it's gonna tip off the tops of those trees."

Lydia glanced back up at TJ and smiled. He had the same attentive look that his father always got when he was focused on something. *He's in his own place now*, she thought. TJ had inherited Terry's ability to zone in and block out everything around him when he was into something. She could see TJ's lips moving slightly as he mouthed something to himself. She started to ask him what he was saying, but decided to just watch him instead. She knew at that moment there was nothing in the world to TJ but TJ and that airplane.

The plane came in low over the trees and sat down smoothly just a little ways before them on the end of the runway.

"How many people do you think are on there?" she asked him just after the tires had barked on the asphalt.

TJ followed the plane's path down past the terminal with the binoculars. "I don't know," he finally answered, after the plane had passed out of sight behind the building. He pulled the binoculars down and let them hang around his neck from the strap. "I think that one will carry about seventy passengers. I was trying to count the windows, but I lost my spot."

"Well, I know a good way to find out," said Lydia, "...Let's go in and watch the people as they come off."

TJ lifted the binoculars and looked out through them one last time and then lifted the strap off his neck and handed them down to his mother. Lydia took them from him and then took a step back as he climbed down onto the spare tire and then hopped down to the dusty ground in front of her.

TJ opened the back door halfway and gestured for Lydia to hand him the binoculars. She handed them to him, and he put them away in the storage compartment in the door and then let it close back by itself. "I wish we'd a'had more traffic here today," he said as they made their way toward the terminal, "I ain't never had that good a seat to watch the planes come in."

"It was very nice of Dip to let us park over here, wasn't it."

TJ looked up at Lydia and nodded his head and grinned, "It's like Grandaddy says, huh?"

"Your grandaddy says so many things," said Lydia, "Which saying would you be referring to?"

"'It's not what you know, it's who you know.'"

"I guess so."

Lydia held her hand out to TJ and he took hold of it as they pushed open the swinging doors and went inside.

"What are we gonna do first?" TJ asked.

Lydia pointed out ahead of them, "Why don't we just go right over there and watch the people come in off that plane that just landed."

"This looks different from the last time we were here," TJ said, "...Look at all the rocking chairs."

"Wow," Lydia said, looking around the waiting area, "They've really made some changes." She looked down at TJ, "This is nice. Why don't we just take a seat and wait for the passengers to come in."

"How 'bout those two right there," he suggested, "We should be able to see everything that's going on from over there."

Lydia looked around, "That's a great idea."

They walked over and sat down in two rockers that were off a little to one side and facing out toward the big windows overlooking the runway.

"These are good seats, TJ," Lydia said as she settled herself down. She looked over towards the doors and then shifted her seat a little so she could see TJ's face.

"Look Mama," TJ said, pointing at the mural that had been painted on the far wall, "That looks like Grandaddy's fish house."

Lydia looked over at the painting. "It does, doesn't it," she said. She scanned the scenes that represented various aspects of her home county, "...And that's the courthouse downtown."

TJ pointed at a picture of a fishing pier jutting out into the ocean, "That's the Scotch Bonnet."

"Yep; and there's the little ferry over Cullett's Creek..." Lydia noticed the people waiting for the plane to unload seemed to be turning their attention towards the runway entrance. She glanced over that way and saw the first of the passengers coming in. "And where do you suppose that farm is supposed to be?" she asked, hoping to keep TJ's attention away from the gate.

"I don't know," TJ shrugged, "Maybe out at McGee, or Tuttle's Mill," he said, "It's hard to tell." He glanced up at his mother and then quickly turned back to the wall.

Lydia glanced back over to the gate and then looked back at TJ. "Are you sure you can't tell," she said, "What's that grey thing in the middle of that tobacco field?"

TJ squinted at the picture and then stood up. Lydia saw Rose come in through the gate and gave her a little wave behind TJ's back.

"That's the Revolutionary War Monument for the Battle of Scripp's Creek, ain't it?"

"It is." Lydia took TJ by the shoulders and turned him towards the gate, "And look down there. What do you think of that?"

TJ stared off toward the far end of the waiting area for a second and then looked back over his shoulder at Lydia, "What am I looking at Mama?"

Lydia directed his gaze back towards the gate with a nod. TJ turned back just as Rose stepped around a kiosk and he took off like a rocket, "*Miss Rose*," he squealed, "*Miss Rose*."

Rose dropped down on one knee and TJ fell into her arms. Rose hugged him tightly, "Mmm mmm *mmm*," she groaned, "Let me see you." TJ pulled back and smiled brightly in her face; "Just look at you," she said, "... So handsome...You look more like your father every time I see you." She pulled him back in to her and gave him another hug, "Are you surprised to see me?"

TJ leaned back, still grinning, and nodded grandly, "Are you here for Christmas?"

"I sure am."

TJ's eyes sparkled.

Lydia came up, smiling down at them.

"And," Rose said, looking up to Lydia, "I have a very special Christmas surprise for everyone."

"*Rose*," Lydia said, "I think you just being here is surprise enough."

Rose stood to her feet and gently laid a hand on Lydia's belly.

Lydia said, "It's incredible, isn't it?"

"It's beautiful."

"I'm huge."

Rose hugged her tightly and then leaned back and looked Lydia's stomach over. "You *might* be a *touch* bigger than the last time I saw you," she smiled.

"*Miss Rose*," TJ said, "She's ten times bigger than the last time you saw her."

~Chapter Ten~

Roger took a deep breath and then opened the door and slid out of his truck, sticking the little box down in his pocket as he climbed the freshly painted steps up to the loading dock out on the front of Harvey Pritt's fish house. Stopping at the top, he wiped his palms on the seat of his pants and took another deep breath as he looked down through the breezeway to the river and went over one last time what he wanted to say. He took a couple steps forward and the door to the cooler swung open in front of him.

"Hey Roger," Maggie's brother Lendon said as he stepped out from inside with a shovel full of crushed ice.

"Hey Len."

"How's it goin'?"

"Pretty good," Lendon replied, "'Cept somebody took my chock again." He bumped the bottom of the thick door with his heel, "Can't keep the dern reefer door open now...You looking for Maggie?"

Roger shook his head. "Uh, no...I was actually hoping to see Mister Harvey," he said, "Is he around?"

Lendon's mouth curved up a bit at the corners, "He's right out here." He gave his head a jerk, motioning for Roger to follow him out to the dock. He dumped the ice into a fish box that was sitting on a table right outside the door and then headed out to the dock with the shovel balanced on his shoulder, "He's wiring a new radio up in *Addiction*."

Roger glanced down into the box on his way past, "Those yellowfins?"

"Yeah," Lendon said, "Me and Tommy ran out this morning and caught a pile of 'em...Nothing real big, but some nice fish. I'm fixing to run 'em all up to Ormond."

"Where you taking them?"

Lendon stopped at the edge of the dock and glanced back over his shoulder at Roger, "Royal Schooner," he said. He banged the shovel against the stern of his father's boat and called, "*Hey Cap*."

Harvey Pritt's face appeared in the open door to the pilothouse, "What'cha need Len?" he said, "Oh, hey Roger."

"Hey, Mister Harvey," Roger said, "You got a minute?"

Harvey stepped out onto the deck and smiled at Roger, "I shore do," he said, "Come on aboard."

"Thanks Len," Roger said. He grabbed a piling and lowered himself down off the dock. Lendon stood there for a moment, grinning at his father.

Harvey made sure Roger wasn't looking and winked at Lendon; Lendon pumped his eyebrows up and down. "Come on in," Harvey said to Roger, "I'm just about finished with this new radio." Roger followed as Harvey turned and went back inside. Stepping up onto his fold-out step stool, Harvey pointed at the captain's chair with a screwdriver, "Have a seat."

Roger climbed up into the seat and let his feet hang in front of the foot rest.

"I appreciate you getting that fence fixed for me," Harvey said, as he went back to stripping wires in the overhead console.

"Have you had a chance to see it?"

"As a matter of fact I have." Harvey took his pliers and crimped two wires together and then stopped and looked at Roger, "I went over to the cemetery yesterday," he said, "... You did a fine job on the gate too." He stopped and pushed his cap back off his forehead with his pliers, "That thing's been stuck, rusted open since I was a young'un."

"It took a bit of doing to get it off," Roger said, "But that was really the only hard part. All I had to do after that was grind off the old hinges and weld some new pieces of rod and tubing on."

Harvey said, "I like that weight you put on it, too...It pulls it right back closed nice and smooth."

"You didn't happen to hear where I found that did you?"

Harvey shook his head.

"Out at the mill," Roger said, propping an elbow on one of the arms of the captain's chair. He leaned a little to one side and held one hand up about head high and made a motion like he was grabbing something off a shelf. "There were six of them lined up on a rafter down at the wheel end of the building," he said, "There's a high stand on that end for monitoring the wheel that if you stand up on it you can see up there. Well, there's these little divots carved out in a line down the middle of this rafter, about a dozen of 'em. There were six of those cast iron balls sitting up there, and for the life of me, I couldn't figure out what they were for." Roger chuckled, "I couldn't tell you how many hours I spent reading up on old mills while I was working on that thing and nowhere was anything like those mentioned. I even sent some pictures to this guy in Indiana who's supposed to be *the* expert on these old mills, and he was stumped."

"How about that."

"So, anyway; that one I used on the gate was sitting on my workbench at the shop and Joey had the idea to use it on your gate, so we just welded that chain to it and then welded that loop for it onto the fence and...there you go."

Harvey reached back up into the console and went back to work, "Well, it works like it was made for it," he said, as he stepped up onto the top step of his stool and stuck his head up inside the hole over his head.

Roger shifted his weight over onto his hip and pulled the box out of his pocket. He straightened himself back up and stared at the box as he passed it back and forth in his hands. After a long moment, he took a deep breath and said, "So anyway, Mister Harvey, I reckon you're probbly wondering why I came by..."

"Not really."

Roger paused a few seconds, wondering if Harvey Pritt had actually heard what he said. "I said, 'You were probbly wondering why I came by...'"

Harvey stepped back down and pulled himself out from the hole in the console. "I heard you," he said. He grinned at Roger through his mustache, "I'm pretty sure I know why you're here, son." He stuck the pliers in his back pocket, picked up a screwdriver, and started screwing the cover back into place over his head.

Roger waited until he was done and had stepped down off of the stool until he spoke again. "I want to be Maggie's husband," he said, "And I'd like your permission to ask her to marry me."

Harvey looked at Roger and smiled pleasantly and then turned and propped on his elbows on the dash and stared out at the river through the windshield.

"I want to come home every day knowing that she's there waiting for me," Roger said, "I want to wake up every morning with her there next to me...I want to have our own little secrets for just the two of us to giggle about together in the middle of a crowded room. I want to warm her side of the bed before she climbs in every night. I want to be the one standing on the church steps holding her hand as Jimmy drives his new bride away...I want to be the one she turns to with tears in her eyes when the nurse comes out and says that Sarah's new baby girl looks just like her mother...I want to know that she'll always be mine..." Roger paused and took a deep breath, "If she'll have me."

When he had finished, Roger stood staring at Harvey, wondering what he could be thinking as he waited in silence for the old man's response.

After a long moment, Harvey took a long, drawn-out breath and then let it out slowly. "Roger," he began, speaking very gently, "My daughter is very much in love with you." He paused and gave his head a little nod, like he was agreeing with himself, and then he glanced Roger's way and continued, "But *obviously*, you must know that." He chuckled under his breath and looked back out the windshield, "A fella that couldn't figure that out wouldn't be worth tending blind monkeys. You make her very happy, and that makes me very happy...I appreciate you coming to me first," Harvey chuckled at himself, a little louder this time, "Not that I even remotely believe my answer would make any difference in what y'all will do." He held up his hand, stopping Roger before he could argue, "You and Maggie both have got good heads on your shoulders and I trust both of you to make right choices, *just as you both always have seemed to do.*"

Harvey stood up and gave his head a little shake and then rested a hand on Roger's shoulder, "...But," he continued, "the reason I say that is not because I am so impressed with either one of y'all's superior reasoning or above-average decision making skills." He paused again and looked closely at Roger, "I believe y'all were meant for one another," he said, taking Roger by surprise, "Y'all were meant to be."

Harvey turned loose of Roger's shoulder, turned around, and leaned back against the console. He folded his arms across his chest, crossed one ankle over the other, and stared thoughtfully down at his feet for a few seconds and then looked back up at Roger, "James was a fine young man," he said, "He was a good husband and a good father... It's all hard to understand, but their meeting was for a reason –if nothing more than to bring those two precious children into this world– it was for a reason...But, I truly believe that there is something special about you two. I believe y'all were chosen for each other and that it's all in the Lord's plan...Y'all are meant to be. It's as simple as that."

Harvey thought Roger looked like he had something to say, so he stopped to give him a chance to respond, but Roger just stood and stared at Harvey, completely lost for words. After half a minute, Harvey grinned and held his hand out, "Let me see what you've got there," he said.

Roger shook himself out of his daze and opened the little box and set it in Harvey's palm. Harvey held it up a little closer to his face and stared admiringly at the ring, "She's a beaut," he said. He turned the box slowly and examined the ring at several different angles, "I don't know as I've ever seen one like it."

"I had it custom made," Roger said quietly.

Harvey handed the box back to Roger, "That's gonna look real nice on my daughter's hand."

"I sure hope so," Roger said. He gave the ring a brief look and then snapped the box closed and stuck it back into his pocket.

"It's natural to be nervous," Harvey said, "but, I don't think you've got too much to worry about."

"All the talking we've done, she's never once mentioned getting married."

"Well, you know Maggie...I don't think she'd want to feel like she was pushing you into anything," Harvey said, "Or even that *she* was the one putting the idea into your head. If it didn't come natural, I don't think she'd want it."

Roger gave his head a little shake and smiled crookedly at Harvey. "She's always said that you know her better than anyone," he said, "I reckon I'm gonna have to trust you on this...But I've got two more people I need to talk to before I get to find out for sure."

Harvey's face lit up, "If you're referring to Jimmy and Sarah, it's a done deal then...Trust me; those young'uns are both happily on board the Roger Lowell fanwagon."

"You're making this all sound so easy."

"Why shouldn't it be?"

Roger shrugged, "I don't know. I reckon when you've wanted something for so long...Something that you thought should have been so simple, but, for reasons outside of your control, you were never able to get worked out..." Roger trailed off and then shook his head, "I don't know...I guess I had just convinced myself that we were never gonna happen, so in the back of my mind I'm still thinking that way."

Harvey grabbed Roger's shoulder and gave it a squeeze, "Don't make life harder than it has to be Roger...You've got something wonderful staring you in the face. Grab it with both hands and don't ever let it go."

Lydia closed her eyes and rocked slowly on her mother's front porch, listening to the chimes ringing softly overhead in the warm breeze.

"I don't think I've enjoyed this kind of weather at this time of year since Leon and I were in Botswana," Rose commented as she came out the front door and sat herself back down in the rocking chair next to Lydia's. She took a graceful sip of the tea she was carrying and then smiled sweetly at Lydia as she rested the glass down on the end of the arm rest. Lydia rested her head back against the chair and ran her hand in soft circles around her belly as she looked back at Rose. "You look beautiful," Rose said, "... *Radiant.*"

Lydia rolled her eyes, "*Oh please,*" she smiled, "I look like I swallowed a *pair* of beach balls."

Rose reached out and touched Lydia's stomach, "That's nonsense...You're marvelous."

"I still can't believe I'm having twins."

"I can understand that," Rose chuckled as she gave Lydia's belly a pat; "But, no one else is having any trouble."

"Ugh," Lydia squeaked. She swatted Rose's hand away and mocked a disgusted face at her, "I thought I was marvelous," she snorted.

"You are," Rose grinned, "...*Big* and marvelous." Rose's eyes sparkled, "I don't care how many times I've seen it happen, or how many babies I've helped deliver, it's still amazing,"

Rose's gaze lingered on Lydia's face for a moment, and then she turned and looked back out over the field towards the pond. She took another sip of her tea and then sighed contentedly.

Lydia looked at Rose's profile as she sat rocking peacefully, with that look of complete harmony that she so often had, and wondered what Rose was seeing in her mind's eye as she gazed out at the pond.

Studying Rose for a moment; with the dry, brown, field grass in the background framing her face, Lydia's mind went back to a black-and-white picture that Rose had hanging in the front hall of her home back in Hadley.

The picture had been taken by Leon, Rose's now deceased husband, back when the two of them were young, newly-married missionaries in Africa. Rose was dressed out in a crisp new safari kit, standing on a tall termite mound, looking off over a scrubby grassland on the edge of the Okavanga Delta. "We were waiting for the car from the Presbyterian mission to come pick us up," Leon had told Lydia, when she first asked him about the picture, "We were sitting there with all of our things in a pile, and I was just loading some fresh film into our camera when suddenly, we saw a group of about twenty Hambukushu Bushmen marching past in a line and my Rose, *all of thirteen hours in the country*, climbs up onto that termite mound and hollers out at them, '*Jambo...Jambo...*Hello... *Hello there*...Hello. Are there any hippos about then?'"

Leon then said that the men had all stopped at the sound of her calls and stood staring at her for what seemed, at the time, a *very, very* long few minutes. He wondered, as Rose waved and *Jambo'd* them again, if they were about to be sent on to their Great Reward, but all the natives did then was glance around at each other, and then without a word, as a man, they turned and continued on their way.

Leon said that he had suggested to Rose, as the men disappeared into the swamp, that perhaps they didn't speak English *or* Swaheli.

"Well of course I didn't expect that they would," Rose replied, "But, I thought they'd at least wave back."

"And no sooner had the words spilled from her lips than the last man in the line stopped, turned around for the briefest moment, smiled broadly at her, and waved. Rose shot her hand up high over her head and waved back as he turned and continued off with his troop. She let her hand fall slowly to her side and took a long, deep breath as she watched them going away.

"She turned round and even though we'd been sitting right there for over an hour, it was as if her eyes were seeing the place for the very first time, and she suddenly saw that she could be a part of it all. A look crept across her face," Leon continued as he smiled adoringly at the picture, "...A look of complete peace...*kinship*...and as I sat looking up at her," Leon paused in his narration and took a deep breath, staring at the photograph and losing himself in it for a moment. "She just looked so *whole*, so beautiful to me," he concluded, "...So beautiful."

"How long was it that you said y'all were over there," Lydia asked Rose, "...In Africa?"

"Twenty two years," Rose said. She turned to Lydia, "We really thought we'd spend our whole lives there. But the Lord had other plans."

"Do you ever miss it?"

"*Sometimes...*" Rose said thoughtfully and turned to Lydia. "You know; you always miss things about any part of your life where you were happy. But God puts you in places in time and gives you blessings to enjoy wherever you go. The thing is accepting where you are and enjoying His gifts there."

"That is so true."

They heard a shot and both looked to see a dove fall from the sky out by the pond. They waited a second and then heard a whistle and saw Huff come bounding from behind the small patch of broomstraw that Buddy had left unmowed at TJ's request, run over, gently pick up the bird, and fetch it quickly back to where TJ was waiting for him in the little blind. "Well," said Rose, "That's seven."

"I reckon I'd better call him in soon...*Oooh look.*" Lydia pointed, directing Rose's gaze up over the treeline, "There's three ducks coming in."

"I wonder if he's seen them–" Rose stopped as they heard a fairly believable quacking call from out near the pond. They watched as the ducks pitched, and then set their wings as they headed down to light on the pond. Lydia glanced back over to the clump of broomstraw just in time to see her son pop up with his little shotgun mounted to his shoulder. *Bam*, the gun sounded, and then, a second-and-a-half later, *Bam*, it fired again. She looked back up and watched a lone mallard flapping its way rapidly back over the pines.

Rose turned to Lydia and smiled, "I reckon he did," she said. She turned back to see Huff come bounding out of the grass again and then dive off into the pond. He swam out, grabbed one duck in his mouth and brought it back to where TJ had come out to wait at the edge of the pond. TJ took the big duck from Huff and waited as the little dog swam back out and retrieved the other. "He looks just like a little version of his daddy out there."

Lydia smiled, "Doesn't he, though."

TJ was now making his way across the field, Terry's heavy canvas hunting vest hanging half-way down his thighs, with his shotgun broken open over one shoulder and carrying the two ducks in his other hand. Huff was prancing excitedly in circles around him as TJ came slowly towards the house, struggling under the weight of his gear. Lydia called out to him as he came into the yard, "That was some good shooting TJ."

TJ looked up from under the brim of his little green corduroy shooting cap and a proud grin crept across his face. "*Enght*," he grunted nasally, as Huff started to run up on the porch. Huff stopped and looked meekly back over his shoulder at TJ. TJ shook his head; "Don't you even think about jumping up there all wet like you are." He stepped up to the edge of the porch and set the two drake mallards down in front of his mother. Huff stood up on his hind legs and braced his front paws up on the porch and sniffed at the ducks.

"He fetched those ducks up for you real good, didn't he," Lydia said.

TJ pulled the little sixteen gauge down off his shoulder and checked the barrels. "I didn't even have to give him a line," he said, snapping the gun closed. "I just told him to '*Hie on*' and he went." TJ patted Huff's head and then handed the gun up to his mother, "Could you hold this for me, please?"

Lydia leaned forward and grabbed the shotgun and then propped it up against the house. "Thank you," TJ said, as he unslung the hunting bag from his shoulder and set it down on the ground at his feet. He reached around behind him and started pulling doves out of the gamebag on the back of the old hunting vest he was wearing. "One...two...three," he counted out slowly as he rested them down gently in a line next to the ducks, "...four...five...six...seven."

"That's quite a bag," Lydia said.

TJ reached in his front pockets and pulled out his spent shells, standing them up on end in a line between the birds and the women.

Lydia leaned forward a bit and held her chin, eyeballing the line of shells. "Hmmm, let's see," she said, and then pointed at each one in succession, "...Nine shots for nine birds." She looked up from the porch to her son, "I am impressed."

TJ grinned sheepishly and then bent down and reached into the top of his hunting bag and pulled out two more shells. "I used these on the ducks," he said, "Steel shot."

"Ahh," Lydia said, "I was wondering if you'd remembered."

TJ grinned, "As soon as I saw them coming over the trees I hunkered down on my knees and popped out the number eights and stuck those in," he said. He patted at the shell loops on the left breast of his vest; there were two shells still in place and two empty loops. "I had those stuck right here just in case," he added, "I been hoping to get a chance at some ducks all year."

"Well, eleven shots for nine birds is still some good shooting."

TJ grinned. "I kinda thought so too."

"Your father would have been awful proud of the job both of you did," Rose said.

TJ looked down at Huff and then patted his thigh. Huff stepped down and then stood back up on his hind legs and propped himself on TJ's leg. TJ patted the little dog's head lovingly and then squeezed a couple times at the base of his floppy ear, "Reckon you deserve a bit of a treat for all that hard work." Huff perked at the word treat and he let out a short yip. TJ grabbed up one of the doves and hooked his fingers around its head.

"*Hold it*," Lydia blurted, stopping TJ just as he was beginning to tug, "Don't you dare."

"But Mama,'" TJ said, "He likes 'em, and I'm just gonna throw that part away anyhow."

Lydia shook her head, "Unh uh..." She caught Rose eyeing her and glanced over and gave her head another little shake, "Just trust me." She turned back to TJ, "Not out here Buddy...not with us sitting right here."

TJ slumped his shoulders and plopped the dove back down on the porch, looking solemnly up at his mother, "He worked really hard today Mama."

"I didn't say he couldn't have a treat...I just said he couldn't have *that* one."

"Is there any bacon left from breakfast?"

Lydia thought for a second and then said, "Seems like I saw a couple pieces in the fridge when we were making dinner."

"Would it be alright if I gave a couple of *those* to him then before I clean these birds?"

"I don't see why not."

"Sit, boy," TJ told Huff, "I'll be right back."

Huff sat quickly down and waited obediently as TJ clambered up onto the porch and ran inside. Rose glanced at her watch as the screen door banged shut behind him.

"TJ likes to, um, *treat* Huff with the heads," Lydia said. She looked down at Huff and smiled squeamishly, "He's a rather indelicate little thing."

"Oh yes," Rose said, "I seem to recall you telling me about that. But, you really didn't need to stop him on my account...I've seen much worse."

"I kind of figured that," Lydia said. "But to be perfectly honest with you," she rested her hands on her belly and opened her eyes wide, "I don't think *I* could have taken it today."

"Understood."

Rose checked her watch again, "Well," she said casually, "It's still a few days 'til Christmas, I know, but the surprise I promised should be here any minute."

"Really, Miss Rose, I wish you wouldn't. It means so much to us just having you here."

"That's sweet, but this surprise isn't costing me a thing."

Lydia eyed Rose, "Now, how can that be? If you're having to have it delivered then it has to have cost you something...At least the cost of the delivery."

Rose smiled mysteriously, "You'll see."

The front door swung back open and TJ popped out with three crispy strips of bacon clutched in his fist. "Hup," he said, as he stepped up to the edge of the porch and waved a piece in Huff's direction. The little dog hopped up onto his hind legs and licked his lips. TJ dangled the piece over Huff's head and he opened his mouth wide. TJ dropped the bacon and in two chomps it vanished down the dog's throat.

"Show Miss Rose that trick you taught him," Lydia said.

"Okay," TJ chirped. Hopping down off the porch, he took a couple steps out into the yard and held a hand out to Huff. He turned around and got down on his hands and knees, craned his neck around, and grinned at Huff, "Ready boy?"

Huff fidgeted a bit and dug his feet in. TJ looked back ahead and stretched one arm out and up as far as it would go, holding one of the pieces of bacon out ahead of him. He paused a second and then clucked his tongue twice and said, "*Hup...hup.*"

Huff lunged forward, ran right up TJ's back, dove over his head, and grabbed the slice of bacon as he flew past TJ's hand. When he hit the ground, he spun around and sat up on his hind legs with his front paws folded up under his chin and the slice of bacon clenched crossways in his jaws. TJ sat back on his heels as Rose and Lydia clapped and cheered.

TJ turned to them and smiled and then looked back at Huff, "Alright boy," he said. Huff quickly flipped the bacon up over his nose, snapped it out of the air, and swallowed it down.

"Wow, TJ," Rose said, "Well done. How long did it take you to teach it to him?"

"I reckon it took us about three days of practicing to get it just right....You want to see him do it again?"

"I'd love to."

TJ spun himself around and got back on all fours. He pulled the last piece of bacon out of his pocket and looked back at Huff; "Ready boy?"

Huff sat back and barked.

TJ held the bacon out at arm's length and was just about to tell his dog to "Hup" when a shining green pickup pulled up into the driveway. "Who's that," he said.

"I believe your surprise has arrived," Rose said. TJ rolled over onto his hip and tossed the bacon to Huff. "Here you go boy," he said, staring at the truck.

A tall, slim, dark-complected, man with neatly trimmed gray hair climbed out of the pickup and waved at Rose. Rose waved back as she stood to her feet. TJ stood himself up and brushed the crumpled blades of dry grass from the knees of his pants as the man strode across the yard.

"Hello, young man," the man said, "You must be TJ." He stuck his hand out and TJ gave it a shake. "My name is Andrew Patterson."

"It's a pleasure to make your acquaintance, Mister Patterson," TJ said stiffly, "I'm Terrence King, Junior...after my father."

"Nice to meet you, TJ. I've heard very good things about you."

Lydia stared out at the man and caught a look in his eyes as he turned and looked at Rose that left no doubt what Rose's surprise was. She stood to her feet as he came across the yard smiling at Rose.

"Please," he said, "Don't get up."

"Oh no," Lydia said, with a self-conscious wave, "I've been sitting too long. I need to get up."

"Lydia," Rose said, "This is Andrew Patterson...my fiancé."

Lydia looked closely at Rose and grinned. "It's is a pleasure, to meet you Mister Patterson," she said, turning to Andrew, "Please come up and have a seat. Would you care for some tea?"

"Thank you," Andrew replied, "I'm fine." Rose stepped past Lydia as he came up the steps and took Andrew's hand. "I see someone's been doing a bit of shooting," he said, gesturing towards the line of birds lying on the porch.

"TJ and Huff usually spend an hour or two out by the pond every afternoon," Lydia said, "When he gets all of his work done." She looked down at TJ and smiled at him, "It's good motivation for him."

"It's good motivation for me, too," Andrew replied. "I'd be glad to give you a hand cleaning 'em if you need," he told TJ.

"You know how to clean birds?" TJ said.

"*Oh, does he*," Rose said. "Did you see the ornament on the hood of his truck?"

TJ looked out at the truck and squinted.

"It's a quail flying," Andrew said. "I'm afraid I'm a bit passionate about my bird hunting."

"That's very kind of you Mister Patterson," Lydia said, "but—"

"Please, call me Andrew."

"I'm sorry, *Andrew*, but you're company. We couldn't ask you to do that."

"Really, I'm glad to do it, as long as TJ doesn't mind me lending him a hand." He glanced over at TJ, then turned back to the ladies, smiled charmingly and added, "And I'm sure you suddenly have lots of questions you'd like to ask Rose."

Andrew stepped down off the porch and started picking up doves, "Where do you usually clean these," he asked TJ.

TJ stepped up beside him and grabbed the two ducks. "We've got a table out back," he said, "I'll show you."

"Alright."

TJ waited a moment as Andrew got all the doves balanced in the crook of his arm and then led him around the house.

"I noticed there were only eleven shells there on the porch," Lydia heard Andrew say as they were going out of sight, "You must be a pretty good shot."

She turned to Rose.

"Charming, isn't he?" Rose said.

"*Oh my gosh,*" Lydia exclaimed, "*Rose!*"

Rose smiled and sat back down. "Let's sit back down dear," she said, and patted the arm on the other rocker. "...And I'll tell you all about him."

"Oh yes, let's do." Lydia grabbed the arm of the chair and quickly slid it around so that it was almost facing Rose and then sat herself back down and stared eagerly at her.

"Well," Rose began, "We met on the plane when I came down the first time last spring. He was on his way home to Ormond from a pastor's conference in Memphis."

"So, he's a pastor."

"Yes. He's the assistant pastor and minister of music at Grace Baptist."

"That's the big one downtown?"

"I believe you're probably thinking of the First Baptist Church. Grace is just as you come across on Old Bridge Street."

Lydia nodded, "Okay," she said, "The sanctuary sits right there on the river. They've got the bell out in the parking lot."

"Right."

"Do they still do the live nativity at Christmas?"

Rose shrugged. "You'll have to ask Andrew about that."

"So anyway...you met on the plane..."

"Yes. He was already on the plane when I got on and his seat was across the aisle from mine. There was a short delay for some baggage loading problem and we got to talking while we were sitting there waiting and the next thing I knew we were landing in Ormond. He said he knew the airport fairly well and volunteered to help me get my luggage and then asked if I would mind him buying me a cup of coffee at the shop there..." Rose paused, leaned in a little closer to Lydia, and wrinkled up her nose, "I knew it was too hot for coffee," she continued, touching Lydia's knee, "I mean, he heard as well as I did, when we landed and they announced that it was eighty-six degrees outside."

Lydia snickered, "There was more than coffee going on, huh?"

"I had a hunch."

"So then what?"

"I told him that I would appreciate it, but that I needed to call y'all to let you know that I was in and that I was supposed to get my rental car and that I was told that the agency was closing at five and it was already ten 'til."

"*Ah-ahh*," Lydia drawled, "Played it a little hard to get, did you..."

Rose smiled slyly, "So," she continued, "After that, he suggested that I go get the car while he got both of our luggage and that I call right after. So, that's what I did, and after I called you, he walked me out to pick up the car and got my things loaded, and then he gave me his card and made me promise that I would call him when I came back into town."

"What was going through your head when all this was going on?"

"I was rather flattered," Rose confessed, "I mean, he is a very handsome and charming man and other than Leon I have never had anyone trying to romance me in the least."

"I'll give him this," Lydia said, "...the man knows a good thing when he sees it."

"He does, doesn't he," Rose laughed.

"So, I guess you called him then."

"Yes. And I couldn't believe I was doing it. I actually left here two hours earlier than I needed to so that I could meet him at his church and then go out for a bite to eat."

"You know," said Lydia, "I seem to remember you being somewhat vague about it when I asked you what time your flight was supposed to leave."

"I'm sorry. I hated feeling like I was being deceptive, but I didn't know where any of it was going and with everything that you were going through, I didn't—"

"Please don't feel bad," Lydia said, "I understand, and I appreciate it, but really, there's no need to feel bad about anything. It's all so exciting and wonderful," she paused and smiled broadly, her face glowing with excitement, "... Then what?"

"We had a wonderful afternoon together and he saw me off at the airport. We kept in touch and talked on the telephone a couple of times a week until I came back in August and we saw each other again. I spent most of the day with him when I flew in and then, to tell you the truth, I stayed in Ormond with him an extra day before I left for Hadley."

Lydia gave Rose a look. "*You did?*"

"Oh you know better than that," Rose said, "...His church has a house for missionaries across the street beside the church office and I stayed there."

Lydia waved her off, "You know I was just messing...Go on."

"He came out to Hadley to see me once in September and then again in October –that's when he asked me to marry him– and then I came back down last month and spent Thanksgiving with him and his family."

Lydia cocked her head to one side, "*Really,*" she said, "All this without so much as a call...My, my, aren't you the sneaky thing."

Rose rolled her eyes, "You make us sound like a dime-store paperback."

"You have to admit," Lydia said, "It is all hopelessly romantic...How did he propose?"

"We took a picnic up to Gabraham's Knob State Park and hiked up to The Overlook..."

"Oh, that must have been beautiful," Lydia interjected, "I heard the leaves were prettier this year than they have been in years."

"Oh it was," Rose said, "And it was so clear that day, all the colors up and around the falls, and off everywhere you turned, in every valley you looked...it was just magnificent."

"Terry and I always loved that place," said Lydia, "It has just about the most beautiful view in all the mountains."

"He took me out to the point of the overlook and got down on one knee with the falls roaring behind him and pulled out a ring–" Rose stopped and her face lit up, "*Oh,*" she said, sticking her hand down into her pocket, "I guess I can put this back on now." She pulled a ring out and slid it onto her finger.

"Ooh, let me see it," Lydia said. She reached out and pulled Rose's hand to her and eyed the ring, "That's beautiful," she said, turning Rose's hand loose, "I love that cut."

Rose held her hand up in front of her and admired the ring, "It's a bit bigger than I would have chosen," she said, "...but..."

"You're not sending it back."

"No."

Lydia laughed, "Well, have y'all set your date yet?"

"January 30th."

"Wow, y'all aren't wasting any time."

"When you're sixty years old it's hard to come up with many good reasons for a long engagement."

Lydia laughed again, "I guess so."

"We're both ready," Rose said.

"So, tell me about him," Lydia said.

Rose took a deep breath, "Well," she said, Andrew's sixty-one; he was born and raised in Pass Christian, Mississippi. He has an older brother and two younger sisters. He went to seminary in New Orleans, where he met his wife...They were married for thirty-six years and he has three daughters: Caroline, Virginia, and Georgia. Caroline and

Virginia married boys from Ormond and still live there with their families; the youngest, Georgia is in Germany with her husband Clifton. He is a C-130 pilot in the Air Force stationed at the Ramstein Air Base.

"Andrew has five grandchildren –all girls– and they are all in Ormond. His wife Carrie passed away four years ago from complications after surgery. He has been serving at Grace for twenty-eight years; loves to sing; plays trumpet, piano, and guitar; loves the outdoors, and is crazy about his granddaughters."

"And you."

Rose smiled blissfully; "And me."

Lydia stopped and her mouth fell open.

"What is it?"

"This means you'll be moving to Ormond!"

"Yes it does."

"Oh, that's wonderful."

The screen door creaked open behind Lydia and Andrew Patterson stepped out onto the porch. "Excuse me ladies," he said. Lydia turned to see him flash a quick wink to Rose before he looked down to her and said, "We've used up all the salt in your shaker and TJ couldn't find a box in the pantry."

"Oh, I'm sorry," Lydia pushed herself up from the rocking chair, "Y'all soaking the birds?"

Andrew nodded, "Yes ma'am."

"I'll get it for you." Lydia stepped around her chair and headed inside, "Mama's got it hidden from Daddy. His doctor told him to cut out salt and he's having a bit of trouble complying."

"I can relate to that."

"Why don't you have a seat, and I'll be right back out."

Lydia went inside and walked back to the pantry. TJ was down on his hands and knees with half the contents of bottom shelf pulled out on the floor beside him. Huff was sitting on the screen porch staring in at him through the door.

"I can't find where MeeMaw hid the salt."

Lydia tickled TJ's ribs and then reached up onto the second shelf and shuffled some boxes around. "It's up here behind the whales," she said, "In this juice box box."

TJ sat back on the floor and looked up at her. "That's pretty good," he grinned, "I'd've never thought to look there."

"MeeMaw's pretty slick, huh?"

TJ pulled out a sea-foam green box and shook it. "I don't know about all that," he said, "I found her taffy stash."

Lydia pulled the salt out and stuck the juice box carton back on the shelf. "You'll stay out of MeeMaw's taffies if you know what's good for you."

TJ slid the box back.

"I'll leave this on the counter. Fill up the shaker after you salt the birds and then stick this back in here," she tapped the juice box carton and then looked at the jars of her mother's vegetables on the floor. "...Make sure you get all that stuff put back, alright."

"Yes, ma'am."

Lydia tousled TJ's hair and then walked back through the house, leaving the box of salt on the kitchen counter on her way out to the porch.

Andrew stood to his feet when Lydia came back out and offered her seat back to her.

Lydia held her hand out and directed them to the swing on the other end of the porch, "Why don't y'all come and sit down here together on the swing," she suggested, "I can just move this rocker over here."

"Let me," Andrew said. He grabbed the rocker and moved it over to the other end of the porch and then waited for Lydia and Rose to take their seats before seating himself down on the swing next to Rose. "That's a fine son you have Miss Lydia," he said.

"Thank you...I'm kind of fond of him myself."

"I was a little worried at first...he was a bit quiet, and I was worried he might not like me messing with his birds. But, in no time, he opened right up to me."

"He likes having a man to talk to –a hunter," Lydia said, "He gets plenty of time with my daddy and my brothers, but they've never been much on hunting...His father weaned him on grouse."

"I gathered that," Andrew smiled, "You can tell he thinks a lot of him."

"He really misses him."

Andrew said, "Without seeming too pushy, I hope –I know that we've just met– But I would love to take him out shooting with me sometime." He looked over to Rose and smiled and then turned back to Lydia. "I don't know if Rose told you," he continued, "But I have been blessed with five beautiful granddaughters...none of which share their grandfather's love of hunting."

"Well, thank you. That's very kind."

"Hey Mama," TJ called, as he popped his head around the corner of the house at the far end of the porch.

Lydia twisted herself around and looked back at him.

TJ stepped one foot up on the porch and held a five gallon bucket up for her to see. "I'm gonna run this over to Mister Curtis's and I'll be right back and get the shotty gun cleaned," he said, "You want to come with me Mister Andrew?"

"Why don't you go ahead, and let Mister Andrew visit a bit," Lydia said.

"Okay," TJ said flatly, "Come on Huff." He turned and headed for the field.

"*Don't forget he set his boar out,*" Lydia called.

"*Yes ma'am.*"

Lydia watched him for half a minute as he and Huff went over towards Curtis Staley's, and then she turned back to her company. "Looks like you made a friend," she said to Andrew.

Andrew took Rose's hand and smiled at Lydia, "I'm glad," he said, "I know that I don't need to tell you how special you and your family are to Rose, and *she* is very special to me...It was very important to me that this meeting went well."

❧

Jimmy and Sarah came running out the front door of their grandmother's house as Roger pulled up in the driveway. Jimmy ran up and snatched the passenger door open, and then waited as Sarah followed up and climbed in. "Hurry up slowpoke," he said.

"Hold it," Roger said, eyeing Jimmy, "Are you reasonably sanitary?"

Jimmy ran his hand across his neck and examined it, "I reckon I am," he said. He looked down at his sister and then back at Roger, "You know Priss is clean."

"Alright then," Roger said, beckoning them in with a flick of his wrist, "Don't forget the seatbelts," He waited as they strapped themselves in and then backed out. Sarah looked up at him, her curly blonde locks falling down in her twinkling blue eyes, "Where you taking us Mister Roger?"

"I thought we could go for a little ride and get us some milkshakes."

"At Mister Randy's?"

"Yep."

Jimmy said, "You know it's almost time for supper, don't you."

"Yes I do."

"Does Mama know about this?"

Roger glanced over at Jimmy, "Not exactly," he said, "But your grandmama said she'd take care of it if there was any trouble."

Sarah gave her head an expressive shake, "I don't want no trouble."

Roger smiled, "Don't worry," he said, "I trust your grandmama...I'm sure there's not gonna be any trouble."

"Why can't we get a hamburger while we're there too," asked Jimmy.

Roger shrugged, "I hadn't thought about it to be honest with you," he said, pausing for a moment, "Well, I have something I'd like to talk over with the two of you and I'd rather not do it right there where everybody else can hear."

Sarah's eyes grew wide, "Is it a secret, Mister Roger? Are you gonna tell us a secret?"

Roger looked down at her and winked. "Kind of," he replied. He put his arm around her shoulder and pulled her close to his side, "You can keep a secret can't you?"

Sarah smiled brightly at Roger and nodded her head.

"I knew I could count on you." Roger looked over to Jimmy and said, "How 'bout you big man?"

"I reckon."

"You *reckon*," Roger said. He stopped his truck in the street out in front of Douglas's and waited for George Pulley to drive past and then pulled up in front of the diner and parked. He looked back over at Jimmy and grinned, "... You're gonna have give me more than that."

"I *really* reckon."

"Well, I was hoping for more, but I reckon that'll have to do for now," Roger laughed. He opened his door and slid out. "It's clouding up a little," he said, looking up at the sky as he waited for Sarah to climb out.

Jimmy hopped out and slammed his door shut and then stood on the sidewalk in front of Roger's pickup. "Can I get a *big* milkshake?"

Sarah hopped out and then skipped past Roger when he closed his door. "What do you think Sarah," Roger asked, "You reckon Jimmy needs a big one?"

Sarah stuck her chin up and stared at her brother through squinted eyes, and then, by degrees she said, "*I don't know...*" She looked at Roger, "He's been a big bossy pants lately...and he wouldn't share his fly cake with me today."

Roger gasped, "*He wouldn't share his fly cake...*What can you do with a brother like that?"

Sarah shook her head dolefully and shrugged, "Ain't nothing you can do."

"You know what," Roger confided, "I've got a sister who's a big bossy pants, too. But, I still love her anyway."

Sarah looked back over at Jimmy and then smiled at Roger, "Can I get strawberry?"

Roger chuckled softly, "Sure...How about you Slick... What kind do you want."

"Chocolate...with whipped cream on top."

"Can I get whipped cream on mine too?"

Roger stepped over and pulled Douglas's front door open, "I don't see why not," he said, "I think I might just get some on mine too."

Jimmy and Sarah walked in and Roger followed behind them. "Hey Randy," he said as he walked up and sat Sarah on a stool at the counter.

"How's it going Roger," Randy said. He looked at Sarah, "Hey cutie."

Sarah wrinkled up her nose and giggled.

Jimmy pulled off his ball cap and climbed up onto the stool next to his sister's, "Hey Mister Randy."

"Hey sport...What can I get y'all."

Roger said, "We are here after some of your prize winning milkshakes."

"*Milkshakes...*" Randy looked at the children and then shook his head somberly, "I guess you didn't hear...All the mothers in town got together with the aldermen and passed a law that I am not allowed to serve milkshakes to anyone under eighteen between the hours of four and seven PM."

Roger sighed loudly, "Oh well. I hadn't heard. But, I can't say as I'm really surprised...mothers and aldermen can be awful meddlesome at times." He leaned against the counter and looked down at the children, "I guess y'all will just have to watch me eat mine then."

Roger reached into his back pocket and pulled out his wallet, "I have my ID right here that shows I'm over eighteen." He looked back to the children, "I wish I hadn't gotten y'all's hopes up like I did, but," he sighed dramatically, "...Such is life."

"It's a real shame, too," Randy Douglas offered, "I've been complimented on my milkshakes three times today." He flashed a big smile at Roger, "I reckon I'm just in my zone."

"Well, since you're in such rare form, and I'm suddenly so powerful hungry," Roger said, "How 'bout you just whip me up *two* of them masterpieces...*No*–" He held his hand up to stop Randy and then massaged his chin, "Make that three —One banana," he glanced at Sarah, "–One strawberry... *and,*" He turned his face towards the ceiling and searched the old tin tiles for clues as to the flavor of the third. Jimmy cleared his throat and drummed his fingers on the counter. "Hmmm," Roger drawled, "What other flavor do I want...*I wonder...*"

Jimmy cleared his throat again.

"I've got some sardines," Randy suggested.

"Sardines," Roger said, "I hadn't thought of that...Maybe that would be–"

Jimmy cleared his throat once more and drummed a bit louder.

"*I know,*" said Randy, "I could drop some weenies into the blender and stir that in."

"Ooh, a weenie shake." Roger paused again and then said, "Will you fry or boil them first?"

"Whichever way you would prefer...I think a boiled weenie would blend up a bit smoother, though," Randy looked over at Jimmy, who was, by this time, drumming the knuckles of both hands on the counter and getting very antsy.

Roger nodded, "You're probbly right Randy," he said, "I wouldn't have even thought about that...I reckon that's why you're the Shake Master."

"It's my life."

"You think maybe you could throw a couple spoonfuls of relish in there?"

"Ooh, give it some texture...nice....I could even put a pickle chip on top with the cherry."

Jimmy covered his face and groaned loudly. "*Chocolate,*" he blurted, "*Chocolate*...won't you just get a chocolate?"

"Please Jimmy," Roger said, "Don't interrupt. Mister Randy and I are having a very important discussion here." He turned back to Randy, "What were you saying?"

"I think I said maybe you'd like a chocolate one," he looked at Jimmy out of the corner of his eye, "With double whipped cream and two cherries...Ain't that right?"

Jimmy nodded, "*Yes sir*...that is *exactly* what he'd like."

Randy turned back to Roger and Roger gave him a quick nod. "Be sure and put plenty of whipped cream on all of 'em," he said, "I really like whipped cream."

"Gotcha."

Roger took a seat next to Sarah as Randy went over a started making up their shakes. "So how was your day, Little Miss," he asked.

"Good."

"Just good?"

Sarah nodded.

"How 'bout you young Master McKenzie? How was your day?"

"It was good."

"Just good?"

Jimmy nodded.

"Didn't *anything* exciting happen to either one of you?"

Sarah looked at Jimmy and then shook her head at Roger. Jimmy shrugged, "Owen Cornel got his tooth knocked out."

"By what?"

"Davy Biggs."

Roger chuckled, "What were they fighting about?"

"They weren't fightin'."

"They weren't?"

"Nossir...They're best friends."

"Then why'd he knock his tooth out?"

"'Cause Owen bet him he couldn't."

"What did Davy get for doing it?"

"Owen said he could have whatever the tooth fairy brings him for his tooth."

Roger chuckled again.

"That's just silly," Sarah said, "Everybody knows that the tooth fairy won't bring you any money if your tooth gets knocked out 'cause you're fighting...Mama said so."

"I don't know as I've ever heard that," Roger said.

"She just said that 'cause she doesn't want me fighting," Jimmy said.

"Well, I think that most likely she was telling the truth," Roger said.

"Me too," said Sarah, "Mama knows about things like that."

Roger said, "You know about the tooth fairy don't you Jimmy?"

Jimmy looked sideways at Roger, wondering how to safely answer the question.

"Here's your first two, Roger," Randy said, sitting two big milkshakes on the counter. "This one's your strawberry," he explained, sticking a straw down into the one on his left, "And," he slid a straw down into the other, "...this one's the banana." Roger looked at them and marveled that whipped cream could be made to stand in a twist so high. He picked up the banana milkshake, took the straw in his mouth, and tried unsuccessfully to draw some up through it. He tried again and then gave up and just pulled the straw out and sucked some from the bottom. He looked at the children, "I think my head would cave in before I could draw up a mouthful of this thing."

Sarah reached up and scooped a fingerful of whipped cream from the strawberry shake and then quickly licked her finger clean, "Mmmm."

"I didn't see that," Roger said. Sarah grinned at him and then grabbed the cherry off the top and popped it into her mouth.

"I didn't see that either," Roger said. He stuck his straw back down into his cup and then leaned over and grabbed a couple spoons from the tray on the back side of the counter. He handed one to Sarah and then slid one down the counter to Jimmy. "Don't let me forget to bring these back," he told them.

Randy came back over and placed Jimmy's shake on the counter in front of him. "You reckon you can carry this out for Roger," he said, "I don't think he'll be able to carry all three without spilling one."

Jimmy glanced over at Roger and then grinned at Randy. "I think I probbly can," he said, wrapping his hands around the cup.

Roger laid a ten on the counter, "Thanks Randy," he said, "I'll try to remember to bring the spoons back this time."

"Good deal," Randy replied, and then to the children, "...Y'all tell your mama I said hey."

"We will," Jimmy said. He slid off his stool and headed towards the door, happily toting *Roger's* chocolate shake. Roger lifted Sarah down and handed her milkshake to her.

"Come back and see us," Randy said.

Sarah smiled up at him with whipped cream on the end of her nose, "Bye Mister Randy."

"Bye Sweet Pea."

Sarah gave him one last smile and then followed her brother out. Roger toasted Randy with his milkshake and then sucked down a mouthful of whipped cream on his way out the door. They all climbed back into Roger's truck and sat silently for a moment spooning heaps of milkshake into their mouths. After a minute Roger said, "Do either one of y'all have any place you'd like to go?"

"How 'bout Herman's," Jimmy suggested.

"You sure do love you some Herman's don't you, Jimmy."

Jimmy slurped down some chocolate shake and nodded firmly. "I shore do."

"Well, sorry Bud," Roger said, "They're closed until the end of March."

"Who wants donuts anyway," said Sarah, "We got milkshakes."

Roger said, "You want to ride over to the beach anyway? Maybe we could come up with something else to do on the way."

"Nah," Jimmy said, shaking his head. "If we can't get donuts, there ain't no sense in riding over...it'd be dark by the time we got over and the water's too cold to go wading."

"How about we just ride down the landing then," Roger said.

Jimmy nodded his approval.

Roger nudged Sarah gently with his elbow, "How 'bout you, kid? You want to ride down the landing?"

Sarah scooped another big spoonful of her milkshake and smiled at Roger as she nodded and swallowed it down.

"Alright," Roger said. He cranked the truck, backed it out, and then headed it slowly down towards the waterfront. He glanced over at the children as he drove along and remembered the first time he had taken Maggie on a date alone.

The two of them had met him at the door when Roger had come by and picked Maggie up at her mother's house. Sarah's nose was pinked by the sun and covered with summer freckles; Jimmy was wearing his father's old Orioles ball cap and had a nice set of tater rows running across his neck.

"Where ya takin' my Mama Mister Roger," Sarah said as she opened the front door and led him inside, "...It better be someplace with food, 'cause she's hungry."

"Is that right?"

"Yeah," Jimmy said, "I heard her telling Grandmama that she couldn't eat a thing all day." He rubbed at his neck and smeared the dirt with the back of his hand. "I shore hope she don't get sick on you or anything."

Roger chuckled, "I do too." He looked up as Maggie came into the room, working at the back of one of her earrings. "Y'all let me know when Roger gets here," she was saying, and then, as she realized he was standing there, "—Oh, hey," she said, letting out a little airy breath. She smiled, and her voice sounded happily surprised, "I didn't hear you come in."

Roger stood at an angle to her, framed in the open doorway, smiling back without speaking. He studied her every move as Maggie finished with her earring and then her eyes sparkled as she slid her hand around the back of her neck and slowly pulled her fingers through her hair. Roger felt a warm rush run through him that made his knees weak. He took a long, slow breath, trying to follow the course of his own thoughts as the choruses of a hundred love songs ran through his mind. He wanted to run across the room and scoop her up in his arms and run away with her...he wanted to take her into his arms and run...run and hide away with her someplace where he could hold her close and feel her breathe, hold her close and never let her go. His chest rose and fell as he looked deeply into her eyes, willing for her to feel the strength of his growing love.

Maggie caught the look in Roger's eyes and her heart fluttered. She adjusted the wrap around her tan shoulders and then laid a hand softly at the hollow of her neck and bit her bottom lip. They took half a step towards each other and stopped. Maggie glanced at her children and then looked back at Roger and blew out a measured, calming breath.

"Well," she said breathlessly, grabbing her clutch from the table as she stepped up in front of Roger, "I guess I'm ready if you are," she said.

Roger caught a wisp of her perfume and breathed in a little deeper. "I'm all yours," he said.

Maggie looked down at her children and smiled. She leaned down and kissed Sarah's cheek and then turned to Jimmy and laid a hand on his shoulder, "Y'all behave for your grandmother."

"We will," the children replied.

She looked at Sarah, "Jimmy's in charge until she gets back."

Sarah looked crossly at her brother.

"He'll be nice," said Maggie.

"He's too bossy."

"He won't be tonight," Maggie assured her. She turned to Jimmy and winked, "...Will you?"

Jimmy gave his head a shake, "No ma'am." Maggie leaned down and whispered "Thank you," into his ear and then kissed his cheek.

"Y'all be sweet," Roger said. He pushed the screen door open and held it for Maggie. "Bye," she said, and then brushed past him as she went out. Roger eased the door closed and followed her out, *Wow*, he thought as he watched her glide down the stairs, the silky hem of her dress swaying just above her knees.

"You look incredible," he told her, as he walked behind her down the walkway towards his truck.

Maggie glanced back his way over her shoulder and grinned, "*Thanks for noticing.*"

Roger stepped past her as she reached his freshly washed pickup, opened the door, and waited for her to climb in.

Maggie stopped in front of him at the foot of the walk and rested a hand on his chest as she leaned up and brushed a kiss lightly against his cheek. She lingered there close to him for the briefest moment, her presence electrifying, and then slid in onto the seat. She held her eyes on Roger's as she pulled her legs in and he closed the door behind her. "You look pretty nice yourself," she told him.

Roger grinned. "It must be my new shirt," he said, running his hand up and down the front of his shirt. He moved his face around in a little circle and batted his eyes at her, "The girl at the store said it brought out the blue in my eyes..."

"As if you needed anything to do that," Maggie replied. She pulled lightly at her dress, smoothing its pale yellow folds across her legs as Roger walked around the front of the shining red pickup and climbed in. "I've got reservations at the Brisa Marina," he told her, "I hope the weatherman got his forecast wrong."

"I don't care," Maggie said. She smiled sweetly at him as he cranked the engine, "...I love the rain."

"You do?"

Maggie smiled, "...There's just something about the rain on a night like tonight..."

"I'll have to remember that."

⤳

Roger drove the children down to the landing and parked his truck out by the little sand beach next to his Uncle Wesley's fish house, backing it in so that the tailgate sat looking out over the river. Opening his door, he looked over at the children, "How 'bout we get out here and sit on the tailgate for a while," he said, "We can watch the ducks 'til it gets dark and maybe figure out something for us to do."

Roger helped Sarah out and then went around and lifted her up onto the tailgate and then sat himself down next to her. Jimmy got out, gathered up a handful of clamshells, and then started slinging them out into the water one by one. Roger stared down at the clean, sandy little beach and marveled at the whiteness of it. It had always struck him how different this one spot seemed from all the other little sandy stretches along the river. The sand was always so clean and white and fine, almost like the powdery stuff he had walked in on the beaches off Corkscrew Key down in the Gulf.

"Bet'cha can't skim one to the marker light," Sarah challenged.

Jimmy had just drawn his arm back to sling another shell out. He stopped and looked back over his shoulder at his sister, "Can't nobody skim one that far, silly."

"Mister Roger could."

Jimmy made a face at his sister and then whipped his arm around, skipping the shell out across the surface of the river...one, two, three skips and then it was gone. He stepped over and propped against the edge of the tailgate next to Roger and took a sip of his milkshake as he stared out at the tall, greasy-green piling standing some fifty yards out into the river in front of them. "You reckon you could skim one that far," he said.

Roger eyed the marker and then took a long pull of his milkshake. "I don't know, Jimmy," he said, "That's' a pretty far piece out there for a skim." He cocked his head to the side and studied it a bit longer, "It'd probbly be a good eight or maybe even ten skips out there." He took another sip of his shake. "Nah," he said, giving his head a little shake, "Not a shell...you give me a good skipping rock and I think I could, but not a shell."

Sarah said, "How come?"

"A shell doesn't have enough heft to it," Roger said, "It won't carry that far."

"What's that mean?"

"It needs some weight."

"Oh."

Roger smiled at her and then turned his cup up and took a big swallow. The sun was setting off in the west and the hazy glow of Ormond was starting to show in the gathering darkness just over the horizon in back of the woods past the far bank of the Cane. Pulling the cup down to his lap, he looked back out at the marker and its green light began to glow. He stared closely at it as it slowly sharpened to its full brightness.

A cooling breeze eased up the river from the east and Roger drifted back again to that night with Maggie.

She had insisted on leaving the windows down as Roger drove her over onto the island to their reservation at *La Brisa Marina*. "Who cares about my hair," she said, "It's just too nice a night for air conditioning."

They could hear the music from the Cuban band that was playing out on the veranda as Roger pulled off the road and into the parking lot. "*Oh*," Maggie said, "*They've got a band tonight.*"

Roger parked out at the edge of the already full parking lot and climbed out. Maggie slid over and got out on his side. Roger closed the door and stuck his elbow out for her. "Don't you just love that sound," Maggie said, taking Roger's arm, "Can't you feel the music?"

Roger cocked his head and listened as a trumpeter began blaring out a solo, "He can shore work that horn."

"You'll dance with me won't you?"

"I don't know if I know how to dance to that, Maggie."

"I'll show you."

Roger glanced down at her feet, "Those toes look awful pretty," he said, walking her up the front steps, "I'd hate to scuff up that fresh nail polish."

Maggie rolled her eyes at Roger as they went in the front door. A dark little man with a closely trimmed mustache in a white Guayabera met them as they came in and presented himself with a crisp smile, "I am Ramon'," he said, with a roll of his tongue, "Bienvenidos, thees ees my restaurant." He took Maggie's hand and gave it a kiss. "Sir," he said to Roger, "Eef, while you are here, you or the lovely lady are in need of anytheeng," he gave a quick bow of his head, "I am at your service. Please," he continued, handing them off to the waiting hostess, "Enjoy your evening."

"Thank you," Roger said and then turned to the smiling hostess, "We have a reservation for two," he told her, "... Lowell." The hostess checked her book and said, "Yes, we have a table for you out on the veranda...Right this way, please." She picked up two menus and escorted them out back to the veranda that overlooked the waterway and seated them at a table that looked down on the dance floor. Maggie caught Roger's eyes and motioned towards the dance floor as they took their seats. "After we order," she said, "You and me Rico."

Roger remembered their waitress bringing them some really tall glasses of ice water floated full of lime slices and them ordering some spicy grilled snapper and a Caribbean spiny lobster *something* with jerk seasoning that she recommended, and then, before he had taken the first sip of his water, or dipped the first brown sugar crusted deep fried sweet potato wedge into the bowl of crushed-red-pepper-spiced-honey, Maggie grabbed him by the wrist and said, "I didn't get all dressed up for nothing."

She stood up and tossed her wrap across the back of her seat. "It's time," she said, pulling him to his feet, "Let's see what you can do *Senor Suavemente*."

"I can shore do *something* out there," Roger said as he allowed Maggie to lead him down the steps and out onto the dance floor, "...But smooth, I can assure you it won't be." They weaved their way through several couples and took a place out in front of the band and Roger took her hands in his and they moved easily to the music.

"I didn't know you could rumba," Maggie said.

"*I can?*"

Maggie leaned her forehead over onto his chest for a second and then looked up at him laughing.

"I thought rumba was all...You know," Roger lifted their hands up a little higher and swung his hips around shuffling his feet. "...That kind of stuff."

Maggie stared up at him, her eyes wide and her smile trembling on the edge of laughter.

"*What*," Roger swiveled his hips jerkily, "...Ain't that how you do it?"

Maggie shook her head at him and rolled her eyes.

"*Huh?*"

Maggie took one of Roger's hands and put it on her hip and then grabbed his shoulder, "Do this," she said, stepping back to the rhythm. Roger fell into step, mirroring Maggie. "*Nice*," she said. She turned loose of his shoulder and grabbed the hem of her dress as she swept around beside him. Giving a shake to the handful of dress she was holding, she spun herself back into place in front of him and winked.

"Well, ain't you just a sassy thing," Roger said, "Where did you learn that?"

"We had a Puerto Rican couple next door to us in Pensacola," Maggie said, "They were the sweetest people. The husband was a mechanic on base and Miss Areta, *the wife*, was like a mother to all of us young military wives in the neighborhood."

"Do it again."

Maggie did it again.

Roger shook his head. He feigned touching a fingertip to his tongue and then touched Maggie's shoulder and made a sizzling sound.

Maggie shook her head, "That ain't no thing. You should have seen Miss Areta...Sixty two and could dance the paint off the walls."

"*Oh yeah?*"

"Oh yeah...And so beautiful; she had such dark, sultry eyes, and this long, silky, raven-black hair, nearly to her waist. That woman would turn heads everywhere she went...She used to tell us, 'It doesn't matter what you've had to do all day, or what *problemas* you've had to deal with, there's no good reason not to *look* your best and to *be* your best when your Love comes home...' " Maggie said, rolling the *L* on her tongue. She chuckled to herself, "It was always '*Your Love*,' " she said, "Never '*your husband*'...She'd say, 'A lady needs to make sure *her Love* always *wants* to come home to her...And *if* she does...He always will.' "

"Her husband must have been one happy man."

Maggie grinned, "I never saw him without a smile on his face."

ॐ

Roger eyed the bottom of his cup as he slurped down the endings of his milkshake. *Well*, he thought, *I reckon you need to get on with it.* He set the cup down on the tailgate and stood himself up, "Jimmy," he said, "Would you mind sitting down with Sarah for a minute...I'd like to talk to y'all about something."

Jimmy looked quizzically at Roger for a moment and then sat down, "We're not in trouble are we?"

Roger shook his head, "No, I just have something I want to ask you two, that's all."

Jimmy looked relieved. He glanced over at his sister and then back to Roger, "Alright."

Roger looked back and forth at the two faces before him for a long moment and then took a deep breath. "*Wow*," he said quietly, "This is gonna be tougher than I thought." He took a step back and stuck his hands down in his back pockets and stared at the ground.

The children watched him for a moment and then looked at each other in puzzlement.

Roger jerked his head back up and said, "I want you both to know that I am very deeply–" he stopped himself and stared at the two of them again. After a second or two, he gave his head a little shake and pulled his hands out from his pockets and clasped them together in front of him. *I didn't think this was gonna be this hard,* he thought, *it's worse than talking to Mister Harvey.* "Okay," he said, pumping his hands out in front of him. "You know how I f —" Roger stopped again and rubbed roughly at his chin.

Wringing his hands behind his back, Roger paced in front of them; trying to remember what he had worked out in his mind to say. Sarah and Jimmy sat silently, sipping up the last of their milkshakes as they followed his progress back and forth.

Roger stopped his pacing and bent over in front of them with his hands propped on his knees and look at them eye to eye. He took a deep breath and started over again, "*Alright*...I love your mother." Pausing, he switched his gaze from Sarah to Jimmy and then went on, "I love her very much."

Jimmy tipped his cup back and loudly slurped the last drops of his milkshake down.

"You understand that, right?"

Sarah gazed up at him unblinkingly and smiled. Jimmy leaned over and picked at a sandspur that was stuck in his shoelace.

"*Is that a yes?*"

Sarah nodded.

"*Jimmy?*"

Jimmy glanced up at Roger, "Mm hmm," he grunted.

Roger blew out a breath. "Good," he said, under his breath, "We're getting somewhere..." He straightened back up, "Now, any decision, or decisions, your mother makes will affect *you* too. So, I have something to tell you that is very important...But you have to promise not to tell anyone until after I talk to your mama."

Sarah said, "Can *we* tell Mama?"

Roger shook his head, "No not yet. Not until after I've talked with her myself."

"Well when is that gonna be?" Jimmy asked.

"Soon."

"How soon?" asked Sarah.

"Soon."

"Tonight?"

"No, not tonight."

Jimmy said, "Tomorrow?"

"Probbly not tomorrow."

"When?"

"I'm not sure," Roger said, "But soon."

Jimmy swung his legs in and out, clapping his feet together. He leaned over and watched his feet for a second and then said, "What is it you're gonna talk to her about?"

Roger said, "I want to ask her if she'll be my wife."

Jimmy looked up at Roger from under the bill of his ball cap and studied Roger's face.

"What do y'all think about that," Roger asked.

Jimmy sat up straight and crossed his arms, "Would that make you our daddy?"

"Yes," Roger replied, "Sort of."

Jimmy's eyes drew down to slits, "Why only sort of?"

"Well, *if* she says yes, then I'll be what's called your *step-father.*"

"Would I have to call you step-Daddy instead of Mister Roger," asked Sarah.

"Whichever one you want," Roger said, "You can call me Daddy if you'd like, or you can keep calling me Roger...it's up to you."

"Can I call you Daddy-Roger?"

"You can if you want."

"I like that."

"I do too," Roger smiled. He turned to Jimmy, "What do *you* think Chief?"

Jimmy stared down at the sandy ground, "It'll be alright," he replied, "...I reckon."

Roger sat down and put his arm around Jimmy's shoulders, "I don't want you to think that I'm trying to take your daddy's place," he said, "I'd never try to do that."

Jimmy held his head down with his hands lying in his lap, picking at his fingernails. Roger gave his shoulder a little squeeze, "You understand what I mean?"

Jimmy's head dipped slightly, and he gave Roger a barely noticeable nod. Roger watched him, unsure of how to proceed. Sarah wiggled in her seat and then leaned on Roger and grabbed the shoulder of his shirt and pulled herself up and stood beside him on the tailgate. Roger held his arm out, holding the back of it across the front of her waist, "What's your mama say about you standing up there?"

Sarah twirled up Roger's arm and sat down across the back of his shoulders, facing towards the cab of the truck and watched a lone herring gull fly closely over their heads. "Does that mean you'll come to all my ballet shows?" she asked, ignoring his question, "...When you're my new daddy."

"I'll go to as many as I can."

Spinning back around, Sarah ran her hands through Roger's hair and then twirled around in the bed of the pickup, holding her hands up high as she danced. Roger leaned down a little and tried to get a peek at Jimmy's face under the bill of his cap. He gave Jimmy's shoulder a little shake, "What'cha say big man?"

Jimmy slid out from under Roger's arm and walked towards the shore, dragging his feet across the sand as he went.

Following Jimmy's steps, Roger wondered if he had made a mistake in bringing it all up to them like he had. He hopped off the back of the truck and winked at Sarah as he closed the tailgate and then walked out to where Jimmy was standing at the edge of the water.

The toes of Jimmy's shoes made moist depressions in the dark sand as he followed a school of minnows flowing back and forth in silver flashes out in front of him. Roger walked up and stood behind him. "Jimmy," he said, as softly as he could, "You can say whatever's on your mind."

Jimmy picked up a shell and slung it out, side-armed into the river. It skipped twice and then disappeared in the dark water. Roger heard a low chuckling sound and looked over as three spotless, white ducks came out from below the dock and threaded around and through the painters of a handful of moored skiffs, cruising effortlessly towards them, "They must be expecting some bread crumbs," he told Jimmy.

Jimmy looked over toward the ducks and watched their progress for a long moment, their white bodies almost glowing in the inky black evening water.

"I'll never lie to you Jimmy," Roger said, "I'll never try to be something I'm not...I love your mother more than anything...but...if you say no..."

Jimmy spun around and dove into Roger, wrapping his arms around Roger's waist as he buried his face into Roger's stomach. Squeezing tightly to Roger, he began to cry. Roger stared down at Jimmy, and slowly wrapped his arms around the boy's shoulders, "I'm sorry Jimmy," he whispered, "I...I didn't mean to upset you like this."

Jimmy squeezed Roger's waist tighter, pressing his face against Roger's body.

Roger shook his head. *Oh no*, he thought, *How could Harvey have been so wrong...How could I have been so wrong*? He took a long deep breath and shook his head again as he looked down at Jimmy, "I'm sorry buddy, please don't cry...Just forget it," he said, "I understand...I don't have to do this...It's alright..." He hugged Jimmy tighter and patted the back of his head, "We'll just leave it alone, okay? We'll leave it like it is."

"No," Jimmy said, his face still pressed against Roger's body. He shook his head and looked up into Roger's face, "I'd never say no," he said, "...I'd never tell you no...I wouldn't...Won't you please just be our Daddy."

Roger backed out the Pritt's driveway and headed his pickup towards home. "Wow," he said quietly, thinking about Jimmy, and wondering if he was truly ready to be a father to Maggie's children. "You got your first real taste of what it's like tonight didn't you boy?" he said to himself, "It ain't all fishing off the dock and baseball games...And you thought *girls* were the tough ones to figure out." Pulling out onto Plantation, he whipped into the library parking lot and then backed quickly back out and drove toward Buddy's.

Roger's headlights flashed brightly across the front of the barn as he turned up into Buddy's driveway. He cut the lights before they shined onto the front of the house as he pulled up and parked beside Hillary's station wagon. Glancing back over towards the barn, as he shut his truck off, Roger noticed the faint light glowing around the outline of the barn doors, "What *splendid* mysteries yon humble storehouse doth now hold," he chuckled.

Roger climbed out, quietly closed his door, and then went up onto the porch and pulled open the screen door and rapped lightly on the front door with the back of his hand. The porchlight came on, and then Hillary opened the door and smiled out at him, "Hey Roger," she said sweetly, letting the door swing open.

"Hey Hill," Roger said, "I'm not interrupting anything am I?"

Hillary shook her head, "No, not at all," she said, "Buddy's out in the barn...What brings you down to the far end of the woods this fine evening?"

"Nothing much...I've just got a couple questions about some things that I felt like W R V could shed some light on for me."

Hillary stared at Roger for a long moment and then asked, "Are you alright, Roger?"

Roger's forehead creased, "Yeah," he said, "Why?"

"You just look like you've got a lot on your mind."

Roger tilted his head a little and shrugged.

"Anything I might could help you with?"

No doubt you probbly could, Roger thought. He paused a second and then gave his head a shake, "Naw," he said, "It's guy stuff."

Hillary smiled at him, "*You sure?* You know I love giving out opinions."

"Naw, that's alright," Roger smiled, "I appreciate it Hill...I reckon I'll just go on out and see Buddy."

"*Alright*...Suit yourself...But if you change your mind and decide you need a woman's perspective, you know where to find me."

Roger let the door close and gave Hillary a little wave through the screen. "See you Hill."

"Bye Roger," Hillary said. "Oh hey...when you're done with my husband could you tell him that he's welcome back inside any time he gets ready."

"Will do."

"Thanks."

Hillary closed the door behind him as Roger turned and walked down off the porch. He slid his hands down into his pockets and took a deep breath, his mind drifting back to Jimmy and Sarah as he walked down the walkway past his truck. *I hope I did the right thing*, he thought...*It seemed right to talk to them first...They needed to know didn't they? If this goes, it's gonna be a big change for them...*He dropped his head down and followed his feet out across the yard. Stopping about halfway to the barn, he turned his face to the rising moon, "It was a lot to drop on children, Roger," he said, gritting his teeth, "It's no wonder Jimmy went like he did." He shook his head, "What a bonehead you are...He's only eleven years old."

Roger stood there, staring at the moon for the better part of a minute and then shook his head again and went on to the barn. As he reached the door, he could hear a familiar, rhythmic, whipping and tapping sound inside. He reached out and gripped the door handle, "If Coach McLeod could see you now, boy," he chuckled. He cracked the door open and peeked in and saw Buddy in the middle of the barn, just in front of the tarp-covered Karmann-Ghia, skipping a rope. Buddy's brow was furrowed deeply and sweat was pouring down his red-cheeked face. He had a dark sweat soaked triangle that started up at his shoulders covering most of the front of his shirt.

Buddy stopped and a look of surprise mingled with despair came into his eyes as he quickly snatched the rope around and hid it behind his back when he saw the door opening. Roger saw him heave a sigh of relief when he realized who it was coming in.

"Come in and close the door, man," Buddy said quickly, and motioned Roger in. He hurried Roger with a wave and then started back in with the jump rope.

Roger came in and closed the door, "What'cha say there, *El Tigre*."

Buddy breathed in through his nose, blew out threw his mouth, and shook his head at Roger. "Thirty more reps," he hissed.

Roger held up an apologetic hand and walked around past Buddy. He noticed the pull-up bar Buddy had placed in the rafters near the side wall and a rope hanging from the center beam out behind the car. He walked over and did two pull-ups and then leaned back against the wall next to a towel Buddy had hanging on a hook and waited for Buddy to finish his rope work.

Buddy glanced over Roger's way and sped up his jumping, "Watch this," he said between breaths. He crossed and un-crossed his arms and then sped up the rope, spinning it over himself twice per jump for three jumps, then turned loose of the rope, dropped to the floor and did five quick push-ups, clapping his hands together between each one.

Roger clapped quietly, "Wow," he said, as Buddy hopped back up to his feet, "I'm impressed."

"Hold on," Buddy said as he stepped over in front of Roger, "Watch this." He squatted down, and clenched his jaw as he lifted one foot and straightened his leg out in front of him, and then pushed himself back up to standing on the other. He held up a finger, instructing Roger to wait, and then squatted back down on the same leg, switched feet and then stood back up.

Puffing his cheeks, Buddy blew out forcefully; his face now completely flushed a deep red, "Now you may applaud."

Roger clapped again, slowly and loudly, "You are an animal," he said, "How many of those can you do?"

"Eight each leg is the most I've been able to do so far," Buddy said, "I start getting wobbly on the last ones though." He grabbed his shirt and wiped his face on the hem. Roger noticed how much flatter Buddy's stomach was looking, "You're looking right trim," he told him.

Buddy lifted his shirt a little and looked down at his stomach and then grinned at Roger, "You think so?"

"Yeah," Roger said. He cocked his head and squinted and then looked up at Buddy's face, "And darker...You been in somebody's tanning bed?"

Buddy put his shirt back down and then pulled up a sleeve. "Check it out," he said, "No farmer tan."

"Seriously, have you been laying in the tanning bed?"

Buddy shook his head, "Naw, man...You know better than that. There ain't no way I could keep *that* a secret. I've been taking off my shirt on the tractor."

"This from the guy who wears his shirt when he goes swimming."

Buddy shrugged, "Wha'dya know...I figured I better take advantage of the warm weather while it lasts."

"Are you coming out here every night now?"

"Just about."

Roger pointed over Buddy's shoulder, "What's with the rope?"

"I can do that, up and down, five times, just arms, no stopping."

"Wow, that's great."

Buddy smiled, "It is ain't it." He pulled off his shirt and hung it up over his pull-up bar and then grabbed his towel and started drying himself off. Roger couldn't remember the last time he had known Buddy to pull off his shirt in front of *anyone*, himself included.

"What brings you out to the far end of the woods this fine evening," Buddy asked him.

Roger chuckled. *I can't wait until Maggie and me do that*, he thought. "I went and talked with Mister Harvey today."

"How'd that go?"

"Great."

"I told you it would," Buddy said. He spread his towel out on the floor and lay down on his back. Planting his feet up close to his butt, he lifted his pelvis up into the air, "What did he say?"

Roger stared down at him, "What are you doing?"

"My bridge-pose...It rejuvenates tired legs."

"It does?"

"Uh huh...it's good for sinusitis, too."

Buddy blew his breath out slowly as he let himself back down and then lifted his legs up and touched his toes to the floor back over his head.

"Is that good for your sinuses too?"

"This one helps me to sleep."

"Is that because you can't get any blood to your brain?"

Roger heard a muffled chuckle and then Buddy's legs came slowly back up and he rested them flat down on the floor. He pointed at Roger, "Good one." He turned smoothly over onto his stomach and then spread his hands and feet out and pushed his butt up into the air.

"That one got a name?"

"Downward dog."

"You're not gonna lift your leg at me are you?"

Buddy burst out laughing and dropped down onto his knees, "You ort to try some of this, Roger," he said, "It's really relaxing." He rolled his head down between his arms and held his chin against his chest.

"I'm sure it is."

Buddy slowly lifted his head back and held his chin as high as he could, "Let me show you a few poses."

"No thanks...I just came to talk."

"What about?"

"Jimmy."

"What about him?"

"I told him and Sarah that I was going to ask Maggie to marry me."

Buddy let himself back down and sat spread eagled on the towel. Pushing his legs out wide, he sat up very straight and said, "What did they say?"

"Well, Sarah asked if I'd go to her dance recitals and Jimmy started crying."

"Really?"

"Yeah," Roger said, "That's what I wanted to talk to you about."

"Did he say anything or just cry?"

Roger squatted down and sat with his back against the wall in front of Buddy, "He didn't say anything at first. And I was thinking that maybe he wasn't liking the idea too well and I started to tell him that if he didn't want me to then I wouldn't ask her and then, all the sudden, he just grabs me around the waist and mashes his face into my stomach crying." Roger pulled his legs up in front of him and rested his arms on his knees. He shook his head, "I feel like I really blew it, man. I mean, what was I thinking, dropping a bomb on them like that...they're just kids."

Buddy stood up with his towel in his hands and looked down at Roger, "Did you ask him why he was crying?"

"No. I was so shocked that he was crying I didn't know what to say...I told him to forget it and he said 'No, please be our daddy'."

Buddy creased his brow, "*Hunh.*" He hung his towel back up, picked up a dry shirt he had sitting on his workbench, and slipped it on as he walked back over and sat down against the wall next to Roger.

"What do you make of it," Roger asked.

"Well," Buddy said, "As I think about it, I'd have to say that I'm not really surprised he'd react that way."

"No?"

Buddy shook his head. "No...When James died, Jimmy had just turned ten. He wasn't old enough to see that his father was a regular human being with flaws just like everybody else...he was still Neil Armstrong, JEB Stuart, and Robin Hood all wrapped up in one. Jimmy still remembers him as his super-dad...He misses him. *But...* and you might not realize this, because Jimmy's not one to wear his feelings on his sleeve...He idolizes you."

"What makes you think *that*?"

"Hill's told me some of the things that Maggie's told her he's said about you...He pretty much believes you're the best thing to come along since Spiderman."

"That's nice to hear," Roger said, "...So explain to me how A plus B adds up to little boy crying on the riverbank?"

"Remember, Roger," Buddy said, he smiled reassuringly at Roger, "...Like you said, he *is* just a kid...Us adults aren't always the best at handling our emotions...Look at us... we've had thirty some years to learn how to deal with stuff. Think of the dumb things we still say and do. He's just starting to learn how to deal with life and he's looking at you very possibly very soon taking the place of his dead father who he still loves and admires very much and that makes him happy because he has all these strong feelings for you and at the same time he's sad because his father's gone and that confuses him because he's torn between wanting you *for* a father and wanting to be loyal to James." Buddy spread his hands out in front of him, "See what I mean?"

Roger stared down at the floor, chewing on the inside of his lip as he mulled Buddy's words over. "I reckon that makes sense," he said after a minute of silent thought. He looked at Buddy, "Do you think me telling them first was the wrong thing to do? I mean, if Maggie says no then I've just put this thought in their heads that I could be their daddy and it may not happen...Maybe I should've asked her first and then if she said yes then *we* could tell them together."

"I don't think you have to worry about her saying no."

"No?"

Buddy shook his head and turned British, "*Not bloody likely.*"

Roger chuckled.

"I think you did fine."

"Then why do I feel like I have completely screwed everything up?"

"Because you are a nervous, single man in his mid-thirties who is head over heels in love with the woman of his dreams and you have lived for so long with the feeling that she would never be yours that you are having a heap of trouble coming to grips with the fact that it *is* going to happen and that no one is going to come along and pull the rug out from under you."

Buddy put his arm across Roger's shoulders and tugged him over closer, "Just because everything's not your idea of perfect, doesn't mean it's not right...remember that."

Roger looked at Buddy out of the corner of his eye and then smiled, "How did you get so wise all the sudden?"

"I think it's all the blood that's been redirected from my stomach to my brain. It's amazing how clear your thoughts become when your brain is actually getting its fair share of oxygen."

"Just imagine what you could have accomplished had you stumbled upon that little fact years ago."

"Yeah, really, I could have been the next Toshitada Doi."

"*The next what?*"

"Not what...who."

"Huh?"

"The next *who*...Toshitada Doi invented the compact disc."

"Well," Roger said, "Good for her."

"Him."

Roger smiled at Buddy and then pushed himself back up to his feet, "So you think I should just let it go with Jimmy and go ahead as planned?"

Buddy raised one hand and dipped his head, "Iacta alea est," he said firmly.

Roger piqued his brows.

"Caesar on the Rubicon," Buddy stated.

"Ahh," Roger nodded, "Missus Wibb's tenth grade literature...I knew I knew that from somewhere...I forget, what does that mean?"

"The die is cast...In a nutshell, the decision's been made."

"No turning back now," said Roger, he paused and then looked closely at Buddy, "You flunked those recitations."

"I know," Buddy said. He hopped up and brushed off the back of his pants, "I didn't even try to learn." He shook his head, "*A*, I didn't see any reason for them, and *Two*, I really didn't think I could do it...I don't want to be that guy anymore." He motioned for Roger to follow him as he stepped over to his workbench, "Take a look at this." He grabbed the corner of a newspaper that was spread out on the bench and pulled it back. "This is my new motto," he said.

Roger stepped up next to him and looked down at a freshly painted plaque that read:

EXCELLENCE WAS NEVER ACHIEVED BY THOSE WHO CAN'T

"Where'd you get that?"

"I did it myself."

"Where'd you get the quotation?"

Buddy pointed at his temple, "Right here."

Roger looked back down at the plaque, and ran his fingers along the carved letters as he read the inscription aloud, "Excellence was never achieved by those who can't..." He turned back to Buddy, "That's really good."

"I've got it here," Buddy said, still pointing at his head, "And," he moved his finger down to his chest, "I'm getting it here...I made a promise to myself that I will never say can't again. Everything I've ever let beat me...I'm going to conquer. Everything I've ever been afraid to do...I'm going to master."

"Starting with Eugenia Wibb's tenth grade oratory?"

Buddy nodded, "Starting with Eugenia Wibb's tenth grade oratory."

"What's your plan for the plaque?"

"After I romance my wife's stockings off it's going up in the house."

"Are you sure you need to keep this all a secret from her? I think she's getting a little concerned."

"Why's that."

"Maggie's been asking questions about you."

"You haven't told her anything have you?"

Roger shook his head, "Of course not."

"Good." Buddy gave his head a little shake, "It's just a few more days 'til Christmas," he said, "She'll be alright 'til then."

"Alright," Roger said, "You're the doctor."

"You really think I ort to tell her?"

Roger raised his shoulders, "Not everything," he said, "Just maybe a bit about you're trying to change. I think she's worried you've got somebody on the sly."

Buddy burst out laughing, "That's hilarious. I thought you were serious."

"I am serious."

"Oh come on Roger...like anybody believes that would *or could* ever happen."

"Isn't that the effect you're after?"

"No."

"It isn't?"

Buddy's face went serious, "No," he said, "I would never do anything like that."

Roger said, "I know that and Maggie knows it and I think that deep down, if she really thinks about it, so does Hillary, but, the man she has known since four-year-old Sunday School has suddenly made a rather dramatic change which he hasn't even remotely discussed with her and it's got her a little worried." Roger paused and grabbed Buddy's shoulder, "How 'bout this Oh Wise One: Step back and advise Warren Vander the way you just advised Roger Lowell...Look at the big picture and tell me what you see."

"Hmm," Buddy grunted. He crossed his arms slowly and then looked up at the roof and rubbed his chin.

"I'm sure you can see my point."

"Actually, I can't," Buddy said, turning to Roger with a grin, "Your hair covers it too well."

"Har har har."

"Sorry, I just couldn't pass the opportunity."

"Yeah, yeah...but you do see my point don't you?"

"Yeah, I reckon I do," Buddy conceded, "But I've got to tell you; the thought never crossed my mind that she'd think something like that, I mean, ultimately, I'm really doing all this for her."

"I know," Roger said, "And I think that she'll appreciate it whether it's the big surprise you want it to be or not...I mean, she *is* gonna be surprised either way, don't worry, but if you go ahead and tell her a little bit of it...*Just a little* mind you," he added, measuring an inch of air out in front of his face between his thumb and index finger, "Like I said, not the big New Year's getaway with the dancing, or the car...just some of the 'New Buddy' stuff. I think it will go a long way toward you accomplishing what you're trying to accomplish without alienating Hillary in the process." He paused and smiled at Buddy, "A wise man once told me that just because everything's not my idea of perfect, it doesn't mean it's not right." Roger pointed at Buddy and winked, "Remember that."

"That is some very sage advice, Roger," Buddy said, "...I reckon you're probbly right. And if nothing else, it would sure be easier watching my food intake and getting in my exercising if she knew...To be honest with you, living in mortal fear that she's gonna walk in on me sneaking food back into the cabinet or come out here and catch me working out every time I'm out here is about to drive me nuts."

"I bet."

"I'll tell her tonight."

"Good," Roger said. "Well, I reckon I'm gonna hit the road...Thanks for the chat big man," he said, "I feel a lot better about things...a lot of things."

"Good," Buddy said. He smacked Roger on the shoulder, "Anytime...just leave a quarter with the receptionist on your way out."

Buddy followed Roger out and turned off the barn lights and then latched and locked the door.

"*Man*," Roger said, heading back across the yard toward his pickup, "I bet it's dropped six or eight degrees since I've been here."

Buddy looked up at the moon as he walked next to Roger, "That front they been calling for must finally be coming in," he said. He pointed towards a bank of dark, billowy clouds that was moving steadily across the sky. "Look at those clouds," he said, as the clouds moved across the moon's face, blocking the old man from their sight. He took a deep breath, "Smells like rain's coming."

They stopped next to the cab of Roger's truck, just inside the ring of light cast out into the night by Buddy's front porch light. "They been calling for it for three days now," Roger said. He opened up the truck, slid inside, and pulled the door closed behind him. He rolled his window down and propped up in the opening, "You got tomorrow's lesson scheduled for high noon?"

"Yeah...We're starting on the Tango."

"You gonna do the whole long stem rose in the teeth thing?"

"I'm considering it."

"You know what Buddy," Roger said, "I would pay good folding money to see the look on Hillary's face the first time you lead her out on the dance floor and start *shakin' your grove thing*."

"It's gonna be good, ain't it?" Buddy grinned. His eyes lit up, "*Hey*," he said, "I've got an idea. Why don't you take Maggie? I'm sure you can still get tickets."

Roger shook his head.

"Why not," Buddy said, "It'd be a lot of fun."

"Because...As much as I would love to take her out for something like that, it's *your* night...You need to be focused on Hillary, and Hillary needs to be focused on you. You're putting way too much work in for it to be otherwise."

"I reckon you're right again," Buddy said, "I hope she enjoys this as much as I want her to."

"She will."

Buddy propped his hands on his hips and looked down at the shadow his legs were making on the walk, "Imagine that," he said, shaking his head slowly, "My wife thinking I might be catting around." He looked back up at Roger and made a face, "*What was she thinking?*"

Roger said, "I told you back when you started this whole deal Buddy...She doesn't see you the way *you* see you."

"I reckon not," Buddy said, and then he gestured at himself, "...but to think anybody else would want some of this...*Come on.*"

"Buddy, I'm gonna tell you this," Roger said, "Not to change your mind about what you're doing, because I think it's great –it's awesome– but because I love you and you need to hear it. Hillary is a babe. She is good looking, intelligent, strong...talented. Any man would be proud to have her on his arm...And she chose *you*. Now, I know what you say...She chose you when we were kids before she became this person, but the thing is, she chose you then and she's still here now. There must be something about you that no one else has that this woman likes. Be sure you're still the man she fell in love with when this is all over."

Roger walked into his bedroom and fell across the bed on his face. He rolled over onto his back with a sigh and stared up at the ceiling. He put his hands to his face and then ran them slowly back through his hair and lay there for a long time, listening to the clock ticking on his nightstand.

After a few minutes, he pulled himself up and swung his legs around and sat on the side of his bed, listening to the rising wind blowing up through the bare branches of the trees outside as he stared out the window. Hearing the patter of rain as it began to fall onto his roof, he got himself up and went over and leaned on his elbows on the sill and looked up into the sky. The nearly full moon shone brightly down through a break in the clouds.

Leaning his forehead against the glass, Roger's breath made little half-moons on the window as a few raindrops plinked against the windowpane. He slid the window up, letting a strong draft of the moist night air rush into the room. He dropped his head down onto his forearm as the curtains began to sway, and felt it flowing coolly across the back off his neck as it worked its way in like a soothing dream.

Roger remembered sneaking his window open at night when he was just a little boy and scooting his pillow over onto the sill so he could lay there with his face as close to the screen as he could get it to breathe in the cool night air. He loved gathering his blankets in his fists, pulling them tightly around his shoulders and close up under his chin and staring out at the stars for what seemed like hours, just dreaming about the world and thinking that it would never change.

Life is always changing, he thought, *Always...*

The wind gusted and he felt a few cold drops of rain blow in onto his arms as he went back again to that first night alone with Maggie:

She had kept him out on the floor dancing until their food arrived.

"I think our food's here," Roger told her.

"*Already?*" Maggie said, glancing back over her shoulder towards their table. Their waitress sat her plate down and gave Maggie a little wave. Maggie twirled herself around and smiled at Roger. "...I feel like our dance just started."

"We can come back out after we eat."

"Are you sure you'll still dance with me with mojo on my breath?"

"I'll just ask the waitress for another bowl of that papaya salsa," Roger said, "A couple good chunks of papaya ort to take care of your mojo."

"Is papaya supposed to be one of those natural odor neutralizers?"

Roger shrugged. "I don't know," he said, "I just figured I could cram a couple pieces up each side of my nose."

Everything about that night had been so perfect, Roger still thought, better than he could have hoped for. He had been worried, because up until then, every time they had been together there had always been others around, either Buddy and Hillary, or the children, or any number of family members and friends, *somebody* to keep the conversation going or create some kind of diversion or point of interest. But they just fit, he realized, from the moment she walked into the room when he picked her up at her mother's, there hadn't been one random moment where they hadn't been completely in sync with one another. The whole night had just flowed.

That night, Roger thought, that night had clinched it for him. *That night* was the night that he had made up his mind that she was going to be *his* bride...that she was going to be Missus Roger Jackson Lowell and he was going to do everything in his power to make the rest of her life just as perfect as that night.

The music had been perfect, the setting had been perfect, their food had been perfect and the conversation the whole time they were together had been so smooth and flowingly-easy. *I want us to talk like this forever,* he had thought. There was never a lull, never an uncomfortable silence, never a forced line...it was just natural. He had never loved talking to someone like he loved talking to Maggie, but what had come back to him time and time again from that night, was the look on Maggie's face when it started to rain. *That look*, he thought, *I want to keep that look on her face for the rest of her life.*

At first, they could only hear it falling out on the water as it came across the sound and then, after a few minutes, the dance floor began to clear as the first sprinkles fell on the dancing couples.

Maggie stopped in the middle of taking a sip of her drink and looked at Roger when she felt the drops hit her arm.

"What?" Roger asked.

"We can't pass this up," she said.

"What?"

She set her glass down and picked her napkin up off her lap and set it on the table next to her plate, never taking her eyes from Roger's. "The rain," she said as she slid her chair back and stood up.

Roger watched her closely, studying her expression, "You don't want to leave now do you?"

Maggie shook her head slowly and gave Roger a tiny smile, "Not a chance." She slid her chair in and held her gaze on Roger as she turned and went down the steps. *Talk about sultry*, he thought.

The band had already started packing up but they all stopped and started pulling their instruments back out as they watched Maggie step slowly out onto the dance floor as the sprinkles became a shower.

She held her hands up high and crossed her wrists up over her head as she moved her hips to the beat and moved gracefully out to the center of the floor as the drummer started a beat and then a couple of the horn players elaborated on the rhythm. Roger glanced around and saw that every eye on the veranda was on Maggie. She stopped with a flourish out halfway across the floor and then the band stopped as she held a hand out in Roger's direction.

Roger felt a hand rest gently on his shoulder and looked up to see Ramon' standing there at his side. "What are you waiting for, Senor'," Ramon' asked.

Roger looked back out at Maggie.

"...The lady ees waiting," Ramon' stated.

Roger stood to his feet and walked out into the rain. He took Maggie's hand and the band started a slow, horn-filled ballad that moved like a rolling swell on the ocean. They swayed together as the band played out over the sound of the storm. Maggie held Roger's hand up over her head and twirled slowly around and then pressed herself in close to Roger and threw her head back, shaking her dripping hair out of her face. She wrapped her arms around Roger's neck and stared deeply into his eyes.

"*You have no idea,*" he said softly.

He wrapped his arm around her waist and led her over closer to the band and back and then turning her round with a quick step, he dipped her dramatically. When he pulled her up, he lifted her off her feet and then set her slowly back down.

"Is this what you meant, Maggie?"

Maggie smiled as the rain trickled down her cheeks, "This is *exactly*, what I meant."

Maggie took a couple steps back from Roger and spread her arms. She pulled her head back, letting the rain fall fully on her face as she slowly spun around.

"What is it about the rain, Maggie," Roger asked, "What makes you love it like you do?"

Maggie turned to Roger and then moved back in close and wrapped her arms around his shoulders. "It's not just *any* rain," she replied, "...Not just *any* time." She smiled at him and brushed her hair back again. "There's something special about a rain like this. It's warm and soft...like a hundred kisses on my skin...But it's not *just* the rain," she said, "It's the night, the air," she looked closely into his eyes, "It's the way you make me feel."

For the first time in the three and a half months since they had been together, the first time since they were seventeen years old, Roger Lowell leaned down and kissed Maggie fully on the mouth.

On the other side of town, Maggie was sitting in the reading chair she kept in her bedroom, staring out the window at the rain with a little smile on her face, thinking back on the same night.

"I don't know what came over me Hillary," she had told her friend on the telephone later, after she had made it home. "...When the rain started, I just couldn't help myself."

"I know what it was," Hillary said, "You, *Miss McKenzie*, have always had this thing about going out in a summer shower and dancing in the rain that I would argue borders on an obsession–"

"*It's not an obsession.*"

"*No*?" Hillary said, "Aren't you the girl who once said that she wouldn't marry a man who wouldn't dance with her in the rain?"

"Yes, I like the rain," Maggie said, "But, *that* was a metaphor and I really think you missed its point?"

"You think so?"

"Yes," Maggie said, "When I said that I meant that I wanted a man who would do anything for me...Up to and including standing out in the middle of a downpour with the whole world watching just because he knew that it would make me happy. It wasn't so much the dance in the rain that I wanted but the heart behind it."

"*Ahh*," Hillary said, "Now I get it. Please forgive my ignorance; we *were* only sixteen when you said that. I was still very concrete in my thinking then."

"You're forgiven."

"But, I digress...That being said, it's still obvious why you would succumb to such urges."

"*Is it now*?"

"Oh yes," said Hillary, "I think we both know that you are just about to explode over Roger Lowell."

"I wouldn't say explode."

"No?" Hillary said, "Didn't you say to me just yesterday – and I quote: 'When we get married, I hope it rains the whole honeymoon?' "

"I think I said *if*."

"Irrelevant," Hillary said, "The sentiment is the same...*So*, you take a sweltry summer night, Maggie's *non-obsessive*, though *lurid*, fondness for spending her time out in the rain...Add to that her *swelling passion* for Roger Lowell, and then toss some sizzling, steamy, Cuban music into the mix..."

"Why do you have to make it sound so dirty?"

"Why do you have to keep interrupting?"

"Because," Maggie said, "you're making my life sound like a cheap romance novel."

"And your point is?"

"It's not."

"I'll be the judge of that," Hillary said, "...So you take all of those things and mix them together and what do you have?"

"A fool in the rain?"

"You're not a fool Maggie. You just have to accept that this is gonna be hard for you...You've been married and you enjoyed being married *and all that went along with it,* and now, you're having to try to be in this relationship with a man that you are falling head over heels for and *not* treat him like y'all are married."

"I just don't want him to think badly of me."

"I don't think he does."

"Not yet."

"Oh stop, Maggie," said Hillary, "And finish your story... What did he do when you went out in the rain?"

Hillary heard Maggie sigh softly on the other end of the line.

"He did just what I needed him to do."

Hillary smiled. She made a fist and pumped it up next to her head, *Yesss!* "*And*?" she said.

"He took me in his arms...and kissed me."

Hillary raised her fist up high again, *Yesss!*

"Oh Hill," Maggie said, "You're right...I thought I was going to explode. It was the most perfect kiss I have ever..."

Hillary waited a moment and then said softly, "It was the most perfect kiss you have ever had, Maggie...and that's okay."

Maggie sighed again. "Neither one of us said a word the whole way home," she said, "After we kissed, we just stood there in the rain for what seemed like forever, just holding each other and staring into each other's eyes...Roger had this look on his face that, I don't know that I can describe it," she paused again, "You know that feeling you have when you wake up one morning and the gardenias have opened up while you were sleeping and the smell has come in the window to you, and it's the smell of them that's woken you up? You know that feeling?"

"Yeah, I think so."

"That's how he was looking at me."

"That's nice," Hillary said softly.

"The band finally stopped playing and packed up their stuff and we just stood there in the rain for I don't know how long. I don't think either one of us wanted to be the first one to leave, but finally, Roger just took my hand and we walked off the dance floor together.

"The owner wouldn't let Roger pay for our meal and he told us we were welcome anytime and then Roger went and pulled his truck up in front of the restaurant, which, at the time, I thought was sweet but really pointless as I was already soaked to the bone and he got out and handed me into the truck so gently."

"And he didn't say *anything* to you?"

"Not a word," Maggie said.

"And you didn't say anything either?"

"Unh uh."

"Wasn't it hard not to say *something*?"

Maggie thought about it, "No," she said, "It was nice... After a moment like that I don't know that anything really needs to be said."

"*Oh,*" Hillary sighed, "I'd love to have a moment like that."

"You know you've had moments like that."

Hillary chuckled. "Thank you Maggie...I love my husband," she said, "He is a very sweet man. But, being married to Buddy Vander and having moments like that just do not go together."

"Aww come on, Hillary," Maggie said, "It can't be that bad."

"His idea of romantic usually involves mosquito repellant and something deep fat fried." Hillary waited a few seconds for Maggie to stop laughing and then said, "So how did everything end...I mean; he didn't just ride by your mama's house and kick you out the door...One of you had to have finally said something?"

"Well," Maggie said, "He drove me to my mother's and helped me out and then walked me up to the porch and then just stood there on the bottom step, holding my hand looking up at me with that sleepy-happy look in his eyes and then he kissed my hand and really softly said, 'I can't wait for the next rain.'"

~Chapter Eleven~

"I know one thing," TJ said firmly as he pulled off his rubber boots.

Iris stood over him with his little shotgun balanced in the crook of her arm, "What's that?"

TJ turned one of the boots upside down and a trail of mud dripped out onto the ground at the base of his grandparents' back steps in sloppy, black globs. He said, "Slipping down into that nasty muskrat hole sure makes me glad I ain't a butterfly."

Iris eyed TJ curiously, "And just why do you say that?"

TJ shook the last of the thick, mucky ooze out and grinned up at Iris, "'Cause they've got taste buds on their feet."

Iris laughed, "Maybe you should ask Santa for some hip boots."

"I think it might be a little late to be making any big changes to my list...Besides, I've already changed it six times."

"You never know," Iris said, "Seven's perfection."

TJ considered Iris's suggestion as he shucked his socks, "Maybe *you* could let Santa know for me," he said, "I'm sure she'd, I mean, *he'd* listen to you."

"And why would I want to do something like that?"

TJ held up the mud stained socks, "So you won't have to help her, or him," he shook his head, "...Or *whoever* with nasty socks like these anymore."

"I think you make a good point," Iris said, clicking the barrels closed on TJ's shotgun as she stepped over to the back door. Leaning the gun up against the outside wall, she pushed open the door, "Hustle up, now," she said, checking her watch, "We've got exactly twenty minutes to get to Uncle Ned and Aunt Tally's."

"Yes Ma'am."

Iris stepped inside and then stuck her head back out, "You're Mama's already got your clothes laid out on your bed," she said, "I'll go ahead and run you a bath...Just leave your dirty stuff out here and I'll get it all later, alright."

"Yes'm," TJ said, giving Iris a little nod as she went back inside and closed the door. He pulled his hunting coat off and tossed it over by the door and then pulled off his overalls and dropped them in a pile next to his coat. A little breeze picked up and blew across the screened porch, drawing up a crop of goosebumps on his damp legs. He stepped back over and opened the screen door and whistled for Huff. He waited a moment and then whistled once more, just as Huff was coming running around the corner of the house, "Come on boy," he said, his body giving a shiver as another gust of wind blew across the yard.

Huff bounded up the steps and licked at the back of TJ's knees as TJ closed the door and latched the hook. TJ shook his legs, "Quit it dog," he said, "I'm about to freeze to death already."

Huff jumped back and then jumped up and bumped TJ in the stomach with his paws. TJ patted his hip and Huff stood up on his hind legs and balanced himself on TJ's thigh. TJ gave Huff's ears a good squeeze and then pointed at his blanket, "You be a good boy and stay out here 'til we get back," he said, "I ain't got time to clean you up now." He prodded his little dog off his hip with a gentle nudge from his knee, and then grabbed his gun and broke it open as Huff went over and curled himself up on his blanket. Huff watched TJ as he went inside and then laid his head down on his paws.

Stepping back out a couple seconds later, TJ clucked his tongue at Huff, tossed him a treat that he had just grabbed from the pantry, and then pulled the door closed and ran upstairs to his room. He broke his gun down, oiled it, and put it away in its case in his closet, and then grabbed a clean t-shirt and underwear as he headed out his door. "*Fifteen minutes,*" he heard Iris call from downstairs as he ran down the hall to take his bath.

Iris came back over from the foot of the stairs and sat herself down on the sofa. "I'm sorry to holler, Miss Rose," she said, "He'd be up there counting shells, rummaging through his sock drawer, or reading the *Wizard of Oz* if somebody didn't stay on him."

"That's alright," Rose said, "It's either holler up stairs every now and then or stand over him with a prod."

"Are all little boys as distractible as he is?"

"Some of them are."

"I don't remember Will being that way when he was little," Iris said, "But, I was a teenager then so I might not have noticed...Lydia thinks it's because of Terry."

"It could be," Rose said, "He seemed to be able to focus on things a bit better before."

"Lydia seems to have to spend a lot of time keeping him on task."

Rose paused a moment as she looked off down the hallway and then turned back to Iris with a look of concern, "Can I ask you something?"

"Sure."

"How is Lydia doing, *really*?"

"I think she's doing well," Iris said, "It's hard to tell with her sometimes."

"I know. That's why I'm asking you...I know that you're the one person that she's always felt like she could talk to."

"I think she's keeping a lot in," Iris said, "I know she's talked with Maggie some –her cousin Maggie–"

"She's the one who lost *her* husband?"

Iris nodded.

"That would make sense."

"But, I honestly don't believe that she's *really* dealt with it yet...She's *been* busy and *kept* herself busy ever since Terry died."

Rose shifted herself in her seat and then nodded for Iris to go on.

"...Between taking care of TJ and getting ready for the babies, I don't know that she's given herself time to grieve."

"Do you think she's avoiding it?"

Iris thought for a second and then said, "I don't know that she's consciously avoiding it..." She shook her head, "I don't know, she might be...It's like with TJ's school. She's insistent on doing her own curriculum for everything. *Don't get me wrong,* she's doing a great job, but there are some programs out there that she could use that would take some of the burden off her at least until after the babies are born."

"Have you tried to suggest some of them?"

"Yes, ma'am," Iris nodded. "And there's a little group that meets at the library once a week that I've tried to get her to join...they work on things together and help each other out, but she says she needs to handle it herself."

"Is TJ making many friends?"

"He's made a few...Mostly family. He's doing a lot better now than he was back during the summer, though...And he seems to be sleeping better now."

"Is he still having nightmares?"

"He had one a little while back," Iris said, "...Maybe a couple weeks ago...But I think it was the first one he's had in a good while."

Rose leaned towards Iris, "Please don't think I'm prying," she said, "It's just that I've tried very hard not to bring anything up about any of this to Lydia...I know how hard it already is during the holidays without someone adding to your worries."

Iris smiled softly, "I know, Miss Rose," she said, "I understand." She smiled again, "And, I know that I'm not telling you anything that Lydia wouldn't tell you herself."

"*Aunt Iris,*" TJ called from upstairs.

Iris smiled at Rose. "*Yes sir,*" she called back.

"*I can't find my tall socks.*"

"*Aren't you wearing long pants?*"

"*Yes ma'am.*"

"*Then why do you need them?*"

"*I just do.*"

"*Check in the dryer.*"

They heard TJ's footsteps as he came tromping down the stairs.

"He's had this thing about knee socks ever since he read the Narnia books," Iris told Rose, "He's been dressing like a turn-of-the-century English schoolboy since September."

"So that's what that's all about," Rose said, "I was wondering if it was some style trend that hadn't made it to Tennessee yet."

"It hasn't even made it outside of the King family, yet," Iris chuckled.

They heard the dryer door slam shut followed by the back door. "*Got 'em*," TJ called as he ran back up the stairs.

"Well," Rose said, "It looks really cute on him."

"It really does," Iris said, "...And, he's the only ten year old I know of that can tie his own half-windsor."

Maggie went into her living room and switched on the gas logs and then went quickly back to the kitchen and answered the telephone.

"Hello."

"You are *not* gonna believe this."

"Hey to you too Hillary."

"Sorry...*Hey Maggie*."

"Hey," Maggie said. She switched the phone to her other ear and held it in place with her shoulder. "What's up?" she said, bending down and peeking in the oven at the stuffed flounder she had broiling for supper.

"You are *not* gonna believe this," Hillary repeated.

"What?"

"Buddy."

"What's your *Smooth Operator* done now?"

"He's been exercising."

"Good for him."

"...*And* eating salad."

"With gravy?"

Hillary laughed, "No," she said, "No gravy, just salad."

"Good."

"*Uh*, don't you want to know why?"

"To lose weight."

"How did you know?" asked Hillary.

"Because," said Maggie, "The only reason anybody starts exercising and eating salad is to lose weight...am I right?"

"Well, yeah."

"Then, I'll say it again...Good for him."

"Yeah," Hillary said, "Good for him. But, do you know what this means?"

"Umm, you're gonna be married to a stud-muffin?"

"*No*," Hillary said, "It means that deep down I am a bad person."

Maggie chuckled, "How do you figure?"

"I didn't trust him...All this time he's been sacrificing food he loves and spending hours out in the barn working his tail off because he wants to look good for me and all I've done is think he's out messing around."

Maggie pulled the lid off her steamer and checked the vegetables. "Come on Hill," she said, "You know you didn't really think that...I mean we talked all about it."

"I know we did, but you know what? No matter what I said, I still was questioning. All the time Buddy's starving himself and working hard to get in shape, I'm thinking bad things about him...I'm a bad wife."

"No you're not."

"How can you say that after what I've just told you?"

"Because we've pretty much known each other our whole lives," Maggie said, "And you are *not* a bad person."

"I feel like I am."

"Well, you're not, Hillary, so let it go...How much weight has he lost?"

"About fifteen pounds," Hillary said, "*He thinks*."

"That's good."

"He doesn't know exactly because he didn't think to weigh himself before he started."

"What's his goal?"

"He said he doesn't really have a weight goal," Hillary said, "He's got a picture in his head of how he wants to be that he's working towards."

"Did you ask him why he decided to do this?"

"Yes," Hillary said vaguely.

"Well...What did he say?"

"You're going to laugh at me again."

"*Why?*"

"Because."

"What did he say?"

"Promise me you won't start using what I'm fixing to tell you as my new nickname."

"I promise I won't use what you're fixing to tell me as your new nickname," Maggie droned, "...*In public.*"

"*Mag-gie.*"

"Look Hillary," Maggie said, "Y'all have just been too rich a source of material lately...You can't really expect me to just let all these nuggets slide by."

"Oh yes I can."

"What did he say?"

Hillary heaved a loud frustrated sigh.

"Come on," Maggie said, "You know you want to tell me."

Hillary paused a few seconds and then sighed again, "He said I was The *Total Package*...He said I had it all going on and that *he* wanted to look as good standing next to *me* as *I* do standing next to *him.*"

"The *Total Package*," Maggie said, "Yeah, I like the sound of that...Hillary *The Total Package* Vander...It's got a nice ring to it don't you think?"

"Maybe if I was embarking on a career as a professional wrestler..."

Maggie opened her refrigerator door and grabbed out the tea pitcher. "You know," she said, closing the door with her foot, "Roger told me that I was a *Mom Babe* the other day, but, that doesn't sound nearly as cool as *The Total Package*...What exactly does one have to do to become a *Total Package?*"

"If you were here with me right now I'd show you," Hillary said dryly.

"Testy, testy."

"I'm not testy," Hillary said, "...Would a *Total Package* be testy?"

"I guess that would really depend on what you were a package *of.*"

"Oh, you are really on tonight, sister."

"I've had a good day."

"I wish I could say the same."

"You can."

"How?"

Maggie opened a cabinet, pulled out three plates, and then went over and sat them in place on the table, "Your husband just told you that he still thinks you're so hot that he's willing to drastically...and I do mean *drastically*, change himself just to be more attractive to you and you think you haven't had a good day?"

Hillary didn't answer.

"*Well?*"

Hillary said, "I guess when you look at it that way it does kind of change one's perspective on the whole thing doesn't it?"

Maggie walked back into the kitchen and grabbed a handful of silverware from the drawer. "I should hope so," she said, on her way back to the table, "You need to get down on your knees tonight and thank the Lord for a man like that."

Hillary chuckled under her breath, "That's what Buddy said he does for me every day."

"He knows a good thing when he sees it."

"So do I."

Maggie dealt the silverware out next to all the plates and then went back into the kitchen and slipped on an oven mitt. "Look, Hillary," she said, "I know you feel bad for thinking that way about him...it's understandable." She opened the oven and pulled out the pan of stuffed flounder, "...Just tell him what you were thinking, apologize, and move on. It's no good to be blessed like you are if you're wasting all your energy holding on to past mistakes."

"You really think I should tell him?"

"Yes," Maggie replied firmly, as she set the flounder down on a pad on the counter, "I do."

"You don't think he'll be upset?"

"He might be at first," Maggie said, "But I really think it'll be better if you go ahead get it out and over with...Shoot, he might even be flattered that you were jealous."

"I'll do it tonight, then."

"Good," Maggie said, stepping into the hallway, "...Hold on just a sec'." She pulled the telephone away from her face and called for Jimmy and Sarah to come to supper. "Just put the children to bed, put on some of that lovin' music he's been listening to, light a few candles, maybe give him a back rub, and then just...let it go."

"I'm not going to want to talk if I do all that."

"Oh really."

"Oh yeah," Hillary said in a throaty voice, "Buddy's got muscles, now."

❧

"See you in the morning, Studly."

"See you Chief," Joey replied. He touched his fingers to his brow and gave Roger a slightly less-than-regulation salute.

"You better tighten that up," Roger said as he hung his coveralls on the wall and grabbed his coat, "...The O D would have you down on your knees scrubbing the floors with a toothbrush and a bucket of soojie-moojie for a salute like that."

Joey wrinkled up his face and waved a limp hand at Roger, "*Ahhh,*" he groaned nasally, "Scrub shmub."

Roger slipped his coat on and snapped it closed, "I appreciate you hanging around and helping me get those hangers finished."

"No problem," Joey said, "You just tell Billy he owes me a meal."

"I didn't know you had plans...you should have told me. I could have gotten them done."

"That's alright. It wasn't like I had a date or anything... Wildlife Man dropped some contraband drum off at Granny Jack's while I was there at dinner and she asked me to come back for supper."

"Which one was it?"

Joey unzipped the front of his coveralls, "What's his face," he said, "...The one that always seems like he's runnin' out of breath when he's talking to you...Mister Harlan's cousin."

"Big blonde headed guy?"

"Yeah."

"Baker."

"Yeah," Buddy said, "Baker, that's him...Baker Ramsey."

"He didn't get them off anybody local did he?"

"*The drum*? Naw...I think he said he got 'em off some Tow-Rows from up around Millsboro."

"Look, why don't you come on and ride over to Billy's with me and we can drop off his hangers and then run over to the Whistling Pig and get us some barbecue."

"Alright," Joey said, "That sounds good. I haven't had me any barbecue in a while."

"Me neither," Roger said, "And this cold weather's suddenly put me in the mood for some."

"I hope they've got some of that pumpkin bread, too," Joey said, "I could eat me a pan of that right by itself."

"Well go on and get outta those coveralls and come on," Roger said, "I'm gonna go on out and get the truck warmed up."

Joey bent over and unzipped the legs of his coveralls and then stood up and started wriggling them off his shoulders. "Alright," he said, "I'm gonna run up and get my coat and I'll be right out."

Roger walked out and looked up at the low grey clouds sulking slowly overhead as he closed the door behind him. He looked down towards the river as he walked over to his truck and smiled as the decorations on the lamp posts lit up. "It's beginning to look a lot like Christmas..." he sang quietly to himself. The cold cut through his coat as a fresh wind blew up from the river. "Brrrr," he shivered, shoving his hands into his pockets, "It's beginning to *feel* a lot like Christmas."

"*Hey Man.*"

Roger turned and saw Buddy jogging down the street towards him. "Hey Man, yourself," he said, "I missed you today."

Buddy came up and stopped in front of Roger's truck. "Yeah, me too," he puffed, "I hated to cancel, but I decided to talk to Hillary today like you suggested."

"Well, I'm sure Roslynne's toes enjoyed the break."

"Ha ha," Buddy said. He bent over and propped on his knees, "I got to tell you," he said between breaths, "I've been working myself pretty hard...but this running mess is tough."

"Yeah it is," Roger said knowingly, "So what did Hill say when you told her?"

Buddy straightened himself up and took a deep breath, "Not a whole lot really. I think she was a little surprised..." He took another deep breath in through his nose and then breathed it out slowly through his mouth, as he went over their conversation in his mind, "But," he continued, "...Really it was a little strange," he paused again, "...She seemed relieved."

"*Really*?"

"Yeah," Buddy said, "...and I gotta tell you. I'm kindly relieved myself. You were right; this is gonna be a whole lot easier now that I don't have to hide from my wife to exercise."

"I don't know how you've done it *this* long."

"It hasn't been easy," Buddy said, "I don't know how them guys that run around on their wives do it...or the ones that have whole other families nobody knows about."

"Yeah," Roger said, "Just imagine what all they could accomplish if they put all that time and energy into something productive."

"Yeah, *really*," Buddy replied. He looked over and waved to Joey as he came walking around the front corner of the shop, "Hey Joe."

Roger noticed that Joey had changed out of his work clothes, ditched his ball cap, and had wet and styled his hair. Joey grinned at Buddy as he came over to them, "Hey Big Man," he said, "Let me see them guns."

Buddy shook his head with mock conceit, "Sorry Red..." he said haughtily, curling his arms. He raised them slightly, "...But these babies are just for *concealed* carry."

"Oh man," Roger said, "You are just *too* much...I think that muscle between your shoulders has swelled up the most."

Buddy grinned at Roger, "You know I'm only kidding."

"So, are you gonna be running regular now," Joey asked, "Cause if you are I might want to run with you."

"I'm not sure," Buddy said, "I might. I just wanted to do something different tonight."

"Let me know," said Joey.

"I will," Buddy said, "Well, look y'all, I hate to run, but...I need to run. I'm trying to do five tonight."

"We've got to get going too," Roger said. He patted Buddy's shoulder, "See you tomorrow?"

"Absolutely."

Roger nudged Joey, "Be shore and warn Roz when you call her tonight."

"I'm immune to your disdain," Buddy said loftily, "...Y'all be good." He turned and took off down Commons at a trot.

Roger watched him for a moment and then got into his truck and cranked it up as Joey walked around and climbed in. Roger looked at Joey as he was strapping on his seatbelt, "Since when do you want to go jogging?" he said, "I've been trying to get you to go running with me for at least a year now."

"I don't know," Joey shrugged, "Buddy's kind of inspired me...He looks really good."

"He looks *great*," Roger said, "I'm amazed at what he's done in such a short time."

"Well," Joey said, "I figure if he can do what he's done with what he started with, then I ort to be able to something with this." He held his arms out and motioned at himself with a nod, "...You know what I mean?"

"I gotcha," Roger said. He pulled the truck down into gear and drove onto Commons, "You're still welcome to go running with me, you know."

"I know," Joey said, "It's good this way," he said as Roger cruised up to the intersection with Plantation.

Roger turned left onto Plantation without stopping and then made another left onto Lookout Road, "Well, why don't you then?"

"*First* is because you go first thing in the morning and I don't' particularly feel like running –What is it you do?

Five? Six? Ten miles...And *second*, I've kind of gotten used to seeing Roslynne on her way to work every day."

"I don't run *every* morning."

"I know."

"...And it's *five*," Roger said, "But, I do appreciate the compliment."

Roger saw Buddy run through the intersection with First Street out ahead of him and said, "He's truckin' along pretty good, Joey. Are you shore you can keep up with him?"

"I don't know now that I really see him at it," Joey said, "I haven't had to run since P.E. Junior Year."

Roger slowed down and turned right onto First Street, headed out what everyone called *The Back Way* out of Sand Ridge. He pulled his truck up next to Buddy and rolled down his window as he cruised along next to him.

Buddy glanced over and grinned, "Hey," he said shortly, puffing out a breath, "Can't get enough of me...Can ya?"

"You're pushing a tight pace, man," Roger said, "Don't overdo it."

"Nonsense," Buddy said. He gave his head a little shake, "I'm a machine."

"Yeah," Roger said, "I know...Just don't overdo it. You hurt yourself and it'll really mess up your plans."

"I won't," Buddy puffed, "How fast...am I going?"

Roger glanced down at his speedometer, "About ten, eleven miles an hour."

Buddy made a face.

"You alright?"

"Yeah," Buddy said, between breaths, "...I read that...marathoners do 'bout twelve...I was...hoping for that."

"If you had some suspenders we could hook 'em over the side mirror," Roger said, "No doubt we could get you to twelve, maybe even thirteen, then."

Buddy cut his eyes at Roger, "No doubt," he grinned, "...See you Rog." Flashing a quick wave, he cut off to his left down Bridge Road. Roger coasted a bit longer, watching him as he ran over the Flats Creek Bridge. He tapped twice on his horn as Buddy crossed to the other side of the creek and then stepped down on the gas and headed on out of town.

~Chapter Twelve~

Lydia smoothed out the wrinkles on the cover on the changing table and then looked around the room. *What have you forgotten*, she thought. She propped the floor sweeper against the wall, walked over to the closet, and clicked on the light.

The hand-smocked christening dresses were hanging side-by-side on the back wall. The pink and white sheets were all neatly folded and in their places, the diapers where stacked, the boxes of wipes, the bulb syringes, the bottles of baby oil, baby wash, onesies, sleepers, blankets, quilts...all there in their places.

She rubbed her belly and felt one of her girls wriggle at her touch. "That felt like a shoulder," she said. She took a deep breath and whispered, "I think I'm ready girls."

Lydia cut out the light, walked over, and stood between the cribs. She glanced back and forth between them and imagined the girls there asleep. In her mind, they looked just like TJ, only with lighter hair. They were lying on their bellies with their arms and legs curled and tucked up tightly under them, sleeping just the way that he did. She remembered how she had been so worried that he refused to sleep on his back and how Terry had seemed so unconcerned.

"Our boy just takes no cotton to conventional wisdom," he had told her one of the first few nights after they had brought him home. "He likes his belly," he said, "God made him that way...and God will keep him. If He wants to take him Home, He will...belly *or* back."

Lydia started up one of the mobiles and then picked up one of the matching "Sounds of the Womb" lambs she had gotten as a shower gift. She stroked the lamb's back as she listened to Brahms's Lullaby play softly over the crib.

Clicking the lamb on, Lydia listened to the whooshing heart sound for a moment and then hugged the lamb tightly. She remembered Terry lying back in his recliner with TJ asleep on his chest, "Oh Terry," she sighed, "I do wish you were here." Carefully resting the lamb back down in its spot in the crib, Lydia stopped the mobile and then walked back over to grab the sweeper on her way out. She saw the monitor sitting on the shelf over the changing table and remembered that she wanted to go ahead and get the receiver plugged in so she wouldn't forget it when she brought her baby girls home.

Lydia stepped out into the hall and put the sweeper away in the closet, and then went down to her bedroom. She walked in and went around the foot of her bed. She stopped and stood looking at herself in the mirror, "*Law* Lydia...You are *huge*." Turning sideways, she looked at the profile of her stomach, "I really wish people were still making those loose clothes like they did the first time I was pregnant." She pulled her shirt up over her stomach and laughed quietly at her reflection, "TJ's right," she chuckled, "It does look like a giant eyeball."

She pulled her shirt back down and looked at the picture he had drawn for her and taped to the mirror. He had drawn it the day that they found out she was having twin girls, and that they would probably be born right around Christmas. It was a picture of him holding a big box, without a top on it, wrapped in Christmas paper. In the box, you could see two babies with little pink caps, wrapped in pink blankets. He had written *Merry Christmas to You* in big arching letters over his head. Across the bottom of the paper he had written, *To: You From: Us*.

Lydia smiled to herself and pictured TJ giving piggy-back rides to two giggling little tow-headed girls with bright pink cheeks. She felt a strong push against the front wall of her abdomen and then another push against her right side. She patted at her stomach, "Easy does it girls," she said, "How 'bout we keep the rough housing to a minimum just yet, if you please."

She went on around to the other side of the bed and knelt down in front of her nightstand. Grabbing the baby monitor from the shelf, Lydia took the twist-tie off the cord, straightened the cord out, and then sat the monitor on the bed. She looked the nightstand over and moved the half empty box of Kleenex from the top of the stand down to the top shelf below the drawer and then sat the monitor in place where the tissues had been. Letting the cord drop down behind the nightstand, she reached awkwardly around behind it and tried to plug it in.

Lydia fumbled with the plug for a moment, fighting against the bulge of her stomach to reach around to the outlet, and then gave up and sat back on her feet. She shook her head and sighed, "Did you *really* think you could reach back there Lydia?" she said, "...Maybe I should just wait for Mama to get home and get her to do it." She paused for a moment and then shook her head, "*Nah,* you can do it Miss King."

Shifting herself around, Lydia pushed against the nightstand, sliding it out away from the wall as she squeezed herself in behind it. She grabbed the cord again and tilted her head over to get a look at the outlet and spotted what looked like an envelope sitting up on its end on the floor and leaning against the wall. "Hmm," she grunted, "I must have knocked something off the nightstand sometime." She grabbed the envelope and passed it to her other hand and then plugged the monitor in. Static scratched loudly from the monitor as she straightened herself up and scooted back out and then slid the nightstand back in place.

Lydia reached up and clicked the monitor off as she pushed herself back up onto her knees. "Now that certainly is a lovely sound," she said, heaving herself up onto the edge of the bed, "I can't wait to hear babies on the other end." She looked at the envelope. The flap was still sealed. She turned it over and read the front.

Peek

It was Terry's handwriting.

Lydia's heart raced.

She gripped the letter tightly, her mind swimming. *He must have left this for me,* she thought, *...How long has it* *been back there...How could I have missed it?* She stared at her name. *Peek.*

How could I have missed this?

Lydia blew the dust off and then turned the envelope over slowly in her hands and held it to her face. She sniffed it, knowing in her heart that it wouldn't still have his smell on it. She held it back down in her lap and turned it over again and slid a finger in under the flap.

God, how I'd love to be called Peek just one more time.

Lydia slowly peeled the envelope open and gently slid the letter out. Sitting the envelope down on the bed next to her, she took a deep breath and held the note up in front of her.

Eyeing the writing through the paper, Lydia realized that she held her husband's last living communication with her in her hands. "*Wow,*" she whispered.

Lydia took another deep breath, letting it out slowly as she paused for a moment and thought about putting the letter back in its envelope and hiding it in the bottom of a drawer.

Shaking her head, Lydia took another deep breath, "Oh," she said softly, unfolding the letter, "I could never do that." She held it in her lap and smiled at Terry's handwriting as she looked it over. A tear slipped from the corner of her eye and clung, glistening at the tip of one of her lashes as she remembered the first time she had seen her husband's script and how pretty she thought it was. She remembered teasing him about the flamboyant flourishes he used on his capital letters.

Darling, the letter began, the D waving at her grandly, *I'm so excited about this great new adventure we are now embarking on. The possibilities before us are boundless and the Lord only knows what lies ahead.*

I'll miss you so much while we're apart, but I know the days will fly by and that our time apart will only draw us closer. My prayer is that this next month will bring more healing for you and your mother and that your Daddy will be waiting on the front porch to welcome you home when we all get back to Sand Ridge.

I can't wait to get back and start our new life together...for some reason, I keep picturing myself at the helm of a teak-decked sailboat with you perched up on the bow in a white sailor's cap smiling back at me...but I digress...

I'll be counting the minutes until you're in my arms again. You are my world.

Love,

Terry

p.s. Just so you'll know...I'll have ten miles of kisses lined up and waiting for you when you get home.

He had drawn a quick sketch of a sailboat at the bottom of the letter.

Lydia felt a sudden burning of sadness and anger welling up inside of her as she stared at the sailboat. She gripped the letter tightly, gritting her teeth as she closed her eyes and a rage built in the pit of her stomach. She felt a heat rising in her cheeks as her face went red.

Balling the letter in her fist, she slammed it down on the bed and screamed, "*Aaaaggghhh.*" She slammed her fists down on the bed again and threw the letter against the wall.

Lydia threw her head back, screaming up at the ceiling, and then threw herself back on the bed and screamed until her throat burned, "*Noooooo...noooooo...Why...Why...Why... Why God, Why...Why did you do this...Why...Why...Why...*"

She rolled over towards the headboard onto her side and pounded the pillows, beads of sweat rolling down her forehead, mixing with her tears and burning her eyes. She pounded the pillows again and again.

"*No, no, no,*" Lydia yelled as she pounded, her breaths coming in short hoarse gasps. She grabbed one of the throw pillows and fell back, pressing it to her face as she screamed again.

"*Aaaaggghhhh!*"

Digging her fingers into the pillow, Lydia squeezed as hard as she could. She gripped it tightly and started pulling. As she felt the pillow starting to tear she gritted down and pulled at it even harder, listening to the helpless wailing of her own cries.

Puffy, billowing, white, down stuffing flew in all directions as the pillow finally gave way and tore apart. Lydia threw what was left of it across the room as she let out one last gasping cry and then rolled back, exhausted, onto her side and curled herself up around her trembling belly.

She covered her face with her hands and fell into rhythmic sobbing, "I can't do this without you Terry," she whispered, "...I just can't."

Grabbing a handful of the old quilt that was folded across the foot of the bed, Lydia pulled it to her and mashed her face down tightly against the soft squares of the worn fabric she had balled in her fists. She rolled slowly back onto her back, taking the quilt with her as she went, and then clutched it tightly against her body.

She lay there with her eyes closed, remembering the last moment that she saw him alive. She had thought about it so many times that she could still see every tiny detail with complete clarity: him, his arm propped up in the open window, driving the Land Rover out of her parents' yard, his eyes twinkling as he glanced back over his shoulder at her...that curly, little wisp of hair on his forehead, blowing gently in the breeze as he turned back to the road...

Lydia's heart groaned.

Why did you do this to me God...Why did you take him away?

She rolled back onto her side, balling the quilt up in her arms as she hugged it tightly against her chest. Gazing off through the window on the far wall, Lydia saw that it had started to snow. She lay there, her body hitching as she cried quietly, staring blankly out through the foggy pane as a few tiny goose-feather flakes drifted slowly past the window.

She heard a quiet step as someone padded across the room from the door, and then, she felt their weight as they climbed onto the bed behind her. Lydia closed her eyes as she sniffed back a sob and then wiped her face on the quilt as she felt the soft comfort of a body pressed gently to hers.

"I love you, Baby," Mary whispered softly as she wrapped her arms around Lydia and squeezed her close, "I love you so much."

Mary's hand felt cool on Lydia's arms from where she'd just come in from outside. "I thought I was over it, Mama," Lydia whispered, her voice sounding worn and tired. She covered her mother's hands with hers, "I thought I was okay."

"I know, Baby," Mary said, "I know you did."

"I don't understand why God would do this to me."

"I know, Baby."

"I just don't understand."

Mary paused, squeezing Lydia in a little closer. "He loves you, Baby," she said, "More than you know and in ways we can't comprehend."

"But *why?*"

"We can't see the whole picture," Mary said, "We can't see what He sees."

"I don't think I can do this without Terry."

"You can Baby," Mary said gently, "...You have to."

Lydia sighed again.

"Terry's gone Baby, but you're not alone."

"I know, Mama," Lydia said, "...But it still hurts."

"I'm afraid it's going to hurt you for a very long time," Mary said, "...But it will get better." She kissed the back of Lydia's head, "I'm sorry I haven't helped you work this out, Baby...I'm sorry I haven't done more."

Lydia squeezed Mary's hands, "Don't be sorry," she said, "You've done all I've let you do...I guess I'm still not used to you being my mother."

"I know," Mary said, giving Lydia another quick little hug, "We have to work through these things together now." She loosened her arms from around Lydia and sat herself up.

Lydia rolled onto her back and looked up at her mother with bleary eyes.

Mary smoothed down Lydia's hair across her forehead and then touched her cheek, "Promise me you won't try to bear this alone anymore."

Lydia smiled weakly, "I won't."

"Promise me."

"I promise."

☙

"Thanks Jessie," Maggie said as she took the box from the man in the brown uniform.

"You're welcome," the man replied. He gave her a little wave and said, "Merry Christmas," as he turned and hustled himself off Maggie's front porch.

"Wow, it's cold out there," Maggie said as she closed the door and walked over to the dining room table.

"Hard to believe it was pushing eighty just last week," said Hillary from across the room.

"I know," Maggie said as she set the box down on the table, "But I reckon it's time." She looked the box over and then read the return address. "*Yesss*," she said, stretching her arm out and pulling a fist in victoriously.

"What is it?" Hillary asked as Maggie walked quickly into the kitchen to get a knife.

"It's Roger's Christmas present," Maggie replied as she went back across the room to cut open the box. She slit the tape across the top of the box and set the knife down on the table as she flipped the flaps open.

"What is it?"

Maggie pulled an album out of the box and held it up for Hillary to see.

Hillary eyed the black and white picture on the front cover, "That looks familiar."

"It should," Maggie said, turning it back towards herself and gazing at the front cover admiringly, "...He and Buddy played it non-stop for pretty much all of fourth grade."

"Oh yeah," said Hillary. She got up from Maggie's sofa and came over next to Maggie. She looked at the album, "Jackrabbit Slim, right?"

Maggie nodded and smiled brightly.

"Doesn't he already have it?"

"Yeah," Maggie said, glancing at Hillary, "This is it."

Hillary looked at Maggie curiously.

"Didn't I tell you about this?"

Hillary shook her head.

"I could've sworn I did."

Hillary shook her head again.

Maggie said, "I got Joey to *borrow* a couple of Roger's old albums under the pretense of making them into CDs –wait a minute," she interrupted herself, "Let me back up a little bit...Do you remember Pastor's sermon back before Thanksgiving about focusing on *The* Gift?"

"Yeah."

"Well, after hearing that message, Roger and I talked about it, and we both agreed that it would be a good way for us to start things...so we promised not to get anything big for each other for Christmas. We decided to keep things simple to keep the focus on *The* Gift..."

Hillary nodded, "Buddy and I did too," she said. "...Not that that's going to be a big stretch for Buddy."

Maggie cocked her head at Hillary. "You know it really is a blessing to be married to a practical man."

"I know," Hillary sighed, "...I'd just like *a little* romance every now and then."

"No you don't."

Hillary's brow wrinkled, "And why do you say that."

"*Because*," said Maggie, "...for the past few weeks your husband has been talking to you like Billy Ocean and all you've done is conjure up in your mind all sorts of high crimes and misdemeanors."

Hillary heaved a sigh and rolled her eyes.

"Feel free to tell me I'm wrong."

Hillary shook her head in frustration, "You're not," she groaned, "I know I'm an idiot. You don't have to remind me." She shook her head again, "Maybe I do like predictability...but I'd *like* to like romance."

"Maybe you just need to try a little harder."

"Maybe I do," Hillary agreed, "So anyway...back to the gifts..."

"Right," Maggie said, "So we agreed nothing big...So, I really wanted to come up with something *very* inexpensive but *very* creative...Something that would make our first Christmas together memorable." She smiled and laid her hand against the side of her head, "Oh man, I wracked my

brain for two weeks and couldn't come up with anything."
She grabbed Hillary's arm, "*That's right,*" she said, "I *didn't*
tell you...*I didn't tell anyone.* I wanted to come up with
something all by myself...So anyway, I'm driving the
children over to Mama's one day and this song comes on
the radio." She grinned at Hillary and started humming the
song's tune.

Hillary started bobbing her head to the beat and hummed
along. After a couple of lines, she pointed at Maggie and
sang the chorus. "I love that song," she said, "I haven't
heard it in forever."

"It's great, isn't it?"

"It is."

"Well anyway, this idea came to me. When I got home, I
looked him up online," Maggie said, pointing at the dark
haired young man with the guitar on the album cover, "And
I actually was able to get in touch with him..."

"Really?"

Maggie nodded, "Yeah, really," she said, "I contacted him
through his web-site, and we've e-mailed back and forth
probbly five or six times...He is such a nice guy. I told him a
little bit about Roger and us and asked him if he would be
willing to autograph the album for me for a Christmas
present and he said he'd be glad to."

She held the album up again and Hillary noticed the
writing on it for the first time. She looked at it closely, "Oh,"
she said, "I thought that was printed on there as part of the
title. That's awesome." She took the album from Maggie and
read the inscription:

"Roger, I hope you get many more miles out of this one.
Thanks for listening all these years. Steve

"That is really cool," she said.

"It is, isn't it," said Maggie. She looked down into the box
the album had been mailed in and said, "Hey, there's some
more stuff in here." She pulled out a note and a handful of
CDs.

"What's it say?"

Maggie read the note out loud: "Maggie, I hope your friend
enjoys his gift. I'm sending you a couple of my old ones on

CD and a copy of my latest, I hope y'all enjoy them. Best of luck to you both and Merry Christmas, Steve"

She finished the letter and was grinning from ear to ear when she looked at Hillary, "Can you believe that?"

Hillary laid the album down on the table and leaned over towards the box, "See if there's anything else in there," she said.

Maggie handed Hillary the CDs and pulled out some of the newspaper that had been stuffed inside for packing.

"Did you see that he autographed these," Hillary said. She held the CDs up for Maggie to see.

"*Unh uh*," Maggie said. She eyed the covers and smiled again, "That is so cool...Didn't I tell you he was a nice guy." She looked back into the box. "Here's another CD," she said, pulling out another CD, "It's signed, too."

"This was a great idea, Maggie."

Maggie smiled proudly, "I kinda thought so, too," she said, "You think Roger's gonna like it?"

"Oh yeah...He'll be tickled to death with this."

"I hope so."

Hillary dropped the CDs back into the box and grinned slyly at Maggie, "I wonder what he's going to come up with for you."

Maggie shrugged.

"I'm thinking perhaps something small and round and gold."

"I doubt that."

"I don't," Hillary said, "I wouldn't be the least bit surprised."

"We promised not to get anything big."

Hillary held her hand up and waved her wedding rings at Maggie, "Rings aren't very big."

"What are you talking about," Maggie said, "Rings are huge."

"Maybe so," Hillary said, "But don't you think one would be the perfect gift?"

Maggie smiled and gave Hillary a quick nod, "You know I would, but I don't know if Roger's thinking the same thing."

"Maybe *you* just need to try a little harder."

~Chapter Thirteen~

Roger awoke the day before Christmas Eve with the sun shining in brightly through his bedroom window and a stomach full of butterflies. "I reckon this is what I get for listening to the weather before I go to bed," he grumbled to himself as he pulled a pillow over his head to shade his eyes from the crisp rays.

It was the third morning in a row that he had overslept because he hadn't been able to get to sleep at a decent time the night before.

He peeked out from under the pillow and saw his alarm clock lying face down on the nightstand. He reached out and stood it back up. *Five after eight.* "Oh great," he groaned, "...I better call Joey."

Roger flung the sheets back as he sat up and slung his legs over the side of the bed. He glanced over at the little velvet box sitting on top of his dresser, "Yeah right Roger," he said, stretching his arms up high over his head. He yawned deeply, "...Like you're really worried about the weather."

He got himself up and grabbed his bathrobe from the hook on the backside of his closet door and slid it over his lanky frame. Tying the belt loosely around his waist, Roger walked over and picked the box up and pulled it open. "*Whelp,*" he said, staring down at the shining ring resting delicately in its cozy velvet cradle, "Tonight's the night." He held it up and rotated it so that the diamond sparkled as it caught the light and took a deep breath, "Let's hope she likes you..."

Roger clicked the box shut and dropped it into his pocket as the telephone rang. He walked down the hallway to the kitchen and picked it up, "Hello..."

"Buenos dias, El jefe."

"Hey Joe."

"Have trouble getting to sleep again?"

"I reckon so."

"I've got some bacon, egg, and cheese biscuits here for you."

Roger said, "I apologize for standing you up, Hoss."

"That's alright," Joey said, "You been up long?"

"I just got up about five minutes ago."

"You still planning on coming in today?"

"Yeah," Roger said, "I'm gonna get a quick shower, get dressed, and then I'll be over."

"You want me to bring the biscuits over to you...They're still hot."

"Naw, that's alright."

"Are you sure? You know I don't mind."

"Naw, don't worry about it," Roger said, "It's cold."

"I know, but if it's coming in like they say it is, I'm not gonna be riding for a while."

Roger glanced out the front window, "It don't look like we've really got much to worry about if you asked me," he said, "I'm looking out the window right now and all I see is blue sky."

"Where are you?"

"Outside the kitchen doorway."

"Well look out your kitchen window."

Roger stepped into the kitchen and walked over to the sink. "*Ooh*," he said as he looked out the window. Off to the east he could see the dark purple-gray front that was moving in from out over the ocean.

"Yeah," Joey said, "*That's what I'm talking about*...The wind's been blowing off and on from the northeast all morning...We're *gonna* get us some weather."

Roger leaned himself over and propped on the edge of the sink, still eyeing the ominous clouds, "Well, I reckon you can bring 'em on over if you want. You had your coffee yet?"

"I had one when I was waiting."

"I'll get the press out and put the kettle on."

"Good deal...I'll see you directly."

Lydia's knees buckled as the pain shot down violently through her abdomen. She gritted her teeth as she dropped her toothbrush and grabbed the sink to steady herself. "*Oh *my*," she said breathlessly. Spitting a mouthful of toothpaste into the sink, she breathed in deeply through her nose, *I guess that clears that up*, she thought. She straightened up and looked at herself in the mirror, "Yes Lydia," she said to her reflection, "Those *are* contractions."

Picking her toothbrush back up off the counter, Lydia finished brushing her teeth, *I guess it's been about a half hour or so since that last one*, she thought. She leaned over and spit, "Of course that last one wasn't anywhere near as good as this one just was." She rinsed her toothbrush out, swished a mouthful of water, and then heard a knock on her bedroom door as she grabbed the bottle of mouthwash from the cabinet.

"*Come in.*"

The door opened and Iris came in, "Hey Baby," she said, as she came across the room, "I forgot to ask you *–Are you alright*...you look pale."

Lydia sighed softly and patted her stomach.

"Girls a little active this morning?"

"I believe they're looking for the way out."

"Are you sure?"

"I just had a *serious* contraction."

"Are you sure it wasn't another one of those pre-contraction contractions?"

Lydia said, "It feels like there's a wild animal in there trying to rip its way out."

"Yep," Iris said, "I'd say that's a contraction...What do we need to do?"

Lydia took a deep breath, "Nothing just yet. I'm going to finish getting ready and call the doctor's office and let them know what's going on...We'll see what they say before we do anything."

"Alright," Iris said, putting her hand on Lydia's arm, "I'm fixin' to head over to the library. Call me if you need me. Miss Janice said that I could go whenever you need me, so you just call."

"I will."

Iris turned to go.

"Wait," Lydia said.

Iris turned back to her.

"What were you asking me?"

Iris thought for a second, "Oh yeah," she said, "I was going to ask you if you were still planning on coming out with us tonight, but I reckon that's kind of answered itself."

"I *would* like to see the fireworks," Lydia said.

"You're probably gonna be a bit busy for fireworks."

"We'll see."

Iris reached out and touched Lydia's belly, "We will, won't we," she smiled. She winked at Lydia and then went out, closing the bedroom door behind her as she left. Lydia gargled her mouthwash and then put the bottle away, "Well girls," she said, staring down at her roundness, "I reckon we're all about ready to get this over with."

Opening the door to the linen closet, Lydia grabbed the little bag of toiletries she had packed just before Thanksgiving, "I'll get my bathroom bag out and get my big bag out of the closet and stick my slippers in there so I'll be all ready when it's time to go." She carried the pink, floral-printed bag out and set it down on the bed, and then went over to the closet. She heard another knock on the door and reached over and pulled it open. Mary was standing in the hallway smiling with Rose just behind her.

"We hear you've got wildcats trying to bust out this morning," Mary said.

"It sure feels like it," Lydia said, "...I hope it's not a portent of how my labor's gonna go."

"You're gonna be just fine," Rose assured her, "...How far apart are the contractions."

"I haven't gotten to that stage yet," Lydia said, "I think I had one last night or, early this morning rather, and then I just had a really strong one a few minutes ago."

"Can we do anything for you," asked Mary.

Lydia shook her head, "Not yet, I'm just getting my things together, and then I was planning on calling the doctor."

Mary said, "I thought you had already gotten everything packed."

"I have," Lydia said, "I'm just getting my bags together."

"We'll do that," Rose said.

"I can do it," Lydia said.

"Nonsense," Rose said as she and Mary walked into the room past Lydia.

Mary looked around the room, "Where's your suitcase Lydie," she asked, "In the closet?"

"Yes ma'am."

Mary went into the closet and came out with Lydia's suitcase in her hand, "Are you sure you've got everything you need in here?"

"I do need to stick my slippers in," Lydia replied, "...And I think that'll take care of it."

"Where are they?" Rose asked.

"I was gonna take the new ones that TJ and Iris got for me," Lydia said, pointing back inside the closet, "They're in a shopping bag on the shelf over the door."

Mary looked at Rose and grinned, "You'll have to get those," she said, "I'm sure I won't be able reach them."

Rose smiled and then stepped into the closet, looked up over the door, and pulled down the bag, "Do you want these in the suitcase or the other bag on the bed?"

"In the suitcase please," Lydia said, "I want to put a couple pictures in there, too."

Mary laid the suitcase on the bed and stepped aside for Lydia to open it up. Lydia pulled the zippers around, flipped the top back and grabbed the checklist she had stuck inside. "Yep," she said, quickly going over the list, "Just the slippers and the pictures is all I haven't packed."

Rose noticed Lydia's hands were trembling a little. She handed Lydia the shopping bag, "Here you go," she said. Lydia took the bag and then Rose touched her shoulder, "A little nervous?"

Lydia let out a sigh and then looked at Rose, her mouth drawn tight. She gave a little nod, "A little bit, I think," she said quietly.

"You're going to be fine."

"I'm praying."

"You just keep doing that," said Mary, "...And put your mind at ease. We're going to be with you through it all."

Lydia took a deep breath and gave them a tiny bit of a smile. She looked at them for a long moment, and then let her breath out in a sharp puff, turning away as her eyes got glassy. She dropped the bag on the bed and quickly pulled the slippers out and packed them down along the inside of the suitcase, squeezing them in between her clothes and the side.

"What pictures are you taking," Mary asked.

Lydia looked over to her dresser, "Those two," she said, motioning with her chin, "The one of all of us and the one of Terry."

Mary stepped over and grabbed the picture frames that were standing side by side in the middle of the dresser. She folded their arms down and handed them to her daughter, "Here you go, Baby."

Lydia took the pictures and laid them on their backs on top of her clothes and stood, staring down at them for almost a minute before she reached over and pulled the suitcase closed. Zipping it slowly shut, she turned, smiled at her mother, and said, "Thank you."

Rose grabbed the handle and slid the suitcase off the bed, "I'll go ahead and take this downstairs," she said. She smiled at Lydia and then grabbed the smaller pink bag and exited gracefully from the room.

Lydia reached out and hugged her mother.

Mary held Lydia tightly and then softly patted the back of her head, "You can do this, Baby," she said, "You can."

Lydia sniffed back tears.

Mary gave her a quick, gentle squeeze. "You hear me, Lydie," she said, "You can do this."

"Iris just called to let me know that Lydia's probably going to be going in for delivery sometime today."

"That's great," Hillary said, "*I guess.*"

"Yeah," Maggie said, "I kind of got the impression that since they hadn't come yet, she was hoping they'd hold off until after Christmas."

"I got the same impression."

"Well, it's all in God's hands now."

"It's kinda been in His hands the whole time, hasn't it?"

Maggie laughed, "*Yes, Hillary*," she said sarcastically, "You know what I meant."

Hillary chuckled as she looked in the oven to check on the pumpkin bread she had baking. "*So*," she said, as she closed the door, "What's the plan for tonight?"

"Well," Maggie said, "All the Pritt grandbabies are at Mama's, and, *as usual*, she'll be playing Mama Hen to the whole brood all evening...Roger's picking me up at five and we're gonna meet y'all Down Front shortly after that, right? –*Hey! It's snowing.*"

Hillary looked outside, "It sure is...and look at the size of those flakes."

"They're *huge*."

Maggie went over, opened her front door, and walked out onto the porch, "They're sticking." She held her hand out, caught a flake in her palm, and then licked it onto her tongue, "*Uh oh.*"

"What?"

"I just used the last of my vanilla," Maggie said, "...And I know *somebody's* gonna want some snow cream."

"Isn't Roger working today?"

"Yeah."

"Call him."

"*For?*"

"Have him run and get you some."

"I'll just get some from Mama," Maggie said, "I'm sure she's got some."

"Suit yourself," Hillary said, "I was just trying to give you another opportunity to see your man."

"*Aa-aah*," Maggie drawled, "I see...I hadn't thought of that."

"I know...And here I am thinking I had brought you up better than that."

"Sorry to disappoint."

"Oh well," Hillary sighed noisily, "After a while I guess you start to get used to these things. So anyway...You'll see *me* Down Front then. Buddy's pulling the youth group's float."

"Oh yeah," Maggie said, "How could I forget that."

"He's over at the Pastor's rigging up the lights as we speak."

"I reckon we'll just have to save a cup or two of hot chocolate for him for after the parade then," Maggie said, *"Oh shoot."* She spun around on her heels and dashed back inside.

"What is it now?"

"I almost forgot about the chocolate. I've got the cocoa, butter, and sugar melting on the stove," Maggie said, grabbing a wooden spoon as she came into the kitchen and started stirring in the pot, "Good, I didn't let it scorch."

"Aren't you using your double boiler?"

"No, not for hot chocolate," Maggie answered. "Besides, Suzanne's got it. She wanted to try some new recipe she found in a Christmas magazine, and she doesn't have one of her own."

"Well don't you go messing up my hot chocolate," Hillary said, "I don't think I could take you disappointing me twice in one day."

"I've got six dozen white chocolate covered peanut butter balls sitting on wax paper right here in front of me that say that ain't gonna happen."

"I'll have to say that they're probably right."

Maggie smiled to herself and glanced back out her front window, "Man, Hillary," she said, "It is really coming down now...I can't even see the road out in front of the house it's coming down so hard."

Hillary looked outside through her kitchen window. "Everything here's already covered," she said. She pulled the curtain back and leaned over to one side, peering out towards the side of the yard, "The barn's just kind of a big dark shadow out there."

"I don't know that I've *ever* seen it come down like this."

"You don't think it's gonna snow out the parade and stuff do you?"

"I hope not," Maggie said, "Have you listened to the forecast any today?"

"No," Hillary said, "I've had Christmas music playing, and besides, I've been too busy cooking to pay any attention anyway."

"Me too...I think I'll call Daddy and see what it's supposed to do."

"Well, I ain't gonna worry too much...You know as good as I do that it'd have to drop a good four foot of snow on us before they'd even consider canceling the Christmas Festival."

"I know," Maggie said, stirring the pot of chocolate again, "I need to call down there anyway and see if he knows where Lendon is...He's supposed to be bringing me some fresh milk from Uncle Dean that I'm planning on using for this hot chocolate."

"Well, please don't let me hold you up," Hillary said, "I'd just about go milk one of them goats myself to have some of your hot chocolate."

"*That* I'd like to see," Maggie chuckled.

"I wouldn't."

"See ya girl."

"Bye."

Hillary stood watching the snow as she clicked the telephone off and set it down on the counter. She stared out the window as the snow drifted steadily down, grinning to herself as she softly sang, "*...I'm Dreaming of a White Christmas.*"

"Are you sure you don't want to park that thing in the shed and ride back to the shop with me? That snow's coming down pretty good."

Joey gulped down the last of his coffee and shook his head at Roger. "Naw," he said, grinning, "I'm primed for adventure this morning."

Roger smiled, "Since when is freezing your keister off high adventure?"

"It won't be that bad."

Joey stood himself up and sat his empty coffee cup down in Roger's sink. He looked at Roger, "We really need to ditch that coffee maker and get one of those presses for the shop. I believe that was about the best cup of coffee I've ever had."

"Thank you," Roger said, "It *was* good wasn't it."

Joey glanced out the window and then grabbed his coat from off the back of his chair, "I think I'm gonna head on back. It looks like it's starting to come down harder."

"I'm right behind you, Slick."

Joey slipped into his coat and ran his hands back through his hair. "Don't be jealous," he said, grinning at Roger, "*Everybody* can't be this smooth." He grabbed his scarf up and wrapped it around his neck and then pulled his gloves out from his coat pockets, "You still planning on putting the railing up at the library today?"

Roger shook his head, "No," he said, "If you don't mind *too* much, I don't believe we'll be doing much out-of-doors work today."

"That's fine by me."

Joey stepped out into the living room and put his helmet on as he headed for the front door. "Take it easy in that snow," Roger said.

"I will *Grandpa*."

"I've got too much time invested in you for you to go sliding that thing off in the ditch and you breaking your funny bone or something...Not to mention my sister would hold me completely responsible if something happened to you."

Joey nodded at Roger as he fastened the helmet straps under his chin, "I'm really touched by the sincere concern you have for yourself."

"I'm a very thoughtful guy once you get to know me."

The snow had come down steadily all day. Hillary had checked its progress out the window throughout the day as she went about the business of baking two loaves of pumpkin bread, several pies, a three layer coconut cake, two dozen extra-large snowman cookies, and two pans of her "trademark" fudge. Buddy had called her just past noon to let her know he wouldn't be home for dinner; he was running behind because he had had to stop three times already to go pull people out of the ditch along "dead man's curve" just up the Old Town Road from the Pastor's house.

"That's alright," she had told him, "Be sure and get something to eat."

"I will *Sassy Lady*," he said.

Hillary chuckled to herself and then, as she hung up she said, "I love you Buddy, stay warm."

"Love you most," he said back, and then hung up.

Now, some four hours later, she was sitting down for the first time since breakfast, absent mindedly stirring a candy cane in a hot cup of Russian tea and nibbling on one of her Aunt Lula's ginger cookies.

She took a sip of her tea and then got up and went in to the living room to start the stack of old Christmas albums back over on the record player. Pulling the stack back up onto the rod in the middle of the turntable, she set the arm in place and clicked the player back on. She watched as the bottom album dropped down into place and the arm swung down and the quiet crackling began from the speakers as the needle found its place in the grooves. She shook her head happily and smiled, "Gotta love that crackle," she said softly.

Hillary went back into the kitchen and picked up her teacup as Johnny Mathis began his walk through a happy Christmas snow. She pulled the candy cane out and sucked the tea off of it as she walked back into the living room and looked out the front window.

"There's got to be at least six inches of snow out there," she said. She took a sip of her tea and swallowed it down slowly, savoring the citrusy-spicy flavor. Looking around the yard, she noticed that it was already dark enough for the light on the front of the barn to have turned itself on. She squatted down a little and tilted her head as she leaned a little closer to the window to peer around the edge of the porch roof eaves to get a look at the sky. *I think it's slacking up some*, she thought.

Hillary stood back up and looked down the driveway as the lights from Buddy's tractor shined into the yard as he came in off the road. The lights he had strung on his tractor were twinkling brightly in the darkening evening, but she noted that not a single bulb was on on the entire float. "Hmpf," she grunted, "I wonder what's going on there."

Buddy drove on across the yard and stopped out in front of the barn and then climbed down and went quickly inside. Hillary watched for a moment and then Buddy came back out, carrying a couple tools in one hand and a coil of wire in the other. He stopped near the back of the tractor and disappeared down between one of the back wheels and the float for a minute, and Hillary watched as the strings of lights on the trailer flickered and then flashed and then went dark again as Buddy fiddled around with whatever it was he thought was causing the lighting problem.

She saw Buddy's head bobbing up and down as he glanced back and forth, watching for a positive response from the lights to the repairs he was trying to make. The lights flickered on and then shone dully through the falling snow. Buddy got himself up and reached up next to the steering wheel and pulled the throttle back. The lights shone brighter for a moment, then flickered, flashed brightly, and then went dark again.

Hillary saw Buddy smack his thigh and then shake his head. He stood staring at the trailer for a second and then reached up, idled the tractor down, and squatted himself down and went back to work.

Grabbing her coat from the closet, Hillary slipped it on as she walked into the kitchen. She cut Buddy a piece of the pumpkin bread, "Not *too* big," she said, knowing that he'd protest if it was. She dropped the knife into the sink and then wrapped the bread in a paper towel and went outside. Buddy was just stepping back into the barn as she came down off the front porch and didn't see her coming out.

Hillary looked the trailer over as she walked past. It had been covered with sheets of burlap and there were bales of wheat straw placed here and there with plywood sheep propped against them and one big brown plywood cow up towards the front. They had strung up three angels on a wire between two posts at the back of the float and two spotlights were hidden behind bales near the posts, meant to shine brightly up at them. There were strings of lights all around the body of the float and spelling out "Hark the Herald Angels Sing" in an arch up above the angels. The whole thing was rapidly collecting snow.

As Hillary looked it over she figured that there had to be close to ten thousand bulbs on it..."And not a one of 'em wants to shine," she said under her breath. She looked at the tractor and noticed that Buddy had two very big box-speakers rigged up on the back of his seat facing towards the float. She looked at the happily twinkling lights draped strategically across the tractor and grinned, "Well, if they can't have lights on the float, at least they'll have sound." She stepped back and admired the whole rig in total for a moment and then looked at the speakers again, "...And plenty of it."

Hillary shivered, shaking the snow off her shoulders as she turned and walked on over to the barn. She opened the door and stepped inside just as Buddy was coming around the back end of her Christmas surprise, headed back out from his workbench. He looked up from the fuse-link in his hands that he had just crimped together and stopped dead in his tracks when he saw her standing in the open doorway. She was staring wide-eyed at the dark green Karmen Ghia.

"Hey," he said, making a coughing sound in his throat.

Hillary took two slow steps towards the car, "What... What...Who's is this?"

Buddy didn't answer.

She stepped closer and touched the hood.

"You like it?"

Hillary stared in through the windshield for a moment and then looked down at her reflection in the glossy paint of the hood, "It's beautiful," she said, "It's like a dream."

Buddy smiled, "Merry Christmas."

Hillary stared at the car a few seconds longer and then looked blankly at her husband, "*What?*"

Buddy smiled again, "Merry Christmas."

A grin came creeping slowly across Hillary's face as Buddy's words sunk in, "Are you serious...Is this really for me?"

Buddy nodded, "I wouldn't have spent two hours out here yesterday waxing it in the cold if it wasn't."

Hillary jumped over and wrapped her arms around Buddy's neck, squeezing him tightly, "Oh Buddy," she said, and quickly kissed him back and forth twice on both cheeks. She looked back at the car and then turned back to him, her eyes moistening, "It's just like the one I wanted when we were teenagers...*It's beautiful.*"

"The keys're in it."

Hillary gazed into Buddy's eyes and didn't move. Buddy gave his head a little nod, "Go ahead and hop in it," he said, "See how it fits."

Hillary paused a second longer and then went quickly around the back of the car, tripping in the tan canvas cover Buddy had piled up on the floor when he waxed the car the day before.

"Watch yourself," Buddy said, "Sorry; I just slid that off there when I waxed it yesterday."

"That's alright," Hillary chirped as she worked to untangle her feet. She flashed an excited smile at Buddy as she finally kicked herself free and then went on around and pulled the door open and climbed inside.

Buddy squatted down and propped his chin on his arm in the open passenger window.

"This car is just beautiful," Hillary said, caressing the steering wheel. "It's just what I've always wanted Buddy. I can't believe it."

"Almost," Buddy said.

Hillary looked at him quizzically.

"It's not a convertible and it's not black..."

"*It's not?*"

Buddy shook his head, "Unh uh...It's green."

"*It is?*"

Buddy nodded, "Dark, *dark*, green."

Hillary gazed out over the hood, "It's beautiful green."

She touched the dash.

"Fire it up."

Hillary cocked her head over to the left and saw the key in the ignition. She grabbed it and cradled the keychain in her hand. It was a shiny gold "H" with a little Volkswagen symbol engraved on it. She grinned at Buddy, "I like it."

Buddy smiled.

Pulling the door closed, Hillary pushed the clutch in and turned the key. The motor sparked to life and hummed perfectly. She let it idle for a moment and then softly pumped the gas. The motor revved a mellow tone. Hillary looked at Buddy again, her eyes smiling.

Buddy pumped his eyebrows at her, "Sixteen hundred CCs and dual carburetors," he said proudly, "...This thing's *built*."

Hillary grinned a little wider and revved the motor, "Built, huh?"

"Not as nicely as you."

Hillary rolled her eyes.

"Wait 'til you get to drive it," Buddy said, "The guy that built this car said he wanted it to drive like it was on a rail...and it does."

Hillary gripped the steering wheel at ten and two and pictured a sunlit two-lane back road snaking out in front of her, with trees whizzing quickly by. She gripped the pearl white shifter knob as she pushed the clutch back in and ran the shifter through the gears, imagining herself speeding the car along with the windows down and the wind whipping through her hair.

Buddy glowed in her smile.

Hillary drove on in her mind for another mile or so and then put the car in first gear and shut the motor down. She turned slowly to her husband, a sudden melancholy darkening her face, "This is too much, Buddy."

"What do you mean?"

"I mean I can't keep this...I know about what one of these in this kind of shape costs and it's too much."

"No it's not."

"How can you say that? This isn't a need...Your tractor's over thirty years old, your truck's almost as old as your tractor. The station wagon's what? Eighteen...twenty years old? We base our purchases on needs right? That's what we've always done...This isn't a need."

"You are absolutely right, Hillary," Buddy said, "That's what we've always done...That's what *I've* always done." He paused and smiled weakly, "You have gone without wants and likes and frivolities since the day you married me. And before you say anything to me about how that's alright and you've never minded and we have a good life, let me tell you something. You deserve more."

Buddy held his hand up and stopped Hillary as she started to speak, "You are the best part of my life," he said, "God has blessed me with the finest woman *any* man could ever want. You have been so good to me and to my family and to my children...You are so kind, so intelligent, so beautiful..." He paused and took a deep breath, "I know that if you had had an opportunity to go away to school or anything like that, there would be no you and me. If you had not been stuck here in this little Podunk town that I would not have had a snowball's chance with you– "

"That's not true."

Buddy said, "Yes it is Hillary...and don't even insult my intelligence by trying to pretend you don't know it." He paused again and shifted his weight down onto his knees so that he wouldn't have to hunch his shoulders to rest his chin on his arms. He looked directly into his wife's eyes, "You are *so* beautiful. I have never seen anyone in a movie or on television or in a magazine or anywhere that even comes close to you. And me," he shook his head, "I've been a fat, tight-fisted, unimaginative, unromantic, clodhoppin' boor of a husband since day one."

Hillary shook her head.

"You disagree?"

"Yes."

"Have you ever caught another woman looking at me?"

Hillary didn't answer.

"Have I ever done anything that made your heart flutter?

"Have I ever taken you *anywhere* that didn't involve farm implements or lawn care?

"Have I ever taken you out for a meal that didn't consist of some form of ground beef or chopped pork?

"Have you ever looked at me and just *wanted* me?"

"Is that what this past month has been about?" Hillary said, "All the dieting and the sexy talk...You think I'm not happy with you? You think you have to buy me things to make me want you?"

Buddy shook his head, "No Hill, that's not it at all. I know you love me. *Dern*, if you didn't, you've had to been crazy to have stayed with me all this time. *You* do all those things to *me*...Don't you see? I can't think of a single time I have been anywhere with you that I didn't see men checking you out. I can't think of a day that has gone by that you didn't make my heart do somersaults in my chest. I can't think of a day that I haven't looked at you and thought that I must be the luckiest man alive. And I finally realized that I haven't ever done anything to make you feel that same way about me.

"Sure, I take care of you," Buddy continued, "I take care of everything. Our roof doesn't leak and the oven works... that's *real* romantic, Hill. Our cars are old, but I keep 'em clean and they run great...*Ooh the passion,*" he said mockingly, "I'm sure everytime you climb behind the wheel and crank that baby up you think, '*Dern*, I can't wait to get back home and jump Buddy's bones!'"

Hillary covered her face with her hand and stifled back a laugh. Buddy contemplated his words as he watched Hillary choking back her laughter.

"Go ahead;" he chuckled, "That *was* funny."

Hillary let out a quiet laugh, "I don't know what to say to all this Buddy."

"Do you like the car?"

Hillary looked at him oddly. "Of course I do," she said, "Are you crazy..." She looked all around at the interior and then turned back to him, "...I love it."

"Then that's all you need to say."

Hillary looked at him closely for a moment and then reached out and grabbed his hand. Buddy smiled at her and then pulled her hand to his mouth and kissed it softly.

Hillary pulled the handle and pushed the car door back open, turning loose of Buddy's hand as she slid out.

Buddy stood himself back up as Hillary climbed out and stood up. She gave him a steamy look and motioned for him to head around to the back of the car. Buddy grinned at Hillary boyishly and then went around to meet her.

Hillary walked up and wrapped her arms around Buddy's shoulders and kissed him fully on the mouth. Buddy felt the heat of her breath as she moved her face around, pressing her mouth against his neck as she ran her hands up through his hair and pressed her body tightly against his. She unsnapped the front of his coat and ran her hands up under his shirt.

She kissed him lightly on his lips and then leaned back and looked up into his eyes. "My heart's fluttering *now*," she said.

Hillary grabbed Buddy firmly around his shoulders and pulled him down with her, guiding him onto the cover that he had left piled up on the floor. She kissed him again, pressing her mouth firmly to his as she pulled him onto her and lay back on the barn floor.

⟿

"I don't know," Maggie said, "I've been calling over there for the last hour and can't get an answer."

"Buddy's not answering his cell phone either," Roger said, "You think I need to run over there and check on 'em?"

"I don't know; I just got a call from Mary Alice that everyone's getting a little nervous that they don't have a float in line yet."

Roger thought for a moment and then said, "Are you ready to go?"

"Pretty much," Maggie said, "I just need to get everything in the basket and get my boots on and I'll be ready."

"How 'bout I head on out now and pick you up and we'll run over there together? It's a little earlier than we planned, I know, but if something's wrong I couldn't live with myself if I didn't check on them."

"No, that's fine," Maggie said, "Come on over."

⟿

Hillary pulled herself in a little closer to Buddy and snuggled in under his arms, her bare skin flushed and warm against his. Buddy pulled the canvas cover a little higher up around them.

"You're amazing," he said.

Hillary brushed a light kiss against Buddy's lips and smiled at him, her eyes twinkling. She glanced over his shoulder at the car and then looked back into his eyes.

"What are you thinking right now," Buddy asked her.

She ran her hands up through his hair and then rolled onto her back, leading him over with her, "I was just thinking that I *really* should come out to this barn more often."

"There's his tractor and the float," Roger said as he pulled up into the Vander's yard.

"The tractor looks good," Maggie said.

Roger pulled up next to it and cut off his truck. He opened his door and then glanced back at Maggie, "The tractor's still running," he said, sliding out of the truck, "... Maybe he's in the barn."

Maggie watched Roger's face as he stood staring towards the barn, "What is it?"

Roger shrugged, "I don't know," he said, "Something just feels funny about all this." He nodded his head in the direction of the barn. "...The door's hanging half open."

"Well, hold on just a sec then and I'll go with you."

"Alright," Roger said, closing his door as Maggie hopped out on the other side. Maggie trotted around and got up next to Roger, looping her arm through his as she stuck her gloved hands down into her coat pockets. She smiled at him and squeezed herself close to his side.

"I'm sure there's nothing to worry about," Maggie said as Roger led her toward the barn. He pulled his arms in tight, squeezing hers against his side and shrugged without comment.

As Maggie watched his brow crease, she knew that he was remembering the day he had found his best friend lying hurt and bloodied in a field just a stone's throw from where they now walked.

Roger stopped and reached out, grabbing the edge of the door as they got to the barn. He hesitated just long enough for them both to hear what sounded like someone groaning inside.

Glancing quickly at Maggie, Roger snatched the door open and ran inside. Maggie followed close behind him as he went in and ran down past the Karmann Ghia.

Maggie ran solidly into Roger, jamming her face into his back as he pulled up and stopped suddenly as he went around the back of the car.

"Oww," she grunted, grabbing her face, "What is it, Rog–"

"Oh shoot, ya'll," Roger was blurting, "*I swornee*. I...I'm sorry..."

Maggie peeked around Roger's shoulder and gasped, "*Oh no*," she slapped her hands over her eyes, "Ooh I...Oh..."

Roger, still apologizing, had spun around and was tripping over her with his eyes closed as he tried to break himself away.

They stumbled over each other as they awkwardly made their way back out past the car, through the door, and out into the snow-covered yard. They came to a stop a few steps outside the barn, holding their breath as they gazed out over the treetops towards the river. Maggie stood there for a second and then stepped back over and closed the barn door with a shove. She stood leaning against the door for a few seconds, her face towards the ground. When she turned back to Roger, he was standing with his hands on his hips staring at his feet, shaking his head.

Maggie walked slowly back to him, tracing their steps in the snow. She walked around in front of him, stopped, and crossed her arms. Roger kept staring at the ground. Nudging his foot with the toe of her boot, she waited for him to look up at her.

After a few seconds, Maggie gave Roger's foot another nudge.

Roger shook his head, "I can't."

Maggie snickered.

"I think I've gone blind."

Maggie chuckled. She reached up and kissed the top of Roger's head. He shook it again and then slowly looked up at her. Their eyes met and Roger's shoulders hitched. Maggie chuckled louder.

Roger's lips trembled. Maggie could hear the laugh beginning to roll up from deep down in his stomach. He covered his face with both hands.

Maggie reached up and grabbed his wrists and pulled his hands down away from his face. When their eyes met, Roger finally burst out laughing. He grabbed Maggie around her shoulders and hugged her close.

Maggie buried her face in Roger's chest and loved being there laughing with him. *This is our first big funny*, she found herself thinking. She looked up at him, "Talk about a spirit of giving."

They both burst out into a fit of convulsive laughter. Roger squeezed her tightly for a long moment and then pushed her gently away and bent himself over with his hands propped on his knees. His laughter punctuated here and there with dry coughing.

"Are you alright," Maggie laughed.

Roger glanced up at her, still laughing and nodded. "I'm fine," he wheezed. "It's just the cold air." Maggie could see tears on his cheeks.

She dabbed at her eyes with the back of a glove.

Roger stood back up, now just coughing, and shook his head at her, "*Out*," he said, chuckling hoarsely, "...*Out.*"

"Didn't your mama ever teach you it's impolite to just barge in on married folks without knocking?" came Hillary's voice from behind them.

They looked over and Buddy and Hillary were standing in the open doorway, both of their faces still a little flushed.

"Just came to check on y'all," Roger said.

"They certainly got a full checkup, I'd say," Maggie said under breath so only Roger could hear.

He started chuckling again. He cut his eyes at Maggie and shook his head.

Maggie snickered.

"Do y'all want to come in out of the weather?" Buddy said.

"Oh, no," Maggie and Roger both blurted.

Roger held up one hand. "We're good," he said. "*You ain't ever gettin' me in that barn again,*" he whispered to Maggie.

Maggie chuckled at him.

Roger was having trouble looking Buddy and Hillary in the eye. He kept glancing quickly back and forth between them and then looking around at all the lovely snowfall. "Well," he said, "We came by to check on y'all, 'cause some folks were wondering where their float was."

"Oh shoot," Buddy said. He checked his watch, "Oh shoot." He looked at Hillary, "I was supposed to be there forty minutes ago...And I ain't even got the lights fixed yet." He spun around and ran back in the barn.

Hillary pulled the collar of her coat up around her neck and walked slowly out to Maggie and Roger.

"I see you got your car," Roger said.

Hillary smiled.

"*Car?*" Maggie said, "I didn't even notice a car...What is it."

"My Karmann Ghia," Hillary said, her smile widening, "I finally got it."

Buddy came trotting back out with his tools and the fuse link in his hands, "Can you give me a hand with this Rog?"

"Sure."

Buddy and Roger went over to the back of the tractor, "Could you shut that off for me," Buddy asked.

"Sure," Roger said again and shut the tractor off. Buddy handed him a roll of black electrician's tape and then quickly went to work stripping the wires that were leading from the trailer lights to the tractor.

"I'm sorry about the, uh, interruption, Buddy," Roger said quietly, as he watched his friend splice the fuse link into the wires.

Buddy glanced up at him and then went right back to his work. Roger thought he could see a little grin on Buddy's face.

"It's alright," Buddy said, giving his head a little shake, "If that's the worst thing you ever do, then you'll be just fine."

"I reckon she really likes the car."

Buddy chuckled. He held his hand up to Roger and Roger stuck the roll of tape into it. Buddy wrapped up all the free wire and then stuck the roll into his coat pocket.

"I thought she was getting it tomorrow?"

"I thought she was, too," Buddy said. He pointed his thumb at the tractor, "Crank it up for me would ya."

Roger cranked the tractor.

Buddy closed his eyes and flipped the switch. When he opened his eyes the trailer was lit up spectacularly. Heaving a huge sigh of relief, he shook his head and then looked over Roger's shoulder to Hillary, "*What'cha think Babe?*"

Hillary gave him a thumbs up, "*Looks great.*"

Buddy looked back at Roger, "She caught me out in the garage," he said quietly, "I had this whole big plan for tomorrow..."

"All's well that ends well," Roger said, "At least you've still got the other stuff."

"Shhh," Buddy hissed as Hillary and Maggie walked up behind Roger.

"Give me those tools, "Roger said, "I'll go put 'em up and you can head on down with the float."

"Thanks," Buddy said, handing the tools over, "I reckon I'll see you after."

"That's the plan," Roger threw Buddy a wink and headed off towards the barn.

Buddy, Hillary, and Maggie watched him go for a moment and then Buddy turned to Maggie briefly and glanced down at the ground. "Sorry about earlier," he said. He looked back up at her and his cheeks flushed, "I uh, don't reckon you were expecting to go walking in on, uh...uh...*that.*"

"That's alright, Bear," she said. She looked sideways at Hillary and then back to Buddy, "I guess this makes us even, now, huh?"

Buddy's face flushed a deeper red, and he chuckled embarrassedly. "I don't know about all that," he said. He glanced at Hillary and then looked back at Maggie, "I think I might be one up on you."

~Chapter Fourteen~

"I'll just stay here with Lydia," Rose said, "If she feels like it, I can drive her down in her car."

Mary grabbed her coat and slid into it, "I hate to leave you here by yourselves," she said.

"We'll be fine, Mama," Lydia said as TJ came thundering in through the front door. "Come on y'all," he said, "We're all ready."

"I think I'm gonna hang out here for a little while TJ," Lydia told him.

TJ frowned, "Y'all aren't coming?"

"That's not what I said," Lydia replied, "I need to stay here for now." She touched her mother on the shoulder, "Mama's coming, and Rose and I will probably be down in a little bit."

"Why can't y'all come now?"

Lydia patted her stomach, "Because your sisters have been very busy all day and I'm a little tired."

"Your mama needs to put her feet up for a little while," Rose said.

Lydia smiled at Mary and said, "Y'all go ahead Mama. We'll be down in a little bit."

"I'd be glad to stay here, too."

"I know, Mama," Lydia said, patting her stomach again, "...but you've got some other grandchildren that want your attention right now...Once these two get here, you won't have so much time to give them."

Mary glanced down at TJ and then smiled at Lydia, "I reckon you're right," she said, grabbing her scarf and toboggan off the back of the chair, "Tell 'em I'll be right out TJ."

"Yes'm," TJ chirped. He hugged Lydia as best as he could, pressing his face against the side of her swollen belly and smiled up at her, "I love you."

"I love you, too," Lydia said, hugging his head to her side. "Have fun."

TJ turned loose of her and ran back outside.

Mary wrapped the scarf around her neck and then pulled the toboggan on, "Call Iris if you need me."

"I will."

"I can't wait to ride in it, Hill," Maggie said.

"I can't either," Hillary grinned, "But you can bet just as soon as this snow's all gone I'm gonna be lighting up the roads with it."

"Listen at you."

Hillary cocked her head to one side and wrinkled up her brow, "You drive a station wagon for the better part of your twenties and then come back and talk to me."

"I'm not judging..."

Roger was sitting in the passenger seat of Hillary's car with his right leg sticking out the open door. Hillary smiled down at him, "Well, if I ever have a secret I need someone to keep I certainly know who to come to."

Roger twisted an imaginary key in his lips, "When I tick a lock, I tick a lock." He heaved himself up out of the car and closed the door.

"I reckon we'd better get on downtown," Maggie said, turning back to Hillary, "Do you need a hand with anything?"

"I've got everything ready...I just need to get it all loaded up and go."

"I'll give you a hand and we'll go then."

"I'll get the barn shut up while y'all do that if you don't need my help," Roger said.

"Thanks Roger."

Roger walked back to Buddy's workbench and clicked the light off as Hillary and Maggie went out. Walking over, he cracked open the little half-door on the outside wall and checked that the light in the pump house was still on. It was, so he closed the door and headed out, looking back at the Karmen as he switched off the overhead lights. He stepped out into the snow, closed the door, threw the latch, and clipped the little spring loaded dog lead into place, "locking" the door.

Roger climbed in and cranked his truck as Maggie and Hillary came out onto the porch, each carrying a tray full of Christmas treats. He slid back out and asked, "Is that everything?"

"Yep," Hillary replied, "That's everything we need for tonight."

At the sound of Hillary's words, Roger turned his gaze to Maggie and his stomach sank. He jammed his hands into his coat pockets and found nothing but two handfuls of empty dread. He remembered grabbing his keys and his wallet on the way out of his bedroom and he pictured the empty top of his dresser. His mind wheeled, *Oh dern*, he thought, *Where did I put it?*

He took a deep breath and held it.

"What is it Roger," Maggie asked as she came down off the porch.

"Huh?"

Maggie smiled, wrinkling her nose at Roger as she walked past him to Hillary's car, "You look like you just saw a ghost."

Roger blew his breath out slowly through pursed lips as he patted around at all his pockets and tried not to look conspicuous.

"Did you lose something?" asked Hillary.

"*What?*"

Hillary slid her tray in onto the back seat and then stood up and looked at Roger over the roof of her car, "I asked you if you lost something," she said, "You look like you're checking yourself for concealed weapons."

Roger stopped patting himself down and clasped his hands behind his back, smiling embarrassedly, "I, I was trying to find my keys."

"They're probably in there," Hillary said, pointing at Roger's truck, "I mean, I would assume that...since it's running and all."

Roger glanced back over his shoulder and then turned back and shook his head, "Oh yeah."

"Are you alright?" Maggie asked him, "You look a little ill all the sudden."

Roger's brows knitted as he stared at the ground, trying to remember the last place he had seen the little box, *This is terrible*, he thought, realizing that he had gotten so preoccupied earlier with worrying about Buddy that he had completely forgotten about his plan. He gave his head a little shake, trying to clear his thoughts, *Where is it?*

"*Roger.*"

Roger snapped to and looked up at Maggie, "Huh?"

"*Are you alright?*"

Roger shook his head again and then smiled self-consciously, "Yeah," he said, "I'm sorry. I, uh, I just got lost in a thought for a minute there."

"Are you sure?"

"Yeah," he said, "I'm sure...I just realized that I forgot something and I was trying to figure out what I had done with it that's all."

"Did you figure it out," asked Hillary.

Roger looked blankly at Hillary for a second; still trying to remember where he had put the ring. "...Actually, no." His brows knitted again and he bit the inside of his lip, "No I didn't." He looked at Maggie, "I think I need to ride by my house real quick. Do you think you might want to ride over with Hillary so you don't miss any of the parade?"

Maggie glanced over at Hillary and then smiled at Roger, "That's alright," she told him, "I'll stay with you."

"Are you sure," he said, "I'd hate for you to miss it."

Maggie checked her watch, "We've got thirty minutes before it's supposed to start. How long's what you've got to do gonna take?"

Roger shrugged, "I don't know. Maybe ten, fifteen minutes or so," he said vaguely, "I don't know."

Maggie glanced back over at Hillary again and then turned back Roger, "I'll risk it."

"Well, I'll just see y'all down there then," Hillary said, grinning at Maggie as she climbed into her car, "T T F N."

Maggie followed Roger to his truck. He opened her door and then closed it behind her as she slid in.

"Are you sure you're okay," Maggie asked as Roger slid in behind the wheel.

"Yeah, I'm fine," he said, a little distantly. They watched as Hillary backed out past them and then Roger pulled in behind her and followed her car out to the road.

"I could go with Hill if you really want me to," Maggie said as Roger pulled his truck out onto First Street.

Roger shook his head. "I'm sorry Maggie," he said, "It's fine...It's just I don't know how long this may take and I'd hate for you to miss anything."

"What do you need to get?"

Roger looked at Maggie, "What do I need to get?"

Maggie nodded.

"I, uh, I need a, um..." Roger stammered. He looked down at the radio and then reached over and turned it on. Holly Jolly Christmas danced around the cab of the truck. "I'm glad the roads are still fairly clear," he said, "I reckon there's been enough traffic in town today to keep 'em that way."

Maggie eyed Roger curiously, "Yeah."

Roger fell silent and Maggie thought he focused himself a little more than necessary the rest of the way to his house. She started to unfasten her seatbelt as he pulled into his driveway, when Roger quickly said, "Just wait here...I'll be back in a minute."

"*Okay,*" Maggie replied, watching him slide out and trot up onto his porch, slipping slightly in the snow that had collected on his front steps as he went up.

Opening the front door, Roger disappeared inside, and as she watched the front door close behind him, Maggie realized that she really needed to use his bathroom. Crossing her ankles, she squeezed her legs tightly together, "You *really* drank too much coffee today, Maggie." She took a deep breath and looked nervously out the side window, noticing that the snow had fallen off to just a light sprinkling. *Just enough for the parade*, she thought, and then looked back up towards the house.

From where she was sitting, Maggie could see that Roger had turned on the light in the living room, the hall bedroom, and his bedroom in the back of the house. *I wonder what he's looking for...* She took another deep breath and slid her hands down in between her thighs and tapped the toes of her boots against each other. She shook her head, "I can't wait." She opened the door and hurried to the house.

⮨

"Are you sure you're up to this," Rose asked.

Lydia propped herself against the Land Rover's fender and stared down at the snowy ground, breathing deeply. Rose moved in close behind her and laid a comforting hand on her shoulder.

Lydia breathed through the pain and then stood herself back up, "That wasn't *too* bad."

"I won't be disappointed if I miss the parade," Rose assured her.

Lydia turned to face her; Rose's face was already flushed with the cold. "I know," Lydia said, "...Really, that one wasn't that bad. To be totally honest, the last three or four haven't been all that bad...at least compared to what I was getting this morning."

"Still, why don't we just go back inside."

"No, Miss Rose, *really*, I'm good...They're not as strong as they were and there's no consistent pattern to them, and besides, I've been looking forward to this for months."

Rose studied Lydia's face for half a minute. "Alright," she said, taking a serious tone, "If you feel the least bit–"

"I know, I know," Lydia said, nodding her head, "Back in the car and home to bed."

Rose held her gaze on Lydia's face.

"I promise," Lydia sighed, "I'll tell you."

"Alright," Rose smiled, motioning towards the front passenger door, "Let me help you in."

Lydia stepped around as Rose pulled open the door for her. She was just about to climb in when they heard the sound of the siren going off at the fire department. Lydia stopped and looked off towards downtown.

"*What*," she said, glancing at Rose, "...They're starting early." She pulled up her sleeve and checked her watch,

"*Thirty minutes* early." She looked back up at Rose, "They *never* start early."

"Maybe it's the snow."

Lydia's shoulders drooped, "We'll *never* get down there now."

"Are you sure?"

Lydia shook her head. "No," she said, "Not to where the rest of the family is."

"Could we go sit somewhere else?" Rose asked her, "Maybe just go park somewhere along the way, maybe towards the end of the parade...Somewhere where we could just sit in the car and watch?"

Lydia thought a bit, "I reckon we could go park up at Maverick's; that's pretty much the end of it, there...It usually ends up in the field right around past his shop."

"Well, why don't we just do that then."

Lydia took a deep breath, "Alright," she said slowly, "TJ's not going to be real happy about it, but..."

"Oh, he'll be fine," Rose smiled. She touched Lydia's shoulder and urged her into the car as fluffy flakes of snow began to drift lightly down again.

Hesitating, Lydia cast her gaze around the yard, "How pretty," she said. She climbed in and Rose closed the door behind her. Lydia watched as Rose walked gracefully around the front of the car, little flakes of snow catching in the collar of her coat.

Lydia's abdomen tightened suddenly and a sharp pain gripped around her waist. Gritting her teeth, she gripped the dash, and took a deep breath, squeezing the dash tighter as a second wave of pain shot through her.

Rose opened the driver's door and slid in, "*Lydia*?"

Lydia sucked in a deep breath, exhaled slowly, and then breathed in again. She straightened herself up and held her breath a moment before blowing it out noisily. Turning to Rose, she forced a smile, "I'm ready."

"Are you sure you wouldn't rather go on up to the hospital?"

Lydia shook her head, "The nurse said that I shouldn't risk riding up to Ormond with it snowing like this if I wasn't sure it was time."

"That's all well and good," Rose said, "But she isn't the one carrying twins."

Lydia chuckled, "I wouldn't trust a ride in an ambulance to Ormond tonight anyway. There's probably three or four inches of slush and ice on every road between here and the Ocean Highway."

"We can drive this."

"I'll be fine."

"The road won't be any better tomorrow."

"I'm fine...*really*...Let's go see the parade."

Rose gave Lydia a disapproving look and then cranked the car. "Which one of these is for the wipers," she asked as she searched the knobs on the dash.

"That one," Lydia said as she pointed out the switch for the wipers. Rose turned the wipers on and watched as they flicked the slowly falling flakes off to her left.

Lydia pointed at another knob, "And that's for the lights."

Rose turned on the headlights, "...And how do we get some heat going?"

"With the blankets in the back," Lydia chuckled.

Rose eased the Rover back out of the driveway and drove carefully down to the intersection. She pointed left, "This way, right?"

Lydia nodded.

Rose pulled out cautiously, "Looks like there's been a lot of traffic out here today," she said. She drove a short distance and then pointed at a spot on the shoulder where there were marks where a car had slid off the road down into the ditch and had then been pulled out.

Lydia said, "Looks like somebody had a bad time."

Rose nodded her head as she brought the Rover to a stop at the intersection across from Maverick's Service Station, "Where do you think would be the best place to park?"

Lydia pointed down past the parking lot going towards the Landing. "Probably over on that side," she said, "That way we can see everything all lit up as they come around the curve."

Rose looked down to where Lydia was pointing, "Alright," she said. She was just starting the car rolling again when Lydia grabbed at her stomach with both hands and let out a long groan.

Rose pushed the clutch back in and gently pressed the brake, stopping the car. She watched until Lydia's pain seemed to ease off and said, "Lydia, why don't we just drive back up to your mother's where you can get comfortable?"

Lydia sat in silence for a moment, breathing deeply through her nose. Lydia sounded winded, "Can't do that," she said, sounding a bit winded.

Rose looked at her quizzically.

Lydia took another long breath, "My water just broke."

Roger let out a frustrated groan as he finally gave up and just pulled the whole top drawer out of his dresser and dumped it out on his bed. He could feel his plans for the night slipping away as he frantically rummaged through the pile of handkerchiefs and boxer shorts. Scooping up a stack of receipts, he picked out the yellow ticket from the jeweler. "Well, I can always slide the receipt on her finger."

Roger rolled the receipt into a circle and held it out in front of himself, sliding it onto a make-believe Maggie's finger, "Rock, paper, scissors, Maggie...I win, we get hitched, *you* win..." He gave his head a shake as he crumpled the receipt into a ball and tossed it to one side. He bent back over the pile on his bed and continued his fruitless search, "This is just great," he growled, spreading the pile out in front of him, "...*Just great.*

"First the weather and now this," he grumbled, "I've changed my plan three times, and now this...*Just great...*"

Roger froze as he heard the front door creak open. After a second, he heard a light rapping and then Maggie's voice called gently down the hall, "*Roger?*" His heart sank further.

Closing his eyes, Roger took a deep breath. "I'm right here," he called back as he stepped over to the doorway and stuck his head out into the hall.

Maggie was standing just inside his front door, looking apologetically in his direction. "I'm sorry," she said, "But, I *really* need to use your bathroom."

"Okay," Roger said, pulling his door closed behind him as he stepped out into the hallway. He motioned towards the bathroom, "It's all yours."

Maggie closed the front door behind her and stepped quickly down the hall. "Thank you," she said embarrassedly, as she headed into the bathroom. Stepping inside, she went to push the door closed, but Roger's robe was hanging up on the corner.

Maggie grabbed the robe down and stuck her head back out; Roger had already gone back into his room and closed the door. She stared at his door for a moment and then looked down at the robe. She checked the back of the bathroom door; *No hook.* She stuck her head back out into the hall "What do you want me to do with your robe?" she called, "...Or does it matter?"

Roger was down on his hands and knees searching on the floor behind his dresser. He straightened himself up and called back, "*My robe?*"

"Yeah, it was hanging over the door."

He glanced over at his closet door, "That's odd," he said to himself, "I never leave that in there."

My robe, he remembered, *it's in my robe.* Beads of sweat popped out on his forehead as he sprang to his feet, *I left it there this morning...when I called Joey.* He punched his hand.

Maggie started dancing in place, "You want me to just toss it over the shower rod?"

Roger pictured Maggie tossing his robe over the rod and the ring falling out, bouncing off the edge of the bath tub, and plopping down with a noisy splash into the commode. He punched his hand again, "*Oh no.*"

Maggie balled the robe nervously, "*Roger?*"

"Just drop it on the floor," Roger answered hurriedly, "... *Wait*, no, *wait–*"

Maggie started to drop the robe behind the door but then grabbed it up again. She thought she felt an odd, hard knot in the middle of it.

Roger shook his head and smacked his hand to his forehead, *I'll just get it when she comes out,* "Yeah...Go ahead."

Maggie dropped the robe in a ball and closed the door. "*Whew,* Roger," she whispered, "You're killing me."

Roger packed everything back into the drawer and slid it back into place in the dresser. He wiped his face on his sleeve, *She must think I'm an idiot.* He opened his bedroom door, walked out into the hall, and stood staring at the bathroom door waiting for Maggie to come out. He wondered how he could salvage the evening, *The dock at the pond's out...We could never get across the dam with all the snow and ice...Maybe I could take her to the point for the fireworks and do it there.* He shook his head, *No, there'll be a crowd there...*

Roger heard the toilet flush and then realized he probably shouldn't be standing there hovering over the door waiting for her to come out. Hearing the water in the sink come on, he went quickly back into his bedroom and stood at the foot of his bed and waited until he heard the bathroom door open.

He waited a second longer and then stepped back out into the hallway. Maggie picked his robe back up and smiled over at him. "Sorry about that," Roger said, staring nervously at the robe, "I don't usually leave that hanging there."

"That's alright...I'm sorry for interrupting whatever you were doing."

"No big deal," Roger replied. He glanced quickly up and down from Maggie's face to the robe, "...When nature calls..."

They heard the sound of the siren going off downtown.

"Oh no," Maggie said, "Are we late?"

"I didn't think so." Roger looked down the hall at the big clock by the front door, "We're not late," he said, "They're starting early."

"Well I guess we'd better get going then," Maggie said. She went to hang the robe back up and Roger stopped her, "Here Mag," he said, "I'll take that."

Maggie stopped. She held the robe out and took a step towards Roger.

"I'll hang it up where it belongs," Roger said. He took the robe from her and turned to go back into his room, neither of them realizing that Maggie was standing on the robe's belt.

The robe pulled from Roger's hand and fell to the floor between them. "I'm sorry," Maggie said. They both bent down quickly to pick it up, knocking their heads together with a loud bump as they went.

Maggie flopped back onto her rear end on the floor, "I'm sorry," she said again, holding her head.

Roger picked up his robe and stood up, rubbing at his forehead. He grinned down at Maggie and squinted, "Are you alright?"

"Yeah," Maggie said, "Was that hollow sound from you or me?"

"Had to be me," Roger chuckled. He held a hand out to Maggie and helped her up. "Let me go hang this up and we'll swoop," he said, heading back into his bedroom.

Maggie rubbed at the little bump on her head as she went back down the hallway and waited for Roger by the front door.

"I guess you found what you were looking for," she said when he came back out.

"Huh," Roger grunted, fumbling in his coat pocket, "Oh yeah, I got it."

"Good."

Roger opened the door for Maggie and then clicked off the inside light as they went out. They could hear the sound of the marching band drifting up from downtown on the cold night air.

"I reckon if we go sit down at Maverick's we can still see the parade," Roger said as they stepped down off the porch and walked across the yard to his pickup, "...At least the end of it."

"We can park at Aunt Vercie's," Maggie suggested, "...We can just sit on the tailgate in the driveway."

Roger walked around and opened the passenger door, "That'll be good...*If* we can get up there."

Maggie slid in, "Ooh," she said, "It's nice and toasty in here."

"Good," Roger smiled, "It's a good thing we left it running then." He closed the door and then went around to the other side and climbed in. He put his seatbelt on, pulled the truck down into reverse, and draped his arm across the back of the seat, winking at Maggie as he craned his neck to look out the back glass, "Aunt Vercie, here we come."

"I hope we can get over there," Maggie said as Roger backed the truck quickly out into the street.

"I think we'll make it," Roger said, skidding to a stop in the slushy snow. He turned back forward and spun the wheel under the heel of his hand as he pulled the gearshift down into drive. The truck started forward and then just died. Roger scanned the gauges on the dash and then groaned miserably and dropped his forehead down onto the steering wheel.

"What's wrong?"

Sitting back up, Roger let his head fall back against the back glass. He let out a long noisy sigh, "I got so worked up worrying about Buddy I forgot I needed gas."

≈

"Do you want me to call for the ambulance?"

Lydia had her head pressed back against the seat. Her eyes were squeezed tightly closed and her jaw was clenched. She shook her head no and took a short breath, squeezing the edge of the seat on either side of her legs. "I don't trust riding in that thing," she said sharply, "They'd try to cowboy it all the way to Ormond...That I don't need."

Rose reached out and took Lydia's hand. Lydia's hand twitched and then gripped Rose tightly as another contraction shot through her abdomen. She breathed in and out rapidly.

"Easy," Rose said softly. She pushed a clump of sweat moistened hair back off of Lydia's forehead, "Count your breaths Lydia; In...and out...In...and out." She breathed a slow pattern for Lydia to follow...in her nose...out her mouth...in her nose...out her mouth.

"Breathe it in...blow it out..."

Lydia listened to Rose and caught up her rhythm, bringing her breathing under control as the contraction peaked. "Good," Rose said sweetly. Lydia's grip loosened as the contraction eased off.

"Good," Rose repeated, "You'll never have to do that one again."

Lydia took another long, cleansing breath and blew it out slowly. She opened her eyes and looked over at Rose, "I don't think I can make it to the hospital."

"No?"

Lydia shook her head, "No, it feels like they're right there...I feel like I need to push."

"Already?"

Lydia nodded her head anxiously, "Mmhmm." She closed her eyes and squeezed Rose's hand tightly again.

"Take a deep breath," Rose said, "Blow it out...blow it out slowly...blow it away...blow the contraction away... breathe...breathe..." She watched Lydia's face and then checked her watch, *Two, maybe two-and-a-half minutes*, she thought.

Lydia breathed through the contraction and then looked at Rose again, her brow now beaded with sweat, "How many babies have you delivered?"

"Fifty-two...Forty-nine of them in Africa, one in Florida, and two in Tennessee."

"Any of them in the back of a Land Rover?"

Rose smiled, "As a matter of fact, I delivered twins once in the back of a Land Rover," she said, "Two boys...They were the grandsons of the local village chief."

"You think you might be up to doing it again?"

"If it comes to that, but why don't we see if we can't get you to a more accommodating place."

Wincing painfully, Lydia balled up the hem of her coat and squeezed it tightly. She shook her head, groaning painfully, as she sucked in a quick breath, and then blew it out in short, forceful, bursts.

Rose cranked the Land Rover and started to put it into gear. Lydia grabbed her wrist and gripped it tightly. "Unh uh," she grunted, biting her bottom lip. She blew out the rest of her air and then took in another long breath and blew it out slowly. She held her stomach with both hands, "I think you need to check me Rose," she said, "I think you need to."

Rose looked at her for a split second and then went into action, "Where's the first aid kit?"

Lydia motioned with her head. "In the back," she said, "... And there's a flashlight and some hand sanitizer here in the console."

Rose flipped the lid back on the console and grabbed the bottle of hand sanitizer. She pulled off her gloves and tossed them into the back seat and then squirted her palm full of sanitizer and rubbed her hands briskly together, "Are you feeling pressure?"

"Yes ma'am...a lot."

"Down low?"

"Yes ma'am."

Rose pulled the big, black flashlight out and clicked it on. "Alright," she said, opening her door, "I'll come around and check." She slid out and closed the door behind her. Lydia could see the lights from the parade approaching around the bend and chuckled painfully.

Rose opened Lydia's door and she could just hear the sound of the marching band playing a souped up version of "God Rest Ye Merry Gentlemen." Rose pulled Lydia's dress up over her knees and reached up under, "I'm going to slip your panties off," she said, "Lift up a little for me."

Lydia lifted herself up off the seat and Rose slid her underwear down and pulled them off over her feet. "I'm going to check you now, Lydia," Rose told her. She reached up to check her and then leaned in and looked up under Lydia's dress with the flashlight.

"Well, Lydia," she said as she straightened back up, "We need to get you laid down in the back...Let me get the blankets spread out and I'll help you out."

"I feel another contraction coming," Lydia said nervously.

"Don't push," Rose said calmly, "You're already crowning and I'd like to get you laid down in the back to deliver these babies...Do you understand?"

Lydia shook her head yes and took a deep breath. Rose leaned back in over her and shined the light down on the top of the baby's head. She heard Lydia let out a quiet, whiney groan as she fought against the urge to push with the contraction.

"*I've got to, Rose,*" Lydia moaned, "*I've got to...*"

Rose reached down and put her hand against the little head. It had been pushed out a little further.

"Hold on Lydia."

Rose stood up outside the Rover and snatched open the back door. Flashing the light around, she found one of the blankets and grabbed it off the back seat. She threw it down in the floor below Lydia's legs and checked the baby again, "If you can't fight it, then push," she said. She laid the light down on the hump in front of the gearshift and propped it in between the levers for the four wheel drive and the PTO and then propped herself in the door jam with her knee on the sill and stuck her shoulders in with her back to the dash so she could get both hands down in between Lydia's legs to catch the baby.

"We can do it fine right here, Lydia," Rose said, "Don't worry at all...just push."

Lydia looked down at Rose as the band marched past the front of the car, and a fearful look flashed across her face. "But," she grunted, "You said not to–" Her face twisted as another painful contraction bored through her.

"It's fine Lydia," Rose said calmly, "...Just push."

Lydia bared down and Rose placed her hand under the baby's head. As it was pushed out, she supported it with one hand, and with the other, she gently scooped out its mouth. She wiped off the little nose and the baby gasped a breath and its tiny chin quivered.

"Her head's all the way out," Rose said. She glanced briefly up at Lydia and then turned quickly back to the baby, "If you'll give us one good push with the next contraction I think she'll come on out."

Lydia rested her head back and gave a little half nod, "Okay," she said breathlessly.

Lydia's legs trembled, "*Okay*," she whispered, taking another deep breath, "...I'm, okay."

"Give me your hand," Rose said. Taking Lydia's hand, she directed it down and touched Lydia's fingers to the baby's head. Lydia looked at Rose and smiled.

"It feels like she's got a lot of hair," Lydia said.

"She does."

Lydia's legs jerked and she let out another low groan. Clayton Tilley drove by in his new four-wheel-drive Chevrolet announcing over his loudspeaker to the world that Sand Ridge Hardware wished them all a "*Very Merry Christmas.*"

"Alright, now," Rose said, "Give me one good strong push and you'll be holding this little girl in half a minute."

Lydia took a deep breath and bared down again. "Come on girl," Rose said, gently working her fingers around the baby's shoulders, "Push...Push...There you go." She caught the baby in both hands and brought her up for Lydia to see.

"There's a pretty girl," Rose said softly, resting the baby on its side on Lydia's breast. She massaged the little girl's torso briskly between her hands, her fingers working nimbly to stimulate the baby's nervous system.

Lydia stared down at her new baby girl with the lights from the Methodist Youth's float flashing red and green through the windshield, "Is she alright?"

"She's just a little tired from all the excitement," Rose said, "We've just got to get her woken up," she assured Lydia, "That's all."

≈

"Are you sure you're not holding the brake?"

"Yes Roger, I'm sure."

At least it's stopped snowing again, Roger thought as he leaned his shoulder against the tailgate and heaved, his feet slipping in the slush. The truck started forward slowly. "Alright," he whispered, "Here we go…" He pushed a little harder and the truck moved forward a touch faster. Maggie turned the wheel, steering into Roger's driveway.

Roger shoved and skidded until he got the truck up into the driveway far enough for the back bumper to be well clear the road and then he stopped. "That's good, right there," he puffed, straightening himself up. Maggie set the brake and then put the truck in park. She pulled the keys out of the ignition and grabbed Roger's coat as she hopped out. Roger was standing next to the truck with his forehead resting on his arm on the top of the bed.

Maggie walked over to him and rested her arm across his shoulders, "You alright, Babe?"

I love it when she calls me Babe, Roger thought. He rolled his head over to one side and looked at Maggie through squinted eyes. He paused a moment and then sighed, "Tonight is not going how I had planned."

Maggie smiled at him as she ran her fingers through his hair, "It's alright," she said.

"This isn't how I pictured us spending our first Christmas parade together."

"We'll have more," Maggie said confidently.

Roger's heart tilted. He straightened up and smiled at Maggie, "At least we can still watch the fireworks together."

Maggie handed Roger his coat, "Right." She smiled again, "Do you want to just go down to the fish-house and watch them with the Pritts?"

Roger slid on his coat and thought for a moment. He reached his hands into the pockets and found the little ring box where he had left it in the right side. Wrapping his fingers around it, he gave it a squeeze and thought, *I don't reckon this is gonna happen tonight after all.* He let out a depressed sigh.

"It's not *that* bad is it?"

Roger smiled and gave his head a little shake. "I'm sorry," he said, "That wasn't addressed to your suggestion…Well," he paused, "It kindly was, but not in that way…I mean, I was…" He shook his head again and then looked up into the sky. The moon was shining brightly through an oddly shaped break in the clouds and handfuls of stars glistened here and there through their own little breaks. He studied the moon intently for a moment and then shrugged, screwed up his face, and gave his head another little shake.

Pulling his hands out of his coat, Roger smiled apologetically at Maggie, *"I'm sorry,"* he said, "I had big plans for us tonight Maggie." He spread his hands out expressively and chuckled a sad sounding chuckle down low in his throat, "...And I'm just having trouble letting go of them...That's all."

Maggie stepped in close to him and touched his face as she leaned in close and brushed a light kiss against his cheek. Her eyes sparkled, "I just like being with you Roger," she said, "...That's enough for me."

Roger stared into Maggie's eyes and couldn't imagine how anyone could be so beautiful. "You are a wonder," he said, reaching up to take hold of her hand. He held on for a moment, holding Maggie's hand against his face and then he squeezed it gently and pressed it to his lips.

Maggie's face flushed. She took a deep breath and held it. She told Roger, "I could honestly stay right here with you holding my hand and let Christmas pass right on by and I would be just fine."

Roger opened her hand and kissed it again, closing his eyes serenely. He held on again for another long moment and then slowly opened his eyes as he pulled Maggie's hand down from his face, "I think we'd better go."

Maggie watched Roger's mouth closely as he spoke, studying the way his lips formed his words, and wanting madly for him to kiss her. "I guess you're right," she said softly, "...If you really want to."

"You know I don't want to, Maggie," Roger said, speaking so softly that, even though their faces were only a breath apart, Maggie almost couldn't hear him, "...But...we should..."

෨

"Alright," Rose said, "Thank you." She flipped the telephone closed and tossed it onto the dash. "We should be hearing them coming any minute now," she told Lydia, "… That is, if we can hear anything over the parade." She pulled the corner of the blanket down and peeked inside, "How's number one doing?"

Lydia kissed the top of the baby's head and then smiled at Rose, "She's just fine."

Rose slid her hand down the side of Lydia's head, caressing her hair soothingly, "…And how's mama."

"She's fine, too."

"Are you feeling any pressure yet?"

"A little."

"I've got a spot ready for her right behind you if you start contracting before the ambulance gets here."

"Thank you."

"It's not the best of circumstances," Rose said, "But if we need to, we can handle it."

Lydia sounded very tired, "The doctor told me at my last checkup that it could be anywhere from minutes to hours between them," she said.

"As fast as this little one came, I'd guess it's not going to be all that long before you start again."

Rose had no sooner finished the sentence when Lydia's face tensed up and she gave a quick start and squeezed a handful of the blanket the baby was wrapped in.

"Don't hold your breath, Lydia," Rose said.

Lydia forced herself to breathe in deeply and then blow out slowly.

After the contraction passed, Rose leaned in past her and grabbed the bottle of sanitizer. Keeping an eye on Lydia, she held her hands out and over to one side and doused them generously with sanitizer and then briskly rubbed them dry. "I'm going to take a look at you now if you don't mind," she said.

"That's alright."

Rose got the flashlight and leaned back in the car and checked Lydia, "Everything looks good," she said as she clicked the flashlight off and set it back down by the gearshift, "Do you want me to take her before the next one starts?"

Lydia stared down at the baby for a second and then nuzzled her face down on the top of the little head and kissed her again. She looked at Rose and gave her a little nod, "I'm scared I might squeeze her," she said, motioning for Rose to take the little bundle.

Rose unsnapped her coat and then took the baby from Lydia. She smiled down at the little pink face and snuggled the little bundle of innocence up next to her body, shielding her from the cold as she moved around to nestle the precious package carefully into the pallet of blankets she had made in the foot behind Lydia's seat. She heard a low, tense groan from the front seat as she rearranged the blankets away from the baby's face, "Breathe through it, Lydia," she said, "...Breathe."

Lydia gritted her teeth, *If she tells me to breath one more time...*

Floats were beginning to back up on the road out in front of them. *I hope they don't hold up the ambulance,* Rose thought as she closed the back door and went back to Lydia's side, "I'll try Robin again in a minute or two," she said, "Maybe she'll be able to hear her phone then."

Lydia's eyes were closed and she had her head pressed back against the seat. She sucked in a breath and blew it out slowly. Rose slid her fingers into Lydia's balled fist. Lydia gripped tightly, breathed in again, and blew it out, "Oooo eeee, Oooo eeee..."

"Good, Lydia...That's good."

Lydia took a good long breath and her body began to relax. She opened her eyes slowly and gave a little shiver.

"Are you cold?"

Lydia shook her head, "Just tired."

Rose nodded. "This one should go a little easier," she said, "Her big sister already did the work of opening the store for her."

Lydia smiled weakly, "How's she doing?"

"She's fine."

"Why isn't she crying?"

"Some of them just don't...After the initial shock some of them settle right down." Rose caressed Lydia's forehead, "Don't you remember how quiet TJ was?"

Lydia rested back again, "That's right," she whispered, "I didn't remember that...Could you check her for me?"

"Sure," Rose said. She let go of Lydia's hand and peered in through the back window, "She looks fine to me," she said as she came back to Lydia, "...Maybe she's listening to the carols."

Lydia's body quivered again.

"Are you sure you're not cold?"

"Mmm hmm," Lydia mumbled, "I'm sure."

A look of concern swept across Rose's face. She took Lydia's wrist and felt for her pulse. It felt weak. She took Lydia's face and turned it towards her. "Lydia," she said firmly, "Lydia, look at me."

Lydia's eyes looked hollow and drowsy, her skin felt clammy in Rose's hand. "We need to get some fluid in you," Rose said, more to herself than Lydia...*Where is that ambulance*, she thought anxiously, *We should be hearing it by now.*

"*Oh,*" Lydia started, her eyes opening wide as a contraction struck her violently. Rose pulled back as Lydia sat up abruptly. "*Oh...Oh...*" Lydia cried painfully.

Rose wrapped one arm around Lydia's back and held her firmly, "Breath, Lydia...breath..."

"*Nnnnnhhh,*" Lydia groaned through gritted teeth, "*She's coming...*"

Rose held her hand and felt herself straining with Lydia to push the baby out.

Lydia made a high, strained, wheezing sound in the back of her throat as she pushed. Rose leaned in, grabbed the flashlight, and clicked it on. She took hold of Lydia's leg and looked down in to check her progress.

"*Stop, Lydia,*" she said firmly, "*Stop pushing...stop pushing now.*"

Lydia cut her eyes at Rose. She blew a short breath, "I can't," she grunted, "She's coming."

Rose put one hand down between Lydia's legs and leaned up into Lydia's face, "She's breach, Lydia...Stop pushing."

The seriousness of the situation came immediately to Lydia. She straightened her back against the seat and gripped her thighs with both hands. Her face contorted and her body tensed again as she struggled against the powerful urge to push. Tears rolled from the corners of her eyes.

"We can't manage this like this," Rose said, glancing around for someone who could possibly help. A group of Girl Scouts singing in the back of a pickup had stopped just down from them. A couple of the girls' parents were standing in the road next to the truck.

"*Hey*," Rose hollered, and then she heard the sound of the ambulance. She turned back to Lydia, "Here they come," she said, "Here they come...just hold tight."

Rose could see the lights flashing red through the winter-bare trees. The siren grew louder over the sound of the parade as the ambulance came into view down at the intersection. The driver hit the horn twice and weaved his way in between two floats and then sped across to where the Rover was parked. Rose waved to them as the head-lights shined brightly in her face.

A heavy-set man with a young looking face and receding hairline jumped out of the passenger side of the ambulance and directed the driver to spin the truck around and bring the back doors up close to the Rover. "Where's the little one?" he asked Rose quickly.

"In the back," Rose said, "But we've got another one coming."

"Right," the man said, stuffing his hands down into a pair of purple gloves, "How's Lydia?"

Rose stepped out of his way, "She needs fluids right away," she said, "The second baby's breach, in the canal..."

"Hey Lydia," the man said softly, "It's Rob." He took Lydia's wrist and at the same time leaned in to check her presentation. "Hm," he grunted softly.

Rob looked up at Lydia as the ambulance backed in and the back floodlights came on, showering them in brilliant light. In the circle of light, Rose noticed that a concerned crowd was now beginning to gather around them.

"Lydia," Rob said gently, "We need to get you into the ambulance. This little one needs to come on out and we can't make that happen where you are. Do you understand?"

The back doors of the ambulance came open and another man, this one tall and slim, dark complected, and graying at the temples hopped out, pulling the stretcher out with him. He popped the legs down and stepped over next to Rob.

"She's already delivered one," Rob told him, "And the second one's coming...Butt first. We need to get her into the van, and get some saline started and get this baby out."

"How's the first one?"

Rose was just picking up the first baby out from the back seat. "She's fine," Rose said, cradling the bundle close, "I've got her."

The man stepped over and looked in at the baby's face. His eyes almost disappeared in his broad grin.

Lydia came aware again and grabbed a handful of Rob's shoulder. She groaned miserably.

"Don't push if you can, Lydia," Rob said, "I know you can hold it girl."

Lydia shook her head, her face twisted into a painful mask of hopelessness. "I can't hold it," she wheezed. Her breaths came short and fast.

Rob let Lydia squeeze his hand. He leaned back in and held his other hand firmly against the baby. "Greg," he said, "As soon as this contraction's over we've got to get her into the van."

"Right," Greg said shortly. He turned and hopped back into the back of the rescue squad and started pulling instruments and supplies out of various storage compartments and arranging them for quick access.

A man appeared out of the darkness next to Rose. Rose saw the concern on his face. "What can I do, Rob?" he asked. It was Buddy Vander.

Rob glanced up briefly and went quickly back to the baby. "Get in the other side," he said, "After she finishes this contraction we're gonna need to get her into the van. I know we can use your help moving her."

Buddy spun around and disappeared behind the Rover. Rose saw him reappear in the circle of light on the other side. "Back up everybody," she heard him say to the gathering crowd as he pulled open the driver's door, "...We need a little privacy," then, to someone in the crowd, "Johnny Ray. Go down to Will's and get him up here quick."

"The baby's coming out tail first," Rob told Buddy as he climbed in, "...She's already delivering. We need to get her moved as quickly and gently as we can."

"Okay," Buddy said. He looked anxiously at Lydia as she let out another loud groan. Her eyes were closed tightly, "I can't," she muttered.

Buddy slipped his hand into hers, "Squeeze this, Lydie," he said, "Squeeze my hand." He looked at Rob, "Do we need to move her head first or feet first?"

Rob looked around the cab and then glanced out at the waiting stretcher and looked up at Greg who was now standing next to him, waiting, "What do you think Greg?"

"Head first. We don't want to try to pull her out this way," he said, motioning like he was twisting Lydia's legs around, "...Too much pressure on her pelvis."

Rob considered for a moment and then nodded his agreement. Lydia's grip on his hand began to ease. He looked at Buddy, "Get ready, Buddy," he said, "We need to do this quick and easy." He looked over at Greg, "You ready?"

Greg nodded and reached his arms in behind Lydia's shoulders.

Buddy got on his knees on the driver's seat and slid one arm in low under Lydia's hips. He stepped one foot over the hump and set it carefully down next to Lydia's.

"We're gonna move you now, Lydia," Rob said gently. He kept one hand down on the baby and slid his other one under the back of Lydia's legs. "Alright, y'all," he said, "On three...one, two, *three*."

The three of them lifted and moved Lydia with such care and precision that anyone looking on would have thought they had been practicing for this very moment their whole lives. They got her up off the seat, swung her out and around and rested her down on the clean white stretcher in one smooth movement, Greg holding Lydia's upper body, Rob her legs, and Buddy, following across the passenger seat on his knees and stepping gracefully out, all the while tenderly supporting Lydia's pelvis.

"Hop in Greg," Rob said, "Buddy and me'll get her in." He bent down on one side of the stretcher and motioned his head to Buddy, "Get that side, Bear...Smooth and easy again, smooth and easy."

Buddy followed Rob's lead and they shipped the stretcher up into the back of the ambulance. "Good job, Buddy," Rob said, as Greg started an IV in Lydia's arm, "I think maybe you've missed your calling."

"I don't know about all that," Buddy replied, "...You want me in or out?"

Rob tossed a box of gloves at him. "Put some of these on," he said, "I think we can probably use your help."

Buddy's cell phone started ringing. He looked irritated, "*Shoot.*" He pulled the phone out of his pocket and answered. "Hillary," he said quickly, "Yes, I do...I'm in it... No, no, I'm fine, it's Lydia, she's gone into labor...Yeah, yes–"

Lydia let out a wail.

"—we're at Maverick's, I gotta go now...yes...I love you, bye."

"Hold on Lydie," Rob said, "Just one more time."

Buddy jammed the phone back into his pocket and then grabbed out a pair of gloves from the box and crammed his hands awkwardly into them, "What do you want me to do?"

"Switch places with me," Greg said. He stepped back around towards Rob and Buddy scooted up towards the front seats, waited for Greg to move around opposite Rob, and then moved in near Lydia's head. He gave Lydia his hands, "Squeeze 'em hard, Baby...squeeze 'em as hard as you want."

Rob moved around to the foot of the stretcher, "Lydia, just fight this last one," he said, "...Just this last one."

He looked at Greg, "Her pelvis is small but she's dilated real good from the first one," he said, "But she's stuck in there tight...Skin's a little cyanotic." He shook his head, "I think after this contraction I can get her back up some and try to get her head out."

"Please," Lydia whispered, "Please just let me push, let me push..."

Buddy leaned down and whispered into Lydia's ear, "Everything's gonna be alright Lydie. Just squeeze my hands and breathe...keep squeezing and keep breathing." He tried to remember what he had learned years ago in childbirth class with Hillary, "Oooo eeee oooo eeee," he said, "...Like that...breathe with me...Oooo eeee, oooo eeee." He felt a drop of sweat run down from his temple along the side of his cheek.

"Alright," Rob said, "The contraction's easing off..." He patted Lydia's leg, "I'm going to move her back up the birth canal just a little," he told her, "You're going to feel pressure...please don't push against it if you can." He glanced at Greg, "Here we go."

Rob slid the fingers of one hand in along the baby's back and supported her neck as he firmly pressed on her, trying to work her back up inside, "Come on little girl," he said, "Come on baby." He took a long breath and shook his head. Greg could see the muscles in Rob's jaw working as he gritted his teeth. He worked a little more, "This is taking too long," he muttered, "We've got to get her out of there."

Lydia let out an awful groan.

"Come on, Lydia," Buddy coached, his voice cracking, "Just a little longer."

"You've got to help me Greg," Rob said, "This isn't working..."

"Let her push, Rob," Greg said, "Let her push...She might tear, but she's got to get her out."

Rob hesitated.

"She's not turning, Rob...just let her push."

❧

Roger and Maggie stepped back up onto the sidewalk at the corner of Plantation and Commons and watched the rescue squad skid around the corner, its siren blaring, and lights flashing madly. Maggie couldn't help but think of her children.

"I wonder what that's about," Roger said.

"I hope it's nothing serious."

They watched it for a moment and then Roger led her back on their way down Commons. They had only gone a few steps when the first rocket shot up and out over the river, crackling and sparkling brightly in the velvety purple sky.

Roger's head drooped, *Unbelievable.*

"*Man,*" Maggie said, "They're jumping the gun on everything tonight, ain't they?"

"Everything's just screwed up," Roger said, "...Screwed *up.*"

Maggie hugged his arm, "It's alright. All there is to do is just make the best of it." She smiled up at him and squeezed his arm tighter, "...*Right?*"

Roger looked at her sweet face. *I wanted so much to make this night special for you*, he thought.

"We'll just have to watch them from here," Maggie said, leading him out into the street.

Roger looked over at his shop, up into the sky at the next burst of colors, and then back at Maggie. She was still smiling.

As Roger watched her, his mind went back to the day last spring when he had made his first attempt with her. He looked at the outline of her face as it was lit up with the flashings of the fireworks. He chuckled to himself, remembering the look on her face as he handed her the sack full of books. He felt a warm flash run through him. *I can't stand this*, he thought, *I don't want to spend another moment without knowing that you're mine.*

Maggie sensed him staring at her and turned his way. She smiled and then smiled even wider, "The show's up there," she said, pointing up at the sky.

Roger held his gaze on her face.

"What is it Roger?"

Roger took her by the arms and squared her up to him, "You know how so often when we put someone up on a pedestal, when you get to *really* know them; the reality is never what we had hoped for?"

Another big flurry of rockets shot out over the river.

"...Well, I want to tell you Maggie...I didn't build a tall enough pedestal for you."

Flashes of red and green, silver and gold, blue, purple and red splashed across Roger's face as he reached into his pocket, and pulled out the little box. Kneeling down in the slushy snow, he opened it up and pulled out the ring.

The sound of Maggie's heart drowned out the cacophony of the fireworks in her ears as Roger took her hand and offered his to her. "There's everyone else Maggie," he said, "...And then there's you."

Tears rolled freely down Maggie's face as her heart danced in her chest.

"You are all I've ever wanted Maggie...and you're all I ever will want. I can't stand the thought of spending another moment without this ring on your hand."

Roger held the ring out to her, "Will you be my wife?"

~Epilogue~

Iris Faith and Grace Rose King weighed four pounds ten ounces and five pounds nine ounces respectively. Their ride into Ormond was, for the most part, uneventful. Miss Berta had called in a favor from the DOT and a truck with a plow had come out and cleared the road for them to the highway. Iris brought them and their mother home on Christmas day. It took two weeks before Grace could lay flat in the crib.

Maggie and Roger had a small ceremony in May down by the pond in sight of the mill, directly across from the dock over on the hunt club side. As the preacher prayed over their union, Roger smiled at Maggie and motioned over towards it with his eyes. Maggie followed his gaze, and when she looked back at him, he mouthed, "That was the second best kiss of my life."

"*Second?*"

Roger nodded and grinned slyly.

"*What was the first?*"

Roger opened his mouth to answer, but the preacher's *Amen* cut him short. Maggie itched until the ceremony concluded and then Roger, under the preacher's direction, leaned in and kissed his bride. As Mister and Missus Roger Lowell were announced to their families, Roger nudged Maggie with his elbow and smiled, "*That* was the first."

After the wedding, half the town turned out for the reception out at Bird Hollow. When the band started, a very slim Buddy Vander, with a slick new haircut was the first one pulling his wife out onto the dance floor. And, when the band finally finished, three hours later, he was the last one to leave.

Roger and Maggie spent ten days on Jost Van Dyke and when they got home, Maggie told Hillary that it was wonderful, "It started raining when the plane touched down," she grinned mischievously, "...And it didn't stop for three days."

෨